LOVE THE STARS FONDLY

LOVE THE STARS FONDLY

JORDYN BARNES

THE HOLLYWOODLAND SERIES
BOOK THREE

CONTENT/TRIGGER WARNINGS

This book is a romance, and it ***does*** end with an HEA, but there are heavy topics. Please make sure this book is right for you. Take care of your mental health and don't be ashamed to ask for help if you need it. You're not alone out there.

domestic violence, physical assault, suicide (off page), murder/death (off and on page), threat of sexual assault, stalking, gun violence, gang affiliations, miscarriage (off page), kidnapping, hospitals, injury and blood, mentions of drug use, alcohol and marijuana use, anxiety & depression, mental health issues, kink exploration, bondage, anal play/pegging, degradation, paparazzi encounters, body shaming, slut-shaming, workplace sexual harassment, sexism, misogyny, femdomme, breeding kink, suspense

This book is intended for an adult audience. Please read responsibly. If you're not sure about the warnings, reach out to me at any of my social media platforms. For a list of mental health resources, see the back of this book, or visit jordynbarnes.com.

Because sometimes, it just fucking rains.

"*I have loved the stars too fondly*
to be fearful of the night."

EDGAR ALLAN POE

DICKTIONARY

Want to find (or avoid?) the open door chapters? Here is a list of chapters that get spicy!

- Chapter 8
- Chapter 10
- Chapter 13
- Chapter 16
- Chapter 17
- Chapter 19
- Chapter 25
- Chapter 28
- Chapter 30
- Chapter 33
- Chapter 34
- Chapter 43

CONTENTS

1. Dare
Gorillas — 1

2. Brutal
Olivia Rodrigo — 13

3. Hots for Teacher
Van Halen — 25

4. Feeling Good
Muse — 37

5. Time Bomb
Rancid — 49

6. Everybody Talks
Neon Trees — 61

7. The Night We Met
Lord Huron — 69

8. Vroom Vroom
Charli xcx — 79

9. Banana Pancakes
Jack Johnson — 89

10. Dangerous Woman
Ariana Grande — 99

11. Just Friends
Amy Winehouse — 111

12. The End
Halsey — 123

13. Madness
Muse — 135

14. Killer
Valerie Broussard — 145

15. Good Luck, Babe!
Chappell Roan — 155

16. Body Talks
The Struts — 165

17. Tear You Apart
She Wants Revenge — 177

18. Guess
Charlie xcx, Billie Eilish — 187

19. Lunch 197
Billie Eilish

20. Tainted Love 207
Chase Holfelder, Tom Evans

21. Running Up That Hill 217
Placebo

22. Slow Hands 227
Niall Horan

23. Stargazing 235
Myles Smith

24. Gorgeous 247
Taylor Swift

25. Breakfast 257
Dove Cameron

26. Paparazzi 267
Lady Gaga

27. GOSSIP 275
Måneskin, Tom Morello

28. Black Bird 285
Evan Rachel Wood

29. Enjoy the Silence 295
Depeche Mode

30. Lollipop 305
Lil Wayne, Static Major

31. Something In The Way 315
Nirvana

32. I Wanna Be Yours 325
Arctic Monkeys

33. Bad Things 337
Jace Everett

34. Desire 349
Meg Myers

35. The Chain 359
Fleetwood Mac

36. Something 371
Jim Sturgess

37. APT. 381
ROSÉ , Bruno Mars

38. Ain't No Sunshine 391
Bill Withers

39. Some Nights 395
fun.

40. Iris   399
The Goo Goo Dolls

41. Obsessed   409
Olivia Rodrigo

42. Karma   421
Taylor Swift

43. I Wanna Be Your Slave   429
Måneskin

44. Belong Together   441
Mark Ambor

Will Continue   449

Like what you read?   451

Mental Health Resources   452

Acknowledgments   454

About Jordyn   457

The Hollywoodland Book Series   459

BOOK THREE:

CHASE + RENATE

Chase

CHAPTER 1
DARE

GORILLAS

MEMORIES ARE the ghosts of the past stalking us every day, haunting us every night, reminding us we can't elude them. Sometimes we're lucky, and we get the friendly ghosts that come with memories associated with love and joy. Some of us aren't that lucky, though, and we're running scared through life with raging poltergeists strapped to our backs.

I'm the latter of the two, but no one suspects a thing because I'm also a big time Hollywood actor with a house in the Hollywood Hills, fancy car, and boatload of fake friends. I've learned to hide my ghosts and live with them, or that's what I tell myself—and my therapist.

The door of my trailer closes, offering some relief from the noise of the explosions outside. I grab a bottle of water and a piece of fruit from the bowl on the counter like things explode around me every day. Of course they do—it's an action movie set. Even my dog, Pongo, seldom notices them as he sprawls out on the bed after spending the last few hours watching the window for my return.

The schedule for this film has flown by at a brutal pace, and we've been at it since two this morning. Sleep comes in short shifts, so I've been looking forward to the shut eye I'm about to get for hours. Shit blows up, gets put back together, and blows up again for days on end, making me long for a nice, calm indie film. My stunt guy and I have been tag-teaming the scenes and rehearsing between takes for a solid week. We're both exhausted and freezing our asses off, but expected back on the set again in a few hours. I'm glad I don't have heavy makeup in this film. It's impossible trying to catch a nap in that shit.

When another explosion echoes through the backlot, I dig in my pocket for the noise canceling headphones and crash into an unfamiliar bed. The next blast never registers as I tuck two pillows on either side of me to keep me from turning over. I lose consciousness almost immediately, drifting off to sleep with Pongo at my side.

When I wake up, I'm starving. I grope around, finding the apple and my buzzing phone from under the darkness of the blanket. If I do this right, I can keep the sunlight out until I'm better prepared for it. Once the alarm stops, I go through my messages while I eat, wishing I could close my eyes again for just a few more minutes. There are a few messages from my friend, Dani, telling me about some gig that she has but how I shouldn't go. I keep scrolling until I spot Jamie's name. I groan so loud, Pongo looks up. Jamie's going to kick my ass.

> JIMJAM
>
> Hey man, we still on for the school gig tonight?
>
> Planning to leave my place around 4:30

Shit. I pull up the latest schedule to check for changes after last night's shoots. I forgot I'd promised my best friend I'd make an appearance at a charity art function with him. I need to find the PA and verify what time filming wraps today and if there's time for me to make it. Either way, they're always pretty cool about it when it's a kids' event.

I stumble out of my trailer like I've been drinking at a damn club all night with my buddy, Steve. The sun burns my eyes as I slap at my pockets, trying to figure out where the fuck I left my sunglasses. No luck, so instead I'm blocking the late morning sun with my hand as I reorient myself to the forest of identical white trailers.

"Chase, oh my god, is that you?"

I don't recognize the voice, and when I turn around, I don't recognize the woman either. Pongo presses against my leg as I scan around to check for anyone else nearby. The lot is a ghost town right now, with everyone either shooting or sleeping. It's possible she's a new intern or some other staff sent to wrangle me. My gut says she's a fan, though.

She's not wearing a badge—that's a bad sign. We've had some security issues in this location, so I'm prepared for just about anything. Pongo, being a giant Pitbull, helps keep some of the wilder fans a few extra feet back, too. They don't realize he's a big sweetheart, and a therapy dog.

"Uhm, hi, how are you?" I croak out. I swipe at the screen on my phone and send a text off to Megan, the PA who has spent the week keeping me on track and on schedule. She'll act as a buffer and get security here, plus I can list a million other set-related items Megan and I need to go over, anyhow. I'm sure she's already looking for me, but the phone might help give the impression that I'm busy. I lay it on thick, in the hope that she'll get the hint and leave me alone.

I don't think my plan worked, and Megan still hasn't checked her texts.

"OH MY GOD! I can't believe you're here." She bats her eyes at me, trying to be cute as she pushes her boobs out and smooths down her hair. A few years ago, I might have given her an autograph and a selfie as I showed her the way out. Maybe even a tour, since she's kind of cute. The fan entitlement has worn me out since I made it big. They interrupt dinner with introductions, interrupt movies for my autograph, and beg for selfies when I'm trying to pick up my coffee. So now, I try to avoid fan situations outside of official events. "I saw the filming and thought you might be here. You don't remember me, do you?"

"Uhm." I swallow hard. My hard nap brain fog won't allow me to think fast enough to deal with this. Do I know her? "I'm so sorry, I've been filming all night so, can you help me out with that?"

"I'm Shawna!" Her voice borders on a shriek. When I don't respond, she pouts—sticking her bottom lip out so far, it's almost comical. Oh, she's definitely a fan. I glance down at my phone again and I've got bubbles appearing and disappearing from Megan. That's promising. "I can't believe you forgot to call me when you got into town."

She says it like I should understand what that means. I don't. I text Megan again, sending nothing but the word *help*. While I do this, I'm trying hard to remember if I've gotten drunk with Steve over the last few weeks and forgotten about someone he's tried to set me up with, but that can't be right. Steve's got a serious relationship and we haven't done that in months. It's a mystery when, or even if, I've ever talked to this woman before. Too many fans take an innocent wave and twist it into an invitation to my personal life.

"Shawna, right? Hi." Pongo senses my nervousness and nudges my side. I give him a pat on the head and check my phone again.

"You're just trying to be nice. You still don't remember?" The longer I'm standing here, the less I want to remember her. The girl can't be much older than early-twenties, maybe younger— not my type.

My agent will rip some poor assistant a new asshole for this, which I'll feel bad about. By this afternoon, she'll be hitting my new best friend, Shawna, with a restraining order. She's justified in doing so, since breaking and entering on a private, closed set qualifies as stalker-level behavior. "Chase! I met you at Comic

Con a year ago and I gave you the book I made for you with all the pictures of us. It had my number in it, so you could call me."

Oh boy. I hate being that guy. The guy that has to break her heart and tell her I get about two hundred gifts at any signing that range from stuffed animals to personalized books and cards. It's impossible to keep track of them all. Even the people I meet multiple times sometimes slip my mind unless there's some other connection. I wish I could remember every one of them, but I can't. I shouldn't tell her that there's a solid chance I've buried her stuff in a box somewhere in my dad's garage or my agent's storage locker, because that's where most of it ends up going. My house isn't that big. Okay, it is, but some of the stuff people give me qualifies as full-blown creepy.

"Right, the… pictures. Of *us*?"

"You do remember! I was worried you forgot or that the dickhead on security took my book away after they made me leave. Oh my god, did they take the book away, and that's why you didn't call me? Those fuckers! It's okay, I have another one in my car!" She lights up and my stomach drops as a memory clicks in my brain and I recognize her. She's one of the few people escorted away from my table by security during a signing event. She damn near climbed over the table, insisting that we were friends. Apparently, I liked some status she'd tagged me in on social media a few years ago, and she read way too much into that.

Truth be told, if I did like the status she posted, there's a solid chance I was drunk or high, scrolling social media out of boredom.

"Shawna, it was really nice seeing you again." I make a show of looking at my watch. I'm hoping she hasn't noticed it's a prop and doesn't even tell time. "I kinda overslept and they need—"

"Coop! Shit, there you are!" Megan comes hauling ass around the corner, ready for anything. She wraps her arm through mine and starts dragging Pongo and me away from our new friend.

"Doug has been searching everywhere for you. We need that reshoot before the sun shifts."

"Absolutely!" I flash her a big smile and I nod to Shawna. The red in her face should signal embarrassment, instead, she's pissed. Not at me, though, at Megan and the way she holds onto me.

"Okay, well, I can wait in your trailer with Pongo. It's no big deal. I took the week off to spend it with you and I've read up on therapy dogs."

My fake smile drops at the thought of her alone in my trailer with my dog. Aside from a few friends and my shrink, people don't know Pongo's role as a therapy dog. To the world, he looks like any other dog, and I never put a vest on him to advertise what he's trained to do. Shawna's awareness of that little piece of information has me more than a little spooked, and Megan can feel the shift in my mood.

"Coop, hun, why don't you and Pongo go ahead to the set and find Doug? I'll be right behind you." Megan steps between us and Shawna. Megan's not much over five feet tall, but she could kick my ass. She used to be a stunt woman until she had an injury she couldn't come back from. "Sweetheart, where's your badge?"

"Oh, no, it's okay. I'm Chase's fiancée."

That escalated faster than normal. I pretend not to hear what she's saying as I keep walking, holding the phone up to my ear to play it off a little better. I round a corner, and the looming figure of Jerry, head of security, heads my way.

"Sorry about that, Mr. Cooper. I have no idea how they're getting in here. You two okay?"

"Yeah, we're fine. Megan's got her right now. Thanks, man." Before he gets far, I add in, "Hey, if my agent calls and blasts you, I'll buy you dinner to make up for it."

Jerry waves me off. I wait for him to turn the corner before I lean up against the trailer, my hands covering my face. Jerry might be used to these kinds of things, but I hate this shit so much. I love acting and most of the fans are incredible. But man, there's always one that has to ruin it for everyone else. Some days I wish I could just go back to being an unknown, but the rent and bills are a whole lot harder to pay that way.

"You okay, Coop?" Megan asks when she comes around the trailer. She rubs my shoulders, which should be funny since she has to stand on her tiptoes just to reach, but I'm too annoyed to laugh.

"Yeah. Thanks for the save. I was on my way out to find you and she was right there waiting by my trailer."

"She's the third one this week that made it all the way back here. They're getting a little too good at acting like they belong on set. Last night, the guy even had a fake badge. A damn convincing one, too." She gives me a sympathetic smile.

"Did he fuck up any of the shoot?"

"Nah, don't worry. The takes from last night turned out fine, and they're going to use them. I was on my way to your trailer to tell you that you're free to go. Will I catch you in Romania next week?"

"I've got that awards show to hit, so I'll be a day late, but yeah, I'll be there." I bend over and give her a hug, glad she's going to be on site next week. Familiar faces always help me relax. "Thanks again. I owe you and love you forever."

Once I change and turn the costume in at the wardrobe department, I check in with a few more people before Pongo and I head for the car. A piece of paper stuck to the windshield catches my eye as I get closer.

The note reads *I love you Chase!* along with a phone number. I unfold the piece of paper and find an actual marriage license filled out with the personal information of some woman named Julie.

"Jesus..." I climb in the car and toss the letter in the glove box so I can give it to my agent. She keeps things that go beyond the standard note or gift, just in case. I've never asked her what *just in case* situation she's kept them for—well, frankly, I'm not sure why she keeps them, but she has her reasons.

This will join the book from Shawna that security took from me at the convention. I remember it now because my agent said it went overboard in all the wrong ways, but I never flipped through it. I rock my head back against the seat and pet Pongo while we sit for a few minutes to get my head back to reality. After I calm down, I text Jamie back.

> Yeah, I'm headed your way now. Just wrapped for the day.

JIMJAM

> Sweet! Shower's open and fixed if you wanna come straight here.

As the engine revs to life, a question tickles the back of my mind. Has anyone leaked tonight's appearance yet? It's a kids' charity event, and while I wish the paps wouldn't show up to those, they still do. If it's not out yet, I can at least get in and help Jamie set up before someone posts about it and they swarm the school. If they have leaked it, they'll already be at Jamie's house by the time I get there.

"It's no wonder I can't keep a damn girlfriend, eh, Pongo?"

I pick up coffee for Jamie and his wife, Lexi, on the way to the house because I'm dragging ass and need the pick-me-up. When I pull into the driveway and check around the house, I don't find anyone lingering in the bushes, waiting to jump out, so there's a chance this event *hasn't* leaked to the press yet. We get the van loaded up with easels, canvases, and other painting supplies in no time. Once we're done, Jamie takes me to the studio garage in the back of the house. He opens the door and pulls back a sheet that's covering the back wall. My jaw drops as I take in the giant mural he's spent months on.

"What do you think, man? I haven't shown her yet."

"Dude, it's fucking brilliant." Jamie stopped painting after his dad died. That changed when he met Lexi. They have a textbook definition of a whirlwind relationship, sending them down the aisle in Vegas after only a few months. I didn't believe in soulmates till they got together. Now, I can't help questioning if there's someone like that for me.

Someone not named Julie. Or Shawna.

"I figured the cherry blossom tree since it's, you know, what I call her." He walks around and points out the Easter eggs hidden in the mural just for her. "Her boba drink is here by the base of the tree. The train we took down to Oceanside is here in the background."

He goes to point out more, but I step in front of him and pull him into a hug. "Jaim, I'm so fucking proud of you, man."

We met in elementary school after I stuck up for him, and he returned the favor. He's been my best friend ever since—more like my second brother. He keeps me grounded so this whole Hollywood movie star lifestyle doesn't give me too big of an ego, and I do my best to support the shit out of him wherever I can. We came too close to losing him a few years ago, right before Lexi came into his life. I've thanked her every damn time I'm with her for being his ray of sunlight in dark times. I don't know what I'd do without him.

"Thanks, pal. Hey, help me pull this back up so she doesn't see it." We get the sheet back in place and head back out to the van. "How's the shoot going?"

"We wrapped the California stuff for now. Which gives me time to find a tux. I just found out I'm engaged." Jamie stops and stares at me like I've lost my mind. "Yeah, when I got to my car to head over here, I had a marriage certificate on my windshield. Guess I got that going for me now."

"Again?"

"They're nothing if not persistent." The exhaustion comes through in my voice. "I should take a break after this movie and go back to some of the smaller projects again."

"Bro, I'm not sure anyone would hire you for small parts anymore. You've made your name, and it comes with one hell of a price tag." He throws his arm over my shoulder as we walk back into the house. "You've got that award thing in Germany next week, yeah?"

"Yeah. I tried to get out of it, but my agent said I have to go for publicity. Do you guys mind watching Lulu for me?"

"Hell yeah, we'll watch her. She and the pup can cause a little extra chaos. Are you taking Pongo?" I nod. "Hey, we could take a trip up to the mountains when you get back. It's been a while since we did that, and Steve's uncle still has the place up there."

"I wish, but I can't. I go from Germany to Romania, then off to Toronto for a bit, and back to Germany for the closing ceremonies. After that, I'm back for about a week before I'm supposed to head to Atlanta again."

"Shit. Alright, well, how about we hang out this weekend before you leave? Play some video games, get high, clear your head." He slaps me on the back before he checks his watch. "We're early. Let's go hit up Beard Papa's on the way to the school. That shit always cheers you up."

"Dude, you think food cheers everyone up."

"Yeah, and I've been right every time so far, so let's finish loading up and get you some damn cream puffs. Dick."

Once again, he's not wrong. By the time we get to the school, my mood has shifted and I'm eager to get in and hand out the bobble heads I brought to sign for the kids. I love coming to these things. Hell, anything that involves helping kids gives me a boost. There's something about the way they view the world so differently than we do, even when it's dealt nothing but shit to most of those kids. It's like a shot of hope right into my heart.

"Okay," Jamie says as he pulls open the van doors and starts pulling boxes out. "Once we get everything in, I'll go find Dani's sister and find out where we're putting the extra toys you brought so they don't get stolen." He stacks the boxes on top of each other in my arms, grabs everything he can carry, and we head for the entrance to a gymnasium. "Have you met Dani's sister?"

"Nah. Honestly, I forgot she had a sister." We hang out with Dani every chance we get, but she never brings her sister along with her. She's just scared we'll freak her out or something. We're kind of rowdy when we're together. Dani included.

"She's pretty cool. I'll try to introduce you to her later if I get a chance."

HOLLYWOOD
Renate

CHAPTER 2
BRUTAL

OLIVIA RODRIGO

I'M JUGGLING paint supplies that aren't even mine right now, and I swear under my breath as something tries to slip out of my grasp. I hold my breath, waiting for the box to fall to the floor and decorate me and the hallway in electric green paint.

"Renate, what are you doing?"

"Marta! Hurry! It's dropping!"

An older woman with long grey hair in a tight bun comes rushing over to me. Her billowy duster is flowing behind her like a cape, and like a superhero, she swoops in and saves my ass. I wasn't even supposed to be here tonight, but my sister called and said her movie star friend was coming and might need to store stuff in my classroom. Normally, she would be here and take my key so I could go home, but she's at a gig tonight. How convenient.

"I've got it!" Marta shouts, taking the paint jars from my hands. Her soft smile reminds me of my *abuela* and makes me miss her. "Ren, getting the supplies there faster only helps if you don't drop them all. Let the kids help! You know you can't get it all in one trip."

"The kids all fucked off because they said some superhero is

here. I'm just trying to help and get this night over with faster, Marta."

"I heard some gossip about a celebrity sighting. It's going to be a madhouse if the press finds out." She reorganizes the box and takes half of what I was carrying. "I know art isn't your area, but we still appreciate you volunteering to help out."

It's not like I had any better plans beyond trying to catch up on my shows and grading papers. Mama isn't happy about me working late. She has a crush on the man down the street who plays live music at one of the senior centers on Tuesdays. She'll give me hell for not being able to drive her there, but I called a friend of hers and they're going to take her. Maybe that will take some of the heat off me.

We drag everything into the auditorium, avoiding the tripping hazard of the tarps they've put down to protect the floor. As I find a place for the last box, the back door pops open and we both glance up in time to find James Barton coming in, carrying even more supplies.

He's cute, but he has two strikes against him. He dated my sister once, and now he's married. He and my sister stayed friends, though, and a few years ago, my sister ended up setting him up with his now wife. Because of them, I have to listen to my sister go on about her matchmaking skills and how she can help me find a date. I might have to punch her in the face soon if she doesn't stop. Which would be sad—my sister has a cute face, and I have a mean left hook.

"Hey Ren, haven't seen you in ages," James says as he gives me a hug. "I haven't seen you since…shit, Dani's show a year ago?"

"Yeah, it's been a while." I've seen him at my sister's concerts and a party or two here and there, but we're not in the same circle of friends. It's still a little strange to see him all smiles and laughter since he got married. My sister used to call him the brooding artist, but he doesn't fit that description anymore.

"Dani said you were bringing some toys? I have no idea what she's—"

The door pops open again and two large boxes with long legs make their way into the room—along with all the staff members that disappeared about ten minutes ago. I'm not sure why, but they're following the boxes around like they're made of gold. James jogs over and takes the boxes, leaving me staring at over six feet of delicious, tan, pretty boy. He looks familiar, and when he pushes his sunglasses up to hold his hair back, I forget to breathe. I know exactly who those sparkly blue eyes belong to.

I may have pictured that man on lonely, late nights before, too. With much less clothing on.

"Hey Coop, come help me with this," James calls out.

Chase fucking Cooper is standing fifteen feet away from me in my school's auditorium. They must be getting ready to film another action movie, or every department store in Los Angeles is required to sell him shirts a size too small. *Beefy* is the word I heard one of the younger teachers calling him the other day while they were reading the gossip magazines. It's appropriate, and I can't help but imagine what that man would look like on his knees for me.

"Ren, you're staring," Marta teases as she walks by.

"I mean, he's cute for a white boy but—"

"You're a little too close to drooling on my floor, Ms. Silva," says a voice from behind me.

I force my head to turn away, letting the thoughts of running my fingers through that thick, long, caramel hair go up in smoke. Of course, the damn principal, Eric Miley, would catch me staring. I twist my lips into what I hope is a smile.

"Oh, Mr. Miley. I wasn't aware you would be here tonight."

Slimy little shit. Three years in a row, I've had one of the highest ratings of any teacher in the school. Three years in a row, this small dick asshole has denied me a raise. 'We don't have it in the budget' is his fallback excuse every time. His story would change if I slept with him, but that's never happening.

"Yes, well, when I heard we had a special guest, well, I thought it would be wise to have a few more male staff members like myself to make sure you ladies behave."

It's not laced with misogyny, it's fucking saturated in it. He's the poster idiot for why women don't give out their real names on dating apps and pick being alone in a room with a bear over a man. He doesn't know that I've got him on camera in my computer room after hours on one of those pay for play sites. Fucker was even trying to see if staff members were on the site, myself included. As if we'd be dumb enough to use our real names, anyhow. Someday, I'll remind him why you do *NOT* fuck with women in STEAM. Not only are we used to it, but we get our revenge on the worst offenders, like him.

"Ren." James appears next to me, which keeps me from saying something I'd likely regret. "Hey, about the toys. It's the bobbleheads Chase brought for the kids. He made sure there were enough for the students that can't come tonight and Dani told us you'd have a place to lock them up for the night?"

"Yeah, sure. Just uh, have him put the box on the end of the bleachers and I'll make sure it's stored in my classroom. My room has locks and security cameras because of the equipment." I would normally have watched Miley to see if he reacted to the security camera comment, but I'm having trouble concentrating. My eyes keep looking a few feet behind James, where Chase is talking with the kids. He's distracting. Distractingly pretty.

"Great, will do. Thanks for helping out tonight. Oh, Lex wanted me to invite you over for game night. We got the living room redone, finally, so there's more room for everyone." Lex, or Alexis, is Jamie's wife. She's one of the nicest people I've ever met, even though life has put her through the wringer more than a few times. I met her at a company party for the guy my sister works for a few years before I met James. "Oh, uh, have you met Chase yet?"

Before I can answer, there's a loud crash in the back of the auditorium and two guilty looking students stare at a stack of chairs that's fallen. "Angel Rodriguez and Steven Wilson, what are you doing? Were you climbing the damn chairs like mountain goats again?"

I excuse myself and go take care of the boys, helping them get the chairs pulled out and set up while ensuring they're not messing around anymore. It doesn't take us long, but it's long enough for me to get my mind off the movie star in the room. As we wrap that up, a teacher's aide comes over and pulls me outside to help with another situation that she can't seem to describe in a way that makes sense to me.

"It's…There are… people here. Lots of people!"

"What do you mean, *'people'*? The school is closed."

"Yeah, I don't think they're parents, Ms. Silva," Jessica mumbles.

"Where the hell is Miley?" I ask, looking around. Jessica shrugs and looks more worried. "Okay, let's go figure out what's going on."

We turn the corner and I'm blinded by the flashbulbs going off like lightning. People are shouting and trying to open the lock on the gate to the teacher's parking area. Why would anyone want to take pictures of a couple of teachers through a fence?

"Miss! Miss! Can you let us in? We want to get some pictures of Chase!"

"Come on, I'll give you two hundred cash right now. Just open the gate."

"I'll give you five hundred!"

I take a slow, deep breath to center myself before I go off on these fucking lunatics. If they think yelling at me like that is going to have any effect at all, it only shows they haven't met many teachers.

"I don't know what you're talking about!" I yell back. "This is an after school assembly and there are no teachers here named Chase."

"Come on," one of them shouts back. "We got pictures from someone inside! We know he's there! Five hundred cash dollars!"

"Who the fuck says 'cash dollars'?" I ask Jessica, and she chuckles behind her hand. This is why she came to find me and not one of the other teachers. I'm nice when I need to be, and a complete hard ass when it calls for it. "Jess, go find the resource guy. He's supposed to be here for the event. Tell him to get his ass back out here and do his damn job, but in nicer words."

I'm not calling the cops yet because this is Los Angeles, doing that could lead to someone innocent getting arrested or shot. But if we're paying a resource officer for the campus, his ass better get to work. I wait for Jess to get around the corner and yell out to the press, "Get away from the gate. This is a goddamn school and there are laws against you idiots being allowed on campus. Not one of you is getting in, so if this guy you're looking for is here somewhere, you'll have to wait till he leaves."

Grumbles and more yells come from the twenty or so of them at the gate, which makes me think others are sneaking around trying to find a way in or looking for windows. "We've called the police. They'll escort your sorry asses off the property as soon as they get here."

"Damnit, Renate!" The distinct huffing and puffing of the school cop jogging up sounds from behind me—clearly, I've disturbed his evening. "You can't be yelling at people like that!"

"Oh, put a lid on it and get these people the hell away from here. I don't care what Miley told you, they can't be on campus and you can't just ignore them to get publicity for the school."

I turn to Jessica, who's only now catching back up to us. "We need to cover the windows on the doors to the gym in case someone gets in. I swear, these people are vultures." I rub my temples, feeling a migraine coming on. This was supposed to be a nice, easy, after school art class and now, it's a zoo.

This is what I get for trying to help. Fuck.

When asked how Chase's appearance could have leaked to the paparazzi, Miley invents one excuse after another.. He ends up being the coward I know he is, blaming it on a parent. I would bet good *cash dollars* he's the one who leaked the pictures. On top of that, Miley's been up his butt all night. I've had to send teaching aides to Mr. Cooper's rescue on more than one occasion just to give him a break. Miley thinks that they'll be best buddies, and Mr. Cooper will visit here for more talks and boost the school ratings or something. Idiot.

"You know, I read in a magazine he's single again," Marta whispers and nudges my arm as we pack the supplies up. There's a handful of parents still hanging around James, trying to get their kids into the program and a few in other little groups discussing whatever they need to discuss at nine thirty at night.

I glance up to where Marta is gesturing and see Cooper in the last row of the bleachers with four or five kids who are still waiting for their parents to come pick them up. It never fails that there ends up being a few stragglers, and even though it means we have to stay later, I understand the situation. One mother is a nurse and her ex is a complete dick about picking their kid up when she needs him to. Another of the kids in the bleachers is living with his grandmother. The interesting part is Chase doesn't mind at all. He's laughing and joking with the kids, showing them how he did a few stunts, and acting like a normal human being. He's been up there all night, watching signing the toys as he stays out of James's spotlight. It's kind of sweet.

"You should go talk to him," Marta presses again.

"Mrs. Rodriguez," I huff with a smile, so she knows I'm teasing. "What in the world would a man like him be doing with a woman like me?"

"I can sure think of a few things!" She giggles menacingly.

"Marta! You've been spending too much time with the older kids and your romance novels."

"I got those books from you, Renate. What can I say? I'm old, not dead. And if I were younger—"

"And not married?" I tease back. "And be real. Why would I want to deal with that crazy lifestyle? That man lives in a big house with a pool and people who cook and clean for him. I've got a two-bedroom house that I share with my sister and my mother and we can't even afford for the neighbor kid to mow our lawn."

"Ren, it's California. That strip of land you call a lawn is dead already, or will be in a few months."

We both cackle, because she's right. We finish packing up so we can call it a night as soon as we can. Tomorrow morning is going to come far too soon, and at this rate, we'll be lucky if we're out of here by eleven.

I hoist up one of the bulkier boxes of paints, trying to make sure Marta doesn't lift anything too heavy, even though I shouldn't either. I head down the dark, empty hall toward the art department. No matter how long I've been teaching, there's something just a little creepy about an empty, dark school at night. My sister makes me watch too many of those horror movies that end up with the killer stalking someone down a school hallway. I remind myself that those aren't actual schools, and even if they were, it's always in some rural area where no one is around to hear them. If you set off the alarm in this school, you'd have an entire neighborhood here in minutes to see what's happening—not to help you, but because they're all nosey.

I heave the supplies onto a table in the art room, and that's when I notice a familiar box sitting in the back of the room. I walk to the back and lift the lid to see a dozen or more Chase Coopers staring back at me. I'm sure I can guess who stashed these here, and that he's planning on scooping them back up after we all leave so he can them for a fast buck. Unfortunately, we didn't install any cameras down this hall since there's no expensive and irreplaceable equipment, so he would have gotten away with it if I hadn't seen the box. With a heavy sigh and several curse words, I grab the bobbleheads and head out the door.

I'm going to regret all of this lifting in the morning, assuming I can sleep.

I fish my keys out of my pocket as I walk back to my classroom. As I turn the corner, there's a giant figure in the dark, startling me half to death. I can't stop and end up running straight into him. I drop the box, my keys, and damn near pee myself from the fright. I also scream.

"I'm sorry! Shit! I'm so sorry!"

My head snaps up to meet the eyes of my would-be killer, and I'm ready to grab my keys and jab them into his neck. Instead of a spree-murdering psychopath, I'm eye to eye with the prettiest blue I've ever seen before—the ones I've been seeing all night from a distance. They're not like a normal sky blue, but darker, with a pretty rim around them that almost looks green in this light.

I've got to stop watching Dani's horror movies.

I realize I'm staring at him eye to eye because he hunched over, trying to pick up the toys and muttering apologies as he does. He looks back at me, a toy in each hand, and I swear he's peering into my soul. He wets his lips and my entire body tingles. This man is dangerous in all the right ways.

"I, uhm, hi. I'm, uhm, I'm…"

"Chase Cooper."

"Yeah. I mean, yeah, of course you know that. Duh. It's, I was…"

"I'm Renate. Nice to meet you."

"Ren…Rena—?" He gets hung up on the unusual pronunciation.

It's rare people meet a Hispanic woman with a Dutch-Norwegian name that isn't even pronounced correctly because of my father's sense of humor.

"Like Reh and naught. Renate. You can call me Ren. Most people do."

"That's, it's pretty. I… shit, I didn't hurt you, did I? I mean, it's nice to uhm—" He shakes his head and mumbles. For a movie star, he's about as articulate as a two-year-old. "Shit."

Closing his eyes, he runs his large hand through that caramel hair, nice and slow, tucking it behind his ear where it refuses to stay. He's cute when he rambles, and he's got this dimple on his chin and I have to resist reaching out and touching it.

"I'm really sorry, Renate. I was looking for the bathroom and —" He looks around us. "Yeah, I'm totally lost."

"You're close. You're one hallway too far." I direct him before I load the toys back into the box. He wants to help, but I shoo him away. If any of those paparazzi got in here, this is the last thing they need to find. "Don't worry about it. I've got it."

"It's my mess," he replies in that velvety smooth voice that I don't want to stop listening to. It's hypnotizing. "The least I can do is stay and help."

We get the last of the toys in the box and he hands me my keys as he stands to his full height. I swallow hard as the expression *I would climb that man like a tree* finally makes sense to me. He's a giant. Of course, I'm just over five foot two—in heels. As I reach out for the keys, our hands brush together and he holds his there just a little longer than most people would. I've frozen, unable to pull my hand away from his touch.

"Here, I'll carry the box."

"It's okay, Mr. Cooper. I've got it now. Thank you, though." I'm not sure how I'm keeping my cool right now with this hunk in *my* hallway. "You were headed to the restroom anyhow."

"Right, yeah. It was nice meeting you, Renate. I uhm, I'm sorry, again, that I ran into you like that."

He's walking away—but not turning around—just walking backward as if he doesn't want to stop looking at me. It would be kind of cute, but… "Mr. Cooper?"

"Call me Chase. Or Coop. Or, you know—"

"You're about to walk into a wall."

He spins around and sure enough, he's face to face with one of the bulletin boards. He turns around again. "Thanks. Again. I'll, you know, be more… careful."

I watch him disappear down the hallway before I unlock the door to my classroom. As I put the box away in one of the storage closets, I lean against the wall and laugh, giving my heart a moment to slow the heck down.

"Why is it always the pretty ones who are dumb as rocks?" I laugh to myself as I lock up.

HOLLYWOOD
Chase

CHAPTER 3
HOTS FOR TEACHER

VAN HALEN

I CAN'T GET her out of my head. I tried watching TV, reading a book, even wrestled the dogs, and still she's in my fucking head. Now, I'm pacing the living room, trying to figure out what the hell I'm supposed to do next while also practicing how to pronounce her name.

"Re nah tuh. Renaaaht. Naughty Renate—y. Don't be a dick, Cooper. Renate."

It's driving my dog, Lulu, nuts because she's trying to follow me around thinking we might play again. She's a Boxer I rescued a couple of years ago to give my other dog some company, and she's a goofy ball of energy. Pongo, the eighty pound Pit Bull, is the laid back one that's now staring at me like I've grown another head. He's trained to sense shifts in my mood, and I'm pretty sure I'm sending his sensors into overdrive today.

"I should call her, right? Fuck, what would you do?" I ask Pongo, but he just drops his head back onto his paws and pretends to sleep. Some help he is. I rehearse what I'll say on the phone and use Lulu as my stand-in.

"Hi, my name is Chase Coo...nope." I shake it off and start again.

"Hello, I was, uhh, at the art painting thing last...Jesus." I take a few quick breaths, shake my hands, and jump up and down a few times. I've got this. What kind of fucking professional actor am I that I can't even make a phone call? Fuck it! I'm doing this. My hand hits my empty pocket and my shoulders shrug.

I'm not doing this. Lulu yawns at me before she flops onto the floor, bored with my stupidity.

"Yeah, you're right. I suck at this. Thanks for that vote of confidence." I pull my hair up, trying to get it out of my face while I figure out what to do next. "Maybe I should call Dani. Her sister might know who Renate is and Dani would play matchmaker. She loves that shit."

Pongo replies with a huff and rolls onto his back.

A thought pops into my head and I can't help but laugh. "Dude, could you imagine if Renate turned out to be Dani's sister? That would be weird as hell, huh?" I shiver at the thought when I let it sink in a little more. "Don't even wish that into existence, man! One Dani is enough. Even knowing there's another one out there is fucking nuts."

I trudge to the fridge and take out the orange juice, chugging straight from the bottle. Bourbon would hit the spot better, but it's a bit early for that, and it's gym day. If I puke, Steve will fucking kill me after he's done laughing his ass off about it. More quick breaths as I center myself and grab the phone off the charging dock. I haven't been this fucking nervous since…since. Since I had a panic attack in the middle of a damn audition. At least that worked out for the best because the movie bombed hard and I got picked up for an incredible show after that.

This isn't a movie, though. It's bigger.

I grab the phone and open the phone app and freeze. "NOPE! Fuck." I open the messenger app instead and pull up Jamie's thread.

Dude, what was the name of that school?

JIMJAM

Literally called Hollywood Tech and Arts, man.
Are you drunk?

Wait…why?

Nothing and fuck you.   My agent asked.

JIMJAM

Bullshit. Call me later when you've thought of a
better lie.

If I tell him now, he's going to talk me out of this. I could ask him who she was, since he talked to just about everyone last night. But if I describe her as the knockout short chick with the pouty lips and thick thighs? He'd slap me through the phone. He had to have noticed me watching her last night. There was no trying to hide it.

I'm arguing with myself over what I should do, and when I glance down again, I've already Googled the school and my thumb hovers over their phone number. I check the time and scoff. I don't have a fucking clue if the schools are open right now or not.

"Hollywood School for Technology and Arts. How may I help you?"

A real person? People still answer phones? Come on Coop, head in the game!

"Yes, hello! My…wife and I have been checking into schools in the area and we spoke to a teacher at your school the other day. I believe her name was Renate. I don't recall her last name." I'm laying it on thick, slipping into a character I played in a television show years ago and hoping like hell this lady falls for my bullshit. "She teaches something to do with art… or technology?"

Fuck, you're an idiot, Cooper.

"Oh, Renate Silva?" the voice on the phone asks. *"She's the head of our technology department."*

"That sounds right. Hispanic, long hair, in her late twenties or early thirties?" I sound like an absolute douche. I hope this doesn't get back to her. Although, I'm sure it will, since I doubt many 'fathers' call the school with physical descriptions of teachers they're trying to reach. Stalker!

"Yes, sir. That's Ren. Did you and your wife have additional questions about the school or anything else I can help you with?"

I'm about to say no and hang up in sheer panic when I get an idea. "Well, we'd like to send her a small gift, something to thank her for her help. A token of our gratitude. Would that be possible? Not to her home address, obviously, but something to the school?"

"Yes, sir. We would take the deliveries in the office."

"Perfect. Thank you for your time."

I don't even wait for her to end the call, hanging up and cheering like I'd won the lotto or something. "Renate Silva! Head of the Technology department—wait. Silva?" I pull up my contacts and scroll through. Sure enough, there's Dani's name followed by Silva. Oh, I will never hear the end of this. Jamie talked to Renate last night, but they weren't acting all buddy-buddy or anything like I thought he would act toward Dani's sister.

I *cannot* have the hots for Dani's fucking sister. Can I?

Both dogs sit there staring at me like the moron I am as I drop onto the edge of the couch. I let out a slow, deep sigh, unsure what to do next. It's the first person who's caught my attention in years and it has to be my friend's sister? Dani is *like* my sister, which makes this all so wrong.

Am I overreacting? Like I don't do that every damn day of my life.

I'm flipping through flower shops when my kid brother

comes barreling in the front door with a case of beer under each arm.

"C, you here?" As Devin yells out, Lulu leaps from the couch and slides across the floor in a frantic effort to reach him.

"Yeah. Living room."

"I got beer! Oh, and no practice tomorrow morning. The ice is fucked up." There's a thunk as he puts the beer down and the sound of Lulu's feet tap dancing on the tile stops. "The Zamboni caught fire, man," he says, coming into the room.

"What?" I glance up from my phone and see Dev holding my dog like a baby, even though she's almost sixty pounds of muscle. "What do you mean, *caught fire*?"

"I dunno, that's what the ice guy said, man. They were flooding the ice and the damn thing started smoking and then, BOOM! Fire."

"Wait, it exploded?"

"No."

"Boom means it exploded, dude."

"Whatever, man! Can I turn on the game? We're playing against Jacksonville in two days and I want to see if their new forward holds up to the hype. I heard he's killing it, and I don't wanna come off like a damn newb between the posts, you know?."

I nod. I don't think my little brother will ever outlive his frat boy lifestyle. He's a good guy, and a phenomenal goalie, but he can be a bit of an idiot sometimes, but that's goalies for you. Devin puts Lulu down, turns on the recorded game, and goes to put the beer in the fridge. He hands me a cold one when he comes back and I take it without looking up.

"Nah, don't get those. Those are for old ladies."

"What?"

"The flowers. I mean, unless you're getting them for an old lady." He watches my reaction with a big smile, but his face drops when I continue to stare at him. "Dude, what? Those are what you'd buy for someone's grandmother or like a teacher or something."

"Well, maybe she *is* a teacher, fuckface."

"Ohhhh," he nods and thinks about it for a while as he sits. Lulu jumps up next to him, pushing me over as she works her way under his arm and halfway onto his lap, licking the condensation off his bottle. He doesn't even notice as he continues to pet her. "So, why are you buying flowers for a teacher?"

"Because I ran into her last night and—"

"With your car?! Jesus Christ, man! Wait, which one? The Jag?!"

"Shut up, no, not *with* my car!" I push the idiot's shoulder, sloshing his beer, but like a true Canadian and goalie, he saves it. "It's, I dunno, I met her at a thing and I just, I dunno, want to send her something…nice."

"Nice as in *thanks for being a teacher* or nice as in *I wanna get in your pants*?"

"Kind of…in the middle? Why?" I take a long drink as we watch the center take the puck from behind the net, skate down the ice, and score on a one-timer. "Is that the guy?"

"Yeah, that's him." He plays the shot back a few more times in slow motion and hits play again before turning to me. "Dude, if you're not just being nice and you want a date out of this, flowers aren't the way to go. Do that later, but don't go overboard."

"Overboard?"

He flashes me a goofy grin, "You know, like when you bought the cute girl with the accent a whole ass kitchen remodel after you'd dated her for, what, a month?"

"Jessica, and we dated for almost a year." I act offended, even though I'm not. "Man, I couldn't cook in that tiny excuse for a kitchen she had. I made an absolute mess the one time I tried."

"As big of a mess as when you walked in on her getting

railed over that sweet ass marble countertop by the construction foreman you hired? Exactly how many meals did you cook after it was done?"

"Oh, fuck off."

"Not an answer." Devin glares at me before he holds his hands up. He should expect me to swing on him for that, but I cut him some slack. "I'm just saying you should slow it down a bit. It's been a while since you went for more than just a quick hookup."

"I *have* dated since—" I think hard and realize there's nothing. Nothing but regrets and too many faceless women. "—nevermind. Whatever. Fuck you."

"No thanks. So, uh, who is she?"

I toss the phone on the coffee table and sit back with my arms crossed, trying to keep my head out of the past. I don't need Jessica in my head anymore. Her or any of my other so-called girlfriends.

"She's nobody. You're probably right." I should forget the whole thing ever happened. Forget meeting her. I suck at relationships, especially over the last few years. No matter how hard I try or how sure I am that I want something, shit comes back up and bites me in the face.

We sit in silence for a while, watching the game, until Devin elbows me in the arm. "What does she teach?"

"Some kind of tech classes. It doesn't matter. I'm too fucking busy for this shit, anyway." Pongo comes over and rests his head on my leg. I pet his head without even thinking about it.

"Smart board."

"What?"

"Look it up, bro. Stop being so fucking old." He nods down at Pongo before he shifts his attention back to the screen, avoiding eye contact. "I didn't mean to fuck with you that hard, man."

"It's fine. It was me, not you." What he said about the smart board echoes in my head, so I grab my phone to do a little digging. By the third page, I smack him on the arm.. "You're a genius."

"Nah. Some girl at the bar called me a golden retriever, though. I'll take that." Devin takes a drink, almost spitting it out as Jacksonville scores another goal. "Fuck—this guy's good."

My absolute favorite place to be during a big Hollywood party? At home. Alone.

I have to attend these social gatherings, but I don't have to like them. So instead of mingling and getting wasted on cheap champagne, I'm leaning against a wall and playing on my phone to avoid people.

I can bail out once in a while, but if I skip out on too many, I risk becoming irrelevant in the eyes of Hollywood big shots.

I glance around, and as I expected, the whole place teems with boring, pretentious assholes. Just another excuse to throw an obscene, lavish party for a rich old guy who doesn't give a fuck about anyone but himself. But I'm the nice guy—Hollywood's sweetheart—so, at the behest of my manager, I make an appearance. It's amazing how much acting gets done when the cameras aren't even rolling.

More than once tonight, I've let my mind wander back to worrying if the smart board sends the right message. Of course, that implies I have a clue what message I want to send. I'm sorry? I think you're hot? I pictured you when I was showering this morning and imagined those big, pouty lips around my cock?

I shouldn't say that last one. Even if it's true.

"Chase?" I turn toward the voice and force a smile at the woman the agency sent with me, since Cynthia isn't available. She's across the room, calling out my name like I'm not six five and easy as fuck to spot. But I remind myself I retreated into an out of the way corner, so I'm actually *not* easy as fuck to spot. I step out into the crowd and wave when she turns toward me again. Rushing over, she grabs my arm. "Oh, there you are."

"Yeah, sorry. I needed some air and wanted to check the score on my brother's game."

"Great," she says without an ounce of actual care for me or my brother. I could have told her my house had caught fire and she would have given me the same flat response. "Well. Let's get you back in there."

"Sure, yeah."

Hollywood isn't easy when you're like me. I love being on stage; I love acting; I love everything about it, but I'm a bit of an introvert who has to play the role of an extrovert whenever I'm at these events. Sometimes, I need a break to give my internal battery a bit of a recharge, which Cyn knows, but clearly didn't tell this woman—her name might be Katie. Or Carmen. I suck with names.

Except for Renate.

"They won," I offer, hoping to at least bring down some barriers and have her talk to me like I'm more than just a thing she's showing off for the cameras. Show dogs get more respect.

"Hmm?"

"My brother's team. They…nevermind. It doesn't matter to you."

"Oh, there's that new director everyone wants to work with. Let's go meet him." Dragging me across the room like I'm five has me clenching my jaw and ready to bolt. But when she has the audacity to tap my phone? I'm not sure how much more of this I can take. "Don't forget to update your social media feed, Chase."

I hold my phone up and snap a quick, stupid selfie of me, making a face that shows how bored and annoyed I am, and post it with the caption: Best night ever! *#Fun* *#Blessed* *#CanIgohomenow.*

She rolls her eyes. I'll have to do a live video later to make up for that, but whatever. I keep threatening Cyn that I'm leaving social media all together, but she keeps stressing that it's part of my brand. I shake more hands and flash a few more fake smiles before I hear my name.

"Chase! Chase fucking Cooper?"

"Robbie!" We hug, clap each other on the back twice, and pull away with huge smiles on both our faces. Robbie and I did a movie together a few years ago, and we've stayed in touch. "How'd you get suckered into this? I thought you were in Egypt?"

"Filming is on hold while they fight about money and why some white dude was cast as the lead, so I figured I'd enjoy the party. The man of the hour dated my mom, so I love crashing these things and making him relive that and wonder why I keep showing up. It annoys the shit out of him, really. Someday, I'm gonna walk up and call him *Dad* just to see how hard he freaks out."

"Dude, you're insane."

"Come on, it would be a blast watching that rich bastard sweat it out while he calls his lawyers. Anyway, I'm going to rescue you from Robo-Agent. There's a bar in the back with this stunning blonde working the bottles. I also brought edibles, so that should help." Robbie checks around our feet. "Where's my main furry friend, Pongo?"

"Home. I gave him the night off."

"Oh, that lucky dog. Literally!"

We duck to the back, and spend the rest of the night drinking, getting high, and avoiding the agency rep.

HOLLYWOOD
Renate

CHAPTER 4
FEELING GOOD

MUSE

THE ALARM SCREAMS at me until I slam my hand down on the phone, turning it off. I flop back onto the pillow, just wanting five more minutes—I was having the best dream! Hottie Cooper had a starring role in my bedroom for the second night in a row. His sweet little ass and those pretty eyes were on full display for me and me alone. He looked amazing on his knees, which I'm sure is true in real life, too. How could he not?

Begrudgingly, I rub my eyes and roll out of bed slowly. My body takes a few minutes before allowing me to start my routine, which means it must be medication day. I'll have to worry about that later, and if I waste any more time thinking about Chase Cooper's assets, Dani will usurp the bathroom and I'll be late.

After I shower and towel dry my hair, I dig through the closet for something cute to wear. I don't always get to wear jeans to work since the school deemed it unprofessional. However, we're outside today, learning about rockets. No way am I wearing my expensive clothes for that.

After looking everywhere, I finally find the jeans shoved in the back of a drawer. As I open them, I understand why. Gigantic holes slashed through the legs at random intervals stare back at

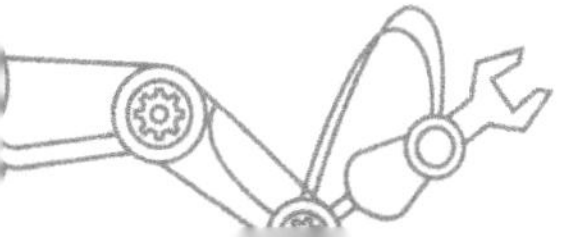

me. I don't have to be a detective to know who did this. She's too damn skinny to fit into my clothes, but that doesn't stop her from playing fashionista in my closet since she could crawl.

"DANIELLA!"

"Sup?" She pops in, her hair already done up in a cute hat. Some days I hate her so much. She rarely goes beyond the smallest amount of effort in her look, and yet it always comes out perfect. Like this morning, she's had shows two nights in a row, which means maybe four hours of sleep each of those nights. But she looks ready for a cover shoot for a magazine.

I managed almost seven hours last night and still look like the remains of a bridge troll after being hit by oncoming traffic.

"What the fuck did you do to my pants?"

"I turned them into *designer* jeans that will look way better on you now," she says matter-of-factly. "What?! You got them for like five dollars at the swap meet and rarely wear them. Now, we can sell them for like twenty bucks and you can get new jeans that are cuter."

"Those were my only pair of jeans I could wear to school, you scissor happy asshole!" I stare at her with my mouth open as she shrugs. "I need coffee before I can handle this bullshit."

"Watch your mouth, young lady!" our mother calls out casually as she walks by to take her turn in the bathroom.

"Grrr, I don't have time for this!" I push Dani out the door and slam it shut. At least she didn't cut them up too high. I swear, she believes two short years in fashion school has turned her into an expert. This is how her world works. She dabbles, becomes bored, declares herself a master of whatever she's dabbling in, and moves on. Fashion school, art, music, she takes nothing beyond the boundaries of her comfort zone. A shame, because she's talented as hell.

I pull on a pair of plaid leggings before the pants and check the mirror. Fuck—they *do* look stupid good.

I drop onto the edge of my bed in front of my makeshift vanity and stare at myself. Dark bags under my eyes tell me I need to take my meds soon. It's probably also why I'm more frustrated with Dani than usual. I move the books and computer parts to the side before I fish out my expensive makeup and stare at it just like I did yesterday.

"Oh, for fuck's sake, girl. It was a dream! He's not coming back to the school and if he did, you're…" I gaze up in the mirror and smirk. "Way too much fucking woman for his skinny white boy ass. Even if he is *beefy* right now." Still, I put the makeup on and check myself out at least four more times before I grab my things.

The delicious aroma of cinnamon and sugar fills the house and wraps around me as I head for the kitchen. Mama gets up every morning to prepare three to-go cups of *café de olla* for us so long as she doesn't have the early shift. The scent brings back memories of my *abuela* and the handful of trips we took to Mexico to see her before she passed. Mama's coffee tastes better than anything I can get at the fancy places, saves me a few dollars on coffee, and it makes her happy. Wins all around.

"Mama, are you ready?" I call out when I don't see her sitting at the kitchen table. "I have to be at school early on Wednesdays, remember?"

"It's Thursday, don't *you* remember? I'm taking the bus today." She's getting old, but still feisty as hell. She glances up as she closes the fridge and whistles. "Mira! All fancy again today just for school, huh? Are you meeting someone special? A new teacher you're trying to impress, maybe?"

She enjoys dancing right on the dangerous edge of pestering me about my love life. Which doesn't exist. Not in a few years, anyhow. I've found better ways to spend my free time like the internet, robots, and naps. Also, the occasional trip to an exclusive club I'm part of. It's not the fanciest place, but it's good enough for what I can afford on a teacher's salary. Mama doesn't know about it and Dani pretends not to after she found a riding crop and a strap-on in my closet once.

"No, mama," I answer as I give her a kiss on the cheek. "I can choose to be pretty for myself and not for a man!"

"You need to find someone and settle down. You're getting too old."

"Uh huh, and where would you live if I did that?"

"Oh shit! Look at you Ms. Hots-For-Teacher!" The whirlwind that is Dani comes through the kitchen, swiping up her cup and waiting for an answer. She leans toward me with a devilish grin, and in a sing-song voice asks, "Is this for your new little friend, Coop? Jamie's thing happened the other night, didn't it? You did meet him, right?"

"What's a *coop*?" My mother asks me as she sits down to read her morning stories. This woman loves her tabloids. "Did you get birds? I thought you played on computers all day?"

"Mama! My friend—Chase Cooper! The Hollywood hottie of the year? The cool as fuck guy that I hang out with?" Dani shoots back, looking at Mama like she's crazy. "Oh my god, you know him! He's in your papers almost every flippin' day! The hot white boy!"

"I can't keep up with your friends, Daniella. You have too many boys. Don't swear."

"And girls," Dani remarks under her breath, and I try not to laugh.

Dani walks over and flips the pages of Mama's paper until she lands on a picture of Chase. My breath catches seeing him in the dark sunglasses and baseball cap with his dog at his side. Clearly, this picture came from the paparazzi. When I glance up again, Dani and Mama are both staring at me with looks that say they know where my mind went. Shit.

"Mama, I don't play on computers all day. And yes, Dani, he

was there," I answer as I grab an apple, attempting to make my escape. But Dani dashes ahead of me and blocks my path, putting her hands out against the door frame. "Get out of my way, Dani! I'm going to be late."

"Not until I get answers! Did you talk to him?" She narrows her eyes, expecting something more. "Out with it! I haven't seen you since and I want the deets!"

"Dani—" I stare harder at her and see the mischief dancing in her eyes. "What did you do?"

"Oh, nothing," she hums, sipping her coffee. "Just, you know, working my magic!"

"Oh, sure. You get one couple together, and now you're some enchanted matchmaking *bruja*? You didn't even have anything to… wait, did you?"

"I may have suggested Jamie take his bestest buddy with him. And which school should they go to next? I also may have told them to ask you if they needed anything—like a place to store way too many toys that Chase brings because I gave him the wrong number of kids."

"When does Xander come back so you can be too busy having sex to meddle in my life?"

"Ouch!"

"RENATE!"

"Oh, come on, mama!" I roll my eyes and push my glasses up my nose so I can glare at Dani. "You're crazy and bored. That's a dangerous combination. I'm going to work. Besides, he's too famous for me."

"Say *hi* to Marta for me!" she sings out as I get to the front door and stop long enough to glare at her. "Yeah. Marta's in on it, too! You need to learn to trust me!"

In the middle of a particularly spicy daydream about a certain Hollywood hunk, a student interrupts me to tell me our remaining robot has finally died. I called in every favor I had to get those robots four years ago since the school won't pay for them, and they're too expensive for me to buy out of pocket.

When I check on the machine to see what I can do, I get an idea and challenge the class to get the thing working again. That should keep them busy and give me a little time to figure out a longer lasting solution—or to get lost in my own mind again.

My phone dings in my desk drawer, and I pull it out to check.

MARTA

Your man is on TV. He's looking fiiiiine.

My what?

MARTA

CHASE!!

Not now, I need to work on a letter to the school board to replace a robot.

My department always struggles, and I've pulled all the strings I can to keep the school from shutting down the robotics program. The kids love it, and so do I. We've even had two students win scholarships back when we could enter the competitions. The school board loves to brag about our STEAM focused middle school and how it helps students, but they aren't interested when we ask for more money to fund the programs.

Maybe I should daydream about getting a bonus this year. With that, I can afford a small drone or one of the basic programmable arms. Or I could sell some things at the swap meet like Dani always suggests. However, I don't have a lot of things to spare. Keeping the roof over our head is hard enough.

MARTA

Yikes. Maybe Chase can get you one?

Yes. *Maybe Chase Cooper could sweep me off my feet and buy every damn student in my classes a robot.* I snicker at the thought as a chime sounds from my computer.

Back to reality, Renate.

OFFICE

You have a package at the front. Maintenance
will bring it by later.

Rather than wait, I assign two of the students to retrieve it, but a few minutes later, they're running back into my classroom, out of breath.

"Ms. Silva! We can't get it!" Carlos announces.

"It's too big, Ms. Silva," Maria backs up his story, adding, "Mr. Jenkins is bringing the box now. What did you get us?"

"Is it a new robot?" Carlos asks.

"A car?" Maria follows up.

I'm trying to remember what the heck I ordered when a giant box appears at the doorway. The box is taller than I am— although that isn't saying much—and close to eight feet long. I definitely didn't order this.

"Hey, Ren," Craig Jenkins, the school maintenance worker, says cheerfully. He maneuvers the hallway and small door, wheeling the rest of the way into the room. That's when I notice the giant red bow on the box and I'm even more confused. "Is today your birthday or something?"

"No, not my birthday. We're sure it's not ticking, right?"

He graciously laughs at my poor attempt at humor as he hands me a card. "The delivery guys said there's information in the box about having them come back for training and installation if we need it."

"Training and installation?"

I take the card without looking at Craig because I'm too busy reading the words *smart* and *screen* on the box. That can't be right. I've requested one of these things every year I've been here and I'm always denied. And the ones I've asked for are much smaller than this one. This thing is going to take up an entire wall.

"Shit. Miley will kill me," I mumble under my breath, trying to remember if I got drunk and ordered things online. Not likely, since my credit cards don't have enough room for a sandwich, let alone a piece of equipment like this.

"Who's it from, Ms. Silva?"

"What is it?"

I giggle as Brad Pitt screams in my mind, *'What's in the box?'* I ignore the eager shouts of the students and open the card, almost dropping it when I read the note.

> *Renate–*
>
> *Sorry for bumping into you last night, but not* <u>*that*</u> *sorry since I got to meet you. I hope you can put this to good use. Any chance you're free for dinner tomorrow night?*
>
> *-CC*

He's included his number at the bottom of the card, but I can't read it with my hands shaking the way they are now. A smart board? Dinner? What the heck happened to flowers or candy? Did this man hit his fucking head last night when he ran into me? Is this some kind of fucked up joke?

Dani.

She's up to something. But how could she afford a smart board?

I sigh and drop my hands to my sides. "Does Miley know

yet?" I'm a little relieved when Craig shakes his head. "Okay. Let's put it in the back. I need to figure out what's going on, and if he sees it, he'll want the damn thing somewhere useless, like his own office."

"Why can't we keep it, Ms. Silva?"

"Who's it from?"

"Is it from your *booooooyfriend*?"

The class becomes a barrage of questions and giggles until I finally turn back around to get them all to sit back down and be quiet. I can't blame them. I'm ecstatic too, even though we can't keep it. It's going to hurt to explain why, though. It's also going to hurt to tell Chase he has to send the screen back. Assuming he's the one who sent the box.

"It's a gracious gift from a…a kind person." Snickers fill the classroom as someone makes kissing noises. These kids are great, but they're also assholes sometimes. "However! It's not fair for this room to have one when no one else does. So we will either be returning the screen or maybe sharing it with other classrooms and students."

I peek down at the card again as they grumble about the rules. I add his number to my contacts while I shake my head—I can't believe I'm doing this. If this ends up being a prank, my sister will not live to see her next birthday. I grab a marker and scribble over his initials and the number in case someone else finds the card.

I open up a new text thread and stare at the screen. This is a horrible idea. He's an actor, and I'm a teacher. He travels the world. It's rare that I leave Los Angeles. He's rich and famous, and I'm barely scraping by. But what if it ends up being nothing but a kind gesture by an out of touch movie star and I'm overreacting? Don't I deserve dinner with a hot man once in my life?

What the hell? Dani is going to think she's an actual

matchmaker now, which means I'll never hear the end of it. But it's better than regretting a free dinner.

I stare down at the card again.

No, this is all too much and I need to tell him to return the damn board and pass on dinner. I don't have the time or the energy to deal with a high-profile relationship, friendship, or whatever else he wants out of this.

Still not sure what to do, I shove the phone in my pocket. I can figure that out later when my mind stops buzzing.

HOLLYWOOD
Chase

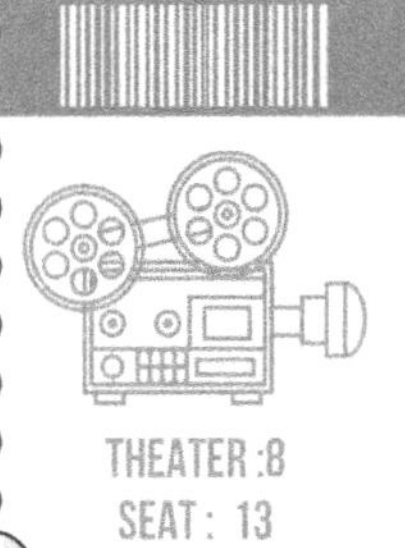

CHAPTER 5
TIME BOMB

RANCID

I DON'T NEED an alarm when Friday comes, since I'm up and out of bed like it's Christmas morning and I'm ten. I picked out the suit yesterday, so this morning I steamed my shirt, picked out a couple ties, and realized I should find out what color dress she's wearing to match it. I'm in the middle of trying the fourth hairstyle when Steve's muscle car rumbles into the driveway.

I forgot all about our workout session this morning.

I stare at the suit and sigh. Renate hasn't said yes to the date. But she hasn't said no, either. In fact, she hasn't even called me yet. If she doesn't call, or if she says no, I don't know what the fuck I'm going to do. Sulk, probably.

"Hey bro, ready to do this?" I ask, jogging down the stairs, meeting Steve in the foyer. Jogging past him, I hold open the door that leads to the garage gym, but he stands there, unmoving. Even the dogs are looking at me with their heads cocked to the side. "What?"

"You're…up?" Steve's been one of my best friends since high school, and my personal trainer for years. He was also my clubbing slash *meet the hot ladies* buddy before he did the unthinkable and settled down with a pro hockey player. Love has picked off two from our circle of friends, leaving only Dani and me as the holdouts. Dani sort of has Xander, even though it's complicated and confusing.

Fuck, that means I'm the lone loser. Phenomenal.

"Yeah." I give him a shrug and nod to the door again, ready to go.

"But…you're not in bed."

"Yeah, I noticed. Come on, let's go. Do you wanna run today? No, it's probably too hot for that. Is it too hot for that?"

"Did you… do your hair?"

"Maybe?"

"Dude, I'm engaged. Why did you wait so long to—"

"What?"

"You're way too happy for this to be one of your episodes, so?"

"I'm not hitting on you, dude! Come on, let's go!"

"Are you on speed? Too much coffee? Who *the fuck* are you and what have you done with my hot Hollywood bestie?" He still hasn't left the front door.

"I'm not that bad! I mean, you don't *always* have to wake me up."

He does.

"Chase Cooper doesn't fucking run unless he's being paid to. He hates it. You've also never once been up before I wake you up. Never. Not since high school, bro."

"Not true. I was up last Tuesday."

"My dude, the nights you can't sleep don't count because we don't end up working out most of those days."

"Heeth gop a bate," Devin says around his toothbrush as he comes out of the kitchen. He's hungover even though he's got a game today, so that's going to go well. He looks up from a box of cereal he's reading and sees the dumb look Steve gives him, walks back in, rinses his mouth out, and tries again. "He's got a date."

"Dude, did you spit out your toothpaste in *my* kitchen?" I swear this guy is ten sometimes.

"Uh, I started in my bathroom but I got hungry, so I kind of walked over here while I brushed my teeth?"

"Use the guest bathroom!"

"Both of you, shut up!" Steve's head turns toward me dramatically, and I brace myself for what's coming. "A *date?* With a *woman?* A *real* woman? An actual date with a human being?"

"Yes. Well, I mean, sort of on the date part. She's a real person, and it's not for a role or a bit."

"Is that a good idea? I mean, the Jessica ordeal was a lot. But Abby? Bro, you just got over her like yesterday. Also, you are, hands down, the shittiest Hollywood playboy I've ever known."

"Yeah, dude. Your dating life is pretty shit," my brother reminds me as he pours the cereal into the bowl, and realizes he doesn't have enough hands to eat it while holding the box and bowl. "Fuck."

I want to argue that this woman is different, but the thing is, I don't know if she is. How can I? I try to think of anything else to say, but I can't counter their points. I *am* a terrible playboy because I care too damn much, and describing my dating life as shit is accurate. Neither of them is wrong.

I almost found myself engaged to Jessica out of sheer stupidity. The media and the internet latched onto the internet idea of a fake relationship, claiming my agency set us up for publicity. Fucking trolls. We dated for a few years, traveled all over the place together, and everything felt amazing. I thought I couldn't be happier. Until she cheated on me with some guy she met at our gym. Steve helped me build the home gym after that.

I went through another epic fail with Abby. We met at a club Steve took me to, and for once I wanted to make it work. Two weeks later, Abby lit that hope on fire, stomped on it to put it out, poured salt over it, and finished by poking it with a stick.

She left a note on the mirror one morning saying she used me to get a part in some shitty film school movie. She even tried to get back with me when the movie bombed. Sometimes she still sends me these strange gifts, but never puts her real name on them. I'm pretty sure she's the one who left me the marriage license the other day.

Just once it would be nice to have a normal, civilized breakup, but those are never in the cards for me.

There's one name neither Steve nor Devin mention because they know it's the one that still hurts. Cassie. She taught me how to love, or at least, that's what I thought she did. She had an incredible personality, tons of friends, top of her class, and beyond smart. She had everything she wanted until I came along and ruined her life. Wherever I go, so goes the media—internet, trolls, even so-called fans. Every one of those vultures drooled over the fresh meat, picking her clean every chance they had. She had dreams of moving out of the city, raising a big family, and enjoying some privacy when we got together. I should have known better.

"Look, it's not even an actual date. It's more of a…hang out."

"She hasn't called you back, has she?" Devin asks.

What if they're right? What if I've built this up to be something it's not to make myself feel better? What if she ends up being like all the others and I'm only doing this because I'm a lonely loser?

"No," My shoulders sink, and I'm right on the edge of overthinking this to the point of canceling everything.

"Where are you taking her?" Steve asks quietly, shoving his hands in his pockets as he watches Pongo walk over to me, nudging my hand.

I sigh and pat Pongo's head, assuring him I'm okay, as I mumble, "Magic Castle. I had to call in a few favors to make it happen on short notice like this."

"Seriously? Fuck!" Steve has me in a bear hug before I can

even register what's happening. "That, my friend, makes it a fucking date. Get your ass in the gym. I need details! *You* don't take just *anyone* there!"

I'm on my last set in my gym, sweating my ass off and wishing I could be anywhere but here.

"Get it! Two more, man!" Steve yells. Some days, I wish he stayed in law school instead of dropping out before taking the bar and getting his certification to be a personal trainer.

My phone rings and both our heads turn toward it, watching it buzz across a table. Steve jumps for it, grabbing it before I can and holding it behind his back so I can't see the ID.

"Come on, fucker! Finish the set and I'll give your phone back."

I push through the set with the last of my strength, drop the weights, and hold a shaking arm out for the phone. Unknown caller. It could be her, though.

"Yeah?" I answer, still out of breath. I'm already prepared to end the call in a hurry if some idiot who paid for my number answers me.

"Mr. Cooper?"

"Depends on who's asking." I'm not sure it's her. I only talked to her for a minute before, but the voice sounds familiar. I take a swig from my water bottle while Steve watches me like he's watching a movie and waiting for the big scene. Now he needs a big bowl of popcorn.

"Uhm, it's Ren—err—Renate. Renate Silva. We, uhm, we met last —" I'm grinning ear to ear while she rambles, until she lets out a heavy sigh of regret. Shit, that's not good. *"Look, the smart board is nice. I mean, like super nice. I appreciate the gesture, but I can't take it. There are policies against gifts like that and it's not fair to the other*

teachers. I hope that makes sense. I don't want to sound like I'm not grateful because, I, you know, I am."

"Shit, I'm sorry, Renate." Even in my panic, her name rolls off my tongue in a way that feels both weird and… right. I want to whisper it in her ear as she wakes up next to me in bed. I've been hanging out with Steve too much.

"I didn't expect you to answer. I assumed this whole thing had been planned by my sister as a messed up joke."

"No! No, not a joke. I hope I didn't cause too much trouble. I should have known better. I, you know, I thought flowers were too old school for a…a woman like you."

"Oh! Uhm, it's okay." The softness in her voice acts like a muscle relaxer and I'm melting into the bench. *"You wouldn't know that kind of thing unless you worked as a teacher. I feel terrible because I do like it. The kids loved it, too. I didn't tell them you sent it."*

"I'll get that taken care of as soon as I can, I promise."

She's silent, and I'm pretty sure she's hung up on me until I notice a kid's voice somewhere in the distance.

"I uhm, did you get… no, you have my number so yeah, obviously, you got the card. Duh."

"I did. I, look, Mr. Cooper, can I ask you something?"

"If I answer your question, will you answer mine?"

"Yes. I think they're kind of, well, related."

"Okay, shoot." I'm trying to act natural and even Steve rolls his eyes at how bad I am at this. The tabloids would eat this shit up if they could see it. *Hollywood Mega Star Crashes and Burns Asking Teacher Out!* Steve adds to my anxiety when he starts making a choking gesture and falling to the floor. Jackass.

"Why do you want to have dinner with me? And don't try the 'why not' or some other snarky answer. Give me a genuine answer."

"Why?" My date hinges on how I answer this, so I take my time to come up with the right way to say it and pray I don't fuck it up. "You… strike me as a confident, independent, beautiful woman and you treated me like a normal human being at the school the other night. I don't get that too often. I'm hoping you'll let me apologize properly both for running into you and for chickening out that night. I'm hoping for a chance to make it right."

"Chickening out?"

"I, uhm, lied the other day. I didn't get lost looking for the bathroom when I bumped into you." I have to close my eyes as Steve throws his hands in the air and walks away like he doesn't know me. "I wanted to, well, to talk to you. I'd been watching you on and off from the bleachers and, I…well, I didn't put two and two together and figured out who you were until after. I'd like the opportunity to get to know you. If you want to, anyhow." That all sounded so much cooler in my head. Steve makes a crash and burn gesture across the room, complete with explosion sound effects.

"Mmm," she hums and I'm not sure if that's a good thing or bad, but either way it makes me remember her lips, full with a bit of a pout to them and red like rubies—but soft. Maybe more like roses? I suck at poetry, but she has prettier lips than most leading actresses I've worked with.

"So? Did I give a satisfactory answer to your question, Ms. Silva?" The way my dick twitches when I say her name tells me I have a teacher kink. Well, a kink for a specific teacher, that's for sure. God, the things she's done to me in my daydreams today. I couldn't help but imagine what we could do together. Especially with the height difference—I'm at least a foot taller than her. Probably more.

"Maybe."

"Oh, *maybe?* That's sneaky." I laugh before dropping my voice, wishing I could see her face. "So let me ask you this. Do you like magic?"

"Magic?"

"I'd like to take you to the Magic Castle for dinner. If you'd like to join me, fantastic, send me your address and I'll pick you up at five tonight." I stop, giving her a moment to think about it, before adding, "If not, well, I'm glad I got to talk to you again and I wish you all the best. Oh, and Ren?"

"Yes?" she answers in a breathy voice.

"Text me the color of your dress. See you at five." I hang up, my heart hammering so hard in my chest it hurts. Fuck, that might have been the wrong move. I flop back onto the weight bench and stare at the ceiling. I had set my sights on going super smooth, but I went mysterious. Now, I've come off looking like a total asshole.

No matter what she decides, I need to take care of this smart board situation for her. I call my agent so she can tell me I'm a moron before we come up with a solution.

"Hey, Cynthia. Can we get some kind of deal with a company that makes those smart board things for classrooms?"

"What are you talking about?"

"The cool high tech dry erase boards. Chalk boards on crack! I dunno, Google it. I need, uhm, I need enough for every classroom at Hollywood Tech and Arts. It could be some kind of tax write off or something? I dunno. I need to make it happen. We can even use Jamie's art school thing as a cover if we need to."

"Oh, my god. Chase Cooper, what did you do?"

"Cyn, it's me. I didn't *do* anything." I don't think now is the exact moment I want to tell Cynthia I've got the hots for a teacher and I'm trying to make a move on her. "It's a tech school where I did a signing the other night with Jamie. I want to, you know, do something nice. Hypothetically."

"Okay, and that's it?"

"Yes." No.

"Stop bullshitting me, Cooper. What happened? Please tell me you only backed into someone's car or something simple like that?"

That's the relationship we have—she knows when to call me on my shit. She also knows that the extent of my embarrassing public behavior as a movie star would be something as mild as backing into someone's car while stone sober and apologizing for twenty years. I'm not here for scandals.

"I kind of asked a teacher out," I say, cringing as I prepare for her reaction.

"You asked her out with a smart board? Points for originality, but, come on, what did you do?"

"I chickened out on talking to her in person. Devin gave me the idea for the screen. He said flowers were lame. I also gave her a card with my number and, uhm, asked her to dinner."

"Wait, you seriously asked a teacher out by sending her a two thousand dollar gift?" She sounds more surprised than upset.

"Five thousand, but, uhm, yeah."

"Chase, that's fantastic! Not the money part. We'll talk about that later. I'll see what I can do about keeping it out of the papers. Where are you taking her? Do I need to set up a security crew?"

"She hasn't actually said yes yet, but she hasn't said no, either. The press shouldn't be an issue since I'm taking her somewhere exclusive. No cameras allowed, and I know a guy who will take us in and out the back way."

"Good idea, hun. Alright, I'll call around about the TV things and see what kind of deal we can work out. Commercials okay? At least voice over?"

"Fuck yeah, I'll be in a damn series of commercials if it helps get those things, sure."

"Chase," I can hear the smile as she says my name. *"She'll say yes, and when she does, have fun, okay? You deserve it. You deserve to be happy."*

"Thanks, Cyn."

As I end the call, my phone vibrates as a text that sends the butterflies into overdrive comes through. She's sent me an address that I'll have to Google later, but she also sent a message.

UNKNOWN NUMBER

Yes, I believe I do like magic.

And blue.

She winked! Okay, it's a stupid emoji, but… she winked. I'm definitely going to read too much into that until I pick her up tonight. My chest feels like it's full of helium or something.

Blue. I can totally do blue.

HOLLYWOOD
Chase

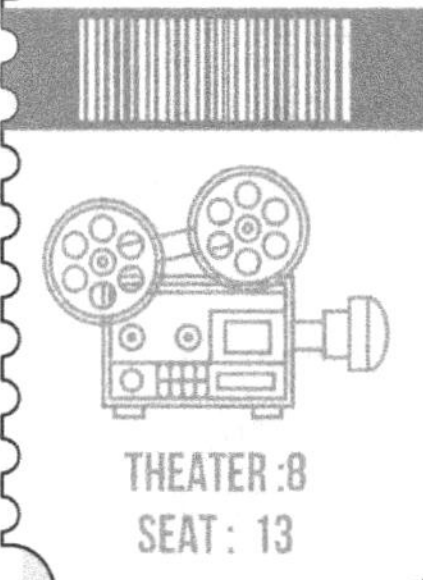

CHAPTER 6
EVERYBODY TALKS
NEON TREES

I'M surprised I'm not dead after the brutal workout this morning. When Steve said we were going fucking hard after my phone call—he meant it. He even made me take a stupid selfie with him and posted the damn thing. That's all over the internet now, which normally causes my phone to blow up, but I deleted the app for the day because I don't want the distraction. I also don't care about anything the press has to say about my body or what outlandish gossip the click-baiters will start today. Today, I'm way too pumped for that kind of bullshit.

So pumped that I've been standing in front of the mirror for fifteen minutes, trying to decide if I should shave or leave the scruff. I end up texting James's wife, Lexi. She says if I shave, she's going to come over to the house and take my dogs. Rude, but she made her point. She was a fan of mine long before she fell for my best friend. Now, she's another sister I never had, right there with Dani.

I drop onto the edge of the bed and pull up the address Ren sent me to see how long it's going to take. For all I know, she could live clear across the city or down in Long Beach, but I have a vague recollection of Dani mentioning they lived pretty close by.

I could have met Ren ages ago if Dani had introduced us, but I was in a shitty headspace before. The decision to take back control of my life took time, and until a few months ago, I wouldn't have given Ren and me a shot in hell. Life is so damn weird, but I'm glad it waited for better times to introduce her to me.

The pin on the map drops near the East Hollywood area—super close. Even with the LA traffic, it should only take me about fifteen minutes to get there, which means I have about an hour before I need to leave and I'm already dressed and waiting. This is worse than prom.

I'm staring in the mirror, and that's when the doubt creeps in. I examine every wrinkle around my eyes and the way my forehead creases when I'm stressed or angry. I over-analyze the way the suit fits me too tightly in some places. I question the way my face looks since I haven't shaved. With a deep breath, I stop and center myself, forcing a smile. But it fades as fast as it came.

What if she doesn't like me or thinks I'm weird? Do I look stupid? What if she finds out that I'm a mess and she decides I'm worth it? What if the paps see us? This is a terrible idea, and it's going to end badly—publicly. Again.

The walls are closing in and breathing isn't as easy as a minute ago. I need to get this suit off and to get some air. But I know the suit isn't the real issue.

What if I hurt her? What if I'm about to ruin her life in the same way I ruined Cassie's? What if she hates me? So damn many what ifs.

A shuffle by the door followed by Pongo's nose on my hand and his ninety-pound body leaning against my leg brings me back out of the spiral. As my breathing steadies again, I crouch down and let him lick my face. I take a few deep breaths to pull my head together. I've worked hard to learn how to pull myself out of the doom spiral.

"Good boy, buddy. Thank you."

"Hey man, all good?" Devin asks as he knocks on the door frame and pokes his head inside. "Pongo jumped up and took off, so I wanted to come up and check on you."

"Thanks, Dev. We're good. Pongo senses the shift in me before I do a lot of times."

After Cassie, I lost a couple of gigs because of my depression and panic attacks. I was sick all the time, lost way too much weight, couldn't even think straight. I admitted I needed help and, lucky for me, I have friends who made sure I got it. A few sessions into therapy, the doc recommended Pongo, a pit bull being trained as a Psychiatric Service dog by a friend of his. The press and public assume I'm another one of those celebrities who gets a dog and takes him everywhere. They had no idea they were a big part of the reason I needed him in the first place. He's been a literal lifesaver on more than one occasion, and Dev knows that. Not a lot of other people do, and I like to keep it that way.

"Maybe you should take Pongo?"

I scritch behind his ears and kiss his head. "What do you think, Pongo? I don't think you meet the dress code there, hotshot." I stand back up and nod to Devin, "It's alright, I uh, I'm a nervous wreck."

"You got this, and if you don't, you got me. I'm headed out to the game, but I'm not starting tonight, so if you need me, call. I'll be there."

"I love you, even if you are a dick sometimes and brush your fucking teeth in my kitchen like a caveman."

"Yeah, yeah. You have to love me, asshole. I'm the baby." He crosses the room and gives me a hug. We've always been close, even if we are eleven years apart. "You look good, man. Go knock 'em dead, but don't knock her up. I mean, unless you want to. You do you, but the kid isn't getting my room. Just saying."

"You…are so strange, man."

I finish getting ready and give the dogs their food before I grab my keys. Twenty minutes later, I'm pulling into a parking lot in front of a veterinarian's office with a Korean restaurant and a fast-food joint at opposite ends. There's a joke in here, but I'm sure as fuck not touching it with a ten-foot pole. I park and realize the Jaguar sticks out like a sore thumb. Instantly, I feel like a douche and the doubt creeps back in.

She's sent me here because I'm an idiot and she doesn't want people to know she's going out with me. Or she's standing me up and trying to prove a point. I should have borrowed Jamie's jeep. She's a teacher and I've seen Dani's car. I'm overdoing it. As always.

Fuck it. She's *my* date, which means she'll get treated like the fucking queen she is. Assuming she's even here.

I crack my neck and climb out, looking around and trying to give off a confident bravado. Inside, I'm jello. As I turn back to the car, the door to the vet's office opens up and there she is. My mouth hangs open, but I can't get my brain to fire off anything, so I continue staring. She's fucking gorgeous, and I can't even tell her that.

She's wearing a blue, floor-length skirt with two slits damn near all the way up the side. I can't breathe as I take in the way it hugs her, showing off that ass and those beautiful thighs. She's wearing a top with fabric criss-crossing over her chest and I can't stop staring at how amazing it makes her tits look. I have *got* to stop staring at them, but holy shit, it's hard not to. She looks like she's headed out to accept an Oscar, not to dinner with some dork like me.

"Is this not okay? I read it's formal attire."

Her voice brings me back to reality as I pull in the breath I've been needing to take for a while now. "I…you…uhm."

"You know, for a guy who basically talks for a living, you're not very good at it," she teases.

I clear my throat as a nervous laugh escapes before I jog to the other side of the car and hold the door open for her. "You look phenomenal, Ren. I mean it."

"Thanks," she replies with a confident wink as she ducks into the car, pulling her skirt in so it doesn't get caught on the door.

"Okay, Chase. DO NOT fuck this up. Do not! Fuck! This! Up!" I mumble to myself as I jog back around and get in. "Sorry if I kept you waiting."

"I showed up early. My neighbor works as a tech at the veterinarian's clinic and she let me borrow these shoes. Since I had to pick them up here, I played with the puppies after work. I even brought a change of clothes, just in case."

"In case of what?"

"You came to your senses and changed your mind. I figured being around puppies would make a satisfactory alternative to the evening if someone stood me up."

I glance at her, still trying not to stare. "You left *puppies* for me? I'm honored."

"Mr. Cooper—"

"Chase. Or Coop. Hell, you can call me anything you want, just, please, not Mr. Cooper."

"Okay, Chase, I don't know if you know this or not, but you're kind of famous and you're also kind of good looking. You're also kind of rich. School teachers don't get picked to accompany Hollywood hot shots to dinner."

"Okay, fair points, but what if she's a smoking hot teacher who looks absolutely stunning in my car?"

Whoa. That… almost sounded smooth. Shit, I might not fuck this up.

She laughs, and she doesn't hold back. I doubt there's a shy bone in this woman's body and it makes me like her more. "Okay, let's be real here before we get too many drinks in us. This isn't going anywhere, and by this, I mean us. You want to show off your toys and your flashy suit that probably costs more than my car. The problem is, those things don't mean a damn thing to me. I'm being nice to the generous—and gorgeous—man who bought me a fucking smart board."

"Oh," I reply, eyes on the road. Maybe I *should* have brought Pongo. No. No, I can do this. "So, if I burn the cars, the house, the suits, all of it, would that give me a fighting chance? Because I can get some lighter fluid while we're out and get started with this suit."

She laughs again and adjusts her skirt in a way that exposes more of her light brown thigh, turning my mouth into a desert.

"You okay, Chase?"

"How about a deal?" I spit out before I can think.

"A deal? Like a bet?"

"No, a deal. Tonight, we agree to be ourselves, have some fun, and enjoy the evening. See how it goes. If I'm a dud, you say so, and I'll leave you alone. You won't have to worry about me bothering you again. I promise."

"What if I don't think you're a dud?" I catch her biting her lip out of the corner of my eye and I pray that I'm not a dud.

"If that happens, I'd like to take you out again in whatever capacity interests you."

She stares at me as we pull into the driveway and up to the valet station. I should have circled the block a dozen more times so we could continue the conversation, but there's no turning back now. Before I can open the door, there's a knock on the window from the valet, Marco, who happens to be buddies with my brother. He waves me around back to a private lot. When we climb out, Marco takes the keys from me with a grin and I hand him two hockey tickets.

"Dev says hi. You should come by next week; I'll be out of town, but he's living at my place now and he'd love to see you."

"Sweet, thanks, Coop. Go ahead inside. They know you're coming." He looks Ren up and down as she slides in next to me and he gives her a coy smirk. "Miss, if it don't work out with Prince Charming, I can get you in here any night you want."

"Seriously, Marco? I invited you to my house two seconds ago, and you're already trying to take my girl?" I laugh and catch the pink spread over her cheeks when I call her my girl. I don't want to scare her off, but I need her to know I'm serious about wanting to give this a shot. I hold out my elbow and she slips her arm through. It's a little awkward and I have to lean down a bit, but we work it out.

"*Your* girl, huh?"

"A guy can hope, can't he?"

"So what happens if the night ends and you realize *I'm* the dud?"

I hold the door open and she steps into the dark hallway, giving us a quiet moment together as our eyes adjust. We're so close I can smell her perfume, and it smells like summer. Like warmth and sunflowers. I want to kiss her so damn badly.

"That isn't possible." I grin, reaching out and letting my finger trace down her necklace. "You're an intoxicating person, Ren. You can't hide that. Intelligent, bold, and absolutely breathtaking. You couldn't be a dud if you tried."

To my surprise, she pushes hard against my chest, backing me up to the wall. Grabbing my tie, she wraps it between her fingers, giving it a pull like a leash. Her rich, brown eyes stare up at me over her gold glasses and my knees are officially weak. I don't think I've ever been this turned on in my whole life, but I'm also terrified I've said the wrong thing. I'm well aware that it's fucked up to think about on our first semi-date, but I can't help wondering how fun she must be in bed.

She leans in and I can't stop staring at her lips as my heart pounds out of my chest. In a low, sultry voice, she says, "Well, you have yourself a deal. Let's see where tonight takes us, eh, puppy?"

HOLLYWOOD
Renate

CHAPTER 7

THE NIGHT WE MET

LORD HURON

NOT HAVING my phone for over four hours should drive me insane, but I've only thought about it when I wanted photos. It's hard not to take pictures in this place. It's a shame, too, because there's been a few times I've caught our reflection in a mirror or picture frame and we look fucking sexy together. Even without the photos to prove it, I'm having the best time I've had in a long time. No one has ever taken me anywhere fancier than a damn Red Lobster. It doesn't even count since my mother took me.

Chase has been like a kid in a candy store, buying us drinks at every bar, bouncing around from show to show, until we have to stop for our dinner reservations. He's treated me like a princess from the moment I sat in his car, and something tells me this isn't an act. This is the real Chase Cooper.

I've got a pang of regret growing in my stomach over not kissing him when I had him against the wall. I would have had to pull him down to my level, but it would have been worth it.

Sometimes I'm a little shy about food because I'm not a skinny girl and I can pack a steak away like nobody's business. Some people find that off-putting, and I find those people to be boring and prudish. But Chase has me laughing and talking so much that I never cared about keeping up some bullshit

appearances that a magazine told me about as a teenager. Half way through the meal, he even offered me a bite of his food and we ended up swapping plates. He ordered us dessert and more drinks, and I thought we'd never leave the table.

For a movie star, Chase is so down to earth and just…sweet. I expected him to have a high and mighty attitude given his place in this town. Instead, he only made me feel comfortable, as if I belonged right there beside him, rubbing elbows with elites.

"Here you go," Chase hands me a martini glass as he sits beside me on a fancy bench. Since dinner, we've watched two more incredible magic shows, but we both need a break and I want to experience as much of this place as I can. "Before you ask, no, I have no fucking idea where he pulled that bowling ball from."

"Oh my god, that was so crazy!" Everything about this place is breathtaking, the staircases, decor, and the number of famous people milling about should have all of my attention. But they can't hold a magic candle to him. I'm not alone, either, because he keeps staring at me, too. Every time our eyes meet, we both smile and giggle until we can't take anymore and we break eye contact, blushing. My eyes drop to my drink as I swirl it around a little and watch the glitter create a galaxy in my glass.

"What is it?"

"Uhm, passion fruit martini. I told the guy you said something fruity, he said they're all the rage. I had him add the glittery stuff, because it's mind blowing, like you." He tucks a strand of my hair behind my ear, and I can feel his hands shake. He downs a huge gulp of his drink to fortify his nerves, and as he goes to set the glass down, I take it from him and steal a sip. The burn feels amazing, and his throat bobs as he watches me lick my lips. "I—I can get you one of those if you want one."

"Nope, just wanted to see what expensive whiskey tastes like." He's watching me, staring at my lips as I sip my fruity glitter. "Do you want to try mine?"

He nods, but when I hand him the glass, he sets it behind him. His large hand slides up my cheek, caressing it gently as he moves his lips to mine. He tastes like fear and danger wrapped up in one delicious package. I'm left wanting more when he pulls away.

"W-why'd you do that?"

"I just wanted to know what *you* taste like."

The room feels twenty degrees hotter, and I don't remember my dress being so tight around my chest earlier.

His hands take mine even though our eyes remain locked on each other. "Will you dance with me?"

"Dance?" I glance around and I don't see anyone else dancing. He nods. "Fuck it, why not? Let's dance."

Leaving our drinks behind, he takes me to a small side room with a roped off piano and a handful of people—none of which are dancing. He walks over to the empty chair at the piano, whispers something, and turns back to me, taking my hands.

"Irma is one hell of a piano player. Watch."

I glance over as the music starts and see the keys being pressed by no one. I'm a science nerd, so I'm sure there's a simple, logic-based explanation behind the trick. But for tonight, I don't want to figure it out. I want to keep this magic alive as we sway, not caring about anything beyond the two of us and the ghost of Irma playing piano.

"Hey, what's the matter?" he asks, reaching up and wiping away a tear I didn't mean to shed.

"Uhm, I...I don't know." I try to laugh it off, but he isn't buying it, so I try to change the subject. "I recognize this song from somewhere."

"Yeah, it's uhm, The Night We Met. I figured it would be, you know, appropriate or whatever. Too lame?"

"No. No, it's...perfect."

People might watch, they might break the rules and take pictures of us, but I don't notice them because this man stares at me like I'm the only person in the room. Hell, in the whole damn world. No one has ever looked at me like that. It's making me a tiny bit uncomfortable. But that feeling can't compete with the soft glow of a crush I might have on him and the relentless beating of wings in my stomach.

"Chase, I… uhm…I'm a dominatrix. Sort of." I spit it out so fast that I slap my hand over my mouth, wishing I could shove every word back into my stupid face. Now he'll run, and I'll be stuck crying in a cab on the way home. *Shit.*

His eyebrow shoots up, and he grins. "Okay."

"No, I mean, like, I'm really a domme. Like, I go to clubs and tie people up and spank them and shit. Not like hardcore or anything, sometimes a lite bondage, and some kink exploration, but—"

"Okay."

"No, it's not okay!"

"It's not? Then why do it?" He's not being cruel or joking around. He's dead serious right now. How can he not see that this could end up an enormous problem?

"No," I take a step away from him and instantly I regret it. "I mean, it's not okay that I do that. I mean, it is for me, but not for you. You can't be seen with someone who does that, Chase. The press would eat you alive. Shit, I ruined the moment with this, didn't I?"

He reaches out and takes my hand, bringing the back of it to his lips as his eyes stay on mine. "Renate, I've let people tell me who I can and can't be, or who I can and can't date for a long time. It's taken me a while, but I'm beginning to learn that I need to stop giving a fuck what people expect of me. Especially people I don't care about. We're adults, we can do whatever we want."

"But the internet will find out and I *do* care what people expect of me. I'm a teacher, Chase! I teach children. It's not appropriate and I—"

"And you're jumping fifty steps ahead, sunshine. Relax, we're only getting to know each other, and I'm sure as hell not about to tell anyone."

He cups my face in his large hands before leaning down to kiss me. This time, it's not a taste, it's not tentative or nervous either. This is deep and serious—more serious than his words let on.

"Do you wanna get out of here?" he whispers against my lips. I nod, still in a daze. He takes my hand, leading me down the stairs and through the winding hallways that have me turned around. We both laugh when he realizes he's as lost as I am, but we've stumbled into an empty room.

He pins me against a wall and we're kissing again, desperate, bordering on depraved as his hand slides up the slit in my skirt. The sound of someone laughing too loudly pulls us back to reality, and we giggle as we race the other way. I can't help but think that I'd have no problem being lost with him anywhere.

He finds the exit, but before going through the door, he spins around and backs me into the same wall I had him against earlier. His powerful arms cage me in, although I'm short enough to slip under them if I wanted. I don't. He licks his lips and smirks. "I don't want to take you home yet. Bar or club?"

"Club. I want to dance with you for real." His mouth slides over mine, teasing without kissing. In that instant, I know exactly how this night will end. We'll fuck. It will be fun and just what we need to get this out of our system, but that's all it will be.

Tonight will be the fairytale I remember for the rest of my life. The night I got to be the princess at the ball. Morning will come, the fancy car will become a pumpkin, and Chase will be a memory I'll cherish forever while he goes back to his palace and a life I could never be a part of.

But for now, he's right. I'm not ready for it to end.

Two hours later, we're both exhausted and laughing at stupid jokes as we fall into a booth in the VIP section of whatever club we're at. I've never been here before, but Chase knows his way around. The giant security guy who could be a pro wrestler keeps the curious away from the area as we make out like teenagers. I grab for the bottle of water on the table, downing half of it before handing it to Chase. As he drinks, I check around before I climb into his lap, straddling him. The empty bottle falls next to us somewhere as I grab his face and crash against his lips while I grind against him. His hands slide up my thighs, squeezing my ass as he moans into my mouth. I love a man who makes noise during sex.

I stop, but instead of pulling away, I move my mouth over to his ear. "Chase, are you a good boy or a bad boy?" I ask before I take his earlobe between my teeth and gently bite down. He grabs my hips, pressing his fingers into my skin and leaving bruises that I'll remember him by tomorrow. He rocks me back and forth on the hard bulge in his pants, and the friction feels sublime.

"I'll be whatever the fuck you want me to be. Just let me be inside you?"

"Not here, Chase." I lean back, letting my finger drag down the buttons on his black shirt. "Take me to bed."

I squeal when he stands up, literally taking me with him. He's staring at me again with that look that says there's no music, no people, no club—only us. He's about to carry me out, but I make him put me down. So far, we've evaded the paparazzi and gawkers, but that's harder to do when he's drawing attention to us.

We're almost to the stairs when he pulls me back for another deep kiss, his hand cupping my breast and squeezing. I am fucking soaked for this man, and I can't wait to get him in bed. If he had his choice, we wouldn't wait for the bed.

"Fuck, you're delicious, like fucking sunshine," he slurs.

"You can't drive. You're drunk."

"Shit, yeah, you're right." He straightens up and gives me a dopey smile. "I can get us a ride share, or a hotel, I guess."

"Or you could give me your keys." I narrow my eyes, expecting him to balk at the idea of me driving his Jag like most men would. He pulls the valet ticket out of his wallet and hands it to me like it's no big deal. He doesn't even ask for the keys when we get to the car, just holds the door open for me and goes to the passenger side like this is standard for him.

This car is worth more than my damn salary and he's trusting me with it after one night of dancing and magic?

"Fucking valet bullshit," he mumbles as he gets in, immediately leaning over and kissing me again. His tongue slides over mine and he whimpers. He fucking whimpers! His hand snakes up my leg and the tip of his finger rubs against me. "If we were in a parking spot, I'd have my mouth between your fucking legs right now. God, you're beautiful."

"Okay, drunky. I gotta drive now before they start to get pissy. And I can't do that with your hands all over me."

"Okay." He pretends to grumble as he sits back and smiles at me with a big, dumb, gleeful grin. He's far too adorable for this world. "Let's go home. My place. I've got all kinds of shit at the house to keep us busy all night. Pool table, pool, dogs. The only thing missing is you."

I should say no. I mean, I haven't known him for more than a few hours, but I knew the second we kissed, I would go home with him. Why shouldn't I have a little fun? Like he said, we're adults. "Alright, but only for the dogs."

"The dogs? Well, what if I get on my hands and knees for you, sunshine? Maybe wear a little collar and wag my ass, all for you."

"Careful, you're writing checks that your dick isn't going to cash when you're this drunk."

He slumps his shoulders and turns away, staring out the window. He isn't angry, but I'm not sure, and looks can be deceiving. I don't know him. I don't know his demons. I don't know what makes him tick or if he's going to turn into a Jekyll and Hyde situation. For all I know, he takes women home to brutally murder them before burying them in the backyard or feeding them to his dogs. It's Los Angeles. Anything is possible.

I check the clock and see it's already after midnight. Even if I don't have school tomorrow, I shouldn't be watching the sunrise with Chase Cooper. But god, do I want to.

"You gonna tell me how to get to your place?"

"Call me that name again."

"Chase?"

"No, the one you called me earlier, at the Magic Castle."

"Puppy?"

He smirks and turns on his GPS before taking a strand of my hair and twirling it in his fingers. "I like it when you call me that, sunshine."

HOLLYWOOD
Chase

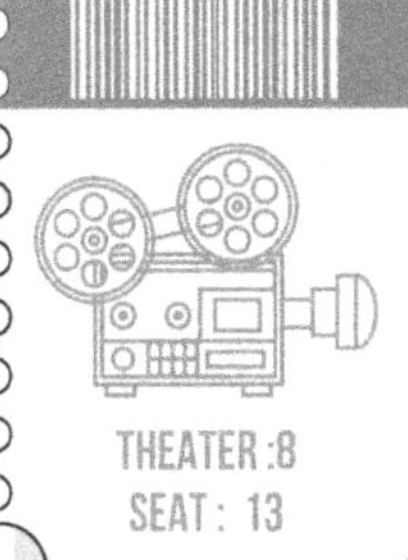

CHAPTER 8
VROOM VROOM

CHARLI XCX

I HAVEN'T HAD this much fun in a long time.

Correction; I haven't *let* myself have this much fun in a long time. I've allowed myself to become so buried in my career and keeping up the illusion of happiness, I've forgotten what it feels like to let go and just *be* happy. Since Cassie, I prefer to spend time with my dogs rather than most people. My friends are the few exceptions.

We alternate between dancing and making out, which brings out a surreal feeling I've been longing to experience again for years. I can't tell if it's the alcohol or Renate causing this sloppy sensation in my brain and butterflies lodging in my chest, but I don't want to let go of these feelings, not yet.

Now she wants to go home with me? And I just handed her my keys? I'm convinced I've died.

She slips behind the wheel like she owns it, and the way she controls the car like a natural has my head spinning. No fear. That's nothing if not hot. Once again, I find myself curious to know what she's like in bed. If I'm lucky, I might find out soon. I have a million questions running through my head about the dominatrix bomb she dropped earlier, and I'm getting a hard on every time she calls me her puppy. Fuck, what the hell got into me? As she drives, I pinch the bridge of my nose, trying to clear my mind, but there's so much running through it.

I've had women over since Cassie, and even dated a few, but always to drown out the pain for a few hours or days. It always left me feeling worse, and them feeling used. Ren is the first one not interested in my money or my fame, and more importantly, she doesn't want to play therapist—I already have one of those. Ren also isn't someone I hope sneaks out in the middle of the night. I want to wake up next to her tomorrow. Hell, for a lifetime worth of tomorrows. I want to dance with her, laugh with her, and just be with her. I want her to be mine, but more importantly, I need to be hers.

But this is all way too fast, and I know she's hesitant.

"You okay, big guy? Or do I need to pull over? Wouldn't want you getting sick in such a pretty car." She glances over at me for a second, then back to the road. I hadn't realized I'd gone still, too busy letting her run around in my mind. She stopped drinking hours ago, because she's a responsible adult. I've been drinking and acting like a fucking frat boy. Like a loser. I'm sure she's being nice and making sure I make it home in one piece. She'll get me to pass out on the couch and leave, never to be heard from again. She'll become the one that got away, the one I let slip out of my fingers because I'm too scared to tell her how she makes me feel.

The alcohol grabs me by the collar and throws me headfirst into a spiral so fast I can't stop it. I'm too drunk to recognize the signs, too stupid to remember what to do. There's a panic attack knocking on my fucking window while she drives through Hollywood.

"I'm sorry. It's uhm." I scrunch my nose together for a second to bite back the coming panic attack. "I haven't been out with someone like you in…shit…a while."

"Like, on a date? Tell me that's not true." She asks as she maneuvers the tight corners. I take her in, the full hips, the thick thighs, the small peak of a perfect soft belly between her top and her skirt. And her tits. I'm still staring at her tits. I'm spiraling into a breakdown and I'm staring at a goddess.

"Huh? Oh, yeah. Yeah, I haven't dated in a while. I mean, I have, but none of them went well." I watch Los Angeles pass by the window. Even the familiar landscape looks foreign in the darkness. Just like in my mind, the world closes in.

"You sure you're okay?"

She reaches over and takes my hand, stroking it with her thumb. The gesture is soft but reassuring and I close my eyes, remembering how to breathe through this as her touch calms me.

"Yeah, I think I'm just..." *In total disbelief that you're sitting next to me, you're holding my hand, you're real.* "You know, drunk."

She continues to hold my hand as I emerge from the spiral. We pass a billboard for the Pasadena Parrots and smack my forehead and whip out my phone. Scrolling through the messages, I can't find Devin's name. Am I that drunk? My memory flashes to him playing with my phone last night, and I scroll back up. Bingo, the blonde knockout named Buffy. Dick.

Hey, bringing Ren home.

ETA, ten minutes.

BUFFY

Roger that. I'm a ghost in the wind!

Leaf. A leaf on the wind.

BUFFY

Whatever dick, I'm gone, and I took the dogs.

I chuckle and look out the windshield. I'm about to give her a heads up about the corners in this area, but she's giving me a look that screams I'm about to be in detention. That's when I notice the console saying I have an incoming message from Buffy. I should be worried, but I'm grinning like a moron.

"Buffy? That's not your wife or something, right?"

"You're welcome to scroll through my messages when we get to my place, if it will help you feel better about it. Buffy is my dipshit brother's idea of a joke. He changed his contact name last night when I told him about our date. Complete with a picture from, well, probably a porn site. Nothing but fart jokes, ETAs, and NHL stats between Buffy and I."

"Oh my god, when you said *brother* earlier, I didn't know you were serious. There's another one of you?"

"Yeah," I laugh, pulling her hand to my lips and kissing each of her knuckles. "My kid brother, Devin *Hollywood* Cooper. Sometimes Mini Cooper." She stares at me until the light goes green, clearly not recognizing the name. "He's a goalie for the Parrots."

"The ice hockey?"

"Yeah, *the ice hockey*," I snicker. She scrunches her nose up, and it's fucking adorable. The panic attack that never fully took hold now fades into the blackness of the night. No Pongo reminding me to take my meds, no calling my doc, nothing but her. She's not the solution to my problems, but, just maybe, she's something better. "You've never been to a hockey game, have you?"

"No. I come from a house of football and baseball boys. Hockey is still a white person's sport."

"Yeah, that may still be true, but if you agree to go out with me again, I think that means you're officially dating a Canadian. We're required to initiate the unenlightened or we lose access to maple syrup. Or something like that."

"Sounds terrible," she giggles. "But we had a plan, remember? The night's not over yet."

"Are you saying I might still be a dud?"

"No, I'm saying we should wait. Get this out of our system so we don't make plans we'll regret later." She furrows her brow and stares ahead at the road. I'm not against what she's saying. It's smart and makes sense, but my irrational brain has the lead. "So, how old is your brother?"

"He's, uhhhh." Math becomes way too hard since my brain has been bouncing from the booze to her breasts. "Twenty-three? Yeah, he'll be twenty-four in a couple of months."

"Wow, that's a big gap. I mean, you are like thirty-something, right? Please tell me you're not in your twenties."

"Nah. I'm thirty-five." I reach over, tracing the edges of the slit in her dress with my finger. "What's with the hate for twenty-somethings?"

"Your brother changes the contact info on your phone to a porn star's tits, and you have to ask me that?" She laughs, and when she looks at me again, it's hard to swallow the lump in my throat.

"God, you're beautiful when you laugh. Actually, you're stunning, laughing or not."

"And you're drunk."

"Not that drunk. I promise."

"You're sure?"

"Yeah, I'm good."

Without warning, she swerves the car into a small section of undeveloped road, throwing it into park. "I will never get over the way you idiots park up here," she mumbles as she unclips her seatbelt.

The GPS shows we're only a few minutes from my house. She can't want to walk the rest of the way. It's steep and brutal. I should know, Steve makes me run it.

"Where are you—" Before I can finish the thought, Ren climbs over the gearshift and into my lap. Our mouths slam together and our hands are everywhere. The tension between us has finally burst, and neither one of us can wait another minute. I want all of her, and she clearly feels the same way.

She grabs my hair and pulls as she moans long and low into my mouth. It's like she's given me part of her soul the way she's kissing back and trying to rip my shirt off.

"Renate," I hum against her ear in time with her hips that are rolling over me.

"Shut up and keep kissing me, you fucking idiot!"

Her hands grab for my belt and she has it undone in no time, so my hands get to work. One squeezes her ass hard, the other tries to figure out how this top works. It looked so easy, but this thing might be worse than a bra. She pulls away from me again, reaching into my pants. I'm gasping for air, but she's not stopping.

"Wait!" She snaps her head up, her face contorted in confusion, he hand pressed against my painfully hard cock. "Ask me again."

"Ask you what?!"

"If I wanna be a good boy or a bad boy. Ask me again."

Her lip curls up in a grin that makes the butterflies in my stomach do backflips. She slips her hands into my boxers as she pushing her tits against my chest. Her lips brushing mine with each word as she whispers. "Chase Cooper, do you want to be a good boy, or do you want to be a very bad boy?"

"Bad," I answer, grabbing her top and pulling it open. "I'll be the fucking devil for a taste of you."

She grabs my bottom lip between her teeth and bites down hard. The pain leaves in an instant, becoming something more, something I've never felt before. I reach down between her legs and under her skirt, sliding my hand up until my fingers find the lace. She's soaked. I could wring out her damn panties level soaked. My thumb finds her clit and before I can slip two fingers inside her, she's got one hand squeezing my cock and the other squeezing my neck.

"The safe word is octopus. If you can't remember that, say red, okay?"

I nod seconds before my eyes roll back. Her thumb drags over the head of my cock so fucking slow, pulling the moan right out of my soul. It's damn near torture, but fuck, I want more. I can't concentrate on what I'm doing, especially when she squeezes my throat harder.

"Oh please! Don't fucking stop, Renate!"

"Tell me what you want, Chase."

"I wanna fuck you."

"Beg for my pussy, Chase."

My mind goes blank for a moment as I'm given an instant lesson on why some women are so into dirty talk. And being choked out. "Fuck, that's fucking hot." I lick my lips and think, "Please. Please let me have you, Renate."

"You can do better, unless you want me to leave you like this." She squeezes my cock again and my ass comes off the seat.

"No! Please!" I yell out, not recognizing the voice coming out of me. "Please, Sunshine. I need you so bad. I can't stop fucking thinking about you. I wanna take you home and let you fuck my face. I wanna drown in your pussy while you scream my name. Please, anything."

"Much better," she says between pants. She leans in next to my ear again, and whispers in the most seductive voice I've ever heard, "You're such a good boy."

She's riding my hand, her head flung back in ecstasy and my fingers curl up, hitting her G-spot and making her scream for me. She's got one hand on my cock and the other cupping her breast, pinching her nipple through the fabric. I grope around, struggling to get the armrest storage open so I can pull out a condom. When it finally pops, I quickly find the foil package, holding it up in triumph. She licks her lips and bites down on the foil's edge while I pull it to the side. She's so fucking perfect.

I move for her tits, but she catches my wrist, pulling it over my head and holding it down.

"Stop trying to take control, Chase. Not until you bury that big cock deep inside me. Do you understand?" I nod. "Good boy, now make me fucking come with your fingers before you fuck me. Earn this pussy you want so much."

Her mouth slams into mine as our teeth clash together when I slip a third finger into her cunt and pump harder. Her nails carve their way down my arm. I'm not even inside her and I'm going to fucking lose it. The wail of pleasure that comes out of her is pornographic and her entire body convulses around me. As she tumbles over the edge, she throws her hands around my neck and holds on tight.

It's like she trusts me to keep her safe in this vulnerable moment, and I sure as hell will.

When her body stops shaking, she lifts herself off my chest and looks at me with those big, brown, sex-drunk eyes and a beautiful smile. "You're turn, big boy. You ready?"

"Fuck yeah."

Her hand wraps around my cock again and I gasp. I damn near black out as she guides me into her. She's so wet I slide right into her and it's beyond incredible. Her head rocks back as she impales herself on me, her noises tell me she likes it as much as I do. The windows steamed up, and the car fills with grunts, moans, and slapping skin as she rides me like a rodeo bull. I fumble around until I find the controls and lay my seat back so I can watch her bouncing on top of me.

Renate isn't tall and skinny like most of the women I end up with. In fact, she's only the second woman I've ever been with who doesn't fit that Hollywood cookie-cutter aesthetic. Watching her body move now reminds me why I love thick women so much more. It's the way her tits bounce when she rocks her head back. How her thighs sound when they slap against my legs. The softness of every part of her my fingers graze. There's so much more to grab, so much more to explore, so much more to want.

We both belt out primal noises as she reaches the peak again and her lips make the prettiest 'O' shape. I don't think she even cares that she's fucking me. I could be anyone. Hell, I don't need to be here at all. Right now, she's taking whatever she needs from my cock as she fucks herself stupid. Knowing that I'm nothing but a toy for her satisfaction is like a sexual awakening in me. This quicky in my car is the hottest, best sex I've had in my whole life.

She's fearless. She knows what she wants and how to take it from me. She's taking me right to the edge and holding me there without pushing me over. Just her, in complete and total control.

"Fuck you feel so damn good, Renate. I'm... I'm gonna come."

She grabs my jaw and stares at me, the street light forming a halo around her wild, messy hair. "You don't come until I want you to, understand, *slut?*"

I nod, but it's not enough. She needs to know I want this, or she'll back off. "Yes...ma'am."

Her small fingers slide down my face, wrapping around my throat again. She squeezes, inching me closer to that release, but I hold back. "Stop having sex with me and fuck me! Make me scream for you, Chase. Do what you've been wanting to do to me all damn night."

She's handing me the keys now, and I'm scared to death I've forgotten how to drive. I pull her top down, grab her hips and thrust hard into her as my mouth wraps around her dark brown nipple. I suck and bite as her fingers rake through my hair. I can't hold out much longer, but I can already feel that I won't have to.

"Oh fuck, Chase, ohhh right there, puppy!" She throws her head back again and I can feel her tighten around me like a vise as another orgasm overtakes her. I'm squeezing my eyes shut and trying hard not to come. I'm focusing so damn hard on not coming, I don't even notice her lean forward and press her lips to my ear until she whispers in this smoky, hauntingly perfect voice, "Fill my pussy like the good little whore you are, puppy."

HOLLYWOOD
Renate

CHAPTER 9
BANANA PANCAKES

JACK JOHNSON

LOUD PANTING PULLS me from sleep and I panic, ready to swing at some motherfucker in my room. Luckily, I open my eyes first. This isn't my room, and the motherfucker in questions is a beautiful white and brown pit standing across the room, watching me.

"You're cute," I mumble sleepily against the pillow. I'm exhausted, but my body feels incredible and the night's adventure comes back to me. I find cold, empty sheets next to me. When I power up my phone, I'm shocked to see that I've slept through the morning. No less than fifteen texts from my mother and sister flood my phone.

> I'm fine, I promise. Sorry!! I slept at a friend's house and didn't hear the phone!!

DANIELLA

HOW DO WE KNOW IT'S YOU?

TELL ME SOMETHING ONLY REN WOULD KNOW!

> Shut up, I haven't had coffee yet, you lunatic.

DANIELLA

Oh, yeah, that's you, alright. My bad.

You watch too much true crime.

DANIELLA

It keeps us alive!!

What time are you coming home? 😌🔪😌

MAMA

DANIELLA DO NOT USE THAT IMAGE!

I'll be home when I'm home. I'm turning the phone off now to save the battery.

I'm still smiling when Chase comes back into the room, whistling. He's wearing lounge pants that hang low on his hips, giving me an eyeful of sculpted perfection. I follow the trail of his six-pack, take in that deep v, and can't stop staring at the patch of hair that disappears into his pants.

Holy shit, I slept with that! Actually, I rode that man like my life depended on it.

The tray he's carrying smells like bacon and coffee that pulls me out of my memories of last night. I like bacon and coffee more than I like dick. Maybe.

"Morning! I told the dogs to let you sleep."

"What's all this?" I ask as he sets the tray down. There's a bowl of sliced fruit, a French press of coffee, pancakes, eggs, bacon, and a beautiful sunflower.

"I woke up early and figured you'd be hungry after last night, so…" He gestures to the tray with a big smile. "Hangover curing breakfast."

"Where did it all come from?" I pick up a piece of bacon, examining it.

"Uh, the kitchen? The sunflower came from the neighbor's

yard, and he'll probably yell at me about that later, but I don't give a fuck. He's an asshole."

"What time did you make the chef come in for all this?" When we pulled up to the house last night, the size of the house surprised me. I expected twenty bedrooms and its own zip code for how famous he is. What he carried me into was not that at all. Yes, there's a pool and a three-car garage, but it's almost modest for Los Angeles. It's still five times bigger than my place, but it's kind of cute.

"He's been here all night." He bows with a flourish. "Chef Cooper, at your service."

"You did this? Seriously?" Everything sits on the plate like he's serving this in a five-star restaurant, not on his giant, comfortable bed that I never want to leave.

"Yeah. I, uhm, I cook. I picked it up a few years ago. It helps with anxiety." He pops a piece of bacon in his mouth and leans in to kiss me. It's gentle and sweet, the way his lips linger near mine. "I'll make you something else if this isn't what you want." He pulls back, shock on his face. He wipes his mouth, looking like he's about to freak out. "Wait, are you, like, vegan or gluten-free or anything? Jewish? I should have asked that before I kissed you. Hell, before I started cooking all this—"

I grab both sides of his face, and his eyebrows shoot up, but he stops talking. "I love bacon. I also love pancakes. But I need at least half a cup of coffee before you can start freaking out over small stuff."

"Yes, ma'am," he chuckles, relieved. Breaking off another piece of bacon, he holds it out and places it on my tongue.

"Holy shit. This isn't bacon. This is heaven."

He puffs out his chest. "It's got a little brown sugar and… never mind, you don't care." He bounces into the bed. "Okay, coffee! I, uhm, wasn't sure what you take in yours, so there's like three different creamers, honey, sugar, and some other stuff." He bites at his bottom lip, trying not to look at me.

I pour a cup and look at him as he watches me. When I set the pot of coffee down, he goes to reach for it and I swat his hand away. "You made me breakfast. I can at least pour you a cup of coffee. How do you like it?"

"Uhm, black. When it's hot anyhow."

"Gross! How do you drink that?"

"Used to it, I guess."

"Next time, I will make the coffee. I'll add a little cinnamon like Mama does and change your whole life."

"Next time?"

"You're not a dud, Chase Cooper." I grin and hand the cup over to him and pour myself a cup. I take a sip before I set it off to the side of the tray and pick up a strawberry, holding it out to him. "We should talk about this, though."

"About breakfast?" he jokes as he leans in to take the fruit from me. "I thought I'd feed it to you, you know.."

"Well, surprise, I like being in charge."

"Yeah, and you're fucking good at it, too. What do you want to talk about?"

He bites down on the strawberry and some of the juice drips down my fingers. He takes my wrist, licking lazy circles along my fingers until they're clean. He never breaks eye contact when he turns my hand over and kisses the palm, my wrist, and works his way up to my elbow before he stops and looks at me with those sparkling blue eyes. I have the urge to cover myself in strawberry juice and let him clean off every inch of me. The devious smile on his face says he's thinking the same thing.

"After breakfast, I can give you the grand tour. We can screw our brains out all over the house. Or we can stay here in bed." He holds out another piece of bacon and he kisses me again after I eat it. His mouth lingers a little longer than before, and it makes my heart flutter.

"Are you going to do that after every piece I eat?" I ask in a breathy voice.

"Yeah, I am. I've never had bacon taste this good before, and I can't get enough." He moves the tray to the side and crawls over me until I'm forced to lie back on the bed. Nipping at my ear, his hand slips up my shirt. "You look so fucking good in my clothes. But you look better out of them."

"Breakfast will get cold." He steals my breath in a kiss as my skin catches fire against his lips. "And spill all over your fancy bed."

He pinches my nipple while his deep laugh vibrates between us. "Ms. Silva, I'm sure *my* breakfast will stay sweet, hot, and soaking fucking wet for me. And I won't let a drop of it hit the bed." His mouth slides down my jaw and I want him inside me again. His fingers dance down my body, and he gives me a needy groan when he finds no lace to work around between my legs. He teases my entrance until the echoing clatter of dishes and hot, panting breaths interrupts us. Chase shoos the dogs off the bed, but the big pit bull wants none of that, and lays down next to me, his head on my chest as he looks up at me with big sweet eyes.

"They want bacon, too, Chase."

"That isn't all he wants. Hey! You cock-blocking fuckers are in so much trouble!" He can't even keep a straight face as he tries to correct them and ends up with the little boxer running away with a pancake. "Lulu! I already fed you!"

"Aww, they're jealous that you don't kiss them like that after they eat bacon, huh, little guy?" I tease as I take the pit bull's gigantic head in my hands. He licks my face and I can't stop giggling. "You are one big ass dog!"

"Pongo, come on, man. You can't steal my girl like that already! Here, bacon!" He tosses a piece toward the end of the bed and pulls me up as soon as Pongo jumps away. Once I'm upright again, he hands me my coffee. "I'm sorry. They get excited when new people come over. I managed to save your coffee, though."

My girl? He's called me that twice now. I'm worried this has already gone too far. Time to ease him into a conversation I don't want to have.

"They're both cute as hell. What are their names?"

"The big one is Pongo. He's the oldest. A guy pulled him out of a local shelter and trained him as a…well, he's, uhm, he's a service dog." His hands knead together as he stares down at the sheets. It's like he's preparing for me to ask why he has a service dog, but I won't ask. He'll tell me when he's ready.

"Well, he's the cutest little bacon thief, isn't he? And the other one?"

"The pancake thief is Lulu. I rescued her about three years ago. She had puppies not long after I got her, and we ended up giving one to Jamie and his wife. Dani wanted one, but your mom said no." He stops, scratching the stubble on his jawline and chuckling. "God, that's still so weird. You're really Dani's sister, huh?"

He leans and tucks a strand of hair behind my ear, but before he can move in and kiss me again, I sit upright with a start. "Wait! *THE* puppies! Chase Cooper! Let me tell you, you started a damn war in our house for two entire weeks with that cute puppy bullshit. Texting her pictures at all hours. Not cool, jerk!" I smack his arm, but there's no force behind it, and he just laughs.

It's easy to forget he's a movie star. Even with the awards in the case downstairs and paparazzi photos. Everything about him feels so different. Ever since we saw each other, there's been a warmth and familiarity around Chase and that extends to his home. Like everything in my life fell into place all at once. As if I can picture myself living here and becoming a part of this. Maybe it's because of his friendship with Dani, maybe it's more.

He leans over again with that smirk. "Now, where were we?"

"Chase." I stop him, holding my hand against his rock-hard chest. I want to tie him up and tease the sprinkling of hair that's growing back after being shaved down for a role. But I have to let him down now before this goes too far. "You're an amazing guy—"

"Oh, no! Come on, finish your coffee before you get to the 'but you *are* a dud' part!"

"I need to be honest with you. I had an incredible time with you last night. But I can't do this all the time. I'm a teacher, and I love my job. You're a movie star. It's going to get complicated even without my whole extra lifestyle thing."

He nods, but I can see the hurt in his eyes. Fuck. I didn't want to break his heart like this, not after the night we had. He's silent for a while and I'm cursing myself for making it awkward. I set my coffee on the table next to the bed and move to get up, figuring I've worn out my welcome, but he stops me by pulling me back into bed.

"Chase—"

"Friends?"

"What?"

"Ren, I like you. I get that all of this is crazy and that we're in two backwards realities right now, but it doesn't mean we can't be friends, right?" Before I can say no, he puts his finger over my lips and stops me. "Come on, please? I just…last night was the best night I've had in a long time. We don't have to be more than that if—"

I raise an eyebrow, challenging what he's about to say. I've done this dance before, and it never goes well. We stay friends, but eventually, he wants more. When I say no, I'm a prude or a bitch. He gets angry and I get another hospital bill.

"Maybe with benefits?" He caresses my cheek; I'm losing this fight. "We'll stop anytime you want to. We'll keep it a secret. We can meet in seedy motels and dimly lit back alleyways. You can drive the Jag to some lonely hillside, climb on top of me, and get yourself off while your hand wraps around my throat."

I should say no, but I don't want to say no. "And when one

of us meets someone else? Say a gorgeous costar with long, beautiful legs and a pair of big, fake—"

"I won't."

"I might!" I try to make it a joke, but there's hurt in his eyes again. He's trying hard to hide it, but I can see right through him. "But when you do? Because you will. That's what happens in friends with benefits, Chase."

"No commitments." He continues to bargain. "We can hang out and see how it goes. I promise I won't do the jealous guy thing."

"Chase—"

"Renate, I am literally begging you. We don't even have to fuck. I mean, I'd like to, but we don't have to. There's something about you that's...that's... I don't even know what it is. I'm happy around you. You're easy to talk to. We have fun."

I blow out a soft breath as I act like I'm thinking it over. I agree with him. There's something, and I want to find out what. It could be a spark that lights a forest fire, or it could be a firework that burns hot and flies high, but falls fast and cold.

"Okay. Friends, possibly with benefits. No commitments."

"YES!" He screams out, grabbing my face and kissing me hard. When he lets go, his face turns from eager to embarrassed, with a dusting of pink on his cheeks. He rubs the back of his neck. God, he's cute. "I mean, yeah. Cool. It's a deal. Super cool."

I shuffle over closer and lean against him while we feed each other what remains of breakfast in bed. Occasionally, one of us will toss a piece of bacon to the dogs, who wait impatiently at the end of the bed. I still can't shake the feeling that I belong here, that everything in the stars lined up just right to bring us together in that hallway.

Dani will assume her magic touch is what brought us together. I'll never hear the end of it.

HOLLYWOOD
Chase

CHAPTER 10
DANGEROUS WOMAN

ARIANA GRANDE

"CAN I ASK YOU SOMETHING?" She nods, mouth full of pancakes. She looks like a chipmunk, and it makes me want to kiss her again. "I'm going to sound like an absolute idiot, and you can laugh at me, but uhm, what did you mean when you said you were a dominatrix? Like what do you do?"

"I, uhm." She swallows down the food and takes a big drink of coffee. "Basically, I like dominating people. That's the short story."

"So, like, pain and torture?"

"No, not torture. Pain only when it's agreed to and done correctly so that it intensifies the enjoyment."

"What got you into that?"

"I was a dumb kid with an ex who I thought loved me; he didn't. My life spiraled out of control and I almost lost myself. I knew someone in the scene and they convinced me to go with them to a club, so I did. It changed my outlook on life and taught me a new dynamic." She reaches over and wipes the syrup off the side of my mouth before licking it off her finger. "I don't think I would have fully escaped that relationship if I hadn't found this lifestyle. It gave me back a part of me that I'd lost. My confidence, self-respect, and my life."

There's more to the story, there always is, but that's what she's comfortable sharing right now and I don't want to press her for more. She didn't press me about Pongo, so I'm returning the favor. She snuggles against me and I kiss her head, catching that smell of a warm summer afternoon just before the sun becomes unbearable. Friends with benefits, I remind myself.

"Would we, uhm, be able to try it? I mean, if we ever, you know, if we're exploring the benefits side of this friendship?"

"Like what?"

I have things I want to say. Things I've seen on different porn sites or read about, but I'm too nervous to list them off.

"You know, whatever."

"We need to work on that answer first." I watch her eyes as she takes in the room. There's not much in here besides a few pictures, some baseball awards I won as a kid, and a dresser with the basics inside. She spots on the suitcases by the windows and her eyebrow raises.

"Ah, yeah. Those. I, uhm, I leave Monday for a three country press tour slash filming, catching my buddy's wedding, and an award ceremony thing," I mumble, hoping I'm not coming off as bragging.

"Wow, that's...a lot. What countries?"

My mind blanks. *Friends. Just friends.*

"Chase?" she asks in a way that tells me I checked out for a minute there.

"Sorry, uhm, Romania first. It's pretty, you'd like it. Maybe you could come with me sometime." I lean against the headboard, crossing my arms to keep me from fidgeting. "After that, I head to Canada, Italy, and back over to Germany. I'm, uhm, going to be gone for three weeks, which I'm now regretting a little."

"Come on, it will be fun!" I only answer with a grunt and a shrug.

She shimmies to the edge of the bed and stretches. I can't pull my eyes away as my clothes hug those hips the way I want to. My shirt is a dress on her, and it's a beautiful sight. When she raises her arms over her head, the hem slips up enough to let her round ass peek out.

"So, you probably want me out of your hair so you can finish packing? Mind if I take a shower first?"

I suck a breath in through my teeth and shake my head. "Mmm, no can do. The shower has a strict two-person minimum occupancy. So sorry about that. It was like that when I got the house."

"Oh, my," she smirks, throwing me a cute little side eye. "So, what? You shower with your brother?"

"Ouch!" I laugh. "Okay, you got me. It's only a two-person minimum when a queen like you spends the night in my bed."

A door opens somewhere downstairs and my brother yells, "C?"

"We're up here. You're okay, man," I yell back.

"Cool, catch you in Italy. I'm off to practice!"

When I turn to face Ren, she's leaning against the bathroom door. She's got the smile of a siren, calling to my soul as she motions for me. I jump out of the bed and as I round the corner; she stops me in my tracks.

"You need to earn this one."

"I didn't earn it last night? Or by making breakfast?"

"Don't be a cocky brat or you won't get anything. Get on your knees and come get me."

My heart drums and I'm rock hard again, which I'm sure she notices. I lick my lips as I drop to my knees and crawl to her like a dog. Like a fucking puppy. I keep thinking about last night in the car and how badly I want her hands wrapped around my throat again. I'm aching for something new in my life, to explore this newfound wild side she's awakened. She's given me a taste, and I crave being a fucking plaything for her. I don't know how to tell her that, though, so I'll show her.

When I'm close enough for her to reach, she sticks her leg out, stopping me by putting her foot on my shoulder. "I need to know how far you want to take this."

"Do you want me to beg again? Because I will, Ren."

"No, but tell me what you want. Use your words, puppy."

I swallow hard and decide to go for it. "I want to take all of this as far as we can. I wanna try everything. Mostly, I want you to use me and toss me aside like a… a…"

"Cheap toy? You want me to treat you like the filthy slut you are?"

"God, yes! Just like last night. Please?"

"Safe word?"

"Uhm, oh! Octopus."

"Good, get in the shower. I'll join you in a minute."

I don't hesitate. I don't even question what the hell she's going to do in my room—or my house—while I'm standing in the bathroom, waiting. When I turn on the water, I get a flash of a thought that she could be out there robbing me blind. I'd be okay with it so long as she left me the dogs and came back to shower with me…eventually. I flip the switch on the side of the showerhead that redirects the water to the rainfall setting. I flip it back almost immediately, unable to listen to the soft sounds it makes. It brings back bad shit, and I don't have time for bad shit right now.

The bathroom door clicks closed and I find Ren standing there with nothing but a nefarious grin and something behind her back. Her dark brown hair hangs past her tits, and the diffused sunlight from the window makes her light brown skin even more radiant. It reminds me of that painting I've seen before, of the woman in the seashell, but even more beautiful. Jamie would kill me right now for not remembering her name, but my mind only has one name running through it right now, and it's not some mythological Greek lady.

She steps to me, her fingers playing with the sparse patch of hair on my chest. I try to peek behind her back, but she won't let me. I shiver as she leans forward and licks the water from my abs and up my chest as far as she can reach before she hands me a piece of cloth.

"Tie it around your eyes. I'd do it, but you're too fucking tall."

It's like I'm drunk, fumbling with the piece of fabric that belongs to an old bathrobe. She checks and makes sure my eyes are fully covered. I'm a little nervous—no—I'm a lot nervous. I can't see her and what she's doing, but I want to. When she rests her hand on my chest, I concentrate on breathing and giving myself over to her. I'd give anything for another chance to experience the release she gave me last night in the Jag.

"Hold out your hands." I do, and she wraps something around them. "It's not too tight, is it? I don't want you to freak out on me."

"It's fine. Has that happened before?"

"A few times. Usually with people new to all this. Trust takes time to build."

"I trust you."

"Do you? Now, carefully take two steps back and hold your hands up," she directs as he positions my hands. "Perfect, slide your hands over the shower head. Good, now be careful. I don't want you to ruin your pretty, two-person minimum shower."

"What…what are you going to—" I gasp and my head rocks back, which ends up with me getting a face full of water. All she did was lick my nipple, and I'm ready to crawl up the wall. "Oh fuck. Wow."

"I'm going to work on gaining your trust." I shake the water out of my hair and nod as she giggles. "Such a cute puppy."

"Okay, so what do I do?"

"You're going to let go for me. Understand? The rules are simple. You don't take your hands down from the showerhead until I say, and the blindfold stays on. Taking away your sight and ability to control the situation is meant to be positive and euphoric, but if it's uncomfortable—"

"Octopus?"

"Good boy."

Her hands play across my skin, tracing muscles and drawing shapes. It tickles, and I'm trying hard not to move too much. She licks and explores, and at first, it's strange because I want to touch her. I lace my fingers together, squeezing them as tight as I can.

"Relax, Chase. Take a big, deep breath, and slowly let it out for me," she coaches, and as I breathe out, her lips play across my chest. "Good, now relax your hands."

She works her way down my body, telling me to relax my head, neck, shoulders, and so on, and each time, she rewards me through touch and praise. After she reaches my feet, everything stops and I don't feel her anymore, but she's still there. I hope.

"Ren?"

She doesn't answer me with words. Instead, she takes me down her throat and I damn near break the fucking showerhead off the wall. I stumble, but there's not far to go before my back hits the icy tiles.

"You okay, puppy?"

"Yeah. Shit, sorry. I didn't expect—" She does it again, taking me even deeper, and when the tip hits the back of her throat, I can't stop myself from yelling out. "Fuuuuuck!" She works her throat and cups my balls as I stand on my tiptoes, screaming her name and listening to it echo off the walls.

"Jesus! Ren, holy shit!" She gags and chokes a little, and god, I wish I could see her. I'm going to come faster than a fucking teenage boy with his first hard-on at this rate. What the fuck? Then she's gone again. WHAT THE FUCK?!

"Ren!?"

"Shh, not yet. I'm still playing with my new toy." Her lips slide over my abs and she cackles when the back of my head slams against the wall. "Do you take your shirt off in the movie you're filming?"

"What? Uhhh, movie…right…y-yes. Yeah. Why?"

"How about your pants?"

"Uhm, no. I have a scene in my boxers."

"What's the safe word?"

"Octopus."

"Are you doing okay?"

"Fuck yeah."

Her nails graze the sensitive skin inside my thighs and I'm on my tiptoes again, thrusting into nothing as she continues to tease me. Anticipation floods my body, forcing fear and anxiety to retreat to the shadows as she replaces fingernails with her tongue. My mind races and my head spins like a tilt-a-whirl—it's incredible. I have no idea what's coming next, but I trust her.

She was right before when she said she still had to gain my trust. I haven't trusted anyone in years. I don't remember how. I didn't, anyhow.

She continues to explore my body with her hands, nails, and her mouth. Electricity coats every kiss, and every touch sets another part of me on fire. The inner demons called self-doubt and shame have fucked off, unable to compete with the way she's rewiring my brain. Something about her, about how open and delicate she's being—it's like she's found the switch that releases thoughts and feelings and fears I've held onto for too long.

Cool air blows over my stomach, followed by a quick burst of pain on my upper thigh. It lasts only a second or two before she does it again. It's a similar sensation to being super high, but better. It's all new to me, these nips and scratches, this whole game. She's keeping the marks high up my inner thigh, ensuring no one will see while I'm filming. I will, though. I can't wait to look in the mirror at how she's marked me. Claimed me..

"Has anyone ever worshiped your cock before, Chase?"

"N-no? I don't… I mean…no."

"That's sad, because you're absolutely beautiful." She's leaving soft, kitten kisses up and down my shaft between words. I can only manage pathetic whines, which she praises me for. "Your cock fits like it was made for me, like the perfect key, filling me up and making me come *so* hard. Did you like that, Chase? Did you like how it felt to fuck me with this thick, pretty cock?"

Words. I can't remember words. "Uh, huh!"

"You have a beautiful cock, Chase. It tastes so good, I can't get enough of it." She takes the head in her mouth, sucking it like a lollipop while she cups my balls, giving them a gentle squeeze.

"Fuck! Jesus fuck!" I almost don't hear the pop when she releases me over the static in my brain. "Do you wanna come for me, puppy?"

"Yes! Please!"

Her tongue glides up and over the tip, sucking hard as she hums and I scream her name. She takes me down her throat again, giving me the most delicious and dirty moan. I want to record her doing this, taking me apart like this. She releases me again and I'm right on the edge of pain. I want to come—need to. But she eases me back down.

"Where do you want to come, Chase?" she asks before moving back to my thigh and biting so hard I yelp. I don't use the safe word, though, because it still feels too good. I had no idea I was into this. "You want to come on my face? Paint my face with your cum? Oh, I bet you wanna come on my tits, don't you, puppy? You really liked those last night. I bet your enormous cock wants to come all over my tits, doesn't it?"

"Yes!" It's a high-pitched yip like some kind of animal. Her tongue laps at the bite marks she's left and I just as I begin to relax, her breath hits my other leg.

"Remember, don't break your showerhead, puppy," she hums the words right next to my dick and bites my thigh.

I'm gonna break the fucking showerhead. She's massaging my balls and jerking me off. Fuck, I wish I could see her. I want to watch her nails rake down my leg, or my pre-cum slick on her fingers. She takes me all the way down again, and when she pulls back, she tells me to come. I lose whatever sense of control I never even had in an instant.

I almost black out, thrusting into her hand over and over as she praises me. All without touching her. Without even seeing her. It's… magical.

When the shrill whistling in my ears stops, she tells me I can put my arms down, and she helps me over to the shower bench and sits me down.

She loosens the blindfold, and it falls away, giving me a look at what I've done to her, the absolute mess I've made. She's fucking beautiful.

"Stay here, don't fall over, okay?"

I watch her walk out of the bathroom, but the world blurs. I squint at the clock, and it tells me we've been in here for almost an hour. No wonder I'm exhausted. There's something else, but I can't put my finger on it. I rock my head back against the tile, still a little sore from banging it earlier.

When she comes back, she's cleaned herself off and grabbed a bottle of water and a bowl of fruit from breakfast. I don't even realize how thirsty I am until I start to drink and down the entire bottle.

"You're probably still dehydrated from last night's drinking. How do you feel?" Her hand cups my face and she's feeding me fruit. Maybe I died and went to heaven.

I close my eyes for a minute and pull her onto my lap, nuzzling into her neck. There's something…different. Like…like I'm about to…cry? My shoulders tense and I try to pull away, but she holds me to her.

"Let it out, Chase," her honey voice in my ear whispers. Not in that sultry voice, but in a warmer, comforting tone that's safe and nurturing. "Sometimes it gets emotional."

That's all I need. Permission. The tears pour down my face. I'm not one of those macho guys who doesn't believe in crying. Hell, I cry for and at movies all the time. But this isn't a movie, and I'm not sad. I'm not angry. I'm not scared. I'm… relieved.

"Good boy, Chase. You did so well, baby. Let it out." She coos, stroking my hair.

Without lifting my head, I say the only words that mean anything to me right now. The only words that make sense. "Don't leave."

HOLLYWOOD
Renate

CHAPTER 11
JUST FRIENDS

AMY WINEHOUSE

I DON'T MISS Chase Cooper. I can't.

He left over a week ago, but he refuses to give me a chance to even start to miss him. Flowers and food show up at my door or my classroom. He calls me when he wakes up and talks to me until I fall asleep every night he can. I wake up to a text from him every morning. I try to tell him to go out and have fun, to not worry about me, to go meet someone crazy and exotic. Yet every night his name comes up on my phone.

I thought it would suffocate me to have someone call me every day and night. I thought I'd want more space, more room to be myself, but Chase cracked the code. Giving me enough room to breathe even when he's clingy. It's a strange juxtaposition that I could get used to under different circumstances. Even so, how could it ever work between us? Me lugging computer parts and broken robots around while he's with his stylist being fitted for a tux to accept his Oscar? That's not the way life works. Not for me.

But I can't stop the *what ifs* from creeping into my brain. What if we gave this a try? What if we filled our nights with movie premieres and lavish parties? What if I wake up and drag myself into class while he's in front of a camera? What if I took

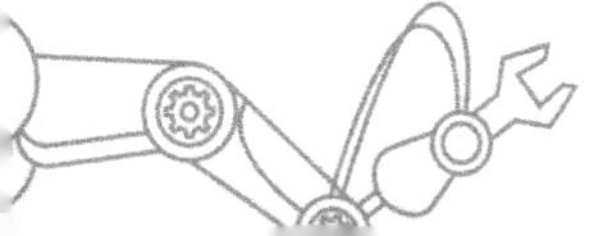

off during spring break and allowed him to whisk me across Europe and dote on me? What if we built a functional relationship built on trust and love instead of the cruelty and ownership I knew before?

Sitting in traffic gives me way too long to daydream about a happy life with him. It also doesn't help that my sister gets to spend time with him at an Italian countryside winery next week while I'm stuck at a school function with Mr. Miley. Not fair. Dani's boyfriend will be there, but it's still not fair. Steve and Ethan, their mutual friends, are getting married in some beautiful, scenic, expensive destination wedding. The most I've traveled is to Mexico to visit family. The squeal of someone's horn pulls me out of my daydream. Bastard.

That's me, Renate Silva, daydreaming of castles, but stuck in a beat-up car in Los Angeles traffic.

When I'm finally home, I lug the box of papers and the day's flower delivery out of my car. Someday, we'll go digital with homework, but we're still not there yet. I leave the flowers by the door and trudge through the house, heaving the box onto the kitchen table. I put on the kettle and change into more comfortable clothes, but just as I settle in with the first paper, the doorbell rings. I'm half tempted to ignore it, but it could be a neighbor.

"Hi!" The woman at the door greets me with far too much enthusiasm and I'm ready to shut the door in her face. She's white with big, blonde hair and an orange spray tan. I'm waiting for the religious pitch that's about to come my way, which always makes me laugh. We live in a Hispanic neighborhood full of Catholics, but these crazies still try. "Are you Mrs. Silva?"

My foot slides behind the door to make it harder for her to push her way in if she tries. I've had a few parents come to my house before, and not to thank me. Working as a teacher has become a little scary over the past few years when parents stopped seeing us as educators and mistook us for babysitters. In the minds of parents, we should pick up their slack for their child's poor grades when they're not bothering to put in any of the work it takes to be a parent. It used to be the rich parents that caused the problems, but now the poor families blame us, too.

"Mrs. Silva isn't home right now. You are?" I reply in a blunt tone while pushing my glasses up my face.

"Oh, well, I'm Rachel Wexell. I work for a local magazine—" She glances down at something on her phone. "Oh, my mistake. You're *Ms*. Silva, right? Ms. Renate Silva?" She slaughters my first name, pronouncing it *Raynawtay*, which I'm used to. I curse my father in my head, knowing he's watching and laughing.

"Whatever you're selling, I'm not interested."

"Right to the point! Well, I'm not selling anything, if that helps to ease this tension. We'd like to interview you about your...class." She looks at her phone to reference what I assume must be notes before flashing her too bright smile. "You're the teacher, right? The technology and computer sciences teacher for Hollywood Tech and Arts?"

"How did you get my address and who do you work for again?"

"Oh, I'm not at liberty to say," her thick southern accent slips a little, and so does her smile. I glance down, noticing her foot tucked inside my doorway. She's done this before, too. "We wanted to do a story about you and the smart boards, do you know who donated them?"

"Some rich lady who died?"

"Ms. Silva, I'll just be blunt here. There's a rumor you're dating Chase Cooper."

"Who?"

"Chase Cooper. The actor? Trusted sources say you two are romantically linked and the smart boards were a... uhm, a romantic gesture or possibly, well, payment for—"

"*Trusted sources*?" I scoff. There's nothing trustworthy about her sources. "The principal, I assume? You may want to check that source again since he's only after attention." If she worked for a newspaper, I would tell her everything about Miley, but I don't believe she does. She's after a scoop on Chase, and she's come to the wrong house for that. "I'm flattered that Mr. Miley thinks I could get a guy like Charles Clarke."

"Cooper. Chase Cooper," she snaps, losing her composure for a moment. "Brown hair, tall, blue eyes? Stars in action movies?"

"Is he the one that drives the fast cars in those *machismo* movies? Or the one that sings and dances, too?"

"So, the flowers?" She nods to the bouquet I forgot to bring in the house.

Shit. Think fast, Ren.

"Ohhhhh. My ex. He's been trying to get back together with me for weeks. He's a little dramatic since he found out about the alimony. I warned him not to leave her panties in my laundry again, but he didn't listen."

"Right, okay, the ex." She's getting frustrated and having trouble staying in character. Such a fake. "And the sighting at the school? You *were* seen with him."

"With who? Oh, some Hollywood guy visited campus the other day. Maybe it was this... what did you say again? Chip Chambers?"

"CHASE!" she spits back. "Chase. Cooper."

"Never heard of him. I'm more of a reader."

"Fine," she huffs, shoving her phone back into her large purse. I don't feel bad for being a pain in her ass. These damn paparazzi will try anything—it's disgusting. "Sorry to bother you."

She turns to leave, but as she gets to the step, she stops and glares at me. It's unsettling.

"I hope you're not lying to me, but either way, you should stay away from Chase Cooper. For your own good."

I'm tempted to respond, but that's what she wants. Instead, I smile, nod, and shut the door before my eyes roll back in my head. I wish she had come out and said it Miley had sent her. That would give me a reason to go after his dumb ass. I'll deal with that later. I'm about to push off the door when there's another knock. I spin around and fling the door open.

"Lady, I don't—" I stop and scream with delight as my cousin holds out her arms and I jump into them. "Oh my god, come inside, quick! There's this crazy white lady around here who thinks I'm dating Chase Cooper."

"Shit, well, I hope you didn't bring him here if you are. She's down the street talking to Mrs. Rosa. That woman would sell out her own kids for a dollar." Terasa looks around as she steps inside. "Wow, you've redecorated!"

"We did?" I glance around at a living room that's sat unchanged for ten years.

"The place looks so much better without that asshole Luis around." She breaks her straight face and cackles like a wild woman. While wiping the tears from her eyes, she asks, "Where's Dani and your mom?"

"Mom's with her new beau. Dani has a rehearsal for a gig. Pizza and gossip?" I avoid her comments about my ex. He's not worth talking about, and she's right anyhow. The house does look better without him in it.

I haven't seen Teresa for at least a year, but we stay in touch enough to send each other memes every few days as proof of life. Before we can order, my phone lights up on the coffee table and Chase's cheesy grin looks up at me. I snatch the phone up and hope she didn't see the picture or the name.

SNUGGLE PUPPY

Am I allowed to miss you? Like, casually or whatever?

"*Snuggle Puppy?*" she gives me the stare that says she's onto me then breaks down laughing. "Not dating my ass! Spill the damn tea. Do you love him? When's the wedding?"

"What?" I yell, exaggeratedly. "It's not—it's the…plumber." I hand her my credit card so she can finish the food order.

"Yeah, Snuggle Puppy, the plumber who needs to talk to you about laying pipes! Please!"

"Oh, hush!" I tease as my thumbs dance over the letters.

No! You should be out having fun. Hooking up with beautiful movie people.

SNUGGLE PUPPY

They're not as fun as you. I should fly you out here right now.

Are you drunk?

SNUGGLE PUPPY

Maybe.

Yes

Can I call you?

Could I even stop you?

I'm giggling like an idiot as I walk across the room to answer, Teresa still teasing me.

"You don't really *want me to fuck someone else, do you?"* He slurs, more than a hint of sadness in the words.

"I do, Chase. It would be good for you!" I whisper as my cousin eyes me with a knowing smirk.

"No, you don't. Don't say that."

"I want you to find someone right now and take them back to your room."

"You're not here. Come on, Ren. Don't be mad. Please?"

"I'm not mad, I'm worried about you. You're drunk and should go to bed. What time is it there?"

"I'm tipsy. It's somewhere around too fucking early in the morning. So, good morning, beautiful! How are you? Did you get my package?"

"I did," I answer as I duck into the kitchen. I want to be frustrated with him, but the butterflies in my stomach have other plans. "Mama almost threw it away. We've never gotten a package from Germany."

"Never? Aww. Send me a picture so I can decide if you're getting a few more packages from Germany, or if I need to send someone over to Paris to pick up something else. Something a little less lacy and more strappy?"

"Do you frequently send women you barely know expensive underwear?"

"No! Only one smokin' hot teacher who will look fucking delicious in them. And out of them."

"Chase—"

"Will you wear them when I get home? I want to rip them off you with my teeth. I'll buy you more. Did I mention I miss you? In a friendly way?"

"Chase Cooper, you are not going to buy me expensive lingerie only to tear it off me."

"I'm not? Are you sure about that? Because I'm pretty sure I already did. Show me?"

"I have a friend over and I'm not getting caught sending you a panty shot."

"So you are wearing them! We should do a video call."

"Oh my god, you are insufferable!" I can't even pretend to be mad at him. He's too damn cute about the whole situation.

"Yeah, but you like it."

"Okay," I giggle. "Get some sleep and I'll call you in a few hours. Okay? I have to go. My cousin thinks I'm talking to a plumber!"

"A plumber? I can get a tool belt from the set and have you bent over the sink while I stick—"

"Chase!"

"I mean, sure, text me when you're free again and I'll call as soon as I can, bestie. Or as soon as I wake up. I think I'm gonna pass out

soon." He doesn't sound disappointed, which makes me feel a little better about rushing him off the phone. *"Hey, uhm, I'm serious, you know? I miss you."*

"Yeah." I bite back the smile, but can't stop the heat from rushing across my face. "I miss you, too."

"You do?! As friends and all, right? Or whatever. Hey, when I get back, I want to take you out somewhere." His words slur together again and I catch the yawn. *"I'll tell you about it later. You'll love it. Pluto… Plato… Platonically. Not a date. We don't even have to bang after, I promise. But we should because you're hot."*

"Go get some sleep," I giggle. The feeling of belonging comes back, a comfortable ease I have when talking with him. I wish I understood it and how his words can touch my soul. It makes me want to say things I don't mean. "I'll talk to you about it later, Puppy. Goodnight."

"Okay, goodnight Sunshine. Don't forget to text me!"

"So?" Teresa asks with a side glance when I walk back into the room. "Girl, you're about as red as a damn tomato. Spill it now, or I'll go to Dani for the details."

"We kind of ran into each other at the school, and he took me out to dinner. Which turned into two days at his house, snuggling and watching movies while he followed me around like a lost puppy dog. It was adorable—and different."

"Different good? No, never mind, I have a better question. Does he treat you right?"

"Flowers and lunch almost daily since he left for his trip. He cooked for me instead of telling me I could lose a few pounds. He tells me I'm beautiful all the time."

"And?"

"He crawled to me on the first night," my face scrunches up in embarrassment.

"Jackpot!" She kicks her feet in the air and screams. "How long have you been dating? Why didn't you call me? How big is his dick?"

"We're not *dating* and you don't even like dick."

"What? Why aren't you dating?"

"Because Chase and I are just enjoying each other's company. I don't need that kind of hassle and extra bullshit right now."

She rolls her eyes, then leans toward me and her voice drops to a soft, secretive tone even though we're alone in the house. "Have you told him about your thing?" She moves her arm in a whipping motion.

I can't hold back the laugh I bark out. "Ma'am, you are forty years old and can't even ask me if I tie his pretty white ass up and spank him." I watch her face flush before she covers it with her hands, laughing. "Now who's red like a tomato? Yes, he knows, and that's as far as I'm taking this conversation. It's nothing serious, no labels."

"Alright, alright. You keep on lying to yourself with that bullshit, but alright."

We talk about our lives in different cities while we share a pizza and some mozzarella sticks, like when we were kids. She tells me about her wife's new job and how much the kids are loving the snow in Chicago. We don't realize how late it's gotten until we hear the car door. A few minutes pass before Mama comes barreling into the house, frazzled and arms full of bags.

"Everything okay?"

"I'm fine!" She shoots back.

"Okay, so why the hell are you charging in here like a bull on fire?" I stand to go peek out the window, curious about who drove her home and what could have her so riled up, but my car sits alone in the driveway. "Mama, did something happen at the senior center?"

"No, everything is fine. I told you." She doesn't even stop to say hello to Teresa on her way to the back of the house. Theresa and I exchange a glare.

"You want to put on the kettle while I try to talk to her?" I ask Teresa, and she nods. Anyone else would leave. But Teresa is family, which means she knows how hard-headed and hot-tempered my mother can be sometimes. I'm just like her in so many ways.

"Mama?"

She spins around before she reaches her curtained doorway. Her words cut deeper than any knife as she yells, "I don't want to talk to you right now, Renate! I know what you did. I know because Luis told me!"

HOLLYWOOD
Renate

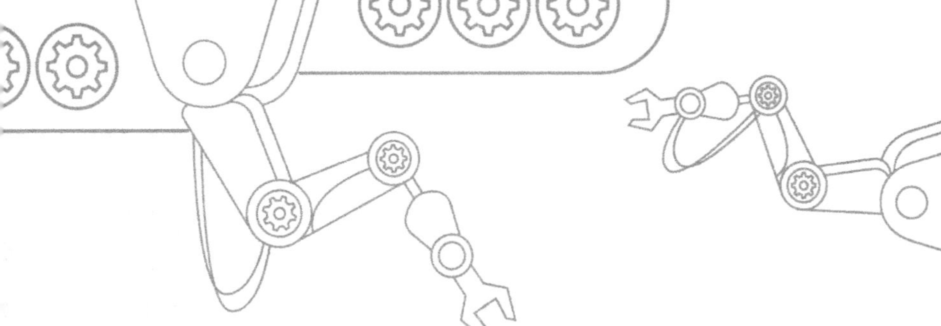

CHAPTER 12
THE END

HALSEY

MY MOTHER LIKES to act as though this is her house, but it belongs to me. I bought it from my aunt with money I'd saved up working two jobs during high school. I wanted a place of my own where I could study and so my boyfriend and I could have some privacy. The bungalow style house isn't fancy, but it has two bedrooms. We planned to turn one bedroom into an office, and after I finished college, a nursery. Two months after I signed the deed, the city condemned Mama and Dani's apartment. Luis hadn't found a job yet, and I worked two shitty jobs while going to class. We needed money, and my family needed somewhere to live.

My office—nothing but a few stacks of boxes—became Dani's room, but when I asked Luis to help us build an extension in the back for Mama, he lost his shit and disappeared. While we had the house to ourselves, Dani and I conned two of our brothers to come down from Montana and help us. In two days, the four of us renovated the back of the house into a separate room for Mama. We've been saving up ever since to get someone to come in and replace the bookshelves with actual walls, but we make it work. I lost a laundry room, but now I spend one night a week at

the laundromat watching Mama gossip with the other neighborhood old ladies.

It didn't surprise me when Luis refused to adjust to the new living arrangements. He liked his space and privacy. He also liked his rules being followed, and things to be done his way and only his way. I paid the price for going against his wishes when he came back. I paid with more than just blood, and I almost paid with my life..

"Luis? What did he tell you? When?"

"Tonight! He drove me to the senior center. He even came in and met Tommy. That's when he told me about your lies."

"What are you talking about, Mama? He's not supposed to be up for parole for almost two more years! What lies?"

"I said I don't want to talk about it!"

"Well, I DO! Tell me what he said!" Mama and I butt heads regularly. It comes with our quick tempers, or that's what my father used to say.

"He said you were trading drugs for...for...*tener relaciones sexuales*!" I stare at her, unable to form a response in my shock. She reaches out for my hand and her voice softens. "Renate, he said he wants to *help* you, wants to take you back. Please, you need to let him help you."

"Tía, no!" Teresa says from behind me. "You can't listen to Luis."

"He wants her back!" she repeats, hope on her face. "He can fix everything. Please, call him and we can get you help! He said he'd forgive you, *mi bella hija*."

I never told my mother about Luis and me. Embarrassment wouldn't allow me to, especially after the wedding. In my mind, he would change if we were married, and I played the dutiful wife. And he did, but not in the ways I'd hoped. Even though I didn't tell her, I assumed she knew at least some of what happened.

The memories flood my mind as she stares at me, willing me

to listen to her. The ER visits, the lies about being clumsy or blaming it on the kids in the school once I became a teacher. How could she not notice sixteen years of abuse?

"Renate?"

"No!" I snap back at her. "I've never sold myself for drugs! That's idiotic! I'm a teacher, for fuck's sake!"

Luis is a manipulative snake and I'm not surprised he tried to pin the divorce on me. But telling people I'm a drug addict and a sex worker? That shit could cost me my job. I need to call my lawyer in the morning to see why they never told us about his release over a year early.

"Don't use that language! Your Papa and I loved—"

"Don't talk to him anymore, Mama. He's not supposed to be here." I turn and see Teresa standing in the kitchen door, gesturing back to my mother. She's right, even without saying a word. I need to tell my mother why Luis and I got divorced. "Fine. Come on, Mama, come out here and let me talk to you about this like adults instead of screaming."

The three of us sit around the kitchen table, drinking tea while my mother nibbles on cookies. She's not looking at me, like she already has her defense against whatever I'm about to say planned out. I need to know if Luis has been to the center before tonight, and what else he's told her.

"You and Papa loved Luis, I understand that—"

"You loved him, too. His father used to work with your father. Back in Mexico when they were young men, always so nice and helpful. I remember how sweet Luis was as a baby."

"Tía, he didn't stay that way," Teresa says before laying her hand on my arm. "You buried this in your heart and your mind because you didn't want to believe it. I told you. My mother told you. You can't blame Renny for this."

My mother ignores her and drinks her tea without looking at us.

"Luis grew up to be a dangerous man with demons, so many demons. He's in a gang, Tía. He's the one selling drugs, trafficking women and children, hurting people and families. You saw at least that much, don't you?"

"No! Don't you talk that way about my Luis!" Mama used to babysit Luis and his little sister, and sometimes I forget how ingrained into my family he became long before we started dating. "He has some ugly friends, that's all. If he was back with you, you could help him."

"He hit me, Mama. He hit me and sent me to the hospital too many times to count. He left me with scars, Mama, and I'm not speaking only metaphorically. He almost killed me. Don't you remember?"

"The drugs did that!"

"You knew he did drugs?"

Her eyes shoot open. "No, baby. You were! He only wanted to help you get off the drugs, and you attacked him. He defended himself. He worried about you, that you were going to hurt yourself."

My brow furrows as I stare at her from across the table. I glance at Teresa and she's as surprised as I am about the news that I took drugs and attacked Luis. When Mama sees us exchanging glances, she gets annoyed and fidgets with the tablecloth. She doesn't want to believe me, but it's not like her to think I'm lying.

"Luis said you went to the hospital so much because of the drugs. He said they wouldn't allow visitors while they helped you."

"Well, that's not how any of that happened," Teresa replied. She stayed with me the entire time, keeping Luis from doing anything more to me. "What about when he broke her wrist for the fourth time? That was only a few years ago."

I'm ashamed to think back on all of this, at how long I let it go on. Years of beatings and abuse before I finally got help. I recognize the same shame in Mama as she avoids looking at me. She knew, but she couldn't stop it, so it became easier to pretend not to see it. Maybe he threatened her, too.

"What else did he tell you?"

"He said when you got home, you stole money from him to get drugs on the street when you took all yours from the doctor too fast."

"He stole them before I ever took any. Sold them while I suffered, miserable and in pain." I rub my wrist as the memories of how badly it hurt come back to me. "He thought he could be a drug runner for the gang, that it would make him rich. He sold them my prescriptions to impress them and said he would get more. He wanted to keep hurting me until I died!"

"My Luis wouldn't do that."

"You're right, *your* Luis wouldn't. But *your* Luis no longer exists." I hold my hand out, offering it to my mother. She stares at it for a while, studying it like she's checking for teeth. I don't want her to blame herself for any of this; he hides his true nature from people, uses them. "We married too young, Mama. Neither of us were ready, and Luis didn't treat me very well even before that. All those times I couldn't come over, couldn't eat, couldn't take off my jacket? Luis did that. He stole from me, lied to me, lied to my family."

"He used to be a good boy," she whispers.

"Tía, if you see him again, you need to tell the security guard, okay? If you can't find them, well, call the police or stay near people." She squeezes my hand as she tells my mother of hospital trips, walk-in clinics, and driving me all the way to south Orange County to see new doctors when the ones here stopped treating me.

She's reluctant, but after Teresa talks to her, my mother gives in and promises not to talk to him anymore. It's hard on her because she only wants to remember Luis as a young boy, because those are memories with Papa. My father treated Luis like a son, always saying Luis made him proud and how one day, Luis would build me a castle and make me a princess. I wanted to believe that fairytale would come true. Or maybe I missed my father. I always believed things would have been different if Papa hadn't died.

It's after midnight when Teresa and I say our goodbyes. We make plans to get lunch before she heads back home to Chicago. After she leaves, I start a fresh pot of coffee and take my meds out of the fridge. My head aches, and my body is sore from the stress. I take my injection, hoping it will stave off the flare that's coming. I try to convince myself it won't be so bad the day after an injection, but that's not true. Those are some of the hardest days for me and we still don't understand why.

I sit down at the table with my coffee, a piece of pizza, and a box of grading I need to get through. I'm only three tests in when my phone chirps, but I ignore it. Chase will understand. It chirps again and I sigh, staring at the paper in front of me and trying to read this student's handwriting. Next year, no more paper tests. I've had enough of this. The third time it chirps, I scoop it up in frustration, but it's not Chase.

> DANIELLA
>
> Dude, where are you?
>
> Wake up, I need to know you're okay!
>
> Luis is here, and I'm freaking the fuck out!

When she answers, it's difficult to hear her over the noise of the club, but I can tell she's walking as the sounds become distant and muffled. *"TELL ME YOU'RE AT HOME!"*

"I am, and you don't have to yell. Are you okay?"

"Yeah! Xander and his weird ass rich white boy posse are watching

him. I'll probably go to his place tonight. Hey, look at us, both catching a rich white guy!"

It's been a running joke between my sister, my mother, and I that her kids only date white people since all of my brothers are with white partners. Mama loves to joke back, saying she doesn't know where she went wrong. She says that even more with Dani, who has spent months trying to explain that pansexual doesn't mean she enjoys cooking.

"You're crazy. Be safe and stay away from you know who. I love you."

"You too! I'll call if shit gets too weird, but so far, he's hanging out by the bar. He knows I've seen him. Fucker."

I hang up and open my laptop, writing a quick email to my lawyer, telling her Luis has been contacting my family, or at least hanging around where they'll see him. It's a scare tactic, and we're not falling for it. Mama, well, I'm not sure what she thinks after everything tonight. When I'm done, I go back to grading.

The next time my phone chirps, I'm startled by it, fully in the grading zone and nearly done. The clock tells me it's after three in the morning.

SNUGGLE PUPPY

Hey, beautiful. I wanted to check in. Hopefully, this doesn't wake you and you're sound asleep after having a wonderful night with your cousin. Sorry about the drunk call. I hope I wasn't too much of an ass.

I flip through the last of the tests and decide to finish them tomorrow on my lunch break. I pack everything up and as I go to stand, my body reminds me I've been in that position for far too long. My joints gelled from lack of movement and none of them will move. I hobble to the bathroom, skip half of my nightly routine, and crash hard into my bed. If I'm lucky, I might get three hours of sleep, otherwise, the pain will keep me awake until the alarm goes off.

Twenty minutes later, I unplug my phone and curl into a ball under the covers.

> Sorry I didn't text. Late night. You weren't an ass.

SNUGGLE PUPPY

It's almost four in LA. Why are you up?

> Too much coffee?

SNUGGLE PUPPY

Are you pissed about the call earlier? I'm really sorry about that.

> No, it was nice to hear your voice. I had a rough night.

SNUGGLE PUPPY

Anything I can do?

> I'll be fine. I just wanted to say goodnight. How was filming?

SNUGGLE PUPPY

I can tell you about it tomorrow night. Get some sleep, Ren.

I'm glad you're okay. I got a little worried. Call me if you want to.

Goodnight, beautiful.

> Goodnight, Chase.

I want to tell him to call me so I could listen to the comfort of his voice again. I'm in pain physically and emotionally, and I'm confused about how I'm supposed to feel about the boy who's texting me late at night, who worries about me, who I wish was here to hold me when we're just supposed to be friends.

I cry myself to sleep for the first time in months.

My alarm goes off far too early, and as I reach for it, I force my arm to straighten out. It takes three tries to stand up from the bed before my knees decide they do, in fact, remember how to behave. When I get to the bathroom, I stare at the tub and shake my head. I won't be able to climb into it for a shower, so I wet a washcloth instead. The bags under my eyes are dark, and I add a little extra makeup to cover it. Learning how to cover bruises and black eyes has its advantages…I guess.

I get dressed at a snail's pace before trudging out to the kitchen. To my surprise, Mama sits at the table, my travel mug of coffee there in front of her with steam rising from the lid. I can smell the cinnamon.

"You were up too late. I knew it would be a rough morning, so I wanted to make sure you had time to get something to eat on the way."

"I told Marta I wouldn't be in early this morning. Care to join me for breakfast and I'll drop you off at work?"

"Can we go to the fancy place?" I laugh and nod. Mama's idea of a fancy place for breakfast is a Taiwanese bakery with case after case of sweet and savory pastries. Mama always loads an entire tray for her co-workers. I'll admit it's delicious, but it's not fancy.

I should take Chase on a date to the *fancy* bakery and see how he reacts.

Mama and I load my papers into the car and, as I'm adjusting my driver's seat to handle the stiffness, she takes my hand and squeezes it tight.

"Luis's father wasn't a nice man either, and he tried to hurt me. It's why your father turned him in, but we never told Luis about that, or you." She smiles at me. "I should have listened to my heart and not his son's lies. I shouldn't have doubted you."

"It's okay, Mama." I reach over and give her a weak hug, and she rubs my back. "Now, let's go buy up a shit ton of pastries."

"Renate, you swear too much!"

"Every damn day, Mama. I love you.

HOLLYWOOD
Chase

CHAPTER 13
MADNESS

MUSE

IT'S CLOSING night in Toronto and the after party is insane, as expected. The DJ has the dance floor packed, and the bartenders are staying busy. People who aren't dancing or drinking have found dark corners to make out in. I've run into a few people I've met before on a film set or at other functions, but most of these people I don't know. That doesn't stop me from dancing, drinking, mingling, and drinking some more. I continue to remind myself to play it cool around the big names, kind around the lesser known, and gracious when possible. Doing that has gotten me where I am today.

Given my hectic schedule and lack of sleep, I fly right past tipsy and into drunk as fuck. My buddy Steve calls this 'fun times Chase,' but Jamie calls it 'dumb Chase that thinks with his dick.' I call it not giving a fuck about anything anymore. I tip back my drink, but it's empty, so I head for the bar again. This time, I've got the drunk confidence to head for the cute chick pouring drinks instead of the dude.

"What'll it be, Mr. Cooper?" the knockout of a redhead says to me in a cute French accent. She leans over, licking her pouty lips and pushing her tits together.

"Oh, I've got some ideas, but how about another drink first? G&T."

"Really? I would have guessed you were a whiskey man."

"It's what I want, but my trainer would absolutely murder me if I slam those back tonight." I lean over the bar and read her name tag in the dim lights. "Chloe. How's your night going so far?"

"Fine, but it could get so much better." She slides me the drink, her fingers brushing over mine, holding them there a second longer than she needs to as the electricity crackles. "I've got some ideas for a new workout you could try. I could show you while I'm on break?" She winks and turns away. She sticks her ass out when she bends over to reach for her bag, damn near flashing me. I don't think she's wearing anything under that skirt.

Chloe gets to a hallway and turns back around, holds up a pack of cigarettes, and nods to a back door. I finish my drink and slip away from the bar, glancing around before I follow her down the hallway and out an emergency door that she's propped open.

"You want a smoke?" she asks, holding the pack out to me. She's got gorgeous green eyes, like emeralds, but it's that mouth that has my undivided attention.

"I don't smoke."

"Good, neither do I." She tosses the pack over her shoulder and I've got her pinned against the wall in an instant. Our mouths crash together, and the moan she gives me hits all the right notes. My knee slides between her legs as I grab a handful of her ass and squeeze hard. Fuck, she's beautiful.

She giggles, popping open the buttons on her top. I latch onto her tit in seconds, swirling the piercing with my tongue. She's rubbing her cunt against me to get herself off as her long leg wraps around me. She's soaking my pants with her bare pussy, so I let go of her. I smirk when my fingers find more piercings.

There's at least two piercings down there, and I wanna play with them. My brain buzzes from the alcohol and the world spins out of control, so I close my eyes and let my body take over as she fucks my hand.

She unzips my pants and shoves her hand in. The gasp she lets out boosts my confidence, but that could be the booze.

"You're a big boy, aren't you?"

"Think you can take it, baby?"

I let out a low, deep moan when her fingers wrap around my cock, releasing me from the boxers. "I wanna take every inch of this cock, Daddy. Please?"

I curl my fingers inside her as my mind slips a million miles away from this small alleyway, letting my body do its thing. It's hard to pretend there's a connection in meaningless sex, so I've learned how to take my mind out of it and not overthink everything. She's clenching around my fingers, begging for my cock, and I'm wondering what time I need to wake up to catch my early morning flight.

"Oh god, harder, Daddy! Don't stop!" She comes apart before I've even got my dick in her. She's still grinding her clit against my palm, working herself through the orgasm when I freeze.

Renate.

"Shit!" I mumble, the fog leaving my brain. I haven't seen Ren in two weeks, and the last time we talked, she'd told me to go out and screw other people. I'm doing what she wants— railing the hell out of this pretty bartender against the wall. To get Ren out of my mind and replace her with someone whose name I won't remember in a week?

The air thickens and I can't breathe. I need to run. I need to get the fuck out of here.

"Everything okay, baby? I have a condom."

"I, uhm, I can't do this." I gulp for air, stepping away from her and shoving my dick back into my pants. "I want to, you're fucking beautiful, but, I kind of… there's this girl back home, and we're… friends, but I—shit. I'm so sorry. I'm…drunk. I'm sorry!"

"Don't sweat it, baby. Chase Cooper just got me off in a back alley. That's a win in my book." She laughs, picking up the pack of smokes and tucking them into her back pocket. "Good luck with the girl back home. Although, I doubt you need it. You know where to find me if you change your mind and need someone to take care of that." She glances down at my pants and winks. Heat climbs my neck when she gives me a kiss on the cheek and walks back inside.

I find the nearest bathroom, wash my hands, and splash ice cold water on my face. My stomach clenches as I stare into the mirror. *Asshole.* I pull out my phone and text Cynthia, telling her I'm going back to the hotel. This pit in the bottom of my stomach and the need to throw up won't leave, even though I didn't go through with fucking the bartender. If Ren and I are only fooling around, why does this guilt weigh on me? If we're nothing more than friends, why does what I did with the bartender feel like cheating? Why can't I get Ren out of my mind?

"Chase?"

I glance up as I'm leaving the bathroom and Cynthia stands there in a sparkling gold gown with her hair still pinned up in a neat bun. It gives her the appearance of being in her late thirties, not her mid-sixties. I rub my temples as she walks toward me, trying in vain to straighten out my shirt and get me to focus on her.

"You've got the look of someone suffering from an existential crisis." She teases. "Did you get stuck in another conversation with Julio Alvez?"

"I fucked up." I hand my phone to her, showing her a long text thread between Ren and I. Nothing dirty, just innocent conversation and flirting.

"I don't get it? It sounds like you two are hitting it off. What did you fuck up?"

"See the tall redhead behind the bar?" Cyn glances around me and nods. "I almost fucked her out in the alley a few minutes ago."

"Not the smartest move, but not the worst." Cyn knows about my exes, the therapy, my brain constantly trying to implode on me. She's even seen me break down a few times and had to cover for me. "You know what the problem is, right?"

"I...I like Ren? I like her and yet I'm out here getting drunk and—"

"No, sweetie, you don't *like* her. You're trying to sabotage what you have because it scares you, doesn't it?" My head drops to my chest and I nod. "I could have told you that before you had me get 40-something smart boards, babe."

"What do I do?"

"Go back to the room and call her. There's only a three-hour time difference tonight. I'll order a pizza to help you sober up while you talk to her."

I purse my lips and nod. Why does everyone else in my life see what I need or what I should do, and I never do? The entire world has read a page ahead of me in the script and I can't seem to catch up, no matter how fast I read. I'm not an idiot, even though I'm being one right now. I'm a chronic over-thinker with severe anxiety, which means I can't see the obvious answers sometimes.

I take my phone back and head for the elevator. I've been keeping myself off the playing field and out of reach for so long now, I've forgotten how all of this works when the feelings hit. I need to tell her how she makes me feel. I need her to know that friends with benefits won't be enough, but I'm worried she'll run away.

I'm on my fifth read-through of a contract Cynthia dropped off in the hopes it would put me to sleep. I toss the thing next to me in the bed and sigh as I rub my face. I'm still in my dress slacks and shirt while Pongo and I lay in the bed and he watches a documentary about sharks since I can't find Dev's game. I've eaten almost a whole damn pizza in my attempt to avoid making this phone call. Steve would have me downstairs in the gym for the next five days because of that.

Out of excuses, I pick up the stupid phone and scroll to her name.

It rings. It rings again. I'm about to hang up when she picks up, and the entire world stops spinning. I can breathe again.

"Hey!" She sounds bubbly and with that one word, my entire body relaxes. *"What are you doing up?"*

Thinking of you. Trying to figure out how to make this real. Wishing you were here.

"I, uhm, couldn't sleep." Not a total lie, but not what I wanted to say. My brain goes blank, and nothing I rehearsed comes out of my mouth. "Did I wake you?"

"No, I just finished grading the last paper before heading off to bed. I've been waiting to see if this hot guy I met calls me tonight."

There's a pang of jealousy before I ask, "To avoid putting my foot in my mouth and sound like a self-centered, arrogant ass clown, would the hot guy—"

"Yes, Chase. It's you." She giggles, but stops when I don't react. *"Hey, are you okay? You sound, I dunno, off."*

"No," I admit, thinking back to the bartender, whose name I've already forgotten.

"Chase, what happened?"

I want to apologize to her, and tell her about the bartender. I want to ask her to reconsider our situation. I need to tell her I didn't mean to fall for her like this. I want to ask her if she misses me the way I'm missing her.

"Uhm, it's nothing. Tired, I'm sure. Tell me about your day."

Why am I acting like this? I want a connection again, but I'm fucking scared. I want mundane conversations about buying groceries and ordering Chinese food. I'm tired of worrying that every woman I meet will leave me. I'm tired of being alone. I'm damaged goods, but Ren doesn't see me like that or as a meal ticket. She makes me feel all the things I've kept buried away for four years—or maybe my whole life.

"It was…a day. You don't want to hear about that, Chase. It's boring. Not like you and your awards and flashy clothes. I saw you the other day. The interview where you had on the shirt with sunflowers?"

I picked that shirt out for her, thinking she'd never notice. It's crazy how much Ren cares about me and my life. Ren understands I'm different and instead of running away, she still answers her phone and listens to my schedule. I couldn't do that with Cassie. I couldn't tell her how often I lose my shit, because Cassie didn't understand me. She came from a close knit family that didn't believe in sharing feelings. She never tried to understand my life or my struggles. I didn't realize that until Ren.

"Yeah?" A cold, wet nose nudges my hand. "I almost threw up at that interview. That guy has a huge following over here, and I felt like a nobody."

"Oh, Puppy. You're not a nobody." Her soft voice comforts me from thousands of miles away, and she doesn't know how much I needed to hear it.

"Cyn says I might be up for an award tomorrow night. I don't get why. I mean, I'm just a dumb action movie guy. Some of these people have made some incredible movies. They're art. Beautiful and moving films that make you feel alive, or angry, or sad. I don't belong here."

"Chase, you belong. I've seen you move entire audiences to tears with an expression on your face and not a single word from your mouth. Stop listening to that voice in your head. You're not a dumb action guy. Your IMDB page will show you that. I bet your movie will

wow the shit out of those people tomorrow and if they don't give you the award, well, fuck them. I'll give you an award when you get home."

It's like someone has held up a mirror and they're forcing me to see this for what it could be and not what we're trying to force it to be. "Ren...I wish you were here."

"No, you don't. I bet you've been up every night with some beautiful Canadian girl riding your cock like a moose or whatever. That's why you can't sleep."

"No. Almost, but no."

"Well, get that pretty face out there and get yourself someone. Have fun!" There's something off in her voice. It could be my imagination, me dreaming up what I want to hear. Or it's hesitation.

"I tried, you know? At the bar tonight, during the industry afterparty. I met a bartended, we flirted for a bit, and I followed her outside. We were—"

"Chase—"

"I couldn't do it, Ren!" I yell into the phone. She doesn't respond, so I keep going. "I kissed her and I swear to god I had every intention of banging her. I wanted to prove something to myself and I failed. I wanted to prove that I could forget about you like you want me to. That we could go on being friends with benefits. But I don't *want* that and I don't want her."

"I understand."

"Do you?" I'm off the bed and pacing now, Pongo trying to keep up with me. I have no idea what I'm doing, but I can't hold it in anymore. "I get it. We're different in so many ways, but that doesn't have to mean we can't try, does it? If you break it all down to just you and I, does anything else matter?"

"We talked about this, Chase."

"No. No, we didn't. Not really." I didn't want to do this over the phone. I didn't even know I wanted to do this. "Renate, I... I'm so sorry. I want more."

The line goes silent and I pull the phone away, checking to

make sure the call didn't disconnect. A shaky breath from her breaks both the silence and my heart simultaneously. I poured out part of my heart, a part I didn't think even existed anymore, and now I'm holding my breath waiting to see if she shatters it again or takes a chance on those broken, fucked up pieces.

Before she can answer, there's a knock on the door. I turn toward it and stare. I want an answer, but she needs time. "Uhm, R-Ren, I need to go. I'm…I won't call again if that's what you want. I'll leave you alone and let you go on with your life. It's up to you and I'll respect whatever your decision is. No matter how much it hurts."

I hang up the phone and turn it off before tossing it on the bed. Pongo follows me to the door, nudging me, but I'm ignoring him. I shouldn't.

"Chase? Honey, what's the matter?" Cynthia sounds like she's underwater and I'm drowning. I can't breathe.

When I look up at her again, I'm sitting on the edge of the bed and she's draping a cold cloth over the back of my neck. It's a trick she learned a few years ago when I had a freakout before an event.

"Hey, breathe and focus. You had another panic attack, a nasty one. I almost called the Doc." She's seen some of my worst, some I don't even remember. "How long do you think you've been sitting here?"

"Uhm, a few minutes maybe?" I pat Pongo's head, assuring him I'm okay.

"Sweetheart, you've been sitting there for almost thirty minutes. Do you want me to call Dr. Clay or would it be better to talk to me?"

I lean forward, feeling sick to my stomach, and put my face in my hands before I tell Cynthia everything I told Ren.

HOLLYWOOD
Renate

CHAPTER 14
KILLER

VALERIE BROUSSARD

THE EARLY MORNING cacophony of the small cafe is deafening, that makes it the perfect spot. Trying to grade at the kitchen table didn't work. Neither did my room, even with headphones and music on. The echoing marble and tables full of chatting people are much harder to ignore, which makes the grading take longer, but at least I'm too distracted by the world to think about Chase and his little phone call stunt.

I don't want a relationship. I don't want the hassle of giving my time and energy over to another person for them to mishandle. I've already lost enough of myself to one toxic, horrible relationship. I fought for my freedom, struggled to keep any piece of myself intact, grasped for air while clinging to the last strings of hope. I won't do that again.

Chase might be nothing like Luis. What if he respects and accepts me?

Is a movie star and all his baggage worth the risk? The paparazzi will catch me. They'll blast my extracurricular activities all over the tabloids, and Miley will fire me. Or worse, he'll hold my job hostage with the hope he can blackmail me into sleeping with him. Gross.

I'm arguing with myself like Gollum deciding the fate of a hobbit. But I have too much of a past to jump into anything that

even resembles a relationship. It's too risky. I have my work, my clubs, and my family. I'm making excuses, but deep down, I'm worried someday I'll step into another trap.

I can't afford to make the same mistake again.

Luis and I were teenagers—young and clueless about life. We were supposed to spend our younger years meeting friends, trying new things, and learning about love through the eyes of innocence. Dating as a teenager has the same feeling as dousing yourself with gasoline and walking through a crowd while hoping nobody has a match. It's hell. Especially when you're not one of the popular kids.

The other people in school teased me for my weight, being poor, or my accent even though the school had plenty of other Hispanic kids. The braces and puberty made everything a thousand times worse. I struggled to find a place to belong and when I thought I'd found it in a familiar face; I ended up in bed with the devil.

I fell for him, because there had never been anyone else. I thought he loved me when he said I'd be pretty if I lost a few pounds. I did everything he asked because I wanted to make him happy because in my impressionable mind, that's how love worked. I became a prisoner under his rule, and after my father died, it became physical. Luis could lay the charisma on so thick, it fooled everyone around us. We played the part of a happy couple, and I learned how to hide the bruises behind a smile.

The crash of a glass shattering against the marble floor silences the room long enough for me to realize I'm doing it again. Drifting off into my mind and bringing up a past I want to bury. I'm staring at the same test I've been struggling to grade for almost forty-five minutes.

I worried this would happen, and I should have stuck to my rules and trusted my boundaries. I went on that date hoping for a good dicking down and a bit of fun. But hadn't prepared for the guy doing it to knock down my mental walls, exposing feelings I hadn't prepared for. I don't want to admit I'm terrified I'll fall for another man's lies.

My phone buzzes on the table and I have to close my eyes and push out a slow breath to calm the butterflies. When I glance down at the phone, I'm relieved to read my sister's name, but also disappointed at not see his name.

"Hey, Dani."

"Yo! How did the meeting with the lawyer go? They throwing his ass back in jail?"

"No. He fooled them all with that fucking charm. They put him on probation and we're working on a better restraining order."

"Pshh, as if those work. Fucker." She yells to someone in the background to stop being so loud, the hypocrisy makes me laugh. *"I'm gonna get so many restraining orders on him, you could use them to plaster the fucking Great Wall of China twice over! Watch me!"*

"I'll let the lawyer, and China, know. How's your trip going?"

"It doesn't suck. Okay, one part kind of does suck. Can you please talk to Chase?" I don't answer, and she gets the hint. *"Seriously? Shit, I'm going to google the term spinster and find your picture right there, big as day!"*

"Daniella, you're just mad I didn't fall for your stupid matchmaking bullshit. Besides, I'm too damn old to be a spinster. I prefer the term forest crone."

"You're afraid of the forest, you crazy city hag!"

"Only because you watch too much horror and murder shows where everyone fucking *dies* in the forest!"

Laughing feels incredible. There's been too much on my mind, which aggravates my immune system and causes flares no matter how much medication I'm on. This morning, I almost didn't bother to get out of bed. All of this because of a stupid boy and his stupid smile.

"He's a nice guy, Ren. And you can't tell me the sex sucked. Are you going to do the 'I don't need anyone' dance for the rest of your life?"

"Yeah, this coming from the girl dating a… what does Xander call himself again?"

"Artistic free spirit of the digital age, don't change the subject. This isn't about us."

"Is free spirit a new term for unemployed, freeloading, rich brat who goes to rehab the way normal peasants take vacations?" I wince. That came out far more harsh than I had intended. "Sorry, I haven't had enough coffee yet and I'm snippy. You know I love Xander."

"It isn't rehab." She waits to see if I react, but I don't. Xander's bad boy aesthetic has no bite. He's a bored, rich kid trying to act like a badass when he spends weekends at ski resorts in sweater vests. I've never called him on it because most people are dealers who lie and pretend to be anything else. I don't want to learn about what went so wrong in his life to make him pretend to be a dealer. He doesn't even try that hard. He's little more than a nineties goth leftover that someone returned to Spirit Halloween and my sister picked him up on clearance. Dani believes she's destined for stardom and riches, so in her mind, they're equals, unlike Chase and me.

"Please, just call him?"

"He's with you right now and that's why you're asking, isn't he?"

"No! Okay, maybe! He's across the room, sulking, and the guys and I are worried about him. Fuck, he's so boring when he's in a mood." She lets out an exasperated sigh. *"He's putting on this happy front for Stevie and Ethan when he can because he doesn't want to fuck up their wedding and all. But he's a fucking mess. Like, Pongo won't even leave his side. He's so worked up. Not like in a Luis mess way, like a lost… I dunno—"*

"Puppy?" The whisper comes out too easily and I can only

hope Dani hasn't heard me. "Well, it's better for him that we got this over with before either of us could get hurt."

"Oh my god, you're both so dumb!"

"I love you, too. Tell me more about Italy." She's been texting us pictures non-stop. I give her and Xander a lot of shit, but he makes sure she's got everything she could ever need. Including a beautiful hotel room with an amazing view. I'm more jealous of their relationship than I care to admit.

"Oh my god, I love Italy and you should have come!"

"They're your friends, Dani. These are your people. They're not mine."

"They could be."

"I need to go. I have to finish grading."

"Don't deflect! You don't want to admit that Chase could be the guy!"

"For someone else." She's a busybody and nosey, like Mama. She's going to be up my ass until either Chase moves on or I give in. I've got a stubborn streak she can't touch, though, and she knows it. "We've talked about this. No more matchmaking! Let the man mourn the incredible sex, and move on with his life."

"Gross, but also valid. Have you finished mourning his big dick?" She counters in a yell, and I have to pull the phone away from my ear. *"Come on, your ex-asshole doesn't deserve to get any more of your life, and you don't even see you're giving it to him!"*

Once again, she's right. The youngest of all of us and yet, she's the oldest soul. I never thought about it that way, making excuses every time a man showed interest or limiting it to friends with benefits. I mull over the idea of calling him, but I shake the thought from my head.

"You still there, or did I cross a line?"

"Dani, you always cross lines, and I hope you never stop. I gotta go." I try to rush her off the phone, but she gets one last dig in.

"Ha! I knew I could get you to call him. Matchmaking fucking bruja!"

"I'm going to work, not calling anyone."

"Hey, wait! I need a date for a dinner party next week! Xander can't make it. Please say you'll come with me?!"

"A dinner party?"

"Yeah, with some of my artsy creative friends. You'll love it. I thought about asking Kennedy, but she's actually sticking to this sober lifestyle, which is great, but—"

"Fine."

"Wait, really?"

"Yeh, tell me what to wear and when. I need an excuse to get out of the house for a bit anyhow." I love recharging and staying home when I can, but sometimes, to get a better charge, I need to drain my battery down to nothing. Besides, how crazy can a dinner party be?

When I get to my classroom, there's a note on my door asking me to see Mr. Miley, the principal, as soon as I'm in. If he didn't suck at his job, he would know I came in two hours ago. I don't go to my room first thing most mornings because I'm in the cafeteria making sure all the kids are getting something to eat, or in the library running tutoring sessions. It's been this way for the last few years.

I pull the note off the door and crumple it up. If he can't bother to learn schedules, he can wait until I have my things settled before I give him my time. I flick on the light and head straight for the back room and open a storage cabinet, where a dozen bobbing heads of Chase Cooper stare back at me. They're judging me. I can tell.

I've been meaning to give them to Dani, but keep forgetting to bring them home. I grab one and stare at it. "Those bastards even got your stupid eyes right." I sigh and lock the cabinet, still holding onto the toy. I walk to my desk and put it on the corner. It's a terrible reminder, but it also makes me smile.

I almost knock the toy off the desk when I go to write something on the board and see what's taking up over half of my wall. As if I need another thing to remind me of him, I'm staring at the shiny new smart board Chase promised he'd take care of before he'd left. I'm not sure if I've got Miley or Chase to blame for this, but I don't need the wrath of other teachers coming down on me because I got the cool new toy, and they didn't. Fuck that. I grind my teeth while I march up to the office to clear this up.

Miley spots me as I walk into the main office. He's sitting on the edge of his assistant's desk, flipping through a supply catalog like he would have a clue what supplies it takes to run this place. Idiot. "Ah, the stunning and talented Ms. Silva!"

"Sir, if this has to do with the smart board, I didn't—"

"Boards. With an *s*, Ms. Silva." He drops the catalog into the trash and nods to the door. "Let's talk in my office."

I follow him into the office, hesitating when he motions me to close the door.

"You're not in any trouble, Ms. Silva. In fact, I want to commend your school spirit." His chair screams for mercy as he throws himself into it. The walls are full of old trophies and awards from his youth, like a shrine to himself. None of the pictures are from the last ten years, and the body language of the people in them says he's always been a creep. "This could be very beneficial for the school if you play your cards right."

"My cards?"

He licks his lips and my stomach turns. "You must be damn good to earn yourself an entire school worth of smart boards. I signed off on having the remaining boards installed over the weekend. Pity you haven't shown this kind of *ambition* before."

My nails dig into the palms of my hands when he leans

forward, pretending to adjust his glasses while he stares at my tits.

"You could have used your charms to get yourself a raise. Or a promotion. But I can understand using them on Chase if he's going to repay you like this."

"Mr. Miley, I don't appreciate what you're insinuating."

"You're denying using your feminine ways to, eh, convince Chase to drop this kind of cash?"

"You sent that reporter to my house, didn't you?"

He sighs and leans back in his chair as he scratches his scraggly beard. I've heard he's in his early fifties, but he looks at least ten years beyond that. He's balding, but trying to cover it with a hideous comb over and always stinks of cheap cologne. I should buy a beat up, windowless, white van to park outside of this guy's house as a warning. I've seen what he does online in his free time here at the school. I can't imagine it's much better at home.

"What if I did, Ms. Silva? You may not wish to disclose intimate details of your life, but I'd recommend you keep providing Chase with your… *services*. We need the press in order for me to request a larger budget. A budget that could help with your review this year. But only if you keep him in a happier and more generous mood than you do the other men in your life."

"Excuse me?" Oh, I'm about to shove a pencil right into this man's eyeball. "Mr. Miley, I will not be—"

"Getting a raise anytime soon if you keep up the attitude?" He smirks, and my lip twitches into a snarl. "Try wearing something a little lower cut from now on, yeah? The children do love those new boards, so think of it as doing it for them. Besides, I'm sure he's giving you much more than smart boards, honey."

I stare at him, mouth open at the pure audacity. As I turn for the door, I glare over my shoulder, and reply, "If you ever insinuate anything else about my personal life or my attire, I will report you to the board with proof of your inappropriate behavior toward the female teachers and what you've been doing on the school computers. Also, he's *Mr. Cooper* to you."

He's sputtering something that I don't care to hear as I slam the door behind me. The receptionist offers me a knowing shrug and whispers, "Are you really dating Chase Cooper?"

"Allison, you're a lovely person. Mind your own business."

"Yes, ma'am."

HOLLYWOOD
Chase

CHAPTER 15
GOOD LUCK, BABE!

CHAPPELL ROAN

MY LEG WON'T STOP BOUNCING. EVEN when I hold it down, it's bouncing like I drank three pots of coffee. I hate waiting rooms for so many reasons and I should have phoned this appointment in, but I promised Cynthia I'd do this in person. Pongo puts his head on my leg and I grimace. "Sorry, bud. I'm trying to stop. I swear."

I haven't talked to Ren since I fucked up. I heard Dani tried to convince her, but she didn't budge. I don't blame her; even if she hates me now.

"Coop?" My head snaps up at the voice. "You ready?"

Dr. Theo Clay isn't much older than me, but he's got one of those faces that says he's lived an interesting life and seen a lot out there. It's part of why I trust him. His salt and pepper hair makes him appear older and wiser, too. A smart thing to have going for you when you're a psychiatrist in the middle of Los Angeles. He doesn't say much until we get into his office and the door shuts. I take my usual seat and look around. He's added some new artwork. He takes photos when he visits different restaurants and kitchens in Europe and fills the walls with them. There's nothing personal, but no stupid motivational shit either.

And he can, and will, tell you about every picture he's taken and what they were making or how incredible the food was.

"So, what's new? I assumed you'd be on a set somewhere?"

"The indie movie has a few special screenings. I just got the script for the next one."

Our sessions always start off this way. Small talk at first until I'm ready to dive headfirst into the deep end. Sometimes I never do, but he says those are still productive appointments because it's bringing whatever's bothering me closer to the surface.

Pongo walks across the room and curls up in his usual sunny spot on the couch. There's a window and he can watch the squirrels play in the tree outside. I envy how quickly he can relax and fall asleep in almost any situation. Most nights, I can't even sleep in a bed that costs as much as a car.

Theo offers me some kind of baked thing he's made. I'm not hungry, but I don't want to come across as rude, so I take it. Plus, he trained in France, so he knows what he's doing. He baked an epic cake for Jamie's wife, Alexis, last year for her birthday. He's been seeing her as a client for a while to help her get through some fucked up stuff with her family.

"Coffee?"

"Nah. I'm alright," I answer, nibbling on the cookie.

"So what's with the bouncing leg?" I stare at him, confused. "The new receptionist is very perceptive. She's practically Sherlock Holmes, and when she sees something like that, she texts me. Mostly because you all love to come in here and lie about how you're doing while you're falling apart on the inside. How are the madeleines?"

"Who? Oh, the cookie thing? No, it's...buttery. Thanks." We've been doing this for a while now, so he knows my tells and most of my dark secrets. It's weird, because in this office, he's my therapist, but once we step outside, he's become more of a friend. We both know that could jeopardize the whole therapy thing, but for now, it's working.

"Good, so what are your plans for tomorrow?"

"Why, you asking me out, Doc?"

He doesn't laugh, doesn't even smile. Instead, he sits there and stares at me. "Just curious what you're doing in your free time, since you're not shooting."

"You're the second person to ask me about tom—" I swallow hard as my mouth goes dry. Tomorrow. Fuck. I should have known why Jamie called me to ask about my plans and decided on dinner at *my* house, but he does that all the time. I shake my head and pick at the crumbs on my jeans. "I totally forgot."

How could I forget? I mean, it's not like I keep it on my calendar. What would I even write there? *Reminder, it's the fucking worst day of your life?* That's why I'm here, to keep myself from putting those exact words on a damn calendar.

"Hey, breathe." He's handing me a cup of coffee. I never even noticed him standing up and crossing the room. "That's an improvement. A big one, at that. The act of mourning a loss should have ebbs and flows. You've been stuck on a plateau for so long, it's nice to see some movement in the needle, alright?"

"Not remembering the day someone kills themself isn't exactly an ebb and flow situation, Theo."

"It means you're letting yourself move on, what we've been working on from the start. The ability to accept that she's gone, but you're still here. Did you make plans for tomorrow that weren't your standard idea of mourning her from the bottom of a bottle?"

"Friends are coming over for dinner."

"Okay?"

I shake my head. "I need to talk to you about something else first. And I'm not deflecting. I promise."

"Okay, go ahead."

"I met someone and I kind of asked her out on a date. I'm pretty sure that's why I forgot about tomorrow."

"No shit? Like a *date* date? Dinner and dancing or whatever you kids do these days?"

"You're not old enough to say that to me," I point out and he holds up his hands. "Her sister and Jamie kind of set us up to meet. She's a teacher at a school where Jamie had one of his art classes."

"How'd the date go?"

I let out a long breath and sit back in the chair while I run my hands through my hair. "Here's the thing, she uhm," I stop and laugh again. "Shit, I can't believe I'm about to tell you this but, she's into some kinky stuff. She's a domme...dominant... dominatrix? Whatever it's called." I swallow hard and lean forward so my elbows are on my knees. "Theo, I cried in the shower after she—uhm, well, to be blunt—after she tied me up, blindfolded me, and gave me the best blowjob of my life."

"Why do you think you cried?"

I stare at the floor for a long time, processing the question and the feelings I've had over the weekend. "I felt...free. Like I let something huge go. That's fucking stupid, huh?"

"That's not stupid, Chase. I've talked to plenty of people who've found healing in the kink community. It's not for everyone, but it's also not only about sex, pain, and bondage. It's deeper for most people. You said she's the dominant one, which means she's helping you work towards letting go of that death-grip you have on your past and things you can't control."

"It's not a *death-grip*."

"And your leg wasn't bouncing because I made you wait an extra two minutes past your appointment time?"

"Fair. Rude, but fair." I run my hand through my hair before I wipe my face, trying to focus and not daydreaming on the shower. "She told me she had been stuck in a shitty relationship, and that she lost part of herself until she found a way to take back control. Do you mean something like that? Like, self control?"

"So long as it's safe and consenting, it could be therapeutic, yeah. Just make sure you listen to her and your body. Don't be afraid to use your safe word." He scribbles a few notes while I nod. "I consider your willingness to let go of any measure of control a big step. You don't need to jump in with both feet before looking, though. Take your time."

"Don't get too happy. I already fucked it up."

"Ah, okay. Spill it. What did you do?"

"Why does it have to be me?!" I stare at him, but give in because the look he's giving me says it all. "You're right. The king of self-sabotage strikes again. I asked her—no, I begged her for more."

"More?"

"More than friends." My mind flashes to the shower, and how she held me after. The constant reminders of all the ways we took care of each other over the weekend while avoiding the personal, painful questions. I remember how comfortable it felt having her around the house. She never coddled me. I would have hated that.

Friends. Shit, are we even friends anymore?

"She wanted it casual, and I failed. Every time something good would happen on my trip, I wanted to tell her all about it. I literally ran back to my room one night so I could call her before she left for work."

"And how did she react to all that?"

"She kept telling me to go out and meet someone new. To let loose and enjoy life. I tried one night, drunk out of my mind. I almost hooked up with this chick."

"What made you stop?"

"I didn't want the bartender."

"You wanted this new woman?"

"Yeah, I headed back to my room and called her, told her what happened, and she sounded, I dunno, happy for me." My heart sinks again, remembering the conversation. "That's when I told her I wanted more. I wanted a chance, and I blew it."

"Have you asked her why she only wants the relationship to be casual?"

"No, because I'm an idiot."

"You said she got out of a rough relationship. Did you stop to consider she's in a similar situation as you? Stuck on someone or something in the past and unable to move forward yet?"

"We didn't get too deep into personal stuff, so no, I should have thought of that." I curse myself under my breath. "You know, she never said octopus."

"Hmm?"

"The safe word. She told me to use it, even when we're not… you know." I can feel her even though she's not there. How her fingers played in my hair while we watched movies. The feel of her arm curled around me when we slept. I can hear her laugh, and if I close my eyes, the scent of summer fills my head. It's been like this since I left Los Angeles. But now that I'm back, it's worse. "It all feels so…different with her. She didn't say it though, when I told her I wanted more. She didn't say our safe word. So maybe, there's—"

"Chase?"

My throat tightens and the next thing I know, Pongo's head sits in my lap. "I'm sorry, buddy." I whisper as I lean down, holding my head against his until I can breathe again. He licks my face and goes back to the sunny spot.

"What happened just now? Before Pongo nudged you?" He hands me a tissue and nods to my hands. My thumb has a bead of blood forming where I picked at it. I haven't done that in months. *Fuck.*

"I don't know. Realizing how bad I fucked this up. She hasn't called me back, and I told her I would respect her decision, no matter how much it hurt."

"I'm going to start off with the obvious—You should have

called me sooner. I could have told you that a friends with benefits situation would be hard work for you. It's why you couldn't take on Steve's lifestyle successfully, you're a commitment guy. You don't want to waste your time with games, you saw your mother do that and your brain actively fights against it."

"I wish it didn't have to end. Not like this, anyhow." He jots down a few more notes and tips his glasses down so he can look at me over the top of them. "In her mind, we're too…I don't know…different. But not super different, just, like, I'm a fucking movie star and she's a teacher. For her, that spells disaster.."

"And you disagree?"

"Yeah. I don't get it. I mean, she opens my eyes to possibility, she talks to me, she cares, she helps me feel safe. I like her, and I want to give this a shot, you know. See where it goes."

"Did you open up about your past or the things we're working through?"

"No. I wanted a clean slate. I liked her not knowing how fucked up I am?"

"Why do you think there's something wrong with you? Because you were rejected?"

"Fuck you. She didn't reject me. She just—" I purse my lips and groan. "Dammit. You did that on purpose." I pick up another cookie and shove the whole thing in my mouth. I eat when I'm nervous and it buys me time to come up with an answer. "I hoped this time I wouldn't fuck everything up like I did with Cassie, since we'd have no relationship *to* fuck up as friends with benefits.."

"Full circle." He leans forward, tossing his glasses on the table. I've gone back to square one. "Chase, we've talked about this, and you're not responsible for what happened to Cassie. The woman who did that will die in prison, you watched her get a multi-life sentencing."

"Not one of those convictions has a damn thing to do with

Cassie's case! They didn't find anything to tie her to Cassie or me other than Jamie, and that's not enough for closure!" I yell before throwing half a cookie to Pongo. I take a few deep breaths to calm myself.

I wring my hands so hard it hurts. "I hope someday I'll believe it when you say I didn't hurt Cassie. If she hadn't been dating me, it wouldn't have ever happened. I'm the cause, I'm the whole reason she—" I close my eyes and picture Cassie. The memory of my screams rings in my head. The strange way the cries echoed as they mixed with the sound of rainfall from the shower. The taste of iron lingers in my mouth. The ghost that still gives me nightmares. Pongo sits at my side again, leaning against my leg when I open my eyes.

"One step forward, two steps back. It's a struggle, but I promise you're making progress, Chase. We need to find a way for you to accept that you did everything you could to protect Cassie. You were a little misguided in that protection, but certainly not to a level of hurting her." He writes some more in his notebook. "Be proud of yourself, Chase. You've taken a big step, even if it didn't work out the way you wanted it to. You opened yourself to something new. That's brave."

We ease into a more relaxed tone for the rest of the session. We shoot the shit about Devin and how he's handling the season, and about my filming schedule. He gives me a new website to try for recipes; we argue the merits of baking and cooking. He insists I try baking, but I tell him he's nuts. Baking comes from science, cooking comes from the heart.

When I get down to my car, there's a large brown envelope on the windshield. I open the door and let Pongo hop inside while I toss the envelope in the passenger seat. I close my eyes and do my breathing exercises while he gets comfortable in the back. When I'm done, curiosity gets the better of me. Inside the envelope, I find a few pictures and another marriage license, which I'm about to laugh off until I read the names..

I grab my phone off the dash.

"Morning, Coop. Did your session go well?"

"Fine. Cyn, I got another fan thing for your collection, but this one you might want to look into. There are photos no one should have of Cassie and I." I swallow hard before I add, "And a copy of our marriage license. The real one. Can you see if anyone has heard of Julie Horowitz?"

"Doesn't sound familiar, but I'll send someone over to pick it up and check it out." She's protective, like the mother I wish I had. That's why I've never entertained offers from other firms, no matter how big they are. *"You could use some uplifting news. Are you sitting down?"*

"Yeah, I'm in the car. Why?"

"Well, Marc Stone got a hold of me this morning. They're taking the movie to France."

"What?" The director has been generating some buzz around the small movie I had the lead in recently. It's why we were in Toronto. But taking it to Cannes? I've never been to Cannes, only ever watched clips of the carpet on my computer. This is…big.

"Your name has come up in discussions, Chase. You're the reason they want to show the movie. They're saying it's your strongest performance yet. This will be a damn huge year for you, kiddo. Not bad for a movie that you filmed in less than a month."

I hang up with Cyn and stare at my phone. There's one person I want to celebrate this with before anyone else. My finger hovers over her name.

HOLLYWOOD
Chase

CHAPTER 16
BODY TALKS

THE STRUTS

PONGO RETREATS to the safety of the house after another giant splash sends water sloshing over the edge of the pool. Lulu swims to me, licking my face as she climbs up on me. Pongo does an amazing job at keeping me calm, but Lulu? She's perfect at just being a dog. I hoist her up and out of the pool. Water goes in every direction as she shakes and gets ready to jump in once more.

The buzzer for the front gate interrupts our playtime, but it's too early for Jamie to be here, and Devin has already left for practice. It must be Dani, but she never uses the buzzer. I open the app on my phone and when I spot the car; I hit the button without hesitation. I hurry out of the pool and run for the door, my hands shaking and my stomach in knots as I reach for the knob. I throw the door open just in time to see Ren park her car.

"Hey," is all I can squeak out as I stand by her car door, still dripping. I clear my throat. "I, uhm, didn't know you were, uhh—"

"Dani invited me. She called it a dinner party with artsy people." She hasn't looked up at me yet, and she sounds annoyed. "I guess she didn't expect me to recognize the house in the daylight. Based on the lack of cars, she also lied about the time."

"I didn't tell her to do that, but I... I'm glad you came. I mean, I get it if you want to leave, but you can, you know, stay." I can't even make sentences. "Food is good."

My shoulders slump and the butterflies get stuck in my throat, but she laughs and shakes her head. I missed that sound. She climbs out of the car, and, risking it all, I take a step forward. My arms cage her against the car, but she still doesn't look up.

"Chase, don't do this."

"You haven't said it." She shivers at my voice, but there's no fear in her face. We haven't seen each other in almost a month, but it's still there. That crackling spark, that desire, that need.

"Said what?" she asks, her voice breathy. Her fingers twitch, fighting the urge to reach out and touch me. Taking another risk, I slide my finger under her chin and tilt her head back. Her long lashes hide what I want to see until they flutter and lift. We're reflections staring back at ourselves, hunger and lust filling both of us. I want to rip her clothes off right here; bend her over the hood of the car and show her how much I want her.

"The one thing you know will stop me." I lick my lips and cup her face, staring into those deep brown eyes. I cash in my last hope, praying to every god I've ever heard of. "If you're uncomfortable, you say the word. You say 'octopus'."

"Coming out here with your shirt off was cruel. You're all... wet."

"I thought that was my line?" My head dips down, and there's an intense jolt of electricity that hits when our lips crash together. Fuck, I forgot how good this felt. Without breaking the kiss, I pick her up and her arms wrap around my neck.

"Wait!" she yells, and my heart sinks. I overstepped, and she hates me even more now. "I need my bag."

I grin as I carry her to the back, pop the trunk open, and

throw her bag over my shoulder. She screams and laughs as I run her into the house. The second we're inside, I have her against a wall and her legs wrap around me like they belong there. Because they do.

"You taste like a pool."

"You taste like a fucking drug." I slide my hand down her leg, but I can't find an end to the fabric. I glance down and shake my head. "Pants? Really? I mean, I want *in* your pants, but how the hell am I supposed to do all these things I want to do to you against this wall when you're wearing pants?"

"You're ruining my clothes. Not in the way I like, either." She kisses the tip of my nose. "Put me down, Chase. We should talk first."

"Is this a terrible idea?"

"Without a doubt." Her eyes follow her fingers down my bare chest, and I push my hips into hers. "We need to get it out of our system, right? That's all?"

"I'll never get you out of my system, Renate Silva. You're there, you're etched on my fucking heart. But if this is it, if all you'll give me is this one last night, then yeah. Sure."

I kiss her until neither of us can breathe. The dogs are going nuts and running around us wanting to get her attention, too, but I outrank them, at least for now. When I put her down, she takes the bag away from me and heads upstairs to my room. I, of course, follow her like a lost puppy, with Pongo and Lulu on my heels.

"You know, the way you follow me around earned the name *Snuggle Puppy* on my phone."

"Really? I've got you listed as *Hots for Teacher* on mine. I even downloaded the song for your ringtone."

"You keep your phone on mute."

"Yeah, but it's the thought that counts, right?" She laughs as she heaves her bag onto my bed. "Should I make a joke about how much you packed for a dinner party with artsy people?"

She keeps her hand on the bag, and sighs. "I had planned on heading out to the club tonight after. To blow off some steam."

The club? Oh fuck, she means the sex club. My eyes flick to the bag again and my heart races at the thought of what's in it. I step toward her with a wicked grin. "Why don't you pretend you're at the club now? With me."

"Aren't you supposed to be cooking?"

She's right. Jamie will kick my ass if I'm up here with my dick out and don't have dinner ready. But there's a devious shimmer in her eyes as she stares at my bare chest. She's in my room with a bag of toys meant for a sex club. I'm not about to miss this opportunity.

"Yeah, I should probably get changed," I say, staring right back at her and dropping my swim trunks. Her eyes drop along with them and she bites her lip.

"Me, too."

She looks me dead in the eyes and pulls her soaked top over her head, tossing it at my feet. I can see her large brown nipples through her wet bra, that gorgeous soft belly—god I want her. Her thumbs hook into the band of her pants, and she pushes them down until they pool at her feet. My jaw drops, but my cock stands at full attention.

Let the games begin.

"What are we going to do now, Puppy?"

"Fuck Jamie *and* dinner. We can order pizza."

"I'd rather you just fuck *me*."

We're on each other in seconds, ripping her bra off and tossing it over my shoulder while he squeezes my ass. I reach for her panties, but she stops me from pulling them down. I whine in response. I'm rock hard and my cock begs for her mouth, her cunt, hell, my hand—anything.

"Tell me you're a bad boy, Chase," she says in a sultry moan. My name sounds so fucking pretty on her lips.

"I'm... I'm a *bad* boy." She looks into my soul while her

fingertip slides up my shaft. "S-so fucking bad. Let me make it up to you. I'll do anything for you."

"No more relationship talk." I swallow hard, and she raises an eyebrow, waiting for my answer. I drop my shoulders and my head, not wanting to answer her. "Not yet."

My head snaps up. "What?"

"I need time, Chase. I need to figure this out on my own terms."

"Yes. Yeah. Okay. I promise I'll drop it until you're ready. I swear. I'll be so good to you, beautiful."

She nods and I lift her up and carry her to the bathroom counter. With my hands on her knees, I spread her legs wide and swallow hard at the head to toe goddess in front of me. I hesitate, though, as what she said sinks in. I have to prove to her I'll treat her like the queen she is. We can have sex, but I still can't have her. *Yet.*

Our tongues tangle and I grab a handful of her hair, pulling it hard as she moans. I try to break away from the kiss, but she bites down on my bottom lip, holding me there while her nails claw down my chest. Just as she releases my lip, my hips crash against hers, grinding my cock against her panties.

"Now you're all wet, Ms. Silva. But I'm gonna make sure you soak these panties for me."

"Good, Mr. Cooper. Then I can shove them in that brat mouth of yours."

She rolls her hips and rubs her pussy along my shaft. The sparks between us are enough to ignite the fire that's about to consume us both. I grab hold of her ass and move her closer to the edge of the counter. My teeth drag down her jaw and to her ear and I bite down as her nails dig into my shoulders.

"Tell me you want me, Renate." I whisper, feeling her clit pulsing with each thrust. If I keep this up, I'm going to come before I'm even inside her.

"I want you, Chase. I want your pretty cock splitting me in

two. I want you to fuck me so hard you break your counter." She grabs my cock and squeezes it hard. "Now, how bad do you *need* me?"

"You're all I've wanted for weeks. I should have never let you leave the house. I can't even come unless I'm thinking about how fucking perfect you are. Your big tits, your sweet pussy, your dirty mouth, everything about you."

"Mm, tell me more."

"I dreamed about the way your cunt feels when you squeeze my fingers before you come. About your hands around my throat while you ride my cock. I came so fucking hard in the shower when I imagined going to an audition with your lipstick all over my fucking cock."

"You're a dirty little boy, aren't you?"

"No. I'm *your* dirty boy."

"Get on your knees and show me, Puppy."

The name has my knees shaking, and I drop hard. She's my altar, and I am more than ready to worship. I stare up at her like she's the sun. "Tell me what you, my queen. Tell me how to please you."

She smirks. "Oh, you already know."

The tip of my tongue slides through her panties and when I make it to her clit, she grabs a fistful of my hair and moans like an angel mumbling about her bad boy. I'll be the devil for her if that's what she wants. I suck hard through the lace as I push the fabric to the side and slip two fingers inside her soaking cunt. I curl them until her back arches and I thrust nice and slow, building up an electric current that has her squeezing my head with her thighs. She pulls hard on my hair. I've got her knocking on the door, so I keep fuck her deeper and faster.

She clenches my fingers so hard I almost can't pull them out. I release her clit, but don't stop my fingers. "What's my name, my queen?"

She cackles as her head rocks back, screaming as loud as she can. "PUPPY!"

"Good girl. Now, eyes on me."

I use my teeth and free hand to rip her panties off, tossing them aside. The tips of my fingers slide through her slit as she moans. I hold them up and watch her red lips wrap around them, humming while our eyes remain locked on one another. She releases them with a pop, and I lower my head, kissing up and down her legs until neither of us can take it anymore. The sweet, sharp taste of her hits my tongue and my arms wrap around her thighs, holding her in place so I can feast. And I do. I want her legs to shake for me; I want her back to bow so hard it almost breaks. I want her to deafen me with her siren's screams.

"Oh god! Oh, Chase! Just like that!"

Her thick thighs squeeze my head and both of her hands have a firm grip on my hair. She's at her own private carnival and my face just became her favorite ride. The heels of her feet dig into my back as I reach up, pinching her nipple. She's close.

I use my one remaining brain cell to concentrate on holding back my own climax as she fucks my face. With one last flick of my tongue, she explodes in my mouth, holding my head to her as she rides out wave after wave. I don't stop until her eyes close and her body goes limp. She smiles down at me through sex drunk eyes, so I lick her clean as she lazily strokes my hair and mumbles blissed out nonsense.

When I stand, she reaches out for my cock, but I step away, shaking my head. She looks equally confused and ruined as she leans against the mirror; it's fucking glorious. Her legs still spread wide, inviting back for more. It's tempting as hell, but I also need to show her I understand my role.

I open a drawer and fish out a condom, tossing it next to her on the counter. "For later, assuming I earn it. I should finish dinner."

"Puppy?" It's a pitiful sound I've never heard come from her before.

I put my hands on the mirror next to her head and lean in, nudging her nose with mine. She tries to wrap her legs around me, tries to pull me into her, but I'm too tall.

"I will worship you in every way I can. I will devour you, shatter you, and tear you apart. I will do everything and anything you want, my queen. Including denying myself for you. I'm your toy, and all I need is your satisfaction. But right now, I need to go make dinner. And if I'm a very, very good boy, I hope I'll earn the need to open more than one foil wrapper tonight."

Her eyes are wide and her mouth hangs open as the reality of what she's unleashed hits her. Without another word, I pick up my t-shirt and leave her there in the bathroom. I toss my swim trunks in the hamper and pull on a pair of jeans before I head downstairs.

I'm trying hard to think of things like cold showers or sports statistics as I organize everything I'll need to finish dinner. But my brain keeps going back to how perfect she looked, dripping wet on my bathroom counter for me. My dick begs me to go back up there and finish what we started, but I told her I would behave. I told her I would earn it.

I take a deep breath and let my shoulders relax. This is my space, my sanctuary. I check the short ribs that I'd put in earlier, and as I'm getting into the groove, two small hands wrap around my waist and her head presses against my back. Warmth floods my entire body, and it's not from the oven.

"Are you okay, Chase?"

I turn around, pulling her closer as I smile. I like how she has to put her chin on my chest to look up at me with those big doe eyes. "I like it when you make me work for it."

"Good to know." She glances around the counter. "So, what

should I do to help with dinner, since Dani had me show up way too early?"

"You came right on time, Sunshine."

"You are so cheese, Chase Cooper."

"And yet, you came back for more, Renate Silva."

Why am I such a fucking mess?

"Renate, I need to…I should…" I need to get this out. But it's hard to concentrate when she's in one of my shirts again, and no pants. How am I supposed to have a serious conversation with her when I can't stop picturing her riding my dick? I turn back around and lean against the counter, letting out a slow breath to focus. "Look I, uhm, I don't—"

"Want me in your kitchen?" She asks, taking a handful of blueberries. "I mean, I'm a shit cook, but I can chop a mean onion."

"No, that's not it." The conversation gets away from me again. I have to get this right, but I blurt out, "I have a therapist!"

"I assumed," she shrugs, unbothered, as she reaches around me and grabs a spatula. I cock my head to the side, and she cackles. "Chase, you're a Hollywood actor with a support dog and deep-seated anxiety issues."

"Deep-seated anxiety? Is it that obvious?" She's not wrong. I pick her up, putting her on top of the counter and spreading her legs wide. "I'll fucking show you deep-seated."

"I've seen you cry, tough guy."

"Once! It wasn't… it's not like I—" Her smile turns me to jelly, and I press my forehead to hers. "Yeah, okay. So, I told him about you and about our *friendship*."

"Situationship," she sighs.

"Yeah, well, he told me I need to be more upfront with you. To be more open and tell you about my past." I kiss her forehead gently before turning and hopping onto the counter across from her. "Yes, I have anxiety and a plethora of other diagnoses. Some I've always had, some are kind of new and I'm still learning to deal with them. I've had some shit relationships, not as bad as yours—

"Luckily, it's not a game of who had the worst relationship."

"Fair. You should know about a few of them before you make your decision about our situationship. Well, one of them—Cassidy Landon."

Ren leans forward, listening in a way I'm not used to from the women in my life. This conversation should have a lump in my throat and my head spinning, but there's something in the way she's looking at me that makes it...easier.

"She came from a tiny town in the Midwest to study art. We met at a gallery and ended up talking at a diner until sunrise. The media dug into her past the moment we went public, but she didn't have skeletons to expose, so they made things up. They attacked her body, her clothes, her career daily in the magazines. To my face, she ignored them, pretending it didn't bother her. Spoiler alert, it bothered her.

"After she moved in here, some sick fuck hid up a tree that used to be outside and took a dozen nude photos of her while she showered upstairs. The press ate it up, posted them everywhere. Even her parents saw them. The humiliation ended up being more than she could handle. She stopped going out, stopped talking to friends, stopped eating. We got her a therapist that made house calls, and she made improvements, but it ended up being too much for her."

"That's awful." Ren hops off the counter and puts her hand over mine. "Hollywood has never been easy on people. Remember, I grew up here."

"I did a bunch of stupid shit in the name of keeping Cassie safe. In the end, none of that mattered. You said you lost part of yourself in your relationship? Well, I kind of did, too. When I lost Cassie, something broke inside me. It made problems I could handle before worse. That's why I have a therapist. And Pongo, too. But I don't want to fuck things up like that between you and me. I want to apologize for Dani tricking you to come here. I'm sorry she did that, but I'm also glad she did."

"I'm glad you found help, Chase. And I'm glad you trust me enough to open up like this. Also, Dani is my sister, so you don't have to apologize for her. I'm glad she did that, too."

"You are?"

"You're cute when you're confused," she says with a smile. "Now, how can I help?"

HOLLYWOOD
Renate

CHAPTER 17
TEAR YOU APART
SHE WANTS REVENGE

HE PULLS a knife from the magnetic holder and grabs an onion from the counter, holding them both out to me. "Show me what you've got."

"Okay, I may have lied about that part." I grimace. "Kitchens, uhm, scare me." It's a weakness I hate admitting and can sometimes hide. But Chase's kitchen looks like it's straight out of some five-star restaurant and I don't know what any of this stuff does. I can't even find a microwave in here.

"Okay, well, we need to fix that. Come here, I'll help you."

He starts off by showing me how to hold the knife, demonstrating the rocking motion I'll need to make. It looks easy enough, but as soon as I take the knife, I become all thumbs and can't recreate what he just showed me. I make a mess. He must think I'm an idiot and I don't like that feeling. My shoulders tense and my jaw ticks as I fight with this stupid vegetable. I'm about to scream when Chase presses against me, taking my hand in his and moving me through the motions with an ease and calm I don't recognize.

The distracting stiffness poking into my back makes it hard enough to figure this out, but when he leans down, dipping his mouth to my neck, it becomes dangerous. Between his hands

wandering all over me and the throbbing between my legs, it's a wonder I haven't cut myself.

"Did your mom teach you how to cook?" I ask, trying to refocus him.

"Nope. Concentrate, or you'll cut your finger off."

He sucks on my pulse point and I don't even realize I've stopped cutting, too focused on his lips and his hands. My chest heaves and my heart races.

All this over an onion.

"How long will all this take to cook?" I ask in a breathy voice.

"An hour," he answers in a gravelly whisper. His hand tucks between my legs and I gasp, gripping the counter tight. "I love how my shirt looks on you. And how wet you still are."

"This isn't sanitary, Chase."

"I'm not touching the food, and I'll wash my hands when I'm done."

He pulls the shirt up over my ass, grinding against it. Such a fucking brat, but I don't want to stop him.

"And what time are Jamie and Lexi going to be here?"

"No idea. They have a key." He makes a disapproving sound in my ear, adding, "I'm going to need to get you a step stool."

"Why?"

"So I can bend you over this counter and fuck you properly."

With a huff, I slam the knife down on the counter. I grab his hand, pulling it out from between my legs even though I don't want to, and face him with a stern look. It's the one I give to my students when I need them to know I mean business. He straightens up, but flashes me a wicked grin. Before I can say a word, he lifts me, spins me around, and drops me onto the other counter. I can't stop the scream that comes out of me, or the giggles that follow.

"There, now you can look me in the eye when you give me

the lecture that's coming about distracting you while you have a knife."

I roll my eyes and bite my lip. His big blue eyes sparkle at me as he licks his lips before dragging his bottom lip through his teeth. I wonder what Lexi and Jamie will think if they come in and I'm on the counter, impaled on that big dick of his. I wrap my legs around his waist and pull him to me while my arms go around his neck so I can play with his soft hair. "I could lecture you, and you'd like it, but I have a better idea."

Our mouths collide and he's grinding against me when his hand slips up my shirt, cupping my breast and squeezing. "Fuck, I need you, Ren. I thought I could wait, but I can't. I need to worship you, to be inside you. Why don't we go back upstairs and you show me what you packed in that bag of yours?"

"I'll make you a deal," I breathe against his mouth between kisses. I'm not sure we're going to stop, but this might at least slow us down. "We get the food ready, and you and I will go back upstairs."

"Stay the night," he moans, pinching my nipple until it's pebbled, still kissing and grinding against me. Out of nowhere, he whispers, "Tie me up and make me yours?"

The thought of his hands bound to the bedposts makes me shiver, but his shoulders stiffen as the words come out, and he pushes away from me.

"I'm sorry…that came out weird, huh?" He swallows hard, avoiding eye contact and shuffling back over to the sink. "I didn't mean…never mind."

"Chase?" My fingers dance over his tight arm as he scrubs his hands, but he doesn't respond. "Look at me, handsome boy."

He turns his head, but can't quite meet my stare. I expect Pongo to be at his side any second now, but this might not be his anxiety. He's embarrassed. I reach up and cup his face.

"Honey, you don't have to be embarrassed about wanting to experiment. Not around me, *mi lindo cachorro*. Never in front of me." He nods while my thumb slides over his pouty bottom lip and I smile at him. "Let's finish cooking, so I can give you a present."

"P-present?" he stutters as I play with his hair. "You brought me a present?"

I pull him down and kiss the tip of his nose, watching the lopsided grin come back to his cute face. "I'll let you pick out one toy for me to use before dinner."

"Damn it. You're making it hard to get things done around here." He grabs my face in his giant hands, pulling me into a kiss that curls my toes and nearly has me melting onto the floor. He whispers as he pulls away, "I'm suddenly very, very hungry again."

We hurry to finish prepping, even though it's him doing the work and giving me tips while I sit on the counter and feed him blueberries. The tension and the rain clouds have melted away and the ease of talking to him returns. I'm in the kitchen of a movie star's house, but it feels more and more like home every time I'm here. Like I'm supposed to be here.

So, why am I pushing it all away so hard?

The logical side of my brain knows better. It's a horrible idea for us to be together, even just fucking around, because that's how people mess up and get caught. I've got too much on the line—my career and my reputation—to let one silly man ruin it for me just because of what his tongue can do. Or because he's cute. Or sweet. Shit, he's damn near perfect.

My heart wants me to let him ruin every part of me. But my brain knows he'll grow tired of me. He'll find some cute little Hollywood girl that the press will fawn over. We'll drift apart, and I'll go back to my robots and kink clubs. I understand robots more than I understand most people anyhow. Robots won't stomp on my sandcastle and remind me I'm not a princess. Computers won't break my heart.

"Hey, you okay?" He asks, putting the leftover ingredients into the fridge.

"Hmm? Oh, yeah. I'm fine." I shake the thoughts of heartbreak out of my head for now, determined to enjoy this while I can.

After I dry the last knife and put it back on the rack, I lead him upstairs with Pongo and Lulu following close behind. They jump up into the bed, but instead of chasing them off so we can have our playtime, Chase pulls me into the bed.

"Talk to me?"

"It's nothing, Chase. I just stood for too long."

He lifts me onto his chest, and I curl up on top of him like a cat. We watched movies like this the day after our date. He plays with my hair as we lay together in comfortable silence. It's peaceful, relaxing.

"Tell me about your brother," I ask as the dogs settle in next to us.

"Devin? He's a nutcase, but he's an alright kid. I can't wait for you to meet him more than just a few shouts down the hallway." He laughs and rubs Lulu's head. "I don't know how we're related sometimes. Devin's always been the life of the party, always the happy, fun guy to my grumpy, standoffish internalization of everything."

"He's still young, right? And playing professional sports?" Chase nods against my head. "He's still a baby, but he's not going to grow up till he retires." He laughs, and it reverberates through me.

"I hope he never does. I hope he always sees the world for its happiness and the good in people. That's what you do for me." I lift my head and he's staring down at me. It's that look he had on our date. The one that melts the walls around my heart. "Your eyes are like brownies. Caramel brownies. Not the dark chocolate kind, but the light brown, gooey ones. Fuck, they're beautiful and apparently I'm hungry."

"You're so strange, but you're cute." I lean up and give him a peck on the lips, fold my arms on his chest, and rest my head on them. "Did you play hockey, too?"

"I did, a little. Baseball, too. Could have played pro ball, but went with acting instead. Fewer injuries and bullshit, or so I thought."

"You were destined for fame no matter what path you chose, Puppy." My fingers play on his arms, drawing shapes and writing his name over and over. He struggles to keep his eyes open as the motion almost lulls him to sleep. My ability to calm him worries me the most. I don't want to take that away from him.

"Were your parents into sports?"

"No. My dad worked as a long-haul trucker and my mom was…absent." He kisses the top of my head and hugs his arms around me. "What about you? Did you always want to teach?"

"No. Teacher never made the list when people asked what I hoped to be. It sounded like too much, and I wasn't wrong. I had dreams of becoming an astronaut or invent something revolutionary like Bill Gates. Not for the money, I just wanted to play with all those shiny toys."

"What changed?"

"I had other priorities. I became an adult with bills to pay and my ex couldn't hold down a job. I had started classes for my masters and had a stack of PhD applications ready to go, but we needed money more than I needed to touch the stars."

"I'm so sorry, Ren."

"It's okay. We all make sacrifices."

"You deserve to touch the stars. You deserve to have the stars flown down to you."

"Yeah, well, I'm touching a star right now, aren't I? *Mi estrella del cine.* Besides, I always expected it. I come from a big, broke as fuck family. We struggled a lot after my dad died. We all had to work hard, and it just became a normal thing. I'm the first one in my family to get a degree. He would have been so proud of that."

He stares at me like he wants to say something, like he wants to promise me more than just the stars, but doesn't know how. "That must have been tough, giving up your hopes for someone else. It might be weird, but I kind of envy the big family part. I didn't really have anyone until Devin came along. Dad spent more time on the road than at home. I'd only see him once or twice a month, but he drank. Mom only came around when she needed money. So I raised Dev. Don't ask me how he survived. A twelve-year-old makes a terrible dad figure."

"Hey, I get it. My brothers and I raised Dani, and look how terrible she turned out."

We laugh together, staring at each other again, not realizing how close we are until our mouths press together. We share slow kisses that turn into deep promises and hopes, and back to slow once more. It's like we can't help ourselves, a magnetic force keeps forcing us together.

"How did you end up in Los Angeles?" I ask, shifting my body down so his mouth won't be as easy to reach and so damn tempting.

"Dad had an accident at work. Thankfully, it wasn't the booze. He fucked up his back real bad. The inspector found some faulty part on the truck. Dad found an okay lawyer and, for once in his life, sobered up enough to do something good with the settlement money. My mom's arrest right after his accident opened his eyes. He had a sister in Pasadena, so the three of us moved in with her."

His hands slide under my shirt and he rubs my back while still holding me tight. Pongo paws at him a little before he shoves his face into Chase's neck. They stay like that, and god, it's adorable, but I'm a little concerned this might be a response to stress from Pongo. I've seen him come to Chase so often in the short time I've known them. I hope it's not my fault, and I didn't ask him anything too upsetting or personal.

"Are we okay, Renate?"

"I…I don't want to hurt you, Chase. Relationships are hard for me because of my past."

There's a long pause as he continues to stroke my hair. "Maybe I'm okay with you hurting me," the heavy sadness in his soft whisper almost brings tears to my eyes. "You, uh, you wanna show me what's in your bag so we can stop talking about this for a bit?"

"Are you sure?"

"I don't open up about that stuff too often except with my shrink, so I kind of need some of your sunshine, gorgeous." He takes hold of my hips, moving me back and forth and sending sparks down my spine. "Or I'm gonna have to take care of you without the bag of goodies."

"What if your friends get here while I'm…distracting you?"

He rolls us over, disturbing poor Lulu and caging me in between his powerful arms as he stares at me, dropping his hips to mine. He reaches down between us, shimmying his jeans off. I have no idea what I've done right in this life to deserve this Adonis with a kind, sweet soul, but I'm so glad Dani arranged for us to meet. I wish things were different. I wish societal norms would give us a chance instead of pulling us apart, but it's an inevitable conclusion that we would never work out. I wish we could give this a chance and see where it goes. I don't know if I can handle it, though. I don't know if I'm ready.

"Upstairs belongs to me." He explains, opening the drawer in the night table. "They don't come up here unless it's with me or an emergency. Except Steve. He does whatever the fuck he wants because he's Steve. Besides, they'll see your car and know you're here, and don't worry, they won't hear anything from down there."

"Are you challenging me, Mr. Cooper?" I reach between us

and pull a whimper from him as I help him roll the condom on while I nip at his chin.

"Yeah, Ms. Silva, it was. Wrap your legs around me, beautiful."

My back arches as he pushes inside me, rocking his hips and groaning as he fills me. He pauses, staring down at me with hope etched across his face. "Sing for your dinner, my queen. Tell me how much you like this. How good I make you feel."

His thrusts are deep and slow, and his eyes don't leave mine. I sing the song he needs to hear as his muscular arms flex next to my head and the muscles in his shoulders ripple. His mouth teases mine and his teeth catch my bottom lip, biting down just the right amount. When he lets go, his hips move faster. I reach up and grab his face, keeping him focused on me.

"Watch me, Chase. Look at how pretty you are with your enormous cock inside me."

"Christ, you feel so goddamn good, Renate. The way you take me…so fucking good." He leans back, not missing a beat as he pushes my shirt over my tits and pinches my nipples. "You're so beautiful."

I reach up and grab his chin. "Shut up and fuck me harder, like the slut you are. I want your cum dripping out of me all through dinner. Do I make myself clear?"

"I mean, I'm wearing a condom—" I squeeze his chin and narrow my eyes. "Yes, ma'am!"

His arms wrap around me and he buries his head in my shoulder as he fucks me into the mattress. The headboard's relentless slams against the wall add a rhythmic drum beat to our salacious duet of moans and whispers.

"That's a good boy. My perfect pet." I fist his hair again and pull hard. Damn, I love men with long hair. "Now, break this goddamn bed, Puppy!"

HOLLYWOOD
Renate

CHAPTER 18
GUESS

CHARLIE XCX, BILLIE EILISH

HE WANTS to cuddle after sex, but that will lead to falling asleep or more sex. So I convince him to bring my duffel bag to the bed and show him my toys. His eyes light up at the rope. But when I pulled out the vibrator, dildo, paddle, and collars? This man might be about to cancel our dinner plans and lock the door to the room. He's more than a little curious; he's downright eager to try them.

"You can pick one out later, since your company should be here soon."

"Okay." He's still staring at everything, taking it all in. I don't bother telling him there's more at home. I'm tempted to make him wear my remote control cock ring so I can fuck with my pet over dinner, but it can wait for another time. He's holding up a collar when his phone vibrates on the table.

"Jamie. They're on their way," he informs me as he tosses his phone aside and kisses along my neck. "Twenty minutes isn't going to be enough time to use any of this, huh?"

"No, Puppy, it isn't."

"Shame. I thought the collar could be a fun place to start." He slides his hand between my legs. "I can do something else in

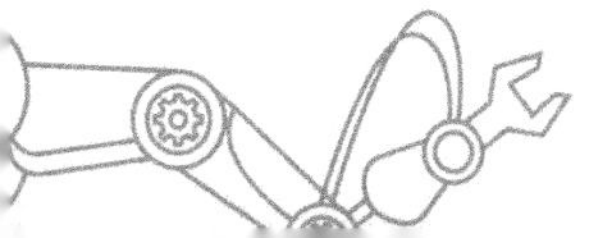

twenty minutes, though. Like make you come a few times for me."

"No, Mr. Cooper." He whines at the name, and I kiss the tip of his nose before crawling out of bed. "We both need to get dressed, and you need to go downstairs and check on dinner. I'm glad I brought spare clothes since someone got my other clothes all wet."

"Aww, but I like you in my clothes. And I like you all wet." He scoots over to my side of the bed, throwing his long legs over the side and grabbing my hips. In an instant, I'm jerked forward and between his strong thighs. I want nothing more than to drop to my knees for this man and worship him the way he has me over the last hour. "My clothes are nice and tight on you in all the right ways."

"Do you say that to all the fat girls you bring home?" He rolls his eyes at me.

"Ren, you're not—"

"Oh, no you don't. I love my body, and I'm just stating facts. I'm not ashamed. Why would I be ashamed of a body that looks this damn good when I'm bouncing on your cock?"

"You're perfect. You're fucking immaculate, Ren. I'm gonna tie you up one night and bite the hell out of that ass and those amazing thighs. I'm gonna suck your pretty tits and listen to you whine for my cock. I'll make you lose yourself the way I lose myself for you. I'll worship you night after night. Every damn inch of you."

"Someday I might let you." I'm trying to keep it light even though my heart pounds so hard it might break through my ribs. He's flying too damn close to the sun and we're going to get burned. "Besides, I need an ice pack and some food. Also, I don't get tied up, you do."

"Ice pack? Did I hurt you?"

"Only in the best possible way. Don't worry, I just need a little recovery time." I palm his half-hard cock, causing his eyes to roll back and a moan to escape those pretty lips of his. "I still have plans for you. Now go on, get dressed and get downstairs before your friends are here."

His eyes beam with happiness before he cups my face and kisses me hard. "See you downstairs, my queen."

He pulls on pants and grabs a shirt, giddy from the ideas I've put in his head. I shake it off and dig through my bag for the outfit I packed. Instead, I pull out a note and one of the skimpiest dresses I've ever seen.

To my lovely, stubborn, Renate-
I found you some different clothes for dinner. Oh, and I won't be there, because I have a gig. Obvi!! Stop with the stupid excuses and get that dick! But also, give him a chance.

P.S. What is all the stuff in this bag!?! If you don't fuck Chase, I'm telling mom what's in here! Mwahahaha! Love you!

P.S.S.- I borrowed a collar. You're not gonna want it back.

I hold up the dress with a groan. Chase will spend the next several hours begging me to take him upstairs so he can rip this off me. I like a man who begs, but I enjoy wearing clothes that fit more. I hold it up and check the mirror with a sigh. It's beautiful, but tight.

Fuck it. I'm in a damn mansion; I can wear pretty clothes and pretend to be a princess for a night. Or, for Chase, a queen.

As I finish pulling up my hair, I stand in front of the giant bathroom mirror and take it all in. The short, baby blue dress hugs every part of my body like a damn glove. The part Dani added—or more accurately, subtracted—has turned the top of the dress into a one sided halter with an open slit across my chest from my shoulder to my waist to show off my boobs. The heels give me an extra four inches, making them fucking delicious. I'm a damn knockout.

That poor man down stairs doesn't stand a chance when he sees this.

I carry the shoes with me down the stairs, not wanting to fall and kill myself. When I get to the bottom, I stop to put them on and listen in for the right time to make an entrance.

"No, man, why the camera?!" Chase's voice comes from the kitchen.

"Chase, dude, we're fucking celebrating. I want to document this!" That's Jamie's voice.

"Jamie, don't be dramatic," Alexis says teasingly.

"She says to the guy who proposed, piled us all into your boss's SUV, and took us to Vegas while still in a sling and with broken ribs. Jamie only knows how to be dramatic, Lex."

"Yeah, and you're a mellow mushroom, huh, Chase?"

"I get paid for my dramatics!" Chase's laugh sounds relaxed and happy, and I catch myself smiling as my heart races. "Fine. Oh, Jimmy Jam, can you get me the number for that Mills guy that worked your case?"

"Yeah, sure. Something up?"

"I dunno. I'm getting weird messages and shit lately and I might need someone to check it out. The other day I got some pictures of Cassie and I. I'm getting phone calls at weird hours. It's right on the edge of freaking me out, so I want Mills and Cyn to talk."

"Pictures? How?"

"No idea. When I got the gifts, I assumed an ex did it. But

that doesn't add up anymore. Don't tell Ren, though. I don't want to worry her."

"Is that a smart idea? Keeping it from her?"

"I want to talk to Mills first. If he thinks it's serious, I'll tell her. I don't want to freak her out over nothing, you know?"

I figure that's my cue and let my heels announce me as I walk into the kitchen. Lexi turns first and a huge smile spreads across her face when she sees me. She and my sister work together and became fast friends. She's been to enough family parties for Mama to consider her a third daughter.

"Shit, you look fucking amazing, Ren! How's your mom?"

"Ornery as ever," I answer as we hug, and I do the same with Jamie. I haven't looked at Chase yet, but I'm sure from the silence he's been eye fucking since I turned the corner. So when I make eye contact with him and lick my dark red lips, he stares with his mouth wide open. "Chase, don't burn the food."

"Food. Yeah," he replies, but continues to gawk at me. Jamie slips past me, his shoulders shaking with a laugh he's trying to hold back, and checks the food. The wave of hot hair from the oven hits Chase, bringing him back to reality. "Shit! Yes, the… right."

Lexi snickers and takes me by the arm. "Come on, let's leave the men to handle the kitchen and go grab a beer out on the patio."

"Brilliant idea. Don't burn the house down, boys!"

The four of us sit out by the pool having drinks and passing a joint around while we wait for dinner to finish. There's small talk and a little teasing from both Lexi and Jamie directed at Chase, which he dishes back. The dogs run around the pool, chasing and playing fetch. That feeling of belonging comes back again, and I wish I could follow my heart. It's all I've ever wanted, to belong somewhere.

"So, where are you headed next?" Jamie asks, blowing out a

lungful of smoke before passing the joint to Lexi. They've been holding hands while we talk and it's adorable.

"I've got a TV spot in Atlanta in a couple of days, then I'm back in LA for a bit. Oh, and I uhm, Cyn says I'm going to Cannes."

"No shit! For that indie flick?"

"Yeah. From what she told me, it's on fire and everyone has been talking about it. Cyn's suckered me into an event that's supposed to be for charity, but it's nothing but as ass kiss party for a bunch of old Hollywood guys. She says it could end up finding more funding for the release since those guys have deep pockets." He turns his focus back on me. "I could really use a not-date to go with me in a few weeks. Jamie refuses to go to those. He claims it's because he's busy, but secretly he's scared to wear the dress. I keep trying to explain that I'm the movie star, so I get to wear the suit."

"Dick," Jamie flips him off with a laugh.

"That's a little...public, isn't it?"

"Shit, yeah. You're right. Duh. I'm too high to brain right now. Cyn will probably come with me anyhow, or she'll send one of her people."

A timer goes off, and Jamie goes to get up, but Chase stops him. "Stay put, chill out. I've got this."

After he disappears, there's a moment of silence between the three of us until Lexi breaks it. "Ren, what the hell? When did you start dating Chase, and why didn't anyone tell me?" She laughs. "Did Dani the matchmaker have anything to do with this?"

"Yeah, she set Chase and I up." Jamie answers before I can. Realizing how that sounds, he laughs. "Wait, not like that. I mean, that's why she suggested the art class at Ren's school. Sneaky minx. I thought she'd be here tonight?"

"Well, first off, we're not dating, but yes, that's when we met." I take a drink of some fruity but delicious wine Chase brought out earlier. "Dani is, uhm, she's at a show. She kind of set me up tonight, too. Telling me she'd be here and not telling me where it was."

"Wait, you're not dating?"

"No. Just friends." I smile, but they're trying to understand why. "It would never work between us. A-list celebrities don't date school teachers who like to play with robots."

"Oh, come on," Lexi argues. "There have been a few movie stars with us lowly working class types!"

"You sound like Dani," Jamie chuckles. "And you can't claim working class anymore, babe. We're upper class now. Sorry, that's entirely my fault, but you did marry me."

"Yeah, when you were still a broke ass artist. And I'd do it all again. Okay, maybe not all of it, but the whole marrying you part, totally. Wait, don't change the subject!" She glares at me, or that's what she thinks she's doing. The face she makes has both Jamie and me giggle.

"Pretty white boys with blue eyes and a smile that outshines the stars like Chase don't date short, overweight, poor Mexican girls. We're too spicy for their delicate nature. In another life, maybe, but in this one, we're doomed."

"Well," Jamie says as he goes to stand. "I'll be right back. I'm going to the kitchen to beat the ever-loving shit out of him for being too fucking pretty. Fucking moron."

"No! Wait! It's… it wasn't his idea. It's mine. It's what I want and what we agreed to." He flops back into his chair and looks dejected. "I have no desire to be wrapped up in that chaotic lifestyle. He's a wonderful guy, and he deserves someone amazing at his side."

"You're amazing! And that dress!" Lexi yells.

"Yeah, Dani changed out the clothes I planned on wearing tonight, too." I sigh. I have to remember to smack that girl when I get home. "But I live in a tiny bungalow with my mother and sister in East LA. I don't need the press dangling off our state-of-the-art rusty ass chain-link fence or spooking Mama when she thinks she's sneaking outside to have a cigarette like we don't know. The school doesn't need that either. We'll have our fun, and after that, who knows?"

"Well, for what it's worth, I agree with my beautiful wife. You're fucking stunning," Jamie replies with a half smile. "I hope you two change your minds, but I get it if you don't. His life isn't easy, but ole Pongo over there helps."

"God, you're a perfect example of why I don't wear dresses. She look so fucking good! I would never look that good."

"Cherry Blossom, you would put me in an early grave if you had that dress on. I mean, hell. I wouldn't hesitate to bend you over this table right now, even if you were wearing living room curtains from a retirement home." He takes her hand and kisses each of her knuckles.

For two people who have been through so much, you wouldn't know anything bad had ever happened to them. The world did them wrong, but they found each other and fought back. Even I'm swooning a little over how they stare at each other. Like no one else in the world exists, just them and the stars.

It's the same way Chase stares at me.

Shit.

"Okay, you fuckers better be hungry. Come in here and grab a plate." Chase yells from somewhere in the house.

Every few minutes while we're eating, Chase's hand wanders onto my lap, squeezing my thigh. Each time, it gets a little higher. It's not long before he leans over and whispers in my ear, "You're killing me in this dress, my queen. I want to rip it off you and fuck you right here on the table."

I hold my hand over my mouth and giggle. I push his hand off my leg, I reply, "You have guests, Mr. Cooper."

"I lied before. I like it when you call me that. Especially in that teacher's voice you use." He cocks his head to the side.

"Besides, they wouldn't give a shit. They'll be fucking in the back room before the night's over. They're part rabbit."

"Oh, and you're not?"

"That's fair," he chuckles. "Can I ask you something?"

I nod, a little concerned about his tone.

"How expensive was that dress?"

"I'm not sure. Dani picked it out." I furrow my brow. "Why?"

His mouth curls into a wicked grin, and now I can guess what's coming.

"Chase, do not!"

It's too late, though. He's hoisting me into the air and making a break for the pool. I yell about my shoes and Lexi catches up in time to pull them off my feet before Chase leaps into the pool with me. I should be livid. If any other man had tried that, I would bury him in the backyard. But when I come up, gasping for air, he's there, cupping my face and smiling at me. I can't hold back the laughter, and I wouldn't want to. The dress was cheap; the makeup wasn't, but none of that matters. The way he makes me feel, the way he opens my heart to pour his feelings into it, is worth so much more. I've spent so much time worried about him falling for me that I didn't realize I had fallen hard for Chase Cooper.

He pulls my face to his and kisses me with a fierceness I've never experienced before. It's fiery and passionate, with so much meaning behind it. "Too much?" He asks as we float together.

"No," I whisper timidly.

"Good," he sighs as our noses brush together. "I thought you'd hate me for that."

CHAPTER 19
LUNCH

BILLIE EILISH

TWO YEARS AGO, my best friend met a woman and fell in love in less than a week. I gave him so much shit for that. Within weeks, we were all piled in a car and headed to Vegas to watch the two of them get married. They're still happy and going strong.

A few months ago, I saw the same thing happen to one of my other best friends, though not as fast. Steve and Ethan have their difficulties, but I pity anyone that ever tries to get between them. They're talking about starting a family now.

Dani and Xander got together in high school, and those two are their own special mess. They've been experimenting with becoming a triad, and break up every six months. But when the dust settles, they've still got each other.

Which leaves me. There's a pang of jealousy when I watch them, but over the last few months, that pang has grown into a pit in my stomach. Until I met her.

After I threw us both in the pool, the look she gave me shocked my brain into catching up with what my heart already knew. I get it now. How people fall so hard and so fast when they find their person. That's what's happening to me. Not as fast as Jamie and Lexi, but that's alright, because we're working at our own speed.

But what am I supposed to do now? What if she decides she doesn't want me for anything but an occasional fuck? She doesn't see a future between us; I've found heaven and possibility in her eyes. I've always been a little extra in relationships. What if my inability to let go caused these feelings? I just wish my brain would shut up for two seconds and let me enjoy this moment with her instead of overthinking it.

"Chase, I—"

She's going to leave me. She hates me. She's going to break all of this off. She knows I'm only going to hurt her.

"JAMES GRAHAM BARTON, DON'T YOU FUCKIN—" Lexi doesn't get the rest out before they're in the pool with us. I can't remember the last time I laughed this much, and I'm understanding the ebbs and flow Doc told me about. Holding a little space for Cassie, but not drowning in her memories. Building something new and not letting my past become the foundation for it all.

Of course, I've just jumped into the pool with Ren, so I'm already trying to sabotage the entire thing. Part of me expected to be punched in the dick as soon as she came up for air. Instead, she's looking at me and laughing that beautiful laugh. The kiss that follows would have knocked me off my feet if I were standing instead of floating.

There's the tiniest hope she's the one. It's kind of fucked that it finally hits home on the anniversary of my fiancée's death. Life has one fucked up sense of humor.

"Jerk!" Lexi yells with a laugh, splashing water at Jamie and me.

I'm about to swim over and dunk her under when I notice Lulu jump up and run inside. Devin must be home. There's a loud crash inside the house, and our heads all turn to hear my brother yell out.

"FUUUUUUUCK! I'll pay for that! OW! LULU!!"

I bolt out of the pool, running into the house with Jamie hot on my heels. We find Devin on the floor inside the front door with Lulu climbing all over him. His phone has shattered, there's a hole in my wall, he's sporting a nasty black eye.

"Oh, hey, man." He's got tears in his eyes, but his balled up fists say he's ready to throw down.

"Hey, what happened? Who the fuck punched you?" I crouch down next to him, trying to get a better look at his eye.

"The guys and I went to a bar. I got in a fucking fight."

"And you had to take that out on the wall?" Jamie asks, rubbing the back of his neck as he checks the damage.

"I said I'd pay for it!" He throws his arms up. "I didn't know Xander would be there."

"Where? At the bar?"

"Yeah! We went to see Dani's show. We had a few too many and, well, one thing led to another and—"

"Wait, our Dani?" I ask as my face twists up in confusion. "What are you talking about?"

"Seriously, Devin? Why don't you just wear 'Xander please deck my dumb ass' on your shirt?" Jamie throws his hands up and shakes his head. I'm so lost.

Devin's shoulders slump as my head pivots between him and Jamie. "She winked at me, and, fuck, I kind of kissed her and—"

"You what?!" I yell.

"They hooked up last year." Lexi shrugs as my jaw hits the floor. "Oh, you didn't know? Shit, I'll go get the first aid kit."

"They'll trade me if that fight made the news."

"Dev, you're the third highest ranking goalie in the league right now." I try to reason with him. "You've been on fire—No, what the fuck does she mean you hooked up with Dani?"

A cold beer comes from out of nowhere, and when I follow

the arm to the source, I find Ren, dripping wet. She's shivering and makeup runs down her face, but fuck, she's beautiful.

Devin looks up at her with his good eye and scrunches his face up. "Who the fuck are you?" I forgot they haven't met yet. "What's with the fancy swimsuit?"

"I'm Ren." She crouches down next to us with a little wave. "I don't know why I never put two and two together to realize you're the Dev she talks about."

"She talks about me?!"

"Calm down, lover boy." Ren shrugs and gestures with her hand. "Do yourself a favor, don't get messed up with a Silva. We're crazy."

"Wait... Ren? Dani's sister? The teacher?" His eyebrows shoot up. "Chase's teacher? That Ren?"

"Something like that, sure," she laughs. "Trust me when I say Dani and Xander like to pretend they're an open relationship. But they suck at it. Both of them are too jealous." Her voice soothes Devin from a giant mess to his goofy self in no time at all. Dev and I aren't used to someone being this warm and gentle with us.

He flashes her a lopsided grin. "You're nice. I'm sorry I swore so much. That's fucking rude. Did you fall in the pool?"

"Your brother put me through the pool party initiation ceremony," she giggles and ruffles his hair.

Lulu pushes past Ren, knocking her into me, and we fall to the ground. When I stare up at the perfect woman in my arms, she's beaming at me again, and my heart skips to a new beat. Hers. I pull her down and kiss her hard as a soaked Lulu smothers my brother in licks and pool water.

Devin has spent the last hour trying to teach Jamie the guitar while Lulu sleeps beside them, snoring loud enough to wake the dead. Lexi and Ren are talking, and I'm relaxing next to them in the hot tub. Pongo lays behind me, watching a family of bats flit around. We've gone through another case of beer and passed around another joint. I'm not sure if it's the beer, the high, or the hot tub, but I'm having trouble keeping my eyes open. I pull Ren onto my lap and rest my head on her shoulder as I wrap my arms around her.

"Put your fingers here, you've got to finger it right or there's no way you're—" Devin's head drops when he hears us all snickering at him.

"I've got the fingering down just fine, man," Jamie teases back while Lexi turns every shade of red going from embarrassed to laughter. Jamie watches her climb out of the hot tub in her bra and underwear, which leaves little to the imagination, especially his. She wraps her steaming body around him and he kisses her cheek and hands her a towel.

"In fact, you know what, Dev? I'm going to take my wife to bed right now and prove it."

"He's going in there and falling asleep the second his head hits the pillow," Lexi teases, wrapping the towel around herself and sitting next to Devin. Jamie scoffs, but doesn't bother arguing since we all know she's right. "Go ahead, big talker. I'll be there soon so you can prove yourself, pretty boy."

Jamie says goodnight and heads back into the house while Devin and Lexi chat, but I'm not interested in them. The second Lexi climbed out, Ren grabbed my hand and shoved it between her legs. Now her head has rocked back onto my shoulder, and she's doing one hell of a job acting like my fingers aren't inside her. Until my thumb brushes her clit.

"Shh, keep it down, Sunshine. You've got to be nice and quiet for me."

She turns her head, and our mouths slot together, so I can swallow her moans. I'm tempted to pull my swim trunks off and let my cock slide right into her, but we can save that for another night when we're out here alone. She's clenching around me and I can feel she's close, and I suck on her neck, leaving a trail of marks. Before she topples over the edge, she stands up and turns on shaky legs to stare at me.

She leans forward, shoving her tits against my chest and whispering in my ear, "Take me upstairs and bend me over the counter so you can ruin me the way you ruined my fucking dress."

"Yes, ma'am!"

I pick her up and toss her over my shoulder as she screams. Devin and Lexi both laugh as I carry her into the house. dripping water everywhere. The sharp slap of my hand on her round, wet ass echoes as we go up the stairs, and her laughter fills the hallway. Kissing her right now feels like she's sucking out pieces of my soul. I'd let her have every bit, especially when she plays with my hair and teases the back of my neck with her nails.

I fish a condom out of a drawer, grab it between my teeth, and she reaches up and tears the package open. I tear the flimsy panties from her and drop my swim trunks to the floor in a wet splosh. Her mouth chases mine as she slips the condom on and lines me up. Our moans echo off the tiles when I push deep into her, holding myself inside her wet, greedy pussy.

My heart lodges in my throat as she clenches around me so hard I'm seeing stars. I never turned on the lights, leaving her bathed in the moon's glow. There's only one thought in my brain as she begs me to move, to fuck her.

"Mine," I'm surprised by the deep growl in my voice. The immediate sting on my face does nothing to phase me as I refuse to move. She yanks my hair, pulling my head back until I can't see her. Her teeth graze up my neck as her body rolls beneath me like waves.

"Try again, Puppy," she snarls in my ear, her nails digging into my bicep.

"You're mine."

She slaps me again, and I swear I'm getting harder. I thrust hard and fast into her, pressing her against the mirror that's already decorated with our handprints.

"I don't belong to you," she says between clenched teeth, defiance in her voice.

"Fine." I thrust again, knocking the contents of the countertop to the floor. "But I am yours. You can't deny that."

"You're getting a little too cocky, Mr. Cooper."

"Maybe I am. Maybe you should punish me for that. But not until I'm done ruining you, just like you asked me to."

I hold her hips so hard I'm leaving fingerprints, and she returns the favor with her hand around my neck. I'm slamming into her so hard she'll feel me for a fucking week."

"Fuck, right there, Chase! Make me come all over your whore cock!"

"You have such a dirty mouth. Never change."

I grab the low-cut neckline of the dress and rip it down, forcing her breasts to literally pop out as she gasps. Fuck, I love her in tight clothes. I lean over and close my mouth over her breast through the bra, biting down and sucking. Her back arches, forcing me even deeper into her as she yells.

"Harder, baby! Oh, fuck."

I pull back the lace and slide my tongue over her pebbled nipple, flicking it a few times before I bite again. She screams and clenches around me, grabbing my head and holding me to her chest.

"More!" she screams as her body shakes and her ankles lock behind my back. I force my way out of her hold and, in one fluid motion, I pull out and flip her onto her stomach. Her toes don't even touch the floor, so I grab her legs and bring her knees up so I don't hurt her.

I stare at her in the mirror, my eyes adjusting enough to make out the streaks of mascara, the smeared lipstick, the look in her eyes that dares me to go harder. She watches me in the reflection, waiting with anticipation for me to start fuckin her again.

"Oh, you wanna watch me destroy you, huh?" She smirks and I spit on her ass before pressing my thumb against her tight hole as her pussy clenches around nothing. Her head rocks back and she fucking sings for me and only me.

"Fuck, you feel so good, Ren." I moan, watching my cock disappear inside her. "Your greedy little cunt wants every inch of me, huh, Sunshine? You like me fucking that sweet little pussy of yours until you scream?" I tease her asshole with my thumb again, making her claw at the mirror and scream my name. It sounds incredible.

"Don't stop! Fuck me like you mean it! Like you wanted to fuck that bartender, you dirty fucking whore!"

I grab her hair and yank it back. She's kneeling on the counter as I slam harder into her, holding her up with my arm across her chest. "Call me that again!"

"Is that what you are?"

"For you? Fuck yeah. Now remember, eyes on me, my queen. I want you coming all over my cock while you stare right at me."

"I'm so close! Fuck me harder, slut!" We both race to the edge of the high and jump off, yelling and moaning, feeling the ecstasy ripple through our bodies as I hold her tight.

"Holy shit!" I gasp for air and drop my head to her shoulder, waiting for my vision to clear. I blink hard a few times, and she laughs, reaching up and playing with my hair. I help her turn back over so she can sit on the counter while I clean us up. I slip off the condom, tie it off, and toss it in the trash, but before I can grab a towel, she's got my wrist.

"You're not done."

"I'm not?" I'm drooling over her smeared makeup, the way her tits hang out of the dress that's bunched around her soft belly. I won't be ready to go again for a while, but I'll do whatever she wants. I kneel in front of her, the goddess on her makeshift throne, as she spreads her legs wide. I lean in and she grabs my hair, holding me back just out of reach of her glistening pussy.

"Don't you dare be gentle, slut!"

I dive in like a man starving, hoisting her legs up on my shoulders and pulling her to the edge of the counter. I might be crazy, but there's something about feeling a woman fall apart against my mouth that drives me wild. Given the choice, I'll take eating her pussy over getting my dick wet every damn day of the week. Breakfast, lunch, and dinner.

She pushes my head down, fucking my face as she tightens her grip on my hair. Once again, I find myself at Ren's mercy— right where I want to be. My tongue circles her clit while she rides my three fingers until she comes for me, and I keep going.

"FUCK! Oh god, just like that, Puppy!"

When she comes down from her third orgasm, she strokes my hair and calls me a good boy. It makes my cock jump and I want her to call me that again and again.

Good boy. Jesus, she's got me by the dick.

I stand on shaky legs and undress her, carrying her to the shower. I hold her until she can stand on her own, washing her hair and body like she's a queen, because she is. She's my queen, even if she won't admit it. After I dry her off, I carry her into the bedroom and sit her down on the edge of the bed. Once I make sure she has everything she needs—water, her phone on the charger, and a snack—I climb in behind her and comb out her long hair before we curl up together under the covers, stealing soft kisses as we doze off. We'll save her toys for another time.

HOLLYWOOD
Renate

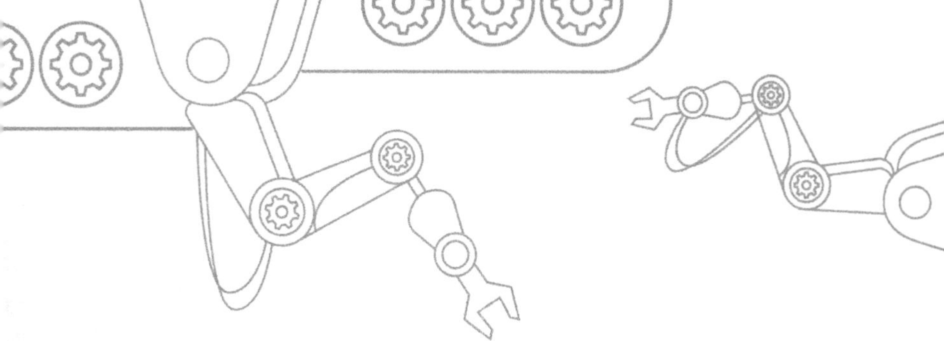

CHAPTER 20
TAINTED LOVE

CHASE HOLFELDER, TOM EVANS

MONDAY MORNING GREETS me with a pounding headache and stiff joints, so I'm relieved to find a handful of students already trying to figure out the smart screen. I crawl on top of a table with the instruction manual and the remote and I get everyone involved so we can learn together. I need to figure out how the damn thing works since I'll be the one giving a crash course to the other teachers. Students helping means I'll have two dozen mini tech support agents at the ready to assist the other teachers and staff.

It takes three class periods before we get a handle on how the board works and what it can do. It's pretty amazing—I can't lie about that—and the kids are loving it. I end up giving them assignments for extra credit to research and present programs and applications we can use in the classroom. It makes my work a little easier and makes them think about practical uses of electronics outside of robots and drones. As the classroom empties for lunch, I head to the back room and pull out my salad and my phone.

> Good morning. You know I hate you right now, right?

SNUGGLE PUPPY

Morning, Sunshine. What did I do this time?

> I now have to teach a school full of teachers how the fuck to use these things.

SNUGGLE PUPPY

Shit, I forgot all about the boards. Well, if it helps you feel any better...

[Image Attached]

I almost choke on my apple when the picture loads. He holds up a script for the company that makes the smart boards while he makes a goofy face. It never dawned on me he would trade his talent instead of just returning the one he got for me or dropping the cash. This man has more layers than Shrek. And the goofy face he's making has me blushing.

SNUGGLE PUPPY

Can I call you after you get out of work?

> You can call now if you're free. I'm on my lunch break.

The phone rings almost immediately and I'm giggling as I answer it. "A little jumpy, *Mr. Cooper*?"

"*Is it wrong that I want to record you saying my name and just listen to it over and over again?*"

"Depends on what you're doing while you're listening."

"*Fuck, you're dirty in all the right ways. When can I see you again?*"

"I saw enough of you yesterday."

"*Yesterday? One shower and a little messing around in the car? And here I had me believing you're as insatiable as I am.*"

"Depraved, Chase. Anyhow, Dani and Mama binge your movies, and they made me join in the marathon."

"All *of them?*" His voice drops and if I wasn't in school right now, so would my damn panties. His voice alone could make me come. We should try it sometime. *"Even the ones with the sex scenes?"*

"Mm hmm. Like that one where your head ends up between that skinny girl's legs while she moans out your name. I got several choice looks from both my sister and my mother when they watched that." I let the next part come out soft and breathy, well aware it will drive him wild. "I get so fucking wet seeing you like that, knowing exactly what your tongue can do when you shut up long enough to use it."

"Don't make me drive to that school to do very unethical things to you on that desk after you punish me for being a bratty student."

"You're cute with your little teacher fantasy. If you were here, I'd have you screaming my name, *Papi.*"

"Fuck, you're making it hard to drive right now."

"So pull over and show me—crap, never mind. The students are shuffling back in early to play with the screen. I need to go. I haven't put security features on it and these kids will totally try to pull up porn."

"Okay," he laughs. I'm about to hang up when he shouts out. *"Wait! Real quick, uhm, do you want to go to a hockey game tomorrow night? Not a date. We're using the box tomorrow to watch Devin, so it will be a bunch of people."*

"Tomorrow? I would, but I think Dani has a gig, so I can't use her car."

"No problem, I'll pick you up! I'll be there around six."

"Make it six thirty if you can. We have a couple of meetings after hours tomorrow."

"No problem, gorgeous. I'll even bring you a jersey." He sounds giddy over the idea of me in a jersey. I've unlocked another kink on this pretty boy. *"Have an amazing day at school, Sunshine."*

"Dani?" I flip on the lights when I get home from work the next day. As I walk around the house, I pull out my phone and text my mother to see if she made it to her sister's safely. As I get to the hallway, there's a noise from the back of the house. I yell out for Dani again, but again, no answer. This old house loves to make noise.

I follow the noise to the kitchen, where I find a stack of Mama's gossip magazines on a side table. Chase's smiling face looks up at me from the cover of the tabloid and I can't help but smile back. Curiosity gets the better of me and I grab the magazine to flip through it. As I do, something slides out and falls to the floor. I pick it up and find it's a photo from my teenage years. I'm dressed in my conservative white gown and I'm beaming. I wish I could go back to that day and tell the younger me to run and never look back. He'll change, but it won't be for the better. He never loved you.

"Huh." I flip the photo over to check for writing. "How did that get in there?"

"I put it there." I freeze at the voice and don't turn around. If I don't see him, maybe he isn't real. Maybe I'm having a nightmare. His boots land louder with each step as he walks up behind me. "Hey, pretty mama. Miss me?"

"What the fuck are you doing here?"

"I saw your mom leave, so I figured I'd come over and keep you company. Like the old days. You remember the old days, don't you? How I'd sneak in your window and crawl into your bed? Take off that pretty nightgown while your parents slept in the next room. Fuck, you smell good." He spins me around and smiles, his two gold teeth glittering in the overhead light. He pulls a small bouquet from behind his back. Sunflowers. "I saw that tattoo you got yourself after we separated. Figured these would help you see that I still love you, baby."

"We're divorced, Luis. We're not separated, and you're not supposed to be here."

"You're my wife! This is my house!" he screams before he glances down at the picture in my hand. "I just want my lady back where she's supposed to be. My fucking bed!"

"I'm not yours anymore, Luis. You need to leave." My voice shakes as I panic. He has me blocked in, my cell phone tucked away in my purse across the room.

Luis grabs me, pulling me up off my feet and slamming my head against the fridge again and again. Five years of recovering, finding myself again, and therapy, all gone in an instant as I revert to the scared young girl that learned about the real him. Just like before, I'll do anything he wants to stop the pain. Anything.

"You don't talk to me like that, you fucking *puta*." I turn my head as he slides his nose up my cheek. His breath smells like cigarettes and booze. "My boys tell me you're with some rich white boy now. You fucking him?"

"It's nothing, Luis. I swear."

"No shit, baby. Nobody could love your fat, disgusting, stupid self but me. Do you hear me?!" he shouts into my face. "Do you need a fucking reminder of who the fuck you belong to?"

"Luis, please? Please don't."

"You worthless bitch! You were whoring around behind my back?" I can't tell what he's on now, but when we were together, he took every drug he could get his hands on. He smacks me across the face, and the copper taste fills my mouth. Nothing has changed. Not even me.

Luis came with so many red flags, so many signs that I should leave him, but I never did. I wish I could say I left him once I found out about the gang and the drugs. I didn't though. I didn't leave when he hit me. I didn't even leave when he threatened to shoot me. That wasn't enough for me, I guess.

"W-we're divorced, Luis. We're not together anymore. I don't belong to you." I fight back tears. He wants me to cry, to break down. It turns him on. Sick fuck.

"You belong to that fucking white boy now? Don't talk like that! You're my girl, baby. Till death do us part, remember?" He tries laying on the charm like he always did. He slides his nose along mine and presses against me as he squeezes my breast. I want to throw up. "You know what? Your papi knows what you need. I'll give you another baby right now. Maybe this time, you won't be a stupid bitch and I won't have to hit you so hard."

"No—" I whimper.

He grabs me and spins me around, groping my breasts and pushing my face against the fridge door as he grinds against me. His hand drops as he tries to undo my pants. "Fuck, I missed that fat ass bouncing on my fucking cock while you cry. I'm gonna fuck the memory of that stupid white boy right outta your head. And if that don't work, I'll beat him outta you and go fucking put a bullet between his damn eyes. Bye-bye, movie star."

I try to push his hands away, but he's strong and presses his body harder against me, making it hard to breathe.

"Stop fighting me, bitch. Just admit you want this. You need me to remind you of your place, huh, baby?" His hand wraps around my throat and squeezes hard. "Don't you remember the last time you tried to run away from me? You're fucking mine, whore."

I remember.

I had shut myself in the bedroom and called the police. He didn't even care that had the dispatcher on the phone. He broke the door down and dragged me out of the room by my hair.

Throwing me to the ground, he kicked me in the stomach over and over. He grabbed me off the ground by the hair again, threatening to kill my family if I tried to tell the cops what happened.

Bloodied and bruised, with chunks of my hair pulled out, I lied for him. They believed my lies without question and threw me in the back of an ambulance. They never even looked at him, at my blood on his knuckles and the toes of his boots.

I tried to tell them the truth at the hospital, but they didn't believe me. They listed my miscarriage as caused by an accident. A fall down the stairs. My house only has three steps, and they lead up to the front porch. They didn't care. I finally tried to tell the truth, and no one listened to me.

There's a noise outside, the crunch of tires on the gravel that pulls me out of my memories and back to Luis and the pain.

Please, don't be Chase. Not yet. Luis will kill him without a second thought.

"You want me to have my boys over? Give your fat, useless ass to them for a few hours? You'll learn real quick how nice I am to my baby girl—Who the fuck?" I hold my breath and wait as Luis releases me and darts into the living room. There's a loud knock, followed by a voice I don't recognize.

"Yo, Dani? It's Martin. Are you home?" I don't make a sound while Luis panics, mumbling about the cops. He's so high, he can't tell reality from hallucinations. "Come on, we're gonna be late for the gig."

Another voice calls out, further away and higher in pitch. Dani.

"Marty the Party! Shit! Sorry, I swung over to see Ms. Ruiz because she makes these amazing empa—never mind. You've had some. Come on, I'll show you the equipment so we can load up and get on the road."

I yell out as she opens the door. There's the sound of a scuffle and Dani swearing. I crawl to the kitchen door and see Luis push past Martin and run out of the house.

"And stay out, motherfucker!" Dani yells, throwing a flower vase after him.

Blood slides down my neck from where he smashed me against the fridge, and I can't hold my head up any longer. A dense fog coats the world and I feel Dani's hand in mine. Black creeps into the edges of my vision as I try hard to not pass out.

"Ren?" The voice makes my heart skip a beat.

"Chase!" my sister yells. "She's hurt, bad."

"Fuck! What happened?"

"Her ex. I don't know how he got in."

"Ren, can you hear me, baby?"

Baby. It should sound sweet from Chase, but I only hear Luis calling me that as he hit me. Pain and blood are the only things I can concentrate on now.

"Okay, come on." Chase scoops me up like I weigh nothing. I want to wrap my arms around him and cry into his shoulder, but my body isn't listening to me anymore. "I'm taking her to the hospital."

"We called for an ambulance," Martin says, but he sounds like he's gone underwater. Odd since we don't have a pool.

"They'll take too long and take her to the wrong fucking hospital. Dani, text me all of her info. Your mom probably has it."

"What info?! My mom is in Mexico visiting my tía!"

"Find your mom. I need her medical history!"

There's more they say, but I can't focus anymore. The sunlight burns my eyes even though they're closed, and my head throbs, but even as I struggle to stay awake. I'm not scared anymore, though. As Chase carries me out of the house, I only feel one thing beyond the pain. Safe.

"I'm sorry. I'm sorry, Chase," I mumble as he gets me into the car and buckles me in. "No! I'll get blood on your seats."

"Seriously?" He cups my face and I try to look at him, but I can't figure out which of him I should focus on. "Hang on, Renate. Just hang on, okay?"

He kisses my forehead, and the world goes dark.

215

HOLLYWOOD
Chase

CHAPTER 21
RUNNING UP THAT HILL
PLACEBO

I CLIMB in the driver's side, pulling her to me and trying to wake her up. "I've got you, Sunshine. I've got you," I hum softly in her ear. As I rub her back, feeling something wet and sticky. When I pull my hand away, it's red.

I slam the gas and peel out of her driveway, kicking up rocks and gravel. I'll pay for damages later.

"I'm here, Renate. No one will hurt you, understand? He's not going to hurt you anymore. Never again. I'm going to take care of you." I'm making her promises I hope I can keep. The tires squeal as I hit the main road and take off. Tears sting my eyes, but I don't have time for them, not now. Not with the woman I love bleeding out in the seat next to me.

"Mmm," Ren moans and tries to move. "Chase? I'm sorry. Please don't send me to jail. Are you mad at me?"

"What? Fuck," I whisper and pull her close again. "No, Sunshine. No. How could I be mad at you? This isn't your fault. Just try to stay awake, okay? We're almost there."

I avoid the under-funded, understaffed local hospital and head for Beverly Hills. I keep her awake, talking to her and holding her hand. She's having trouble focusing and I'm trying my best to not panic. When we get to the hospital, a nurse recognizes me and we're taken to a private room out of the public eye. Ren can't even fill out her own name, so I take the forms and call Dani to get any information she's found. Once I get Ren checked in, it all becomes a waiting game I don't have the patience for.

As we're both finally coming down from the adrenaline high, Ren bolts off the table and runs for the private bathroom. I hold her hair back, and when she's done, I clean her up and carry her back to the bed. The black eyes and swelling in her face make her almost unrecognizable. Almost.

Doctors and nurses come in and out of the room. Followed by a detective, more nurses, tests, and more questions. The dread creeps in, and the helpless feelings take over. I should have gotten to her house earlier. I should have picked her up from school.

When the doctor finally comes in and says there's no bleeding in her brain, I drop hard into the chair behind me, relieved. She's got a concussion, and they want her to see a specialist as soon as possible. I make the appointment, get the discharge papers, and listen to the instructions to wake her up every two to three hours.

She looks like a shell of herself, and I'm ready to get the fuck out of here. She says the dizziness and nausea have passed, but the doctor said the headaches will last awhile.

She's not talking—just staring off into nothing.

"Ren? The orderly will take you downstairs so I can pick you up away from the main entrance, okay?" Security chased three people out of the hospital earlier after catching them trying to sneak in for pictures. Ren nods, but she's not listening, so I step in front of her and tilt her head up. "It's gonna be okay."

"I didn't even tell you about him," she says in a hoarse whisper that sounds painful.

I sit beside her and take her hand. "Sunshine, I'm going to say to you what everyone says to me, and I sure as hell hope it sticks for you better than it has for me. It's not your fault. You didn't do anything wrong, not a damn thing. Blame him, but he's not getting to you again."

"I...I need to go to work in the morning. I need—we were...I can't remember."

"It's okay. The doc said that will happen for a bit. You're coming home with me."

"But Mama and Dani! What if he comes back?"

"Dani packed some things for you, and she's going to stay with Xander. She convinced your mom to stay in Mexico until we're sure he's gone."

"Chase, we're not... I can take care of myself."

"You can. But I'm asking you, please, let me take care of you." I brush a loose strand of her hair behind her ear. "I can stay at your place later, but tonight at least, stay with me."

The orderly comes in with the wheelchair and she stares at it like he's asking her to climb onto a mechanical bull. I help her down from the bed and into the chair, and crouch in front of her.

"Good. Let's get you home, get you better." She tries to smile, but it's half-hearted. I kiss her forehead and head for the car.

As I walk to the garage, I grab my phone and turn it back on. I'm expecting voicemails and texts from Cyn's office, and I'm not disappointed. Over twenty missed calls and messages. I shoot her a quick text.

CHASE

I'm okay. Ren got beat up by an ex. I'll call you when I'm back home and have her settled in.

BOSS LADY

You damn well better call me. Be safe.

As we pull into the driveway, the door to the house flies open, and Pongo bounds down the steps, Devin hot on his heels and yelling after him. I stop Pongo before he jumps on Ren, but he still licks her face when she leans over to greet him. It's the first genuine smile I've seen on her today.

"I'm sorry! I told him to *stay* but he straight up said *fuck that* and bolted. He's been pawing at the door since he heard the main gate."

"He's okay. He knows people he loves are worried, that's all." Ren rubs the dog's head.

"I ordered pizza, so you'd have something to eat. I hope that's okay—do you even like pizza? Fuck. I can go get something else if you—"

"Thanks, Dev. That's sweet of you," she responds flatly and walks toward the door like she's in a trance. Pongo stays right beside her. She needs him far more than I do right now.

Dev turns to me and whispers, "What the fuck, man?"

"I'm trying to figure that out, Dev," I snap, pushing past him and following Ren into the house. I watch her disappear into my room before I turn back to Devin. "I'm sorry. I didn't mean to be a dick, it's just...a lot."

"She doesn't like pizza, does she?. I kind of...panicked. I thought about ordering something better, but I don't know what she likes and I figured everyone likes pizza. Don't they? I cleaned up the guest room, and I cleaned up my apartment so Dani and her mom can stay in there if they need to." He's talking a mile a minute and I can't keep up with him right now, so I put both hands on his shoulders and look him in the eye.

"D, I need you to chill." He nods and takes a deep breath. "Dani and her mom aren't coming over. We've got that covered, but thank you for straightening up. How did the game go?"

"Uhm, we lost. In a shootout. Guy went left when I could have sworn he showed right." His shoulders slump and he leans back against the wall, running his hands through his hair. "Fuck,

Chase." He rubs the back of his neck and looks back at me, fear and worry on his face. "I don't want her to leave us. You. I mean, Pongo likes her and I...it's... you've been happy, like, really happy since the other night. I don't want...what if she—?"

"Hey, hey." I grab the back of his head and pull him in for a hug. This has less to do with Ren and me and more to do with the two women in our lives that left the biggest scars on both of our hearts.

Our mother left him in grocery stores, bars, and even the car once or twice while she danced through life in a drug soaked haze. I grew up knowing our mother had an addict and needed help. Devin grew up thinking mom never wanted him. Cassie and Devin were close, too. She cared about him and for him better than I did sometimes. Devin found her that morning, and I don't think he's ever recovered from that. He hides it well. Better than I do, anyhow.

"I'm gonna go up and stay with Ren." He nods and I take the stairs two at a time. I poke my head in to see if she's already asleep. She's sitting on the edge of the bed, staring at the floor. She jumps when I sit beside her, putting my arm over her shoulder and pulling her closer. "How are you holding up, Sunshine? Hungry? Thirsty?"

"I shouldn't be here. He threatened you. Said if I didn't do what he wanted, he'd shoot you in the head."

"He's not going to do that."

"You don't know him!" she yells, wincing as she does. "He's in a gang, Chase. I should have told you, I should have told you everything, but I'm terrified of him. It's why I thought we should stop at friends. I didn't want you to find out about this. To find out how weak and pitiful I am. I convinced myself you'd leave me. Or Cynthia would tell you we couldn't be together. I should have told you."

"That's the concussion talking, Renate. You're strong, smart, brave, and not the one to blame in this situation. Besides, you're telling me about him now. We'll be okay, Ren. He isn't going to scare me away." I kiss the top of her head. "You don't owe me explanations. I want you to be happy and safe."

"But…you shouldn't have to deal with this. With me. I'm not good for you and your image. I'm not what you should have." She reaches for her things, shoving them into her purse. "I should go. I shouldn't be here."

"You just got out of the hospital, Ren! He broke into your house!"

"It doesn't matter. He can't find me here. He'll hurt you, and you and I aren't even dating."

"Why does that matter? Why are you so worried about that?"

"I can't do this to you."

"That's fucking bullshit, stop lying to yourself. You're making excuses and running away, and I don't understand why. Am I that fucking bad? Do you hate me or something?"

"No, Chase, it's not like that."

"Explain it to me!" I yell, standing and throw my arms in the air. My head drops because I shouldn't yell at her. I crouch in front of her and take her hands. "We're punishing ourselves for our past, for things we couldn't control."

"We're—"

"Too different? No. Me and your fucking ex are different! He's a prick and a moron. He threatened you and beat you. He's an asshole, and you got away from him. But you put up these fucking impossible walls. I want a chance to show you how much I lo—" I catch myself before I say it, swallowing hard. "I just want a chance. I want you to be my queen."

"Oh."

I pull her closer, nuzzling her head with my cheek. "Do you know why I call you Sunshine? Because you've lit up my life since the moment I laid eyes on you. Cliché as fuck, right?"

"I've heard worse."

"My shrink likes to remind me, sometimes, it just fucking

rains and behind the clouds, the sun still shines bright as fuck. Only we can't see it because of the clouds. You don't have to tell me about your clouds until you're ready—it's your timeline, no one else's."

"Chase?"

"That…sounded so dumb, huh? Theo makes it sound cool, and I sound like a cheap fortune cookie."

"No, you don't." She sighs and plays with the buttons on my shirt, slowing my racing mind and drumming heart with that simple touch. "We got together when we were kids. Hell, we got married when we were kids. I went to college to learn about computers and try to build a better life while he learned how to sell drugs and hide from the cops. At first, he only threatened me, but the real him came out after my father died. My family and my friends believed his bullshit, not me."

"I believe you. I'm also proud of you for being brave enough to leave that shithead."

"Anger helped me leave, not bravery.."

"Sometimes, those are interchangeable feelings."

"I tried to call the police, but that didn't stop him. Hospitals turned me away because I came so often they thought I only wanted a fix. After that, it got worse because I—"

Her hand slides over her stomach and mine lurches.

"I wanted a family, like what I had growing up. But he only let me have fear and sadness."

I don't know how to respond to that. *I'm sorry* isn't strong enough for that kind of pain and trauma; no words are. I hold the sides of her head, pressing my forehead to hers. "I can't fix the past, but I can promise you with all that I have and all that I am, I will never hurt you. You're my goddess, my sunshine, my queen. If we're only meant to be friends, fine. But Ren—oh, fuck it. I'm falling for you. Hard."

"You shouldn't though."

"Well, I suck at listening to what I should and shouldn't do."

"Why aren't you mad about this?"

"Mad? Oh, I'm livid, but not at you. I'm mad at the cops, the hospitals, and that asswipe motherfucker."

She tries to laugh, but winces, holding her head. "Ugh, that hurts so much."

"Migraine?"

"I'm not sure. I've never had one."

"Take off your shirt."

"Chase, now really isn't—"

"So I can get you changed! Geez, I'm not always horny! I mean, I am, but…hold on." I go to the other side of the bed and pick up a basket of things I keep there and a pillow. I set up the pillow and help her lie down. "Okay, there you go. The shape helps with migraines. Oh, lift your head for a second."

She gives me a concerned look as I slide a knit hat onto her head.

"I, uhm, I get migraines. Always have. I'm gonna make the room cold and dark. It will help, but the hat works for me, too. The sleep mask thing takes some getting used to, but it's like a massager for your eyes. If none of this works, I'll run you a bath." I get her tucked in, close the curtains, and turn all the lights in the room off except the one by the bed, that one I set the color to red. I make sure there's water nearby and Dani comes up with tea when she comes by to drop off Ren's things. I add timers to my phone for her medication and waking her up, and I stay with her until she falls asleep.

Once she's sleeping, I head straight for the garage, Pongo following right behind me. I can feel the breakdown coming, and if I can't be in my room, the soundproof gym will work. When the door shuts behind me, I slide down the wall and stare over to the room where I hide my demons. I promise myself once I get Ren past hers; I need to work harder against mine.

I bury my head in Pongo's fur and let go of everything I've held in since I saw Ren on her kitchen floor. I don't hear the door open, but I recognize the arms that wrap around me as my shoulders shake. I used to wrap around him like this as a kids.

Another, smaller set of arms envelopes me and I recognize them, too.

"I called Jamie and Steve, but I told them not to come over tonight. And to not make a big deal out of it unless Ren's ready."

I can't stop the sobs—I don't want to—so I just nod.

"We'll take care of her, Chase. We'll take care of all of them." My brother pulls me to him, pressing a kiss to the top of my head as he sniffles back his own tears. "We're a fucking family, now. Even you, Dani."

"Shut up, dickhead. You're ruining the moment."

HOLLYWOOD
Renate

CHAPTER 22
SLOW HANDS

NIALL HORAN

I'M SITTING ON A BARSTOOL, scrolling through Amazon while Chase cooks. It's been almost a week, and I haven't been home since. I'm still afraid to be there. Even here, where I'm safe, I'm still jumpy. Chase pulls down a couple of plates and gives me a wink. He's been incredible, and he enjoys taking care of me.

"I'm here! Hold your applause, please." Dani announces as she joins us in the kitchen and drops a small bag in front of me, bowing with a flourish. "Your medicines and tinctures, m'lady. How's life in the castle treating you, Renny?"

"I don't have a castle, Dani. Breakfast?" Chase asks, grabbing a third plate when she nods excitedly. Dani only stayed the first night before taking off to Xanders. Living with Devin in the same house became…trying.

"Would it be okay to keep these in the fridge?"

"Sure, what is it?"

"Medication. It needs to stay refrigerated."

I watch that crease in his forehead deepen at the word medication. He blinks a few times and shakes himself out of the spiral that his mind tried to take him down. Spending more time

with Chase means seeing him at his worst and his best, and Pongo has helped me learn Chase's anxiety tells, too.

"Can I ask, or?"

Dani cackles. "Look, Hollywood. I totally had you put these on her medical forms the other day. All good in the hood. Or the hills? Whatever, you know what I mean."

"Devin goes by Hollywood, not me, fucker." He hands her a plate and flips her off. I've also witnessed more of the way his friendships work, and realized that some of them are more family than they are friends.

"It's a shot I have to take once a week. I'll tell you about it later."

He's done nothing but dote on me since the hospital. Twenty variations of *how are you* in bed, a break for sex, and twenty more questions in the kitchen. I don't mind because he's not being weird, he's only being…nice.

"When's your next shot?"

"Today. I had Dani bring them over so I wouldn't miss a dose."

"Okay, well, I've finished breakfast, so how about you come over here and show me what to do?"

"Eat it?" Dani snorts a laugh as Chase flips her off again.

"With the shot, fuckface!"

"Chase!" I laugh, shaking my head. "Don't worry, I've been doing this for years. Kind of a one person thing, not two."

"Are you sure? Have you ever tried?" I'm not sure how to react to that, because I haven't. Not since the nurse showed me how to give it to myself. "Come here, I'll show you what I mean, and if you hate it, I'll stop. Okay?"

"NOPE! I'm not about to be scarred mentally for life as you make her shot a sex thing." Dani grabs another waffle off the stack and heads outside.

He watches me prep everything, asking questions as I go. He

has me stop just before I'm about to poke myself in my belly. His arms wrap around me and he whispers in my ear that I'm beautiful and perfect. He's kissing his way down my neck, jumping a little at the loud pop the injector makes, and then it's over. But I don't move. He shuffles around me and tilts my head back, drying the tears.

"Does it hurt?"

"N-no," I sob. Burying my head into his shirt while I fist the fabric in my hands. "I'm sorry. I don't...I don't normally cry when I do this."

"Didn't like me holding you?"

"No. I mean yes. I mean, I did like it. It's just, there's so much going on lately and, I...I..."

He pulls me close and rocks me, "Come on, Sunshine. Let's go eat by the pool and figure out your schedule and mine so I can get a driver for you on days I can't take you to work."

I sniffle, following him out to the pool. "I can drive myself to work, Chase. We both would benefit to getting our lives back to, well, normal."

The sun's come up, but there's a nip to the air and steam coming off the pool from the heaters Chase had on for his morning laps. I expect the dogs to be at our heels with the food, but we're pretty sure Lulu slept in the pool house with Devin, and Pongo paces out in the yard chasing a bird he'll never catch. I shiver as I sit, and Chase grabs a throw blanket off a chair and wraps it around me.

"Alright, no shoots till Thursday," Chase announces after taking a big drink of coffee and checking his emails. "How about I stay at your place for a night or two?" I roll my eyes and he holds up a finger. "Hey, Xander did it for Dani. Also, it will make me feel a lot better knowing you're not alone. I promise, only a night or two. You need your space."

"You're going to hate the bed."

"I'm sure I've slept in worse. Oh, like the weekend Steve,

JimJam, and I decided to go camping, and it rained, so the three of us slept in Jamie's old as hell VW Bug!"

"JimJam?"

"Jamie. It's a childhood thing that stuck. Kind of like him calling me Coop. Or Dipship McFuckface when I really fuck up." We both laugh as I hug my coffee close to me, enjoying the warmth. The chime on his phone dings and he groans as he reads the message.

"Uh oh," Dani smirks. "Wait, let me guess, the blond with the personality?"

He nods and rolls his eyes, and I'm looking between the two of them, trying to understand.

"Charity event," he answers after swallowing a mouthful of waffle. I haven't touched mine yet, but they smell delicious. "There's like four interns at the office they can send out with us when we need a plus one. This chick fucking hates me for whatever reason."

"Uh, because you insist on posting stupid shit on her watch!" Dani reminds him.

"Whatever. She treats me like a five-year-old."

"Because you social media like a five-year-old. Or a fifty-five-year-old."

"I mean, unless you've changed your mind about the charity event?" He asks me, and my eyes go wide. "Go public and show your ex and the whole fucking world—"

"Who I *belong* to?" I ask, one eyebrow raised.

Chase laughs, almost choking on his food. "Oh shit, that's funny. I was gonna say who *I* belong to. You belong to no man, Ren."

"Nice, LOTR reference, nerd. Shit, I gotta go to work. See you guys later!" Dani scoops up her plate and takes off for the kitchen. She pops her head back out before she goes, "Yo, don't forget Mom's birthday next week. Can you pick up a cake?"

"Sure." I answer, but my mind lingers on what Chase said

about belonging to no man. I'm not sure why, but the thought makes me smile a little, then a little more. No one has ever said that before, especially no man I've ever known. A few men I've met would choke on their *machismo* if they tried to even say that out loud.

"You'd have fun…att the charity thing,"

"Sure, and how do you introduce me? The teacher you're banging? The woman causing you more headaches than anything else?"

"Well," he looks me right in the eye as he picks up a strawberry and holds it out for me. "The words you're looking for might be *your boyfriend*, so I would introduce you as my *girlfriend*, right? Or date, if you prefer to go gender neutral."

His phone vibrates with an alert that someone has pulled into the driveway, and he excuses himself to let them in. Pongo stays behind, staring at me with a little drool bubble on the side of his mouth. I toss him a small piece of bacon and pet his head.

Girlfriend. Boyfriend. Public. It's a lot.

I pick off a pepperoni and feed it to Chase while he, Devin, and I watch a slasher movie from the eighties. Devin always picks horror when his turn to pick movies comes up, even though he and Chase have seen this one a hundred times, according to them.

I'm heading home tomorrow, and I even convinced Chase to not stay at the house with me. It's not that I don't want him there, but Mama just returned from her trip, and I need some mom and daughter without the *boyfriend* time. Time to explain that Chase and I are now a couple, I guess.

"Hey," Chase whispers, nudging me. "What's the name again? The thing you have?"

"Rheumatoid Arthritis. That's what they assume, anyhow."

"Arthritis? You're, what, twenty-five?" Devin asks with a yawn.

"You're sweet. I'm thirty-two. It's not arthritis, but it's kind of like it. Anyway, some days it's hard to move, like arthritis, and that's why I give myself shots. I'll be on it my whole life or until it stops working. If that happens, they'll try something else or transfusions."

"Yeah, so don't fuck with her meds in the fridge when she's here."

"Be nice, Chase," I give him a soft smack on the arm. "It's a shot, not a bomb."

"Wait, you have to give yourself a shot?" He asks in shock. I nod and Chase kisses my head. "Shit, that sounds serious."

"It's an immune system thing and it kind of sucks, but life goes on and I deal with it. Some days are better than others. And the shot isn't that bad. Especially now that Chase helps."

"Of course, my queen. I put your next one on my calendar already."

A few minutes pass, and my eyelids are getting too heavy. I'm almost asleep when Chase nudges me again.

"Do you have a lot of flare-ups?" he whispers, staring into his phone.

"What?" I ask, surprised, not expecting a question like that. "Are…are you reading about RA during the movie?"

"Yeah, I've seen this movie. I can quote the whole thing."

"But, why?"

"It's a classic? I hate the part with the dogs, but it's still—"

"Chase."

"Oh, not the movie. Uhm, because…I'm not a dick?"

No one outside of my mother and my sister ever offered to help, look up, or try to understand my condition before with any sincerity. Plenty of people give me unsolicited advice, like telling me to lose weight or do yoga. Unhelpful, every one of them. To think, a week ago, I wanted to push this man out of my life. I'm glad he fought me so hard on that. He didn't give up on me, and I'm not about to give up on him.

"Tomorrow, before you go home, I want to add anything you need for the nights you stay here to my cart and I'll order it, okay?"

"What stuff?"

"Well, it said if you have a flare up, it can be harder to open things, so probably a couple bottle opener things, something to help you if you drop something. I can get handrails put in the shower. Those could actually be fun."

I'm in shock as he rattles things off that he's found online. He must notice, because he puts his phone down and hugs me close before pulling the blanket over us.

"Renate, you're my queen in more than just the bedroom. So get used to being treated like one."

"Okay," I squeak out.

"Good, watch the movie and let me take care of you. Obviously, I like doing it."

"I can take—" He cuts me off, covering my mouth with his hand.

"We established that, but you don't have to do it alone. Never again." He lets go of my mouth and his hand slips under the blanket, snaking its way between my legs. "Now, stop arguing and try to keep your voice down while I make you come again. And again. And again."

"What about Devin?"

"When he's snoring, nothing can wake his ass up. Now, spread those pretty legs for me."

HOLLYWOOD
Chase

CHAPTER 23
STARGAZING

MYLES SMITH

THE SHOWER BECAME useless the second we stepped in, since we've been standing under the water kissing the entire time. Slow, sensual kisses. Hard, needy kisses. We're doing our best to make up for the days she's been back home instead of here with me.

Until we hear Devin and the dogs come home.

"Oh, come on, man!" he yells from downstairs. I assume he's in the kitchen. I'm not sure where her panties ended up, but the rest of our clothes are there on the floor.

"Should I tell him we already did?" She laughs and pulls me down for more kisses.

When neither of us can stand the water anymore, I hop out and tell her to wait there. When I come back, I've got the softest, most comfortable robe I could find and wrap it around her. It's black with small sunflowers on it, and it's beautiful on her.

"Do you like it, Sunshine? Had it custom ordered for you."

Her fingers trace over the embroidery before she throws her hands around my neck and squeezes me tight. "These things never fit me, Chase. How did you find one so perfect?"

"Lucky guess?"

"Did you call Dani?"

"Dani's lucky guess?"

"She's so sneaky. I love it, Puppy!"

"Good. Uhm, I also bought you this."

Her eyes light up at the dress I pull from the bathroom closet. I'm an idiot when it comes to fashion and dresses, but this thing has a slit up the side and as soon as I saw it, I wanted to see her in it. She runs her hands over the black sequined top and the feather details on the shoulders before giving me a look when she eyes the deep v-cut in the front. I don't care how much it cost, it will be worth every damn penny when I fuck her stupid in it before I rip it off her.

"You'll look stunning."

"Chase, I can't accept this."

"You can, because you're my queen. Unless you were yelling YES earlier about something else." I tease.

"Well, it might have had something to do with your head being between my legs."

"Why, Ms. Silva, are you accusing me of using sex to get you to attend this event with me?" she rolls her eyes and I'm not sure if the look she's flashing me means she's about to end me, or she's playing with me. "If you don't want to, we don't have to, but whichever you choose, I'm not returning the dress. I've asked my stylist to send someone over tomorrow to adjust it so you're not tripping over yourself."

"Jerk." She smacks my arm playfully for the dig. "Whatever!

"Anyway, she's going to bring some jewelry too. If you like any of it, I'll buy it so you can wear it to other events. Whatever you don't like, she'll take it back after the event. Cyn said she'd come over and help get you ready for what the press will be like, too."

She stares at me and I go head first off the deep end diving board of an empty pool. "Fuck, it's too much, isn't it? I'm sorry.

You're probably right and I should, I can, we can do this another time. It's fine. I'll just—" Her hand on my chest stops me, but it also helps me calm down. I lean over, dropping my forehead to hers.

"There you go. Breathe for me. I love the dress, Chase," she coos, rubbing circles with her hands. "It would be an honor to attend the event with you, beautiful boy."

"Wait, you're sure?" She nods and I spin her around, holding the dress up to her. She's going to look stunning, and I tell her that as I kiss up and down her neck.

"Okay, you're going to mess up the fabric and get it wet," she laughs.

She squeezes my hand hard enough to get my attention in the back of the SUV as we head to the charity event. It's still weird having her hand in mine and not a cold, wet nose. I'm still adjusting to Pongo not being here with me tonight. I avoid bringing him to smaller events. It's more difficult to pass him off as a pet. They're expecting a huge crowd tonight, though, just what he's trained for.

I love my dog, but having her here with me tonight is far more important. Besides, I'm pretty sure he's been teaching Ren some of my tells. She's picked up on them over the last few weeks and sees right through me when I try to hide. She can tell when the self-doubt, the worry, and the massive imposter syndrome take hold of me.

It's been a while since I had someone I cared about come to an industry event with me, especially one as big and high profile as this one. Usually it's my agent or someone else from the agency. I've brought a girlfriend or two before and had a few break up with me because I wouldn't bring them. Cassie hated these damn events with their glitz and glamour, so I stopped asking her to go. That should have marked the beginning of the end of our relationship, but I'm too stubborn to see warning signs and she was too stubborn to realize she couldn't change me.

The press noticed right away, and our apparent breakup became the running headline for weeks. It made the paps even more desperate for pictures of us out in public. It's crazy to see some of the supposed experts they get on body language to discuss the photos and try to make out details that just aren't there.

Our hands were too far apart when we sat at dinner. I wasn't standing close enough to her when we were out around town. We never looked at each other with love in our eyes. That's what they ran with from a handful of blurry, shitty photos. They never mentioned the triple-digit heat wave outside or how we'd kissed, but they hadn't timed their shot right. That didn't generate sales as much as our implosion as a couple. That's when they manufactured a fake dating rumor. They still throw that one out from time to time.

I climb out of the car and a frenzy of flashbulbs blind me; I'm used to it. They limited the number of press photographers in this section of the property, so it's only a handful and a something of a warmup for Ren. When I take her hand and she steps out of the car, she exudes royalty and her eyes never leave mine. Her confident smile brings the same out in me. I don't even hear what the photographers are yelling at us. I don't care.

"I'll never understand why getting out of a car became so photograph worthy," she asks, looking around but trying not to be obvious about it.

"Ask the female celebrities," I reply with a wink.

"Oh. That explains why you stood so close to the door when you opened it for me."

"Damn right. They're not taking underwear shots of my girl. Hell, are you even wearing any?"

Her devilish grin tells me I'm right and my heart drums against my ribs. I'm going to spend the whole night thinking of excuses to sneak off with her to a bathroom or down some back hall. I should ask if this place has a wine cellar.

Once we're inside, there's an area designated for the guests to meet and mingle before the dinner. It's so loud, with conversations and laughter echoing off the walls, I don't know how anyone hears each other. However, most of the people in this room are only here to listen to one person—themselves. I snag two glasses of champagne from a tray as the waiter walks by.

"Is this champagne?" she asks, taking a quick sniff of the glass I handed her. "I've never had champagne. What's it like?"

"It, uhm, tickles? I dunno. I'm not a big fan, but you kind of get used to it after a while." She smiles and everyone in the room disappears. I lean forward and kiss her on the cheek, whispering, "I can't take my eyes off of you, Ms. Silva."

"You never can, Puppy." She winks. She's not wrong. Her fingernail taps on my glass. "So you drink things even though you don't like them?"

"Yeah, comes with the territory. Weird food, too. Some on set, some at parties. You kind of learn how to stop tasting things, I guess." She raises an eyebrow and I laugh. "There are still things I can taste just fine. The food I make, a smooth whiskey, oh, and you. And if you keep looking at me like that, I'll toss you on one of those platters and show everyone just how hungry I am for you."

She takes the champagne flute and tips it back. I don't know what she's expecting, but her hand touches her nose and she giggles. Electricity collects at my spine before bursting through my body. I want her. Now. I want to drop to my knees and worship her right here in front of the entire crowd of stodgy, rich people.

"Yeah, you were right. It tickles!" The giggle ripples through her, and they're contagious. She takes my hand and drags me away from the wall, and further into the room where everyone mingles and mulls about. "I want to see you at work, Puppy. I don't mean the movies, I've seen those. I want to see you become this Hollywood golden boy right here in front of me."

I shrug and look around, but before I can find someone I trust, people crowd around us, asking both of us questions and chatting away as we float between cliques.

I'm impressed when I see how easily she fits in with wave after wave of famous Hollywood types. She's effortless. Unfazed when she's socializing with the rich and famous, as they brag about their wealth or fame. No one knows who she is, but they all assume she's on their side and not their staff. She commands the room with a glance, and tomorrow morning, while these assholes are sleeping off cocaine hangovers, she'll be driving her sputtering, broken down Fiat to teach at an unassuming grade school. It would blow their minds.

"So what do you do?" One of the big shot producers asks, as if he can read my mind. We met at another industry event, and I'm not thrilled he's here. He's part of the upper elite of Hollywood to survive the *Me Too* movement unscathed. Well, not entirely. They took him down a few pegs, but he could stand a few more. They should have taken him down to hell and locked him away for good.

"I teach." She's brilliant. She's mastered giving them enough information to answer their question, but leaving them wanting more.

"Ah! A scholar amongst men! Brilliant! Let me guess, art history? Something as beautiful as you?"

I step closer to her, my hand resting on her hip with a gentle squeeze. She makes a show of moving her drink to the other hand so she can reach behind me and grab my ass. I don't think I've ever had a woman claim me like this in public. Grope without permission, yes. I want her to do it again. I can't stop fantasizing about her leading a pack of these clowns on leashes and collars down Hollywood Boulevard. Humiliating them the way they deserve. It's giving me a hard on and making my head spin because I'd beg to be right there with them.

"Ah, no. My degree in robotics."

"Chase, my friend," the guy slurs, and he definitely isn't my friend. He's ogling her and I don't like it. "You are one lucky son of a bitch to be climbing into—"

"Watch yourself, Eddie."

"Fair!" He holds his drink up as his eyes travel to someone new and shiny, and he's stumbling across the room to drape himself all over a young blonde.

"Did he make you jealous, Puppy?"

"You shouldn't call me that here." I stare down at her, watching her hips sway to the music as she presses her body against mine. Fuck.

"Oh, there are rules now? *Puppy?*" Her fingers wrap around my tie slowly, pulling it out of my jacket and giving it a little tug.

"No, ma'am. You can call me whatever you want, whenever you want."

"That's better." She pulls me down to her and my head fights for blood flow since it's all gone to my dick. "So, Puppy. What if I were to put your collar on you, pull you up on stage, and spank you like the needy little slut you are in front of all these people?"

Fuck! I'm so hard right now, and she knows it. Her glossy lips ghost mine, my eyes darting back and forth between hers. I want to pick her up and carry her to the nearest table. I want her to scream my name and call me a whore. No—to call me *her* whore. I want her to smack me in the face, spit in my mouth, and tell me to get on my goddamn knees and worship her.

She's opened Pandora's box inside of me, and I have no idea what I am anymore other than hers.

"Careful, Puppy. We don't want to have to leave the party

early, and I doubt any of them will buy the old, *'ran to the store for smokes'* excuse anymore."

"There's a bathroom—"

"Chase Cooper! There you are!"

I'm only pulled halfway out of my trance as my eyes search out the source of the voice. I groan when I find it. Richard Lawson, big time movie producer and the guy who heads up this fundraiser every year. I'm about to hide a raging hard on from the biggest Hollywood royal pain in the ass. Fun.

I promised Cyn I would be on my best behavior with these guys since they still have pull when they want to use it.

"I've been looking for you, buddy." Lawson has never, and will never, be someone I called *buddy.*

I'm thanking Ren with my smile, because the second I stand, she steps in front of me enough to keep my secret. I reach across and offer my hand. "Mr. Lawson, nice to see you."

"Say, where's the muscled out guy you brought with you last year? Sean, was it?"

"Steve. He's married now, and I brought my date, Renate, instead. Renate, Richard Lawson."

"Shame, he had…talent. Call me Richie." He doesn't say it to her, he says it to me, because Lawson still thinks we're in 1952 and he matters.

There's something about older men tossing 'ie' at the end of their name that always weirds me out. Like they're grasping for the last strings of youth, which they haven't had in decades.

"Look, I booked Ashton Vincenti to give an award tonight after the dinner, but he called me five minutes ago. Can you believe that shit? Do me a solid and take his spot, yeah?"

Lawson isn't even trying, laying out the shoddy groundwork for an old Hollywood bait and switch. Vincenti found himself on the wrong side of a warrant last week, and he'll have a hard time finding jobs after what they say he did. Lawson needs to distance himself from Vincenti, and I'm the perfect guy to help with that. Hollywood's golden boy instead of the child groomer.

I glance down at Ren and shrug. I can tell she's surprised that I'd even ask her. Of course I'm asking her, she's my date. My queen. She nods and I flash her a grin before looking back at Richie boy.

"Sure thing. Anything special?"

"Nah, we've got the teleprompter for the intro. It's a couple quick lines, you announce the name, bingo, bongo, you're back next to your, uh, lady friend here."

He hasn't even looked at Ren, and he's tiptoeing that line between things I'll let slide and things he'll regret. "Fine, you know where I'll be."

"Fantastic, I gotta run!" He ducks back into the crowd.

"I'm sorry. He's always been a prick. It's why I refuse to work with his people or his studio." I ask as I pinch the back of my neck, the nerves kicking in again. Looking around the room, I notice a fair amount of other people I would describe the same way I described Lawson. I hope that I never turn into them, but I'll also take their money when it's offered for the right job. Feed the machine, as they say.

"People like him don't intimidate me, Chase. Besides, I'd make most of the men in this room, including *Richie* Lawson, cry."

"You'd have them on their knees, Sunshine. Come on, I want to see where they've got us, and get out of the crowd for a few minutes." I caress her cheek and it's as if I can feel the dynamic between us shift. She's letting me take the lead, at least for now. I hold out my arm and she takes it with both hands as we navigate the swarm of people toward the photography step and repeat.

She stops before we step out in front of the cameras. Our big moment lies two steps ahead of us. We could turn around now and stay in the shadows, letting the paps make their wild guesses while I claim she's from my rep's agency. But as soon as we step out there in front of the cameras, there's no more 'rumored to be dating', it becomes public knowledge.

"We're good, right? If not, we turn around and walk the other way." I check in with her one last time as she takes a deep breath, lets go of me with one hand, and shakes her hair out. With a wink that says 'Let's do this,' I lead the way into the lights.

HOLLYWOOD
Renate

CHAPTER 24
GORGEOUS

TAYLOR SWIFT

THE FLASHBULBS ARE EVEN MORE BLINDING than when we got out of the car, and I have no idea how Chase is seeing a damn thing or not getting a migraine. After what feels like an hour, but what is little more than a few seconds, the flashbulbs stop, but I can still hear the roar of the shutters as they snap closed over and over. I focus on the blue in front of me and follow his tie until I find his eyes. He's standing in front of me, with his back to them as they yell his name.

"The flashes can be intense," he explains over the noise. "I thought you'd like a moment to get used to them. Keep an eye on the floor when you walk. There are markers where they want us to stop. Remember, at the end—"

"Don't step away when they ask me to."

"Damn fucking right, Sunshine. Let 'em have it."

He spins on his heel and slides back in place by my side. Being a teacher, I can pick out the voices as they shout random things at us. *Over here! Look right! Give us a smile!* Chase has told me he ignores most of them now. They've merged into the background noise except for the few he wants to hear.

Finally, they yell the questions we spent the entire ride here preparing for.

"Who's the lady?"

"Hey Chase, who's that?"

"Are you two a couple?"

"Is she your agent?"

Chase doesn't hear the comments they're making under their breath, but I can. Again, teacher's hearing.

"Wow, why's he with her?"

"This is a joke, right? His cousin or something?"

"Was this staged? He can't be dating someone like her."

"Bet she sucks dick like a Hoover."

"I told you he was gay."

With each flippant comment and backhanded compliment, my smirk grows until I'm grinning like a cartoon villain. Everything they say feeds my confidence, because I'm used to this bullshit. Those pricks can think whatever they want to about us; I'm going home and riding this man's cock tonight. They're not.

We make it to the end and sure enough, there's a handler there telling me to keep moving and to step aside. They try to tell me that the photographers need pictures of just Chase, but that isn't what we want, so to hell with them. We're going to force our relationship right down their fucking throats. I prepared for this, but I'm still surprised when Chase grabs the sides of my face and plants a slow, passionate kiss on me that curled my toes and left me breathless as my knees tried to buckle.

"Alright, let's go, goddess," he says with a wink as we pull apart.

"Damn, Puppy," I sputter, trying not to say it too loud. He kisses my forehead and offers me his arm again as our dopey, smiley selves walk away from the cameras, past the annoyed handler, and into the hall.

Once we're in the door, another flute of champagne ends up in my hand. I take a sip, letting it tickle my nose and give me the giggles. The way I scrunch my nose up makes him laugh. It's a warm laugh where his nose crinkles up to match mine, and the laugh lines around his eyes become more visible. He's so fucking adorable, and we must look like a pair of nerdy weirdos who've crashed a very uppity party.

"You're so beautiful."

"I am. Lucky for me, I found myself a handsome man to stand next to me." I take another drink. "Wait, is this stuff free?"

He laughs again, brushing a strand of hair behind my ear. "Yeah, Sunshine. It's been paid for already by the organization throwing this thing. They like keeping us boozed up."

"How much of this shit do they go through at one of these events?"

"More than I'd care to admit. It's not the cheap stuff either, so you're talking around three to five hundred a bottle."

"I've had three glasses, Chase! I'm guzzling down hundreds of dollars!"

"Yep," he says, emptying his own glass and grabbing us both new ones.

"Why hold a charity event when you're letting people drink hundreds of dollars of champagne that nobody even likes?" I glimpse around the room, watching tray upon tray of flutes around the room. "If they cut that, they'd have made more money than any fundraiser the school's ever done. And that's before these assholes even open up their wallets!"

"I guess they think drunk people spend more money? It's all a show, Ren."

"They're right! But you only give them one drink of the good stuff. You water the rest down!"

"Welcome to Hollywood, Sunshine."

"Rich people are dumb."

"Thanks, babe," he teases, pretending to be hurt by my comment. Chase's hand is on my hip as we head over to the stairs, where a woman who looks just out of her teens blushes as she leads us to our seats. Chase gives her a cute little smile because he treats his fans well, so long as they're not assholes. He pulls my chair out with a bow.

"M'lady."

The room fills in a few people at a time as Chase stands behind me, looking around. I'm too busy checking out the table decorations and the other names printed on the cards. If mine didn't say *Guest of C. Cooper*, I wouldn't think twice about tucking it into my clutch. Once again, I'm floored by the expense. There's a gift bag on top of each of the table settings. Chase had told me this happens at award ceremonies and some other events. They could sell what's in these bags and make a fortune, but big name companies just drop expensive gifts right into the laps of people who could already afford it.

Why? I'm understanding why Chase hates these functions.

"Hey," Chase leans down next to my ear. "I'm gonna go say hi and bring a friend over. I'll be back in two seconds. Punch anyone in the balls if they try to talk to you." He doesn't wait for my reply, kissing me on the head before he goes.

I love watching him work. The swagger, the confidence—it's cute and what people expect. But I'm one of few who knows it's all a front. When we go home, he'll be my shy, dopey, idiot boyfriend with his therapy dog at his side. I pick up my champagne glass to take another drink when someone bumps right into my arm, pouring my drink all over the front of my dress.

"Oh…oh no!"

Of course, it's Rich Lawson, the man desperate to cling to his younger years even though they left him a while ago. I'm trying to find something to wipe my dress off while he spins around like a dreidel, freaking out more than I am. I'm just glad it didn't ruin my hair or makeup. The black fabric won't show as wet, and no one will even notice it but me if he'll shut the hell up about it.

"Oh, oh, I am so sorry about that. Why don't you come over

here and we'll see if one of my staff has a towel or something?" I try to shake him off, but he's insistent and pulls me out of the chair. As he drags me across the room, I glance behind me, but I can't find Chase before I'm pulled behind the curtained area. Lawson flags down John Cena's dollar store doppelgänger. Of course, he's the chief of security.

"Ma'am, the fillers aren't allowed in the seats during the diner service." Cena's buddy, ninety-nine cent Macho Man, says. Maybe he's the head of security and not the other way around? Either way, I don't care.

"I'm not a filler."

"The agency should have gone over this with you, miss. Guess they've run out of girls, since they're using you," Not-Cena finally speaks.

"Fourth stringers. They should do better for Chase. Something like this could ruin his image." Richie says, exasperated and as if Chase didn't introduce him to me earlier. He's being dramatic, arms flailing about, huffing and scoffing as often as he can. He sounds like the old jalopy my uncle drives. When I stare him down, he backs away. I have a feeling he doesn't deal with many women who don't intimidate easily. "Are you seriously trying to play that you're really dating him? I'll bet my left fucking nut that—"

"Renate? Are you back here?" Chase comes around the curtain, looking concerned. He spots un-Cena and not-Macho Man, glaring at them until they get the hint and slink away. "Ren, are you okay? What happened?"

"What happened? Chase, it's cute that you brought a charity case, but you know the agency's people stay outside. There are rules for a reason." Lawson's gravelly voice sounds like Harvey Fierstein with a helium balloon. This guy must smoke four packs an hour and use Listerine as a chaser.

"Richie, she's not from the agency. I introduced you to her earlier. She's my girl—"

"Coop, stop fucking playing with me." He sounds disappointed. "You're better than this. I don't care how good a mouth she has, you don't bring them out of the bedroom until the lipo and Tic Tac diet does the job."

Chase drops my hand and steps toward Rick the Dick, going toe to toe. "What the fuck did you just say? I'm hoping it's the alcohol and loud music that makes it sound like you're disrespecting my girl."

Richie glances back at me again for half a second before his lip curls up. "Fine. I sure hope you're paying by the hour and not the pound, though, buddy."

In the blink of an eye, Chase has Richie shoved up against the wall by the lapels of his jacket. The security bros stand by, unsure of which person to take orders from. Three staffers come rushing over to break it up, but they stop when they see who's involved. No one wants to interrupt Hollywood's new royalty as he shows the old guard the way out.

"Jesus Christ! Fine!" Richie holds his hands up. "She can sit wherever she wants."

"It's not about where the fuck she sits, dickhead. It's about respect, something you know fuck all about," Chase snarls, not backing down. "I don't give a shit if other people let you talk to them like that. I'll fucking deck you if you say one more fucking thing, got it?"

"You'll throw your entire career away for a—"

Chase shoves him harder, and I swear he growls.

I am so wet for this man right now.

"FINE! I'm sorry." I'm not surprised that it sounds like a half-ass apology. He probably has to give them out constantly. I should care, but I can't. I'm too busy watching Chase, my Chase, stepping up to someone who could sink his career in a heartbeat. And he's doing it for me. He's defending me, not raging against me. It's hot and terrifying all in one go. Before this moment, I didn't believe anyone would give up a million dollar career for me. How could I be worth that?

I take Chase's arm and squeeze it. "Come on. His small dick energy isn't worth it."

Chase pushes off him and checks on me. "How did your dress get wet? What happened?"

"Dickie here spilled my champagne on me. Tried to play it off as if it were an accident as he whisked be back here out of the public eye." I straighten Chase's tie and tuck it back into his jacket. "Let's just go back to the table, okay? I'm sure he's regretting his decision enough right now."

"Are you sure?"

In a moment of panic and passion, I grab his face and pull it to mine. My fingers are in his hair and his hands press my lower back toward him. When I break the kiss, he stares at me, stunned in the best way, and no longer angry over that piece of shit, Lawson.

"Come on, beautiful. Let's go before dinner gets cold. I want to introduce you to some people that don't suck the life out of a party."

During dinner, where I'm at a table full of Hollywood elites that don't question why I'm here. We laugh and joke, enjoying a few drinks as we wait for what's next, when a woman takes the seat next to me. I'm so star-struck, I almost tumble out of my chair. Rosie Johnston, one of Chase's former co-stars, and one of my favorite actresses, sits right next to me. I could die.

"Rosie!!" Chase yells out, a little tipsy. "Oh, Ren, she's great. I didn't think you'd make it, Ro. Oh, this is my girlfriend, Renate Silva."

"I love your name. It's so beautiful!"

"Thank you, you're beautiful. I love your movies."

Rosie invites me out to Rodeo Drive to pick out a new dress after Chase tells her about the incident earlier. She's even sweet enough to assure me that no one can even tell. She's gorgeous— blonde hair, green eyes, and big lips—but, like Chase, she's stayed grounded among all the chaos and bright lights. We end up talking about my job until the lights dim and a spotlight hits the stage..

We lose track of how many awards and speeches we sit through, because apparently you can't have a charity event without inflating all these egos. Before dinner, I didn't realize how much charity work Chase does. But during the awards, several people at our table make comments or mumble about how he should get these awards.

He's got a big heart, and he cares so much, but a stupid trinket isn't why he does it. I'm learning that the other people in his big action movies are a lot like him, too, as he tells stories during breaks about the work they do helping people. Especially kids.

But this event isn't about kids or helping real people. It's about stuffing pockets, being seen, and making people like Richard Lawson look good because, in reality, he's a horrible person. It's all a show for publicity.

Toward the end of the night, someone comes up behind Chase to let him know it's almost time for him to present. When I turn to wave at him and tell him to break a leg, he's got his hand held out to me and I'm staring at it like it's a live fish.

"Chase?"

"Come on, let's piss some people off."

"Seriously?"

"Yes!" Holden says as his boyfriend, Blaine, cheers us on. They've been an absolute riot all night and I absolutely adore them already.

Chase leans in and whispers, "I promise I won't get in any trouble for this."

Even Rosie tells me to go, as she grins like the devil. Who am I to go against the wishes of the wonderful Rosie Johnston?!

"I can't believe I'm about to do this, but alright, let's go, baby."

His toothy grin makes my heart flutter as I let him pull me up. We make our way around to the side of the stage. Some people are curious, others are passing judgment they have no right to pass. While we wait, Chase gives me a rundown of what's going to happen, but I'm only half listening. I tune out when he says I can follow his lead and I don't need to say anything.

Before we step onto the stage, I catch Mr. High and fucking Mighty as he scrambles around on the other side of the stage, trying to figure out how to stop us. It's not a large stage area and there's no back curtain for him to sneak behind. His options are to run across the stage like a fucking idiot, go out into the audience like a fucking idiot, or don't stop us at all. I like our odds.

There's laughter and clapping as the last person accepting his award finishes thanking people and talking about their charity work. That's when Chase's grip tightens and he's doing breathing exercises that remind me of a birthing class. I need to remind myself later to work on that with him. I have a couple of techniques that have helped students more than just breathing like a pregnant woman.

"Hey, Sunshine?"

"Yeah, Puppy?"

"I'm so glad you're here with me tonight."

HOLLYWOOD
Chase

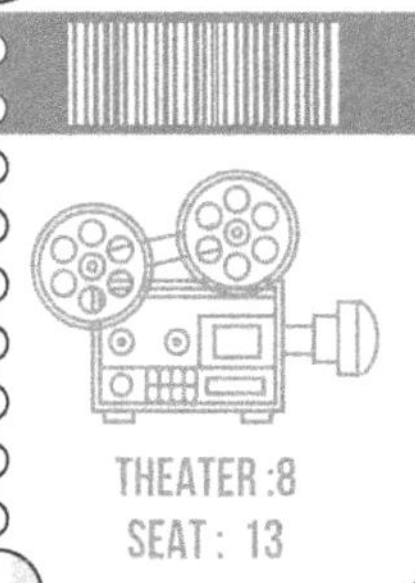

CHAPTER 25
BREAKFAST

DOVE CAMERON

WE TUMBLE INTO THE HOUSE, laughing and kissing, and laughing more. Fuck, I've never felt this good after an event. Usually I'm so beat I come home and crash, but this incredible woman has given me my life back. I don't think I could ever repay her for the ways she makes me feel…alive. Whole. Hopeful for the future.

"Wait, Devin?"

"Nope. Not here. He's on a road trip! Gone for two more days." I toss her heels into the hallway. We'll get them later. "It's just us, Sunshine. You, and me, and that fucking dress."

"And a bag of tricks upstairs that we've barely unpacked," she says with a wink. "How about we grab a snack, make out in the pool, and—"

Lulu and Pongo both barrel down the stairs towards us and I have to scoop Ren up to keep her from getting knocked down, but at least she's laughing at the whole thing. She belongs here, in my arms and laughing like nothing in the world matters anymore.

"Okay, so those two idiots are here, too."

"Aww, be nice to them!" she chides as she wraps her arms around my neck and nips at my bottom lip.

"Nice? Do you have any idea what these two eat? Nice!" I snicker and put her back on the ground, where Pongo immediately starts licking her hand. She drops, and he licks her face. "Hey! Mine! Ya dick. What's gotten into you two?"

I poke my head into the living room and nothing there appears out of place, so I tell Ren to stay with the dogs and I go check out the upstairs. I've got a small den setup with a TV and a bunch of book shelves. There's a pillow on the floor, but Lulu loves to toss them off the couch. Nothing out of place there.. I turn to the bedroom and I throw my hands up.

"Are you fucking serious?"

"What's the matter?"

"Well, I left the closet open. I owe you a new vibrator. Or three?"

She hurries up the stairs and sees the remains of her toys on the floor. All in pieces, all covered in drool and tooth marks. Lulu comes dancing up behind me with a bright pink piece of silicone stuck in her teeth.

"Oh my god, will they be okay?"

"The dogs? Yeah. Your toys, not a chance, sweetheart." I kiss the side of her head before I get the piece out of Lulu's teeth and we head into the room.

This would be one hell of a picture for the paps. I'm in a designer suit, she's in her dress, and we're on the floor picking up pieces of vibrators. Cover story material right there. When it's finally picked up, I shoo the dogs out to their beds for a while. Closing my eyes, my head falls back and thuds against the door while I let out a sigh and enjoy a moment of silence. I enjoy it even more when her hands dance up my shirt and pull my tie off.

"I never even got to play with them. We can order more tonight, anything you want, baby."

"Relax, I've got you now, and I just want to take care of you for a while," she whispers. "Keep your eyes shut—why are you so fucking tall?"

I bend my knees so she can reach and better secure the makeshift blindfold. The darkness makes me sleepy, but my other senses are kicking into high gear to make up for the blindness. She smells like champagne, and every kiss tastes like it, too, only better.

"No touching," she says. I whine, but she ignores me. "If you touch me or yourself without permission, you're not going to come tonight."

"Okay, okay. I promise." She has me stand there while she's rustling around the room, pulling different things out of her bag. I hope the dogs didn't get their teeth into anything she planned to use on me tonight. Part of me still can't believe I'm doing this. The other part wants to please her, to let go and give her all of me.

"Take off your pants, keep your boxers and shirt on. Once that's done, take off the blindfold," she commands, so I do as she asked, feeling around for somewhere to hang the pants. She guides my hands so I can find a chair. When I take off the blindfold, I can only stare. "On your knees, baby."

When I hesitate, she clicks her tongue in disappointment, but it's not my fault. Not really. She slides the slit in her dress over, revealing the bright pink dildo sticking out of her..

"Ren, I don't—"

"It's a strap-on. Don't worry. I'm not going to fuck you with it. Not yet, anyhow."

"Yet?"

"Oh, I have a feeling you're going to beg me for that soon enough. But you already know I'm not going to hurt you or do anything you don't like." She crosses the room and I watch her cock bob up and down. If I wasn't so nervous, I'd be laughing. When she comes back to me, she reaches out and cups my dick.

"We're going to work on this bratty bullshit you keep trying to pull. What's the safe word?"

"Octopus."

"Good, now get on your knees, and don't make me ask you again."

I lower myself. Every muscle in my body tense as I watch her toss a bunch of different things onto the bed. I want to peek, but I can't, having trouble prying my eyes away from that dildo. It's not huge or anything. In fact, I'm not afraid of it. I'm a little freaked out at how turned on I am, watching her walk around with her own cock. I glance around to make sure the curtains are all closed.

"Okay, now, if at any point you can't say the safe word?"

"Tap your thigh three times?"

"Good boy. Let's see how well you can follow some very simple rules. Open your mouth and tip your head back."

I do, and when she spits onto my tongue. An instant later, I'm a moaning mess with my cock throbbing for her.

"Swallow like a good little bitch." I do, locking eyes with her. She gives me a nod of approval and it's not enough for me.

"I can do better!"

"I didn't say you did anything wrong."

"No, but you didn't…you didn't call me a *good boy*."

The butterflies in my stomach kick into overdrive when she kisses me. She doesn't even use her tongue! I want this woman unlocking all of my dirty little secrets. Praise, spit, choking, her dominating the living hell out of me and god only knows what else.

"Let's earn you that praise. Now, spit on my cock and jerk me off." She smirks.

I don't hesitate, spitting into my hand and grabbing hold like I do this all the time. I mean, I do, but to myself. I've got my hand wrapped around the dildo, stroking it while I stare at her, waiting for more commands.

"That definitely earns you a good boy. Doing what I ask without questions. That's trust, Puppy. I need to know you trust me before we can go too far." Her nails on my scalp feel so incredible that my eyes roll back. "Did you play with the toys I left you in the bathroom?"

I hesitate and swallow hard, but she tucks her finger under my chin and forces me to look at her.

"N-no. I wanted to, but you didn't tell me I could."

"There's my good boy." Her nails drag across my stubble as my gaze flicks between her eyes and the pink toy bobbing in front of my face. "Have you ever had a cock in your mouth, Chase?"

"What?" I lick my lips, even though I try not to. "No. No, I haven't."

"Okay, we'll go nice and slow. Open wide," she says in that low graveled voice of authority. She slides the tip of the dildo over my lips before slipping it between them and rubbing it on my tongue. "I'll give you pointers. Now relax your jaw and throat for me."

I lock eyes with her, and she winks.

"Good. Now, if it gets to be too much, you tap my leg three times, right?"

I take as much as I can before I gag and she pulls it out again. I catch my breath while she strokes my hair.

"Color?"

"Green, my goddess."

"Good, again." I thought I'd hate this, but I don't. I want more. More of her, more praise, more of everything. "You're being a perfect slut for me, Puppy. If you suck my cock well enough, I'll give you a nice little reward."

I gag again, but not as hard this time, taking more of it than I could before. I'm weirdly comfortable doing this, even though I thought I'd hate it. Her hands slip through my hair, taking the power back a little at a time. She grips my hair tight, putting a little pressure on the back of my head to keep me in place.

"So pretty on his knees with that mouth around my cock. You like it, don't you, Puppy? You like being a dirty boy for me, don't you?"

I answer with a hum and a slight nod. I'm reminded of the dentist, when they ask a question while they're hands in your damn mouth, only that never turned me on. Her hips rock back and forth as she coos my praise, building my confidence. I've never thought about sucking someone's cock before. I don't go that way, so it never comes up. This should humiliate me, emasculate me, not make me harder.

"Atta boy, suck that cock with your pretty mouth. Choke on it."

I speed up, grabbing her ass and pushing her deeper as I soak the shaft in saliva. I'll do fucking anything to hear the praise from her. Anything. That's when I have the realization that I want her to fuck me with this thing. I want her to take everything from me, every sliver of control I have left.

"Look at you, taking that thick cock like a pro, Puppy. That's it. Take every fucking inch of me into that smart mouth."

She gathers my hair so it's out of my eyes, giving me a better view of her standing over me and that wicked smile that I've fallen for. I'm so fucked. She's not holding back anymore either, the tip hitting the back of my throat and making me gag. Spit runs down my chin, but I don't tap out. No fucking way. I suck harder as she fucks my face, my nose bumping against her soft belly which each thrust. I whimper when she pulls out of me, and whine when she's in me. I fucking can't get enough.

"I'm gonna have you begging for my cock and my pussy." She's right, I already see my future on my knees begging for any part of her, even the silicone parts attached to her.

She holds my head back as I try to chase the fucking thing. There's a string of saliva connecting me to the tip of her cock and

I almost come while staring at it. Her finger collects tears from my cheek as she stares down at me.

"Good boy. Are you close?" I nod with enthusiasm. She unbuckles the harness, letting it drop to the floor as she brushes my sweaty hair back. "Puppy?"

"Yes, my perfect queen?"

"You have my permission to ruin this dress, okay?"

"I'll buy you a new one!" I yell as I lift her over my shoulder and carry her into the bathroom. I turn on the shower and put her down, staring at her like a predator ready to play with his prey. I kiss her hard and deep as I back her into the shower. She's still in her dress, I'm still in my shirt and boxers as the water pours down over us.

She's palming my cock when I stop her. "Shit, I forgot the fucking condom."

She grabs me by the shirt before I can turn around, pulling me back to her. "I want to feel you. All of you." She rubs harder, teasing my head through my boxers before she nods toward the bench. By the time she climbs on top of me, I'm already out of my mind with desperation, grinding against her as I rock my head back and moan like a wild animal.

"Renate, I need to be inside you. Please?"

"Come in your fucking pants. Show me how desperate my little whore is to fuck me. Show me what I do to you, my pretty white boy." Her hands wrap around my neck as she grinds her bare pussy against the bulge in my boxers. I'm fucking gone. Grinding against her clit while she restricts my air. My head buzzes and I come so fucking hard I yell out her name, listening to it echo off the walls.

"I...I wanted to..." I try to speak, gulping down air now that the world slowly comes back to focus.

"Shh, Chase. Don't worry, we're not done yet." We stand up, and she turns around, facing the wall.

I bend her over, pulling the skirt up so I rub her sweet, round ass. She looks back and nods, but I shake my head. I'm on my knees again, spreading her cheeks and sinking my tongue into that slick pussy I can't get enough of. My thumb presses into her puckered hole, filling the bathroom with her moans. She grips my tongue, but I don't let her come. Not yet.

"Chase! Please!"

Spinning her around, I rip the front of her dress open and let her tits spill out before I take a step back and admire her. Her fingers tuck into the band of my boxers and she pulls them down. Now it's her turn to admire me, but not for long, because by the grace of nature and her sexy as fuck body, I'm ready to go again.

I lift her into the air, press her back to the tile, and impale her on my cock. Her nails claw my shoulders and arms and I hold myself steady with one hand and bounce her with the other.

"Yes, Puppy! Oh, fuck!"

I can't hold back the primal noises I make as she wraps her legs and arms around me, and I hold her tight. Each thrust harder and faster than the next.

"Oh, shit, Renate! God dammit, you feel fucking incredible."

"Come inside me, please?"

I carry her back to the bench, gripping her hips and lifting her, thrusting into her as hard as I can. She screams, riding me like her life depends on it. Everything inside of me tightens when her cunt holds me tight.

"Fuck! Fuck! Right there Puppy!"

We come apart together, letting the world spin out of control as the fuzzy sensation in our brains clears. I don't know what I've done right in this life, what I've done to deserve her, but I never want to let her go. Never.

HOLLYWOOD
Renate

CHAPTER 26

PAPARAZZI

LADY GAGA

"SO WAIT, he pulled you on stage with him?!" Dani squeaks over her morning coffee as Mama comes back into the room, hair in a bun and ready for work.

"He did; it was, well, kind of surreal if I'm being honest."

"What happened?" Mama asks, clueless until Dani turns her phone to her and she can read the giant headline for herself. She reads it out loud, *"Hollywood's Golden Boy Turns Bad for Date."*

"I wish they weren't so fucking sexist about it, though. *Mystery woman holds down a career as an underpaid teacher for a misogynist dickhead while finding time to date Hollywood hunk* has a ring to it."

"It's a little wordy, and I don't think even the rags will print dickhead in their headline." Dani smirks.

"Speaking of, did I tell you that dickhead last night had the *cojones* to give himself an award for charity at his own charity event?"

"Stop saying those words! Both of you."

"Yes, Mama," we say flatly in unison.

"At least they don't know who you are yet—and do you really want them to?"

"Fair point. Okay, enjoy your day off, Dani. Come on,

Mama." I grab up my things and head for the door. I'm not sure how long it will take me to adjust to the lifestyle of a movie star's girlfriend. Glamorous events and late night kink sessions are fun, but it makes waking up in the morning and going to work a lot harder. Especially on the nights I want to stay with him. He asked me to stay last night, and I hated turning him down, but I knew I couldn't make it to work if I had stayed. His arms are too tempting in the morning, and too difficult to pull myself away from.

I hook my finger over the door handle and get it open, even with my arms full. I nearly drop my box of papers when the roar of cameras clicking hits me and the strangers on the other side of the fence shout questions.

Are you the mystery woman dating Chase Cooper?

Are you fucking him?

How long have you been together?

How big is his dick?

Have you read the fan reactions online?

Is the agency paying you to sleep with him?

Mama tries to push past me to see what's causing the commotion, swearing in Spanish under her breath at the swarm of people crowding the sidewalk and even the street. A car tries to pass by and they slam on their brakes to avoid hitting a younger guy with a camera as he darts across the street to get a picture of me in all my teacher glory.

"Shit," I snarl and glance at Mama. "Ready to make a run for it?"

"I'll get the gate," Dani announces as she looks over our shoulders at the growing crowd. "Am I allowed to fuck with them?"

"Yes," Mama and I answer together.

"Fuck yeah!" She runs out into the yard, flipping them all off and shouting something about her band's next show. Leave it to Dani to find an opportunity to promote her band in any circumstance. Someday, when she makes it big, she'll know how to handle these clowns, and she's getting her practice in today.

I ease the car out of the driveway while the horde descends on us. Dani yells and swears at them, but I'm too focused on trying not to hit anyone and waving my arm, shooing them away. They don't care, they just keep shouting and taking pictures. My phone doesn't stop buzzing from the cup holder, but that will need to wait. When I'm finally out of the driveway and in the street, I watch in my rearview as Dani shuts the gate and flips them all off again before waving at us.

There's silence as I drive to Mama's work. Normally, I would only drive her to the bus station, but after that mob, there's no way I'm risking it. I swing into her favorite coffee spot, hoping it will give us both time to calm down from all that chaos.

"Renate, baby, maybe you should rethink this guy," she asks as we wait in the line at the drive-thru. It's the first thing she's said since we left the house. "Rich white men are weird."

"Yeah, but I've found one of the decent ones, Mama. I promise, he's worth it." I pick up my phone as we wait to place our order. Four missed calls from Chase and even more texts from him, Teresa, Marta, and a few other teachers from the school. News travels fast, especially here..

I start with Chase's texts.

CUDDLE PUPPY

Are you okay? A friend sent me pictures of your house.

I'm talking to my agent to see what she can do.

I'm sorry about all this. I'll fix this, Ren.

God, you look fucking hot, though. 😈 🔥

I can come get you. In fact, I'm leaving now.

When I read the last one, I quickly reply that we've made it out safely and that I'll call him as soon as I can. Hopefully, he hasn't left yet or gotten too far.

They haven't reached Mama's work yet, and with any luck, they won't. The paparazzi invasion at the school has begun, and I recognize some of the same faces from earlier. Why would anyone want a career like this? Chasing people around, invading their lives, and harassing them for a few dollars? The stupidity of a job like that just makes them assholes. I'm a teacher. What do they think they'll get from me? A lecture and a syllabus?

I guess I'm not as boring to the gossip mags as I imagined.

I'm relieved to see the resource officer doing his best to keep them a safe, legal distance away from the building. He and I don't get along most of the time, but at least now he's doing something productive that doesn't involve harassing my students. I glance around, knowing the paparazzi can all see where I'm parked, and I consider asking for a new spot, but it wouldn't matter. If these people want information and images, there's plenty of staff and even students that would rat me out for a payoff. I leave my grading in the car—I can send someone out for it later or come out myself when they've grown tired of watching a public school's parking lot.

I've never wished for spontaneous rain so hard in my life.

I'd hoped that getting to my classroom would help, but I'm still too frazzled and can't get the image of all of those people hanging over our fence out of my mind. The terrifying reality that my family, my house, my car, everything, and everyone in my life are going to be fodder to those blood thirsty assholes knots my stomach. If I hadn't had that talk with Cynthia last week, I might lose my shit, but she gave me some pointers on how to not get arrested for punching one of them in the nose. I'm not sure how long I'll be able to keep myself from doing that, but I'm going to try my best, for her sake.

I'm almost inside when I glance over my shoulder one more time. That's when I spot the big, fake blonde wig of the reporter that came to my house. I want to gouge her eyes out. There's something off about her, but I can't figure out what, and I can't waste time hanging around to find out. If she's here, I can bet on who ratted me out.

"Miley, you fucking son of a bitch," I murmur as I duck into my class. A few of the students are in class early, milling about. If they hear me, they don't mention it. Too busy on their phones.

Shit. The phones.

"Okay, Hannah? I'm going to put you in charge of this—I want everyone's cell phones on the table in the back of the classroom. Face up, understand? Tell the other students as they come in." This won't go over well. I always allow cellphones in my classroom. Encouraged, even. I use them as a teaching tool rather than taking them away as punishment. Not all teachers can or should do that, but I'm a technology teacher.

"Tell them it's part of a class assignment and they'll all get their phones back in a few minutes, okay?"

I feel awful taking their phones away. Most of these kids can't focus on a lecture; their brains don't allow for it anymore with the overstimulation that surrounds us these days. It's one of many downsides to technology. I'm not blind to that, but I can't change it either. The adrenaline wanes and I head to the back of the classroom to get prepared while there's still time. Locking the door to the storage room, I hop up on a counter I can see out into the classroom from.

"Hey, Ren, I'm so sorry—" Chase stammers as soon as he answers my call. But I cut him off.

"These people are fucking insane!" I shout, looking out the small window on the door to monitor the students. It's only five minutes until class starts. "But, baby, it's not your fault. Stop apologizing."

"It is my fault. I knew this would happen. I knew better than taking you last night, putting you on display for those vultures."

"Are you serious about that?"

There's silence, followed by a heavy sigh as he thinks about it. *"No. I'm glad you were there, Ren. I knew it would all blow up, but I thought it would take a day or two to find out who you are."*

"Miley and that fucking bitch reporter were behind that leak."

"Who?"

"The one that came to my house."

"Fuck," He sighs into the phone, and I can picture the stressed look on his face. *"Come to my place after work. There's a chance fewer of them will stay around your house if you're not there."*

"I don't know, Chase. I don't have any clothes with me or anything."

"You'll be at my place. Why would you need clothes?" His goofy laugh lures me in.. *"I can get a driver to pick up clothes from your house, or I'll order you more. I don't use my celebrity privileges often, so let me use them for you."*

"I have all these papers to grade and…"

"I promise, I'll let you. I'll stay out of your hair. Hell, you can grade them out by the pool. You know you'd love that." He tries to persuade me, and it's working. *"I'll cook us dinner and make sure your mom and Dani are taken care of, too. It's like a vacation, Sunshine."*

"A vacation where I still need to work."

"Please? You don't want the alternative, remember? Cameras, security systems, and cops."

"When do you leave for Atlanta again?"

"A few days. It's a quick trip, reshoots I think. You can stay in the house while I'm gone if you want, or you can go home. It's your call. Hell, you can bring your mom and Dani over here."

"Chase, I just don't know if—"

"I'll give you whatever privacy you need, Renate. I just want to make sure you're safe and they can't get to you for a few days. Give you room to breathe and adjust. Hell, I'll sleep in the den and you can take

the bed with the dogs so I don't keep waking you up for a taste of your—"

"Okay! Okay. Not to you sleeping in the den. I'll come over. Dani can pack some things for me. I'll drive straight to your place after work. I gotta go, but I'll call you before I leave, okay?"

"Perfect. Just like you. It will get better, Sunshine. I promise."

HOLLYWOOD
Chase

CHAPTER 27
GOSSIP

MÅNESKIN, TOM MORELLO

I'M HAVING trouble getting into character for the first time in my career. The worst part? It's a character I've been playing for five years. I know this character inside and out, and yet, I can't find his voice because I can't stop dwelling on Ren. I'm not picturing her naked or what she does to me. I've imagined that a million times over and it never held me back. Instead, I keep picturing her in Cassie's place. The paparazzi breaking her down, the stress of my lifestyle being too much for her. All the nightmarish images of the last time I saw Cassie flood my mind and in every single one, it's Ren's face in place of Cassie's. I blink those away and a new wave crashes into me. The fights, the crying, all the horrible things keep coming back.

Work, home, anywhere I am, those memories have me tense and lashing out. I'm supposed to support her right now. Instead, I'm acting like a fucking dick.

I excuse myself from the table read and step outside, pulling up my therapist's number. It rings. It rings again. I swear under my breath when it rings the third time.

"Morning Chase. How are you doing?"

"Fucking bad, man. You got time?"

"Absolutely. Do you want me to come to you or?"

"Nah, I'm gonna get myself out of this read and come to you. Be there in fifteen minutes?"

"I'll be ready. Hopefully."

I need the stability and structure of his office right now, so I'm glad he has time and doesn't need to do this by phone. I talk to the PA and the director, promising I'll be back tomorrow and that I'm having an off day. They pull in my stunt guy to read my lines for me; he'll crush it. He's a badass like that. Like I'm supposed to be.

I'm numb as I make the blur of a drive to Dr. Clay's office. I've made so much progress over the last few months, this feels like a side swipe from a semi truck. I hoped this relationship could help me get through some of this pent up shit, but I also understand it's a relationship, not a crutch or a fix-all. Ren has been more than understanding, and the release I'm getting from the sex and the role play? Downright therapeutic.

I could handle this better if the gossip magazines were all I had to worry about. But I found another envelope on my windshield after catching some paparazzi loitering outside my house. That sent me all the way back to square one.

"So, what happened?" he asks as I walk in, heading straight for the couch. "Where's Pongo?"

"He's at home. The crew scheduled explosives testing today, so I didn't want him getting spooked." I flop down onto the couch so hard I worry it will break, and when it doesn't, I cover my face and let my breathing take over until I can tell him more. He's a patient man, which comes with the job. But I'm sure minutes turning into money as they tick by helps.

Fuck, I never think of Theo like that.

I uncover my eyes, finding him looming over me with a look that says he understands.

"I'm fucking up so bad."

"You looked like you were both handling it brilliantly at the event. I saw the pictures."

"The event? Yeah. Fuck that thing, that's a whole different therapy session. One where I vent and fucking break things."

"It's one way to complete the cycle. So, what are you here to talk about?"

I pull my phone out and slide it across the table as he takes his seat again and flips through the photos. "That's her front lawn. Look at those fucking parasites. The rest are of the school or taken by the professional dickheads in the middle of the fray. They had the fucking audacity to send me these! Told me I could pay for them if I wanted. It's like they're taunting me at this point." I run my hand through my hair, wishing I had a hair tie with me. "Nothing in these qualifies as print worthy! They're just harassing us for shits and giggles."

"They want to get under your skin because a celebrity meltdown nets them serious money for them. If the mundane sets you off, imagine how you're going to react when they catch her sunbathing in the backyard. You've already done this dance."

"I hoped we had more time before they dug up her identity. That's partially my fault. She's a teacher, not a ninja. That comes with too many variables: students, parents, and other teachers. Any of them can tip off a pap, or take a few pictures themselves and sell them. Hell, I met her at the school and the paps were there that night, too."

"We always think there will be more time, Chase. More time to plan, more time to say I love you, more time to hold someone close. We also like to think people are trustworthy, but you learned from experience they're not. We can plan everything down to the finest detail, and it doesn't matter. Sometimes, it just fucking rains."

I laugh. It's his favorite damn phrase.

"I said that to Ren not long ago after her ex came after her. You make it sound more poetic than I did." When it rains here, the whole town goes under water in no time. I guess his metaphor has more meaning than I thought. He's right, though. Again. I knew it would be fast.

"I keep thinking of Cassie, picturing her there in all that… blood." I swallow hard. My stomach churns, so I drink down the glass of water on the table. "But it's not her face, it's not her body. It's Ren. I'm even having nightmares about it. I can't sleep."

"How is Ren handling things?"

"I'm not sure. I mean, Cassie had a fucking breakdown and I never even saw it. I'm a fucking idiot who can't see shit when it's right in front of my face. I mean, do I even know Ren? Would I notice a shift in her? Would I ignore it like I did Cassie?"

"Chase, we're going to get through this, but we have to do it in steps. You did see Cassie's issues, so did other people, including her own therapist. You did everything you could for her, but you aren't to blame for that. You also have to stop comparing the two. Ren and Cassie are different people."

I stand up and pace. Rage builds and I'm not sure where it's coming from, it just needs to get out. "FUCK! How the fuck am I not to blame for her slitting her fucking wrists in *my* house? My girlfriend fucking killed herself because of me and my fucking baggage. Which part of that am I not blaming myself for? Huh? I can't even go in the fucking room anymore, Doc." I fall back onto the couch, running out of steam, and I mumble, "I sealed it shut so no one could."

"No amount of nails or glue will help you control the world around you, Chase. People make their own decisions. They choose how to live their lives and face their demons, not you. You can sympathize and understand their demons. You can stand at their side as they battle them. But each of us has to battle their own demons." He sets his notebook aside and takes off his glasses. "Chase, let's start smaller. Tell me about what's going on with Ren."

I rub my face and groan. "I had her come stay at my place.

She calls me when she gets to the school, when she leaves, at lunch. She's doing everything I ask, but I'm losing my temper, forgetting lines at work, and being a general fuck up. I'm so damn lost."

"There's where we need to start. Think about what you've told me. You've described Ren as an intelligent, capable woman who hasn't shown signs of mental distress, and yet you're trying to control her life. You're giving her rules and putting her on a leash, but from what you've said before, she's the one who wants you on the leash." I nod and he continues. "Why are you controlling her?"

"I'm not! I want to keep her safe."

"Noble, but it will backfire on you. She's independent and you're trying to force her to be something she's not used to. She needed to take back control of her life after what she lived through. You're taking her away from her life outside of you and forcing her into yours. Does that worry you?"

"It's not… I'm not…"

"Go ahead. Saying it out loud helps."

"I'm trying to protect her! She'll get hurt if I don't do this."

"Who will hurt her, Chase?"

"I don't know! I could have stopped Cassie. If I'd been home, if I'd have answered her call that morning."

"You don't know why she called you, though."

I've never stopped thinking about it. It's hard enough finding the woman you love in a pool of her own blood, but living with the realization you missed the last opportunity to hear her voice? I may never let go of that. I'm forever haunted by this idea of saving her just by answering her call. That's why I get annoyed when people let my calls ring. It's why Dr. Clay never picks up right away when I call him.

"No," I admit. I have my theories, and they range depending on my mood. Some days, in my mind, she called to tell me she loved me. Other days, I'm sure she called to say she hated me and what I'd done to her life. Theo likes to remind me it's possible she called to tell me to pick up eggs on the way home, something mundane instead of dramatic.

"Ren has a life, doesn't she? Family, friends, responsibilities? She'll need her freedom back."

"She goes to work! Her sister comes over, too. "

"Given her past, what she's been through, she's likely allowing you to do this because she understands what you're going through. You're doing this for you, not her, and she's picked up on that. But soon, she'll see you as controlling, and how do you think that's going to work out?"

I can still picture it. The night I took Cassie's keys and locked them in my safe when she wasn't looking. I told her I hadn't seen them and promised her we'd find them soon or replace them. I wanted to protect her, and I ended up becoming her fucking jailor. I don't want that for Ren. Hell, I don't think I could do that with Ren if I wanted to. She'd smack the ever loving shit out of me and walk home in a rage.

"I'm fucking it all up. I don't want her to be a prisoner, but I want to keep those fucking assholes away from her." I rub my eyes with the heels of my hands so hard, I'm sure I'll give myself a migraine. "It's all my fault. I wanted this so bad, and now that I have Ren, I'm so fucking desperate to keep her safe."

"Some sociologists think safety exists only as a social construct. That believing something or someone is safe ignores the potential harm, therefore becoming the harm itself."

"Fuck. So, I'm fucking everything up, like I said."

"Try a different angle. Who keeps you safe?"

"I don't need—" I stop, realizing what he's actually asking me to do. He wants me to think about how to answer, not answer off the cuff. "I'm in the same danger she is, so why am I not locking myself up in the house?"

"You're in more danger, technically. Cyn sent over the notes and pictures you keep getting. After Mills found the microphone in your house? Chase, you have an increasingly aggressive, delusional stalker, and you're worried about pictures they sell online?"

He's right, my priorities are way off. I can't lock Ren away in a tower. I'm not that monster. I've struggled to get past that, and I need to accept Ren would fight before she ends up like Cassie. Bringing her to my house solves one problem and ignores a hundred more.

"What do I do?"

"Again, start small. Are you giving Ren the space she needs?"

"Yeah, I'm trying to. There's been a few times that I interrupted her a little, but I backed off." He stares at me, accusations in his eyes. "Yeah, okay, I get in her way a lot."

"How about designating a space that's only hers? You're not allowed to bother her when she's in there." I argue, but he holds up a hand. "It doesn't need a door, but you will need to adhere to the boundaries she sets. Where do you work when you're at home?"

"The loft. Sometimes the garage. I work out and do my lines."

"And where does she work?"

"The dining room table," I groan. "Shit, okay. I get it."

The more I talk to Theo, the more I'm letting go of the death grip I had on the idea that Ren would follow the same path as Cassie. She doesn't have the same history, the same jaded perception of the world. She's different, even in how she treats me, so why am I not treating her differently?

The crushing weight lifts off my chest as that realization sets in. It's not the perfect solution that I wanted, but it's what I needed in order to help myself get through this again. Because it won't be *again*, this will be different, even if the villains stay the same.

"Thanks, Doc," I say as I rise from the chair as our session ends. "I needed this. I needed that kick in the ass."

"I'm always here to kick you in the ass when you're down, Chase." He picks up his glasses, wiping them on a cloth from his pocket. "So, circling back?"

"Mills hit a brick wall on the name we found. She avoided all the security cameras on the set, and no one has footage of her from the convention a few years back." I wring my hands as I talk, feeling the stress come back. "I block her numbers, but she still calls."

"Take that seriously and trust Mills. He's worked on a couple of stalker cases for other celebrities. It's a cry for help, and I don't like the way it's escalating. Have you told Ren about it?"

"Some."

"Time to tell her everything. For both the stalker and Cassie. Now keep moving forward and stop being the warden."

As we're walking out, something on his desk catches my eye. I recognize the CD cover art from Dani's band. "Interesting music choice."

"Oh, yeah, I got that at a local Battle of the Bands a friend conned me into judging."

"Yeah?" He's hiding something. That's the fun part of therapy. He's getting to know me, but I'm also learning about him along the way. "Well, I'm close with the lead singer if you want to get it autographed or something."

"Came autographed, but thanks. They were pretty good." I could swear he's blushing.

On the drive home, I'm feeling better. I consider going back to the studio to get some work done, but I need to take the rest of the day to get my head straight. I owe it to Ren and myself to fix this. Sometimes I'm excellent at picking up a concept, understanding it, and tossing it right out the window a few minutes later to slide back into old, comfortable habits.

As I maneuver the streets of Culver City, I work on a plan to help make this stick. I'm going to keep to new things today as much as I can to stop myself from drifting off into the past. I've even thought up a new recipe she'll love. But I change my mind because that's not enough. Theo tells me to start small, but that might be too small. I'll ask her to leave the prison, go out to dinner. Look at some new walls for a few hours together at least. Maybe even tell her why I've been such a prick and open another window into who I am.

HOLLYWOOD
Renate

CHAPTER 28
BLACK BIRD

EVAN RACHEL WOOD

AT FIRST, I enjoyed staying with Chase again. The security system and high wall remind me I'm safe, while offering privacy, and I missed coming home to a pool, hot tub, and him every night. But things have become more than just rocky between us.

The day before Chase's flight, we took Lulu to the dog park to play with one of her puppies, the one owned by Jamie and Lexi. We stayed toward the back of the park, keeping to ourselves and letting the dogs play. A fan recognized Chase and he let her take a picture of him with her dog. She looked familiar, but I couldn't place her. Not long after the fan left, Lexi spotted a paparazzi standing on the roof of his car taking pictures of us. It didn't bother me since I'd expected as much to happen, but it set something off in Chase and he hasn't been the same since. He backed out of the project in Atlanta—or that's what Dani told me. Chase told me they no longer needed him for the reshoots, blaming it on funding.

Now I don't know who to believe—my boyfriend or the gossip bloggers my sister reads.

He talked to his therapist, and when he came back, he again promised he'd let me do my work and wouldn't bother me. He spent half a day in the loft with Devin, moving furniture and

painting the walls. He created a space just for me and even made a little reading nook so I could grade my papers while overlooking the pool. Things began moving in the right direction again.

The next day, Chase found a letter on the front door that shoved him back into the dark and moody recesses of his mind. He spent the rest of the day in the gym with the door closed and has been a revolving door of mood swings, getting worse by the day.

Today has been another example of peak moodiness bordering on the male version of PMS. He flips from clingy and horny to sulking and cold so fast, neither Pongo nor I can keep up.

I can't help but think this has something to do with his ex. Did he drive her away with his behavior? Has this side of Chase been a red flag I missed before? The more distant he becomes, the more tempted I am to look into his history. But I don't, because I want to trust him to tell me on his own. I haven't even googled his brother, who has welcomed me into the house with open arms. Devin's part of why I'm sticking it out and not going home. He's a sweet kid, and he reminds me that Chase is like that, too, when he's acting like himself.

The sound of drilling and hammering comes from the loft as Chase installs shelves even after I said I didn't need them, so I'm sitting at the dining room table getting some grading done. I flip open another folder and I can already tell this one will take a while. The student transferred to my class a few weeks ago, and I'm glad he did. His intuition with programming far surpasses that of most of my other students. I have to take my time reading his papers to understand them. I've been trying to schedule meetings with his parents about after-school programs and robotics clubs, but it's been hard getting times pinned down with their schedule and my now hectic life. I make a note on a piece of sticky paper to email them and see if we can't set up a video call instead of being in person. This wouldn't be a problem if I went home. Maybe we jumped into this too fast and we need to pump the brakes on this relationship. Or we should never have listened to our feelings and stopped at friends.

I zone out to the world around me, getting lost in the language of programming. Right as I'm getting to the meat of his report, Chase pulls my chair back from the table in a quick jerk.

"Chase! Fucking seriously?" I yell, upset with him. But when I glance up at him, I catch the glimmer in his eye that's been missing for days. I don't want him to lose it again.

He kneels in front of me, his palms on my knees and eyes getting darker the longer I stare into them. "I've been hard to be around lately, and I don't mean to be—I hope you understand that. You are the warmth and sunshine against the darkness of my mind. I don't want this, and I need to take responsibility for how I've been acting."

"Don't be hard on yourself, Chase. If you're doing your best, that's all I can ask."

"I should be doing better than my best for you. I want to make you happy. I wanna make you laugh again. You look so damn amazing in this bikini. I wanna make you feel good, my queen."

"Yeah, I look good *in* it, so let's keep it ON and in only two pieces." He cocks his head to the side and raises an eyebrow when I pull the crochet lace cover up closed. It doesn't hide a damn thing, but it sends a message. "You big goof."

His face drops to a pout.

"How am I supposed to say no to that cute, pouty face of yours?"

"You're not. Or at least that's what I'm hoping for." His lips travel up my legs, but his eyes stay on mine. "My sexy as fuck teacher, busy grading papers. Interrupted by her naughty student. You should teach me a lesson." His fingers play with the knot in my bikini bottoms.

"I'm going to teach you one hell of a lesson later if you don't stop and let me get through these last few papers."

"I can't wait till later. Please," he begs while his hands slowly push my knees apart. I've stopped fighting, and he's aware he's about to get his way, licking his lips like a hungry dog. This is my Chase, the one I've been falling for over the months. Playful, fun, a bottle rocket full of anxiety, always ready to explode.

I put the folder down, and he pulls me to the edge of the chair. He taps on a folder and wiggles his eyebrows, so I pick it up and start reading to him about the theory of robotics. His head moves to my side as I read, and he bites down on the string, pulling until it comes undone before moving to the other side at a leisurely pace. I like when he takes his time, exploring me like I'm some new adventure he's never had before.

"Are you listening to me, Mr. Cooper?"

"Yes, ma'am. Algorithms. Programs." He moves the fabric that's between him and his treasure, licking his lips before he slides his finger through me. "Beep beep. Boop boop."

"You're going to have to work hard for that passing grade." I lean forward, grabbing his hair and holding his head back. "Really, really hard, Puppy."

"Yes, ma'am."

I want his mouth on my damn pussy, but he's got other plans, focusing on other areas. He's squeezing and biting anywhere he can get a hold of. There's plenty of those on me. I gasp when his fingers do their slow, deliberate dance between my legs. Fireworks shoot through my spine every time the tip of his finger slides through me, ghosting my clit. My head rocks back in anticipation.

"Goddess?"

"Yes, Puppy?"

"Can we play tonight?" We haven't even fucked in two days, but that's not all he wants. He wants his release from the world.

He wants me to tie him up and tear him apart. It breaks my heart that he's asking, but heals my heart to know it helps him.

"What would you like to do, Chase?"

"I'm not sure. I think I'm ready to try something new. I like when you teach me new things." His eyes light up as he remembers to add, "I mean, the ropes have been on the bed for a week now and, well, we haven't used those yet. How do I earn that?"

"Oh, Puppy. We've barely even scratched the surface, but I have a few things in mind we could try. For now, keep doing what you're doing and that will earn you some extra credit in class."

Hunger has come into his eyes and spreads down his body. He hoists my legs up onto the arms of the chair. He pulls me closer, licking one long strip up my center. Something's on his mind. I can tell because he's only giving me half his focus—still a million times better than some men give when eating pussy. Nevertheless, if anyone needed a poster boy for the belief that a man can't think while he's fucking, or fuck while he's thinking, it's Chase. It's also adorable.

"What will you do to me when I'm tied up?" he asks, before licking deeper.

"Oh, I'd start by riding your face so you'd shut up and give me what I want."

"I'll do anything for you," he hums, his tongue sliding through me before he closes his mouth over my clit, sucking and flicking until I'm seeing stars. I'm not sure who taught this man the right way to use his mouth, but bless her. In fact, I hope she's out there giving classes to other men.

He sucks in soft, quick pulses while two fingers part my lips. He wants to draw this out, wants it to last as long as he can make it. Last time he tried this tactic, we ended up with his cock in my mouth. Not that I mind. He has a fantastic cock. He went right back to work after I got him off, making sure I had more orgasms than common sense. Walking into class the next day proved difficult, and I regret none of it.

I play with his hair, twisting it around my fingers and pushing it out of his face so I can watch him. His fingers splay, stretching me open. They push deeper and curl, finding my g-spot with ease as my toes curl. A man who can find both a clit and a g-spot should win some kind of Oscar in my mind. I slide my nails through his long, soft, caramel swirled hair and tell him how good he is. He loves his praise, so I shower it on him.

"Right there, baby. Make me scream for you and your magic tongue."

I'm thankful when he finds the pace he wants to set and lets his tongue draw circles over me. I push his face into me as I get closer to what we both want. "Just like that, baby. Oh god! Fuck me, Chase! Make me come on your gigantic cock!"

He picks me up and drops me on the table. As he goes to pull his cock out, he freezes and looks away from me.

"I can't…do this."

"Chase?" He doesn't answer, swearing under his breath. "Baby? Come on, what's the matter?"

"I can't do this…not again. Not again."

I sit up, reaching for him, but he shrinks away from my touch. This has got to stop, and it has to stop now. "Chase Cooper, you need to talk to me. We've been doing this dance for a week. This has more behind it than just paparazzi or me going home."

"I fucking can't!"

Without looking at me, he storms into the kitchen, leaving me half naked on his dining room table. He opens the fridge so hard the bottles on the door rattle and threaten to break—just like my heart. When he comes back out, he has a beer in his hand and he walks right by me, heading to the patio. I watch Pongo follow him as Chase drags a chair about as far away as he can get, turns it away from the house, and sits with his head in his hands. As badly as I want to go to him, I don't think that's what he wants right now.

I pick up my phone and call my sister.

"Yo, are you ever coming home or should I hire movers for your shit?"

"Soon. Hey, can you give me Jamie's number? Something's going on with Chase and I want to talk to someone who knows him better."

I jot the number down on a folder, and once we're done talking, I call Jamie. He doesn't answer, so I leave him a message.

"James, it's Ren. Uhm, I need some help with Chase. He's acting unusual lately, and frankly, it's getting worse. I'm hoping that I'm not meeting the real Chase right now, because I don't like it." It sounds like I'm calling a parent about a child who's misbehaving, which isn't the tone I wanted, but it fits the circumstances. I keep the information vague while fighting to keep the quaver out of my voice. The familiarity of hiding my fear only makes it worse. "I'm worried about him."

I leave him my number, pull my robe back on, pack up the few remaining papers I need to grade, and head upstairs to the loft. We both need a little space right now. As I set up the pillows and get comfortable, my phone buzzes. It's not showing a caller ID, but it could be Jamie, or a parent, so I answer it.

"Renate?" a familiar voice asks, but I can't place it. *"Richie Lawson here from the studio. I'd like to talk to you."*

Of course, I didn't recognize his voice because he never once said my name. "I believe you said all that you needed to at the charity function, don't you?"

"Chalk it up to me being drunk. Okay, princess? This concerns Chase Cooper more than it concerns you or me. His past, and his future." He says Chase's full name as if I wouldn't recognize the name. I should ask for a sincere apology before continuing, but it will never come.

"What about him?"

"I'd rather discuss it in person. Can I send a car for you tomorrow afternoon?"

"No, I have meetings scheduled." I don't hang up on the prick, and I can't explain why. Curiosity, or the off chance he might be behind whatever's bothering Chase? "What about Thursday? I'll meet you somewhere."

"Thursday works fine."

He agrees to meet at a bar that Dani and tried a few months ago. Public, but not so public he'll refuse. The call ends with an ominous warning to not tell Chase about the meeting. I plan on telling Chase, but not until I figure out what Lawson's up to. I need to see what this fucker wants before I get Chase involved. Especially given his emotional state. I don't want him getting into any more fights with Lawson or doing something stupid. My phone rings again, but this time I recognize the number.

"Jamie?"

Someone giggles in the background before he clears his throat. *"Yeah, hey, sorry about that. I was, uhm, busy helping Lexi. I got your message. How weird is weird?"*

I tell him about everything that's happened since the dog park, about the last few days, and how fine of a line Chase now walks around me. I've got thick skin; it comes with the territory of being a teacher. I can take a lot of bullshit from people, but I have my limits. Even shorter limits for the people who are supposed to care about me. Chase has tested those limits far too often since I got here.

"He hasn't exactly crossed into red flag territory, but he's dangerously close. He's under a lot of stress right now, but it's not an excuse to be a dick." He's stayed clear of the one boundary of mine that has no lenience. Violence. He gets mad, and occasionally has shouted, but he's shown no signs of being abusive, in either the physical or emotional sense, toward anyone but himself. I just wish he'd stop trying to hide his pain from me like I don't see it. I'm not making excuses for him; I've done that before and it doesn't end well. "If he doesn't open up to me soon, or if he crosses any of those lines, I'm not sure we'll be able to recover. I'm not sure I'll want to."

"I understand. I planned on coming over anyhow. I have some stuff I need to run by him for an event. I'll be there in an hour."

"Thanks, Jamie. I hope he opens up for you."

"If not, I'll gladly kick his ass back in line. He's an idiot if he loses you, Ren. You're an amazing person, and you two are good together. Hang in there if you can. I guess you already are since you're calling me instead of walking out, but you get what I mean."

"I do. It will take more than whatever this is for me to walk out on him, but he's getting too close to that edge."

HOLLYWOOD
Chase

CHAPTER 29
ENJOY THE SILENCE
DEPECHE MODE

"WHERE'S REN?" Jamie asks as he walks out and pulls a chair up next to mine. Listening to how long it drags on the concrete deck makes me feel like a fucking dick for doing the same thing earlier, and that's his intention. Jamie doesn't do passive aggressive when I'm involved; we're too close to one another for that shit. We're brothers, and we've always been honest to a fault with each other. It's what keeps us true to ourselves.

"Probably upstairs packing her shit up and getting ready to light the house on fire."

"She wouldn't do that." He drops into his chair and pops the top on his beer before clanging the top against the neck of my empty. "She'd get the dogs out first."

I agree with a grunt.

"So, you wanna talk about it? Steve says you're canceling workouts, the internet says you're backing out of projects, and when I checked your phone, I found ten missed calls from Cyn."

"Whatever."

"I'll give you credit, man. I half expected an outgoing call to one of the, uhm, dating services Steve used to use. I mean, since you want to implode your relationship and life at such an epic level, you might as well go out with a *bang*, right? Pun intended."

"Fuck you."

"You're not my type. What the fuck is going on? I thought you talked to Clay?" I don't answer, so he leans over and ruffles my hair until I swat at him and grunt. "Oh, full caveman, now? Not talking is my gig; you can't have it."

Jamie and I met back in high school. He didn't talk to anyone for a few years, and some dickhead tried to jump him. I kicked the kid's ass, but they tried to suspend me. Jamie spoke up and saved my butt. We've been the dynamic duo ever since, adding Steve about a year later.

"What do you want? Why are you even here?"

"Officially? I got the numbers back on that new grant we talked about for the center and thought you'd like to take a look. Unofficially? Because the best thing that ever happened to you called me worried sick."

"I thought you were the best thing that ever happened to me?"

"I was! Now I'm the second best. You're losing your ever loving mind, man." He sighs when I shake my head. I don't even know what to say, unsure if I'm angry or sad…or both. "Coop, don't let her go, okay? She's not the problem, but she deserves to know what is. Tell her, and not just the sugar-coated version. Tell her everything. The truth. Every fucking word of it."

I wipe my nose on the back of my hand like I'm fucking five. Jamie's right, I'm falling apart just like last time. Worse. This time I can't stop. Ren doesn't deserve that. Ren deserves better. She deserves for me to come clean and open up about what's going on. Or she deserves to move on to someone who can treat her better than I am.

First, though, I need to tell Jamie. "I opened the room." I mumble, but he hears me anyhow. Hell, I'm sure he knew before he even sat down. Of all the people she could have called, Jamie is the only one who can pull me out of this emotional nosedive. Maybe.

"Shit, for real? Okay."

"I talked to Theo, like I told you. We talked about going after our demons and not confusing Ren for Cassie, and it made sense. I promised myself and Ren I'd do better, and I did for a while. Until I saw some of those fucking vultures outside the house."

"So you conveniently waited until she left for work? And made sure none of your support system could stand with you to confront your demons alone? Like the fucking idiot you are sometimes?"

"Seriously, fuck you."

"You should have waited for Devin or Steve. You should have called me, you prick." He stands up, but I don't make eye contact. He sounds pissed. No, worse than that, he sounds disappointed. "The way I see it, you have two options right now, pal. Option one, you get the fuck in there, and you spill your fucking guts like you're Linda fucking Blair. You show her the room and lay all that pain out at her feet while you beg for her to stay. I guarantee she won't leave you for that, man. She wants to help you, but she can't do that if you won't tell her what's up."

"What's option two?"

He groans and shakes his head. "I'll take the bullet for you, but just this once. You're going to owe me so fucking much if you make me do this, and I probably won't talk to you for at least six months." He puts his hands on his hips and stares down at me. "I'll tell her what happened, help her pack her things, and take her home. After that, I'll seal the room back up so you don't have to face the monsters till you're ready."

"Fuck."

"Look, asshole, she's going to leave you anyway if you keep acting like a dick. Please, tell me you didn't lock her keys away?" I shake my head. "Well, at least we're not past the point of no return. Coop, you have a real chance to put your life back together and I don't mean the duct taped, barely holding it together version of you from the last four years. I mean the real you. It's terrifying, and you're scared to shit about the entire thing because it means opening up that part of you that's still hurting. But I'm telling you, that woman in your loft? She's about as far away from Cassie as you can get. Renate will face down your darkest demons and fucking dare them to lay a finger on you so she can rip their throats out and eat their black hearts. She's not a damsel, Coop. She's a goddamn assassin and if you'll let her, she'll fight by your side till the bitter end."

"You don't know that."

"I do, actually! Because I'm lucky enough to have one just like her back home. Thing is, I'd do the exact same thing for Lexi, and you've seen it. So my question now is, would you do it for Ren? Because there are some wicked fucking demons in her closet, and if you're not going to be there when she needs you, let her go. Let her find someone with balls big enough to match her own."

"What?" I stare up at him, squinting against the fading sun.

"I'm saying you don't have to do this alone. You never have, but now you've got her and fuck it, man. Either fight to keep her, or let her go and keep wallowing in your self pity by your big ass pool."

I wipe my face and groan into my hands before I stand up and stare back at the house. There's a light on upstairs in the loft and find her silhouette in the window. My stomach turns as everything I've done since she's been here comes rushing back. The thought of losing her feels like someone twisting a knife in my gut. The problem is, if I were to look down, it would be my hand on the hilt.

"I'll bring the dogs out here and keep them company. If this ends up being anything like Lexi and I when I finally told her everything, you two aren't going to leave the bedroom for a while. Someone should be here to warn Mini Cooper." He squeezes my shoulder with a lopsided grin. I witnessed Jamie putting it all out there for Lexi, and how it laid a stronger foundation for both of them. The irony of both of us being so fucking dumb to think we could lock the past behind literal doors makes me question our sanity.

"If it heads south, I'm here for you, man. You know that. Stop trying to be all weirdly macho and handling shit on your own. It never works out how you think it will, because that will never be you, and it won't ever be what she wants."

She looks stunning as she sits curled up on the sofa grading her papers, so I lean against the wall, trying my best to be silent and not disturb her. Every breath I take reminds me of how much I don't want to lose her. How I'm not ready to let this go. My stomach becomes a battleground of nerves and butterflies, and my heart pulls me in two directions. Or maybe it's that voice in my head trying to sabotage my life again.

"Ren?" My voice cracks. Her head snaps up, no trace of anger in her eyes, only concern. I swallow the lump in my throat. "Can, uhm, can I talk to you for a minute? I can wait till you're done grading if you need me—"

"No, you've waited long enough." I'm glad. I'm not sure how long I'll be able to keep up the nerve to do this. She gathers up the papers and pats the couch next to her.

"I've been acting like a fuckup, and you deserve to know why." I should ease into this, but I'm ripping the bandaid off. "My ex never recovered from what happened with the paps, but I tried to keep her going," I explain as I sit next to her. "I just wanted things to get better, and that's probably why I proposed to her. Neither of us were in the right headspace for that kind of leap. Hell, I'm not sure we ever we loved each other, but I thought it would help give her something happy to look forward to. Something good."

Ren reaches over and takes my hand, which surprises me. It shouldn't, though.

"She could smile again, and spent her free time looking at florists and dresses. We agreed to only tell a few people about the engagement, so it wouldn't leak. A few weeks after I proposed, I drove across town to check on a venue she'd been talking about."

I thought I'd feel nauseous or upset telling her this. I didn't expect to feel numb. It's like I'm somewhere else, listening to someone else tell my story. I get up, still holding Ren's hand, and lead her down to the back of the garage. To the door I couldn't bring myself to open for years. I reach for the knob with a shaky hand, but she stops me, resting her hand over mine.

"While I met with the venue people, Cassie called me," my voice cracks as I continue the story. I step back as the door opens, still expecting the pool of blood. Expecting to see her lying there, cold and lifeless.

"Stay with me, Chase," she says as I fight off the panic attack. My hand absently searches for Pongo and he nudges my fingers. Jamie must have let him in, knowing I'd need him. Ren rubs my other palm with the tip of her finger until I can talk again.

I blink away the nightmare. "I didn't answer her call, too busy talking to the venue manager. Dev blows up my phone about twenty minutes later. He came down to visit during his college off season. The Parrots got permission to invite him out for a workout and he couldn't shut up about it the whole week. He forgot his skates and came back to the house. He should have been on the ice, not at the house that morning.

"The fourth or fifth time he called, I finally answered. I almost yelled at him. I thought he had locked himself out of the house or something stupid. But he... he freaked out when I answered. Crying and screaming at me that he saw something under the door—" She steps in front of me, and for a flash, she's Cassie, her cold eyes staring at me. The face shifts back to Ren again, and her eyes aren't cold. They're warm and full of tears. There's recognition in them as she realizes what I'm about to tell her before I can get the words out. She cups my face and lets me take my time.

"I raced home, found him sitting in the corner covered in blood. She died before he'd opened the door, they said. The shock hit him hard, so hard he forgot to call the cops." I close my eyes, trying to will the smell of bleach away, but I can't. "After they took her, I didn't leave the house for four days. I cleaned the blood, and I sealed the room shut so no one could get in."

"So the demons won't get out," she whispers as she turns and looks at the door. "You opened it last week, didn't you? That's what changed?"

I nod. "I thought I'd handle it better. I thought I needed to man up and get over it, like you got over your ex. Instead, I got scared and tried pushing you away while simultaneously trying to control your life. I couldn't let you...I couldn't let it happen again."

"Well, you forgot to actually have me here with you, Puppy." She strokes the side of my face. "You *can* move on, but you're never going to get over something like this, Chase."

"Her, uhm, her parents...they wouldn't let me go to the funeral. They blamed me for taking her away." Those are the words that do me in, and she pulls my head down to her shoulder, but I crash down onto my knees instead. Burying my face in her stomach as I break down. "I did this to her," I whisper over and over again, but she keeps holding me and stroking my hair. No one has done that since Cassie. No one did that before Cassie. She had so much love to give this world, and because of me, she ended her life.

"Jamie has a sister, Elle, who orchestrated the paparazzi attacks based on what they found in her computers. She had it out for Jamie and tried to attack his friends to make him suffer. I never completely understood it, though, because she went after Steve and his ex fiancé and taunted them over it. She admitted to leaking the nude photos, but never anything else to do with Cassie—including the guy who took the photos and the harassing texts to Cassie's phone." It's the first time I've ever admitted that to anyone. "They never charged her for anything since Cassie died by suicide."

The door shuts, and she tilts my chin up as she brushes my hair out of my face, tucking it behind my ear. "Chase, I need you to make me a promise, okay?" I nod, not trusting my voice yet. I draw in a shaky breath as she takes my face in her hands and stares into my eyes. "Never push me away like that again. Never. If you need to talk, we talk. If you need to cry, fuck this manly bullshit and you cry with me. If you need to yell, we'll both go outside and yell at the damn moon. Just don't push me away, especially when you need me."

"I—I promise. I promise I won't."

"Good, and I need to make you a promise." She gives me that soft, forgiving smile that makes my butterflies go nuts. "I'm not Cassie. I will never be Cassie, and I can't take her place. That means you can't treat me like her, either. This won't be me. I'm too much of a damn pain in the ass to leave before my time, so get that out of your head right now. People keep leaving you behind, Puppy, but you're mine now. I'm not leaving you unless I'm kicking and screaming. Got it?"

I nod, and she pulls me to her, kissing me like she's making promises to me I don't deserve. Making me feel like just this once, I deserve her and this. I pull away because I'm not done yet. She needs to know about the more immediate threat, too.

"Ren, there's…more. There's a stalker. My shrink said since she's gone from leaving me pictures and marriage licenses to more threatening phone calls, it's not something we can ignore."

"Jesus, what should we do?"

"Remember Mills? He talked to you after the whole thing with your ex? He and Cyn are working on it, but they said I should tell you so you can be on the lookout. Mills thinks she's using disguises though, and that's why we haven't noticed her."

"Do you know who?"

"No. Hell, we're only guessing it's a woman."

A car pulls into the driveway and Ren shivers. "Sounds like your brother just pulled up. How about we get some Chinese, get really high, and decompress by watching some of those dumb ass horror movies you boys think are comfort films? I'll even have James invite Lexi over."

I nod, because the words get stuck in my throat. They'll come out soon enough, because she's staying. Maybe not in the house for much longer, but she's staying with me. She's not leaving, and I'm not sure what to do about that other than learn to get used to it. Staying has become a lesson only she can teach me.

HOLLYWOOD
Renate

CHAPTER 30

LOLLIPOP

LIL WAYNE, STATIC MAJOR

I FLIP through the pages of tests I need to grade before the weekend, putting my headphones on and hoping I can get a head start on them while I wait for the Parent Teacher Organization meeting. They used to hold them in the mornings, and the teachers would work together and cover classes so that whoever needed to attend could be there. Now, they hold them after school hours to see if they can boost the number of parents that attend. The problem is, the PTO president owns a business and sets her own hours, so she's been fighting the change tooth and nail instead of listening to the parents who work more conventional jobs. I've talked with a few of the parents and told them I'd come tonight to help push their agendas a little harder.

Yesterday drained me, but I took some medication before it became too much to handle. Chase and I both fell asleep on the couch, and at some point, either Jamie or Devin pulled a blanket over us and left us there to sleep. Unfortunately, I never plugged my phone in and it died. We didn't wake until we heard Steve come over to start Chase's workout, so I had to rush to make it to school on time. It's a challenge, running around that big house and trying to avoid the dogs. While I made it out the door on time to make the first class, I forgot to pack lunch. I almost

ordered something for delivery, but the kids from morning tutoring asked if we could do it over my break since I missed our session. I couldn't say no, but now I'm starving.

I check the time and dig through the drawers, looking for something to snack on. But the kids raided my stash earlier, and I only find a lollipop. I still have an hour before the meeting, so I take off the wrapper with a sigh. As I pop it in my mouth, I get an idea. I snap a picture of my lips and the lollipop, nice and close, and shoot it off in a text. It still shows as delivered after a few minutes, so I go back to grading papers until my phone finally buzzes.

SNUGGLE PUPPY

Fuck...I'm going to jerk off to that when I'm gone next week.

Dinner?

Mind if I'm a little late? Parent's meeting tonight at 7.

SNUGGLE PUPPY

I know. ;)

I jump when there's a knock on my classroom door, and my jaw drops when my eyes meet Chase's dorky grin from the other side of the small window. He holds up a stack of food containers and shrugs, so I hurry over and let him in. I open the door and he pulls the lollipop out of my mouth, kisses me hard, and pops it into his mouth.

"Cotton candy, yes!" he smirks, directing me back into the room as he shuts the door behind him. "You're super hot when you're working, you know that?"

"What are you doing here? Did anyone see you? Please tell me you didn't break into the school?!"

"I slipped the maintenance guy a fifty, and he let me park out back where no one will see. So technically, no, I did not break into anything. Also, hello to you too, Sunshine." He puts the food on a nearby desk, hands me back the lollipop before he cups my face in both of his big, firm hands and devours my soul. I swear, every time this man kisses me, it's like he's scared it will be the last time.

He walks me backwards toward my desk before he lifts me onto it.

"That little picture you sent me had me worried you'd ruin your appetite." His fingers trace down the buttons of my top.

"Oh, baby, I'm going to ruin more than my appetite. I'm going to ruin you." I run the lollipop over my tongue with a mischievous moan. He's drooling as he watches me sucking hard, and I get a terrible idea. My mind flashes back to high school when I snuck into the bathroom to make out with the school's hot bad boy. I grab Chase's hand and pull him toward the door. When I check the hall, it's clear, so I drag him down the hallway to the bathrooms. I'm sure it would make for a funny sight for some people. My short ass pulling this specimen of a man down a darkened school hallway after hours.

The second we're in the bathroom, I lock the door and push him against it, grabbing for the button of his tight jeans.

"I wanna see how much you liked that picture, Puppy. I need to feel how hard I make you." I drop to my knees and take his pants and boxers down with me. I can't help but marvel at his cock. Just the sight of it makes me so fucking wet every time. It jumps when I slide a finger up that thick vein, teasing him. A dull thunk follows his soft moan when his head lolls back. I stand up and hold the lollipop up to his lips. "Show me what you want, baby. Suck it like the good little whore you are."

He watches me crouch in front of him, his eyes wide as he hesitates—just a little. I scratch my nails down his thigh and he responds with a sharp inhale before he gives the sucker a shy lick. I mimic the motion on the head of his cock. He licks his pretty lips and slides his tongue over the round ball before closing his mouth around it and winking at me. Now he's getting it. I copy his motions before I take the head of his cock in my mouth, lapping at it, followed by gentle sucks and kisses, just like he's doing, but I don't stop when he does.

"Oh god!" There's pure sin in the sounds this man makes during sex.

I take him to the back of my throat, reducing him to whimpers. I repeat the motion, letting my tongue drag over the tip of his cock before swallowing him again. His hand finds my hair, and when he pulls my head back, there's a line of spit connecting my lips to his cock and tears running down my cheeks.

"Jesus fuck, you're beautiful." He slides the cotton candy flavor over my lips and pushes it gently into my mouth before he picks me up and drops me hard onto the counter. There's a new look in his eyes. Feral...dominant; a side of Chase he's kept hidden away from me, and I'm curious to see how far he'll take it. He yanks my skirt up around my waist, and I let out a squeak as I hit the counter again.

I want him to tear me apart right now. I glance to the door, double checking the lock, and spread my legs for him. He grabs my panties, ripping them off of me with a snap before he holds them up, feeling them.

"You're all fucking wet, my little tease of a teacher. Were you planning on attending your meeting like this? Your hungry cunt soaking the seat under you while you suck on that fucking candy and think about my cock? Thinking about how good I fuck you?" He takes the sucker from my mouth with a pop and replaces it with my panties, pushing them between my lips with two long fingers. I've never craved a man the way I'm craving him right now.

His fingers trace down to my top again, but this time, he rips it open—something I only thought happened in movies. The buttons clatter across the floor as he stares down at me like I'm a four course meal. Something hard and sticky slides through me and pushes against my clit, but my eyes don't leave his.

"I'll take care of you, Ren. I'll watch you stand in front of all those people with your ruined pussy and my cum sliding down your fucking legs, tasting yourself as you suck on your fucking lollipop." He traces his nose up my neck, making my breath catch. "If you're a good girl, I'll bend you over the desk and fuck you in the ass while you talk to them about school funding or whatever bullshit you need to discuss. Your perfect tits shoved against the desk as you tease them with your lollipop."

I don't know where this side of him came from, but fuck, I want more. I'm so wet it's easy to slide his two fingers in as he continues to tease my clit, swirling the lollipop over it while he watches me squirm. He crouches down, letting his tongue trace up my thigh as he leaves a trail of nips and soft bites. My fingers are in his hair when his mouth finally closes over me and he sucks my clit hard while he shoves the lollipop inside me. He's thrusting it into me, rubbing it and his fingers against just the right spot. I don't know if it's him, the risk of getting caught, or that damn piece of candy I found, but I'm seconds away from falling apart already and he's not slowing down.

I wrap my legs around his head and scream into my panties as rainbows explode in my vision. I'm dragging my nails over his scalp and riding his fingers, unable to let go. I squeeze his head between my thighs, no longer in control of my body, and the tension builds again. I'm a shattered, ruined mess, and he's not done with me.

I'm coming again, harder than the first time. So hard, the panties don't muffle much of my screams. I'm so lost in the high, I don't notice him standing up.

He's digging through his pockets and swearing, mumbling under his breath. "I didn't bring a fucking condom? Planned out an entire dinner and a surprise, but forgot the stupid condoms."

I hold out my hand, pulling him to me on the counter. As

soon as I can reach it, I take his cock and line it up. He asks without words, and I answer in a needy whimper, panties still in my mouth. He doesn't slam into me like I expect, but stretches me in gradual, shallow thrusts. He watches my eyes roll back when he finally bottoms out. There are stars in my eyes, and they're all him. I pull his head down to my neck as he hammers into me in unrelenting thrusts.

"You're so fucking perfect, Renate. You feel like heaven, and you taste even fucking better." His deep, soft voice has a blissed out edge to it and I can feel him throbbing inside of me, ready to let go. "I need you. I need all of you. I wanna make you…mine."

I whimper and make noises I've never heard come out of myself before, all the while trying hard to keep my voice down. I want to scream his name, but I can only scratch at his back in desperation while I try to pull him deeper into me.

"Fuck, I'm sorry… I'm sorry Renate." I'm almost pulled out of the moment with his apology when he adds, "I'm sorry I'm saying this now. I love you. I love you so fucking much. Oh fuck! Fuck!"

His body jerks as he fills me, and his head falls to my shoulder. We stay like that, panting and half naked, until he softens and slowly pulls out of me with a groan, his head still resting against me.

"Chase?"

"I meant it," he pants. "It wasn't just the sex. I meant it, Renate. I won't take it back."

I lift his head and I'm met with those big, beautiful eyes, full of hope but also worry. I cup his face and bring his lips to mine while he pulls me closer and holds me tight, like I might try to get away.

"Say it again."

He looks into my eyes as his nose rubs against mine. "I love you, Renate Silva. I need you and I love you."

"I love you, too, Chase Cooper." His smile has both relief and joy in it, and it's perfect and beautiful. It's my Chase. My beautiful Puppy. "You were so raw and beautiful. Dominant and sexy. You couldn't have picked a better time, Puppy. I assume therapy went well today?"

"Yeah, it did." He looked down at me, at the mess he's made of me. "Uhm, I kind of ruined your panties. And your shirt. And your skirt, too. Fuck, let's do it again."

"You ruined me, too. All of that because of a lollipop? I'm gonna stock up on those things when I'm at the store."

"Please, do."

He kisses me a million times, each one softer and more gentle than the last. He whispers he loves me between every few kisses, and each time, I'm floating a little higher. We giggle together like idiot teenagers, drunk on one another. With one more hard kiss, he finally pulls away from me, turning the water on in the nearby sink and grabbing some paper towels. When I move to climb off the counter, he stops me, shaking his head.

"I'm not done." He kneels in front of me again and cleans up the mess he'd made of me. Starting with his tongue. The lightest touch has me on edge again, right where he wants me. When he's done, he kisses both of my knees, lifts me off the counter, and makes sure I can stand before helping me pull my outfit back together as best as we can.

"Shit. I can't go to the meeting like this. I need to sneak down to the office and get some gym clothes or something." I check the time, my face morphing from bliss to panic because I only have five minutes before I need to be there. Chase pulls off his t-shirt and helps me out of what's left of my blouse. He laughs softly as he looks down at me, swimming in his giant shirt except around my breasts and my hips, where it's tight.

"Fuck, you look damn good in my clothes, Sunshine. Go to your meeting before I get hard again just looking at you. I'll clean up in here and wait for you in your classroom, okay?" He caresses the side of my face and I'm floating again. With a smirk and a wink, he adds, "I'll wait under your desk."

"You won't fit under my desk, you giant." I jump up and wrap my arms around his neck, kissing him hard. "I'll get under the desk as soon as the meeting's over, and you can tell me over and over how much you love your cock in my mouth."

"I love you, my dirty little princess."

I rush out the door and hurry down the hall. I have no idea how I'm going to make it through this meeting because no matter what they're discussing tonight, all I'm going to hear are the four little words in Chase's beautiful voice. *I love you, Renate.*

"Ms. Silva!"

Shit. Mr. Miley. I went from starving to blissed out to pissed off real fast in the last hour and I'm over this roller coaster. Miley strolls up to the door with a smile that's way too big on his face. He never comes to these things, not even when they were during school hours.

"*Lovely* to see you here tonight." He looks me up and down, licking his lips. Pervert. "Interesting choice of attire for a parent's meeting, don't you think?"

I check the shirt for anything vulgar, remembering it belongs to Chase. Lucky for me, it's just the logo for Devin's hockey team. "Yeah, I made a mess of dinner tonight. Ruined my whole outfit. I had to borrow the shirt from a friend."

"Lucky friend." He pulls an envelope out of his jacket pocket and hands it to me. "A friend of mine asked me to give you this. Make sure you look it over before tomorrow's meeting."

"Meeting? What are you talking about?"

"After school, Ms. Silva. Now, run along and tell the parents I said hello."

He shoves me in the room before closing the door behind me with a wave. I hold the envelope tight, wondering what's inside. But I don't have time to look at it now since all eyes are on me and these parents are ready to get this meeting started.

HOLLYWOOD

Renate

CHAPTER 31
SOMETHING IN THE WAY

NIRVANA

BY LA STANDARDS, this bar is dead. But there are still enough people around that will react if I make a loud scene that Lawson won't be too happy about. I've ordered a drink and I've been sipping it for ten minutes while I wait, checking my phone and trying to calm my nerves. The waiter must be bored with the afternoon crowd, since he's come by three times already asking if I want more chips and salsa. I've texted both Dani and Marta, telling them where I am and who I'm meeting, not that I expect it going that far south, but I felt better knowing someone else knew.

I also told Chase's PI, Mills. Better safe than sorry.

This morning when I left for work, I told Chase I was meeting someone and would be home a little later. I hated lying to him, but even Mills said it would be better to see the whole angle Lawson tries to work before we send Chase off the deep end. I have my own reasons, too. They might be immature and foolish reasons that come from watching too much TV, but that's gotten me through the last few years of my life, so why change now?

I'm flipping through social media when a file drops onto the

table. Without a word, Lawson slides into the seat across from me and flags down the waiter.

"Gimme a scotch, and refill whatever fruity shit she's drinking." His gruff tone appalls me, and he never looks up to acknowledge the server. Hell, he's still doing the absolute least to acknowledge me, and I'm the one he's meeting with.

"Whiskey, and I hope you don't expect me to pay for any of that."

"Yeah, that's right. You're a teacher at one of those half-baked inner city hood schools, right? That's what the rags are saying, anyhow. What have you got on Cooper? Or do you suck so hard I should be making you an offer to get under the table for a demonstration?"

"Wow, we're done here already." I go to stand up and he holds up his hands.

"Fine, fine. Learn to take a joke. Whatever." He taps the folder with one of his meaty fingers. If someone told me this sorry excuse for a man had paid for elective surgery to replace his blood with a mixture of cheap hair dye and even cheaper cologne, I'd believe them. He's the epitome of a slimy salesman and I guarantee he's faced sexual harassment charges. "Before you run out on me, though, you should take a look at this. It's the other half of what my buddy delivered to you yesterday."

I put my purse back on the seat next to me and pull the file over while I stare at him. I find a contract with my name on it. I continue to flip through and find more pictures and documents like the ones Miley gave me last night, but instead of being Chase's life before we met, it's mine. Wedding photos, hospital bills, Luis's arrest history. I glare up at him over my glasses with an eyebrow raised. "What the fuck? Where the hell did you get these?"

"Oh, just a few items some little birdy dropped into my lap. Tweet fuckin' tweet."

"This is…" I flip through again as fire fills my veins. "That's fucking blackmail."

"You know, for a teacher, you got one hell of a mouth on you. First off, we do this shit all the time, so don't think you're some big deal, sweet cheeks. It's straightforward. You break up with Chase. I don't care how." His gold rings flash in the dim lights of the bar as he waves his hands around. He's trying to sound and look like some kind of 1970s New York crime boss, but it's all cheap crap. He's a used car dealer at best. "Anyway, you break up, badda bing badda boom, you get a hundred thousand dollars in your bank account. Oh, and Chase keeps his cushy Hollywood lifestyle without having to deal with how the papers are going to tear you to shreds like they did his last girlfriend. Fuck, for an attractive guy, he has terrible taste."

"Fuck you, I'm not—"

"Whoa there, before you get too carried away, listen to what I'm saying here. That kind of cash money could buy you a bigger house, so your mom isn't sleeping in a closet with no doors. Help your sister get that apartment she's been eyeing. You could go back to school, finish up that degree you never got to start or something. Hell, I'll even put in a word for you with the big tech guys. You just gotta stop seeing Chase. You've barely been together for what? A week?"

"How do you know about any of that?"

"Oh, I have sources. Two of 'em, in fact. My little bird friend, and the other one? Bit of a snake if you ask me, but he don't bite when I flash the cash." He grins, pushing up his tinted glasses. I wonder if he knows everyone can tell they're bifocals. "I mean, you could say no if you're that kind of bitch. You're welcome to stay with him if your heart is set on those big blue eyes of his. I'm sure he can find another life somewhere, because he'll lose everything when I'm done with him. He'll be that guy people used to know, the 'What ever happened to him' guy. You know what I'm talking about."

My mind races as I stare down at the contract.. "Why? Why are you doing this over me?"

"Oh, it ain't you, honey. It's Hollywood's glory and honor. I'm not alone in this. I'm just the one with enough balls to make you the offer. We ruin careers left and right in the business. Use 'em and toss 'em, that's how Hollywood works. Cooper ruffled too many feathers. My feathers. Bringing his fat whore to charity events and threatening me? Yeah, tip of the iceberg baby. There's an order to things, a way of life we're all very accustomed to here in LA. He's been threatening that lifestyle for years. If you ask me, he's a ticking time bomb. But if you sign your pretty little name, I'm gonna be the one who swoops in and saves his entire fucking career."

"I'm not signing shit."

"You should take some time to think about it. That signature also buys me keeping my trap shut about certain things I've heard from my little friends. You think I'd give you the goods on the first day? Get real. I can tell the school board about your spy cameras in schools."

He slides something across the table and I'm ready to throw up. He's hacked our camera feed because I'm looking at Chase and me sneaking into the bathroom last night. "Fuck you."

"Ex-husband gang members with a rap sheet two miles long look real good on the cover of the gossip rags." He pulls something out of his pocket and leans in, his smile turning my stomach. "Or I could go right for the jugular and spill the beans on that little club you like to spend time in."

"Go all the fucking way to hell, you pig."

"Okay. Suit yourself. I'll run you both out of Hollywood. Hell, out of California. Before the end of the school year, you'll both be long forgotten shit stains in line for unemployment and. government handouts. Don't worry, I'm sure I can hire you to clean my toilets and suck my cock. It'll be a love story for the ages, riches to can't even afford rags to wipe my fucking boots."

"You can't do that!"

"Oh, but I can. I've made more deals with the devil than I care to admit, and each one has come with more power than god. You try me and see how quickly people can forget. It's a cinch to knock Chase off that pedestal of his and watch him break like a fucking egg. A photo here, a story there. A weeping mother in front of the cameras talking about how her daughter *never stood a chance* with a controlling, abusive prick like Cooper. A sweet story about how he held her daughter captive in his home, doing god knows what to her, until she finally snapped and took her own life. You're nothing but trash to be tossed in the gutter, but him? Oh, I'm gonna enjoy the fuck outta that."

"That's not what happened. That's not what happened and you know it!"

"You assume people give a shit about the truth. You been sleeping through the last few years, sweetheart? No one cares about the truth. They care about the drama, the fighting, the pretend feelings. They care about ratings and gossip. As for you? You won't get another job in any school after those rumors spread. I mean, fuck. My little snake laid it on thick enough to convince your poor, innocent, sweet mother, didn't he? Tell me something though, who the hell did you piss off in the paps?"

"I don't know what you're talking about."

"You pissed off someone with a camera, and juicy isn't even the right word for what they're digging up. What does Chase call you? Mistress? Madam? I bet you got a tell-all book inside of your thick skull that could bury him so fast. But it won't sell when I leak the details of your little hobby with the whips and chains. *Tie me up tonight, Renate!*" His Chase impersonation sucks, but I still want to throw up. When his hand finds mine, I try to pull away, but he grabs my arm. "Maybe we could put that pretty mouth to use. You say no, now. But once I ruin you, you'll both be begging to suck my cock for a couple of bucks."

Screw throwing up. I want to punch this smug, arrogant

asshole in the fucking dick. I picked a public place to protect myself, but in doing so, I guess I made it harder for me to fuck this guy up. I can't think of a damn thing to say, but I don't want to sign this bullshit contract, and he can't make me. I'll call his bluff, because that's what it has to be.

"I'm not signing." I close the folder and push it back toward him.

"Alright. Well, when you want to change your mind and beg for mercy," he sneers, handing me a business card with nothing but his number on it like he's some hit man from a made for TV movie. He taps the folder again. "You know what? You should keep this. Give it a read through while you're eating your bonbons and tacos or whatever the hell you do."

He drops a hundred-dollar bill on the table like it's supposed to impress me and walks away. I keep my mouth shut as he leaves, trying not to show any emotion when I'm full of rage and anger. The second he's out the door, I let out the breath I've been holding and let my head fall onto my arms on the table.

"Miss, do you want another drink?"

I nod. "Yeah. Yeah, I think I need another."

I drink so much at the bar, Chase has to come pick me up. I thought about calling Dani, but she's already busy with her band tonight. I fall asleep in the car with my head against the cold glass of the window and instead of waking me up, Chase parks and comes around to carry me inside. I don't even bother to fight him; I'm in no shape for it anyhow. And he's too damn tall. I'm going to be in a world of hurt tomorrow.

He takes me upstairs and helps me get undressed before pulling one of his t-shirts over my head and tucking me into bed like I'm a child. He even kisses me on the head and leaves a glass of water and two pills on the nightstand before I black out.

I wake up screaming into Chase's arms as he rocks me, slowly pulling me out of the nightmare. When the world comes back into focus, I'm a hot, sweaty mess. I wipe my eyes and pull back a hand streaked with tears and mascara. I'm also convinced someone sat on my chest.

"You're okay, I've got you, Sunshine. I've got you, baby," he coos softly in my ear as the last of the nightmare fades away. Chase looks at me with that smile of his and I get butterflies. "Feel better? You kept screaming about signing something and the devil, so I ran up here to make sure you were okay."

I have to squint to focus on him, and it's not because my glasses are on the nightstand. There's a lump and a bruise forming under his eye. "Who hit you? I'll fuck them up!" I slur, still drunk, but ready to swing.

"Well, I'm not sure you could take her. She's short, but she's fiery."

"Oh my god, I hit you?!"

"Punched me right in the face, but I deserved it. I shouldn't have tried to hold you while you were still working on your left hook."

I reach up, touching his face as panic floods my body. He has a shoot tomorrow. "Chase! Oh my god! I fucked up your pretty face!"

"Good thing we're shooting a fight scene, huh? Makeup will have half the work already done for them. Now come on, I'll start a shower, see if that helps sober you up. I'll even wash your hair the way you like. Okay?"

I nod, but as he goes to move away, I grab his wrist and gasp, "Cynthia! We need Cynthia!"

"In the shower? That's a little weird."

"No, Chase!" I cringe and sink into my shoulders, knowing I

need to come clean. It's better right now anyhow, since I'm still lightheaded and angry from earlier. I'm less likely to chicken out. "I, uhm, I wasn't out with friends, but I didn't want to tell you because I wanted to know what the fuck he wanted first. I told backup to, so I had Mills."

"You mean you told Mills, so you'd have backup?"

"Yeah, that's what I said! Look, I didn't tell you because you'd punch his nose in, which he deserves! I almost punched that arrogant, racist pig."

"Which Los Angeles arrogant, racist pig are we talking about here, Ren? Not Mills, right?"

"No! Lawson!" His face drops and I regret both meeting with the jerk and not telling Chase about it. "I protected you! He called me the other day while you were being a prick, and he wanted to meet. He said it was about you, and I like you, so I wanted to talk about you. You were still all fucked up on emotions, so I meet him somewhere public and try not to kick him in the dick."

"That man has no dick."

I snort out a laugh before my jaw drops and I let out a huff. "That dickless fucker called me fat and offered to pay me to suck his dick! He didn't even offer me a magnifying glass?!"

"He did what?!"

"Shhhh," I slur. At least he's taking it better than I thought he would. "He showed me things from my past that he shouldn't even have, and I think he's working with my ex-husband."

"Fuck that guy, I'll call Cyn and we'll—"

"He's working with your stalker, too. Maybe." He stops, the color draining from his face. "He had Miley give me an envelope last night, and it had pictures of you. You were soooo young! He threatened to use Cassie's mom and make her say shit about you. It wasn't very nice."

"What the fuck?"

"Oh! He wanted me to break up with you for a hundred

thousand dollars because he's mad at you, but also because he has no dick."

Chase whistles long and low, shaking his head as he tries to unravel what I'm telling him. "Fuck. I'm not surprised he'd pull this shit. I don't work with him because of who he is and how he treats people. He's a fucking pig, and I have no problem telling people that."

"I called him a pig, too!" I scrunch my face together, staring at his eye. "Are you sure I punched you?"

"I've cost him a few dozen contracts by telling people how he treats people."

"You're...not mad at me? I punched you and not that fuckface."

"No, Sunshine." His dopey smile comes back. "No, you had valid reasons for what you did. You're right, too. If you'd have told me, I'd be in jail right now for assault. Besides, you're telling me now. It's not like you waited two months to say something, and you told Mills. I'll call Cyn in the morning. She's out of town, but she can at least get the ball rolling."

"Chase, why are you so calm about all this?"

"Oh, I'm not. I'm high, thankfully, but I'm definitely not calm." He leans over and kisses my forehead. "Now come on, beautiful, let's get you wet and naked. Possibly in that order."

"Yaay!" I throw my hands up and burp loudly. "Oops. I think I drank too much, Puppy."

HOLLYWOOD
Renate

CHAPTER 32
I WANNA BE YOURS
ARCTIC MONKEYS

MY ARM FLOPS across the bed, and while I'm expecting to hit the rock-hard chest of my super hot boyfriend, my arm keeps going until the soft, cold mattress finally stops the momentum. I crack an eye open as my hand feels around, as if he's shrunk himself down and I have to find him again, but I don't even find the wet noses of the dogs. I pick my head up and sniff the air. No bacon or waffles detected, so I roll over and grope around for my phone. I find a handwritten note next to it.

Good morning, to the beautiful woman who I found snoring in my bed this morning.

I'm in the gym with Steve, so if you come down naked, he'll stare at you, and I'll have to defend your honor and punch him in the nose a mere week before he's supposed to get married stateside.

Since Ethan, his half-Canadian husband-to-be, plays hockey, this will reprise the Treacherous

Canadian Ice Feud of the households akin to the Montagues and Capulets, but with better pancakes.

Speaking of, I'll make you some as soon as I'm done. In the meantime, since you have a long weekend, pack a bag. I have a surprise for you.

-CC

I'm reminded by the things he says and does that even I fall into the trap of his greatest acting skill—duping people into believing he's just another stupid actor. He plays that part to protect what's left of his sanity and because he's shy. But he's not an idiot—unless he's horny. He reads, follows politics more than most of us who were born in the US, and loves to learn or try new things.

It doesn't matter if he's the goofy idiot who wants to play, or a nerdy guy with his nose shoved in a book. I love them both.

I shower, pack a few things, and stop as the black bag sitting in the closet catches my eye. With a wicked grin, I crouch next to it, pulling out a few toys, and tucking the bag away again when I'm done. I hide everything I picked out in the bottom of my travel bag. He's not the only one who enjoys surprising people.

They're just coming in from the garage when I head downstairs. Chase tries to hug me, but I duck out of his reach and make him chase me around the living room while Steve yells about him having too much post-workout energy. I finally grab a pool towel and throw it at Chase before I race out to the patio and shut the door behind me.

"Don't you dare! You're all sweaty and I already showered!"

"Without me? Aww. Besides, you like it when I'm all hot and bothered for you!" he yells through the glass door before flashing me a pouty face, batting his eyes like a cartoon character. "Come on, beautiful."

"Promise me, no grabbing or hugging!"

"Fine. Come in here and properly meet Steve since his bitch ass didn't show last night."

"What?! I promised Lala I'd be there, bro!"

I'm cautious as I slide the door open, but I give in when Chase holds up the towel with a shrug. He wraps it around me so he can give me a hug without covering me with sweat. "Fuck, you smell incredible. You get my note, Sunshine?"

"I did, Puppy. What's the surprise?"

"Tell you later, but not till I have to." He turns to Steve, who I'm pretty sure has been staring at my ass the whole time. I didn't expect his sheepish grin from all the stories I've heard about him and his reputation. We've met already, but only in quick passing as he's coming into the house and I'm leaving.

I thought Chase had muscles until now, because standing here and staring at Steve? I could do this all day. He's built like a fucking truck and more. Chase has better hair and a better smile, and if I'm being honest, I hope he never has to get my Chase that big. But Steve's still fun to stare at. I'm sure he thinks the same about my ass.

"Hi, I'm Steve," he chokes out nervously before adding, "I have a boyfriend."

"Husband," Chase corrects.

"Only in Italy."

"That's not how that works, dumbass. Now, stop ogling my girl or I'll tell Ethan. And Dev." Chase smacks him hard in the arm, making him wince and pulling his eyes away from me.

"I swear, I'm not! Wait, did you just call me a bitch ass because I went to my husband's game instead of being here?"

"Steve has made progress in his recovery from *fucking anything that walks* syndrome. In fact, he's so busy with his recovery—which I think—involves a lot of sex with his husband, he hasn't even had time to meet my damn girlfriend," Chase explains to me, smiling and teasing Steve the entire time. "I'm sure Dani told you about him, right?"

"She has, but I've also heard a lot about you from Jamie, Lexi, Chase, and Devin. So, don't worry, I'm sure you're nothing like anything they said. Are you staying for breakfast?"

"Yes, he is. Come on, Stevie. Gimme a hand in the kitchen, yeah? Ren, you're the best, baby." He tosses the towel aside and picks me up, spinning me around while he kisses me and I scream at him. He ignores me. "Oh no! Now you need another shower! With me this time. Two-person minimum, remember?"

I've learned that Chase's group of friends all have unique bonds between each other—even Dani. With Jamie, Chase behaves the most like himself, but with the others, he's picked up a part of their personality and made it his own when they're near. Steve gives him an equal amount of shit talking back, and even smacks him in the back of the head a few times for good measure. I sit back and watch the two clowns. It's better than those reality shows Mama watches.

"So," I interrupt after a low dig by Chase. "You have a husband, but you're getting married again?"

"Yeah. Fucking crazy, right? I mean, I tried teaching Chase here the art of the playboy life—no offense. He sucked at it. Anyway, I met Ethan at one of Chase's parties about a year and a half ago. It got off to a shaky start, but I got him to say yes. We got married in Italy last month while Lala—uhh, Ethan—had a break for the All-Star game. We thought about waiting for the off-season, but his folks are in town for the Boston games, so it works out."

"That's so sweet, having two weddings."

"Did you pack your bag?" Chase asks before slamming his coffee back.

"I did, not sure why, though."

"I'm taking you somewhere, obviously. I had to work while

you were on your Spring Break, so think of it as a second, shorter break. Steve's gonna take Pongo and Lulu, and we're going on a little adventure."

"You're sure that's smart?"

"Yep. Mills and Cyn will let me know if anything blows up while we're gone. Oh, and before you ask, yes, you'll be back in time for school on Monday. Promise." He drops another waffle on my plate. "Eat up, because we're gonna have a late lunch. We'll bring the leftovers to snack on in case we get hungry."

Two hours later, we're on the road headed north out of Los Angeles on the Pacific Coast Highway. The weather isn't too warm yet, so the windows are down and I'm watching the scenery pass by as Chase sings along to his playlist.

"Shit, I've never been this far north before. At least not on this side."

"What? Seriously?" He looks over at me for a second. "Okay, eyes ahead. Trust me."

He takes my hand, kisses my knuckles, and nods toward the road ahead. I'm not sure what I'm waiting for, though. So far, I've seen a ton of trees and random freeway stuff, just like it has been for the last hour.

I gasp as we come around a corner and I'm met with a stunning view of the ocean. The beautiful view leaves me speechless.

"You spend too much time in the city."

"Something tells me you're going to change that."

"Damn right."

"We used to go to the beach as kids. I always looked for the animals, but all I ever saw were birds." Even now, I'm staring out at the water, looking for any signs of life. "Mama saw a big shark fin while out fishing with my father once.

"You've never seen anything?"

"I've never even been to an aquarium. I haven't seen much beyond the Shark Week programming I watch with my class."

"Shark week? For robotics kids?"

"I use it to promote pushing the limits of computers and technology. Most of them question it, like you did. Forgetting about submarines and exploratory robots that give us more insight into ocean life we can't safely reach."

"Fair. I never thought of that."

We've been driving next to the water for an hour, and the road ahead turns away from the ocean view. As we continue on our trip, I turn back for one last look. "Oh no, I didn't take any pictures! Shit!"

"We'll be back this way, don't worry. Besides, you're going to take a ton of pictures when we stop for lunch." He glances over and winks at me. His hand wanders up my thigh, squeezing it. The speed that I just went from wishing I could see a dolphin to wishing I could ride this man like a bull makes my head spin.

"God, I can't wait to get you alone later. Maybe I'll pull over and stop at a shady motel for a couple of hours."

"Yeah, I can see those headlines now. Dive motels, sex, and drugs. Cynthia will fire you as a client. How did she even handle you trying to be a playboy like Steve?"

"I avoided stupid shit." He goes silent and I worry I've overstepped, but after a pause, he adds, "I sucked at it. Steve's a natural, charismatic and open to his wild side. Even when I'd work up the nerve to take a woman home, I'd be out of the house before she woke up, leaving her flowers and a note saying it isn't going to work out."

"You'd leave them alone in your home with a note? Brave of you. I'm glad I didn't know about that before I got the note this morning, or I might have done something only slightly out of character."

"One of them took a kitchen knife to my sofa."

"Clever, but amateur," I reply. He smiles at me with a wink. I glance around again and have a full-blown fuck it moment, reaching over and sliding my hand up his leg. "How about I pay you back for still being there when I woke up this morning?"

"Now that's a headline. I'd probably crash the car into a tree with the way you give head."

"Why don't you pull over, big shot?"

"I can't believe I'm saying this, but we can do that later. I don't want to miss…something."

I still haven't figured out where we're going when Chase pulls off the freeway and we drive into this small beach town. I'm so used to the busy beaches of Los Angeles that this slow, relaxed lifestyle could be an alien planet. I gawk at all the little shops, cute homes, and the sprinkling of people wandering about. He parks by the docked boats near a long pier and my head pivots, trying to take it all in. He's opening my door for me before I notice he's even out of the car. He grabs our coats from the back and holds my hand as we walk down the pier. It's old, and the wood creaks a little as we walk by a handful of people fishing off the side.

"I used to go to the beach with my father and we'd build sand castles. Baby Dani cried about the sand for an hour." He squeezes my hand and we stop walking, but I'm too busy watching a young girl reel in a fish to turn around. "I dreamed about living in one of those castles one day. Too many movies with princes saving the princesses, I guess. What about you, what did you dream—" I turn back to Chase, but he's not looking at me. He's staring down at a small box in his hand. There's a lump in my throat and I remember the conversation at breakfast about how quickly his friend jump from dating to marriage..

"I used to dream I'd… I'd have a family. I mean, I have Devin, but that's not exactly what I mean."

"Chase Cooper, if that's a ring—"

"No!" He replies too quickly, and winces. "I mean, it is, but not like that. It's not a, I'm not going to ask you…I mean. Wait, if I asked? What would you say?"

I roll my eyes at the question. "I'd say yes, you're an idiot!"

"I mean, yeah, but…it's definitely not a ring. It's only earrings." He lets go of my hand and opens the box, holding it out for me to see. Two beautiful gold sunflowers with diamonds in the middle sparkle back at me in the late afternoon sun. They're stunning, and they look more expensive than any jewelry I've ever owned. "Do you like them? I figured these would work since I call you Sunshine and your tattoo."

"Chase, you didn't need to do this."

"Buy stuff for my girl? Yeah, you better get used to that. It's kind of my thing. Fuck, by now I would normally have given you tons of flowers and jewelry, but life keeps getting in the way, and you're not like that." He brushes the hair out of my face, but the wind blows it right back. "I want the things I give you to mean something, not compulsory buys because we're dating."

I've never in my life had a man put earrings on me before, but the sparks on my skin and the heat building in my stomach as he attaches the backing makes me think I could get used to it. When he secures the second one, he steps back to look at me with a giant grin.

"You're beautiful."

"*They* are beautiful."

"They're barely noticeable on someone as stunning as you, Sunshine." His hands take my face and he pulls my lips to his, stealing the last pieces of my heart that were trying hard to hold out against his charms. I never stood a chance of dodging him. "Things have been upside down for a while now, and my filming schedule doesn't let up anytime soon. So, I wanted you to know that I love you, and I'm going to do better. For you. For us."

"I love you, too, Chase, and I'll be here with you to hold you to that."

"Say it again…but the other name."

"I love you, too," I grin and pause as he eagerly awaits his name. "My puppy."

"Perfection. Just like you."

We walk hand in hand to a small restaurant at the end of the pier. It's cute, with colorful stools along the pier overlooking the water. There's a noise as we head to our seat, like a strange sounding dog. When I turn to see, I pull Chase to a stop and stand there, fixated on a dozen sea lions, sunning themselves on a floating piece of wood. They're all barking and one of them slides off into the water, splashing around. My heart races and I can't believe my eyes. They're real. The sea lions are real. Not on a screen or a picture, not behind glass, but real and right here in front of me.

"Sea lions. Those are sea lions, Chase!"

"Yep. Hold on, you've never even seen a sea lion? I thought you just meant you hadn't seen dolphins and sharks. Weren't you born in LA?" I nod, unable to speak as I watch them. "Come on, let's go sit and I'll show you the otters."

"The what?!" My eyes are probably bugging out of my head as I stare at him and make pawing motions with my hands. "Otters? Like, little furry…otters?"

He kisses my forehead with a laugh before he drags me off to our table. I don't listen to what he orders, too busy leaning over the railing like a child and watching the marine life go about their day. I damn near fall in when the pod of dolphins swims by. As I watch, I spot something off in the distance and I freeze, staring hard at the water and hoping it happens again. The dark hump comes up again, followed by a giant flipper and a spray of water high in the air. Whales. My whole life, I've only ever seen seagulls and the random pelican. Now, I've seen so many things that my head might explode.

He comes up behind me, wrapping his arms around my waist and resting his head on top of mine as the wind picks up. I never want to leave. The pier. The serene little sea town. His arms. I've never felt this happy, and all I needed to make it happen was the right man, a few hours in a car, and a pier.

HOLLYWOOD
Chase

CHAPTER 33
BAD THINGS

JACE EVERETT

I'VE NAILED this trip so far. I came close to a panic attack when I researched everything, worried she'd find it stupid or boring. The second she spotted the ocean from the car, I knew from the look on her face I hadn't fucked this up. And the animals? I expected a few sea lions, but the whales?! I couldn't have paid for a better turnout. I had to drag her away from the pier, promising we could come back another time—maybe even on the way home.

"Puppy, if you're taking me to some motel to kill me after showing me otters and whales, I'm kind of okay with it." She looks around as we pull into the driveway. She's right, from here the place looks pretty damn strange. Especially with the sun setting.

"Show a girl a couple of whales and she's ready to become a crime documentary."

"Are you saying I'm easy, Mr. Cooper?"

I park and run in to get the key. I spent hours on the website for this hotel after Lexi mentioned the place. She warned me about the campiness, and when I flipped through the pictures, I booked our room right away.

"Room one five seven. Enjoy your stay, sir."

Each room has its own distinct look and theme, but I had more in mind when I picked ours. I almost picked the one with a bed made from what looked like an old stagecoach—we're getting that room next time. Instead, I opted for the room with two king-size beds that face each other, a fireplace, and a soaking tub. It's not the most adventurous room they have, but it's a start.

When Ren walks into our room, she almost falls over, laughing. It's the reaction I prepared for, and I'm laughing right alongside her.

There's a giant stone fireplace that looks like it's part of a damn mountain coming out of the wall. The floor has wall-to-wall deep, plush magenta carpeting, and the furniture screams antique rejects. On the other side of the room sit two four-poster beds, foot-to-foot, with only a small space between them. Impossible, ridiculous, perfect—the accurate definition of campy. I might go down to the office and book out a year's worth of stays in different rooms after seeing this.

"What should we do first? Want me to start a bath?" I ask as I throw myself onto a bed, bouncing a bit.

"Maybe we'll do that later." She picks up the bottle of champagne and walks over to me, climbing onto the bed and straddling my stomach. "How about you open this, and I slip into something less comfortable before I show you what I packed?" I take the bottle as she kisses my nose, my chest, and even the tent forming in my pants before she takes her bag and disappears into the bathroom.

As soon as she shuts the door, I'm uncorking the champagne, pouring two glasses, and ripping my clothes off as fast as I can. I laugh as I pull off my shoes and almost fall over. No one has ever made me this delirious with excitement before. Sure, I've had decent sex before, but this? This is *I'm gonna need a cigarette when I'm finished* sex.

The one thing I'm looking forward to most on this trip has

nothing to do with sex, though. The uninterrupted time together, holding the woman I love in my arms as we fall asleep, and not answering our phones. I run to my bag and dig to the bottom, making sure I remembered to pack the other box just in case.

I'm not sure if my knees or my jaw hit the floor first when the knob clicks and the door opens. She's in pink leather lingerie with straps and chains. There's even a little fishnet skirt accentuating her already perfect ass. I lick my lips as my eyes try to take it all in, but it's hard to think. She's fucking gorgeous.

"Already on your knees for me? Such a good boy." She walks over and ruffles my hair before grabbing a fistful and pulling my head back. "I like when you're below me. Do you like it when I tower over you for a change?"

"Yes, my queen." I'm far too enamored to argue that she's only a few inches taller than eye level. Not exactly towering, but enough.

She takes my chin between her thumb and forefinger, squeezing as she stares into my eyes. "Someone's working hard for a reward, aren't they? So eager you forgot to take off your shirt, Mr. Cooper?" She's using her teacher's tone, and I'm about to melt into this crazy carpet. "Take off your shirt, pretty boy."

I reach back with one hand and pull my t-shirt over my head, holding it out to her like an offering to a goddess. My goddess.

"And what would my good little boy want for a reward, hmm?" She moves behind me, running her fingers through my hair while her nails slide over my scalp.

The question throws me off since I'm used to her asking about my punishments, not my rewards. Of course, I'm usually being a pain in the ass by this point. "I—I want to please you?"

She steps back in front of me and her smile hypnotizes me right until her hand connects with my face.

SMACK.

I almost fall over, not prepared for that at all. She helps me back up, checking my face with soft, warm hands. The coldness leaves her eyes as she makes sure I'm okay.

"I'm sorry, baby. I shouldn't hit you in the face."

"It's okay, my queen. I...I want...will you do it again?"

Her head pulls back in surprise. "Chase, your face is kind of your brand, honey."

"I don't have any shoots for a few days, so long as you only use your hand, we'll be okay."

"You're sure?"

"Yes, my queen," I smirk. "Smack me, spit in my mouth, do anything you want to me."

"Alright," she smirks as she stands again. "I have some toys in the bag. Why don't you crawl over there and pick out the ones you want to play with?"

"Yes, my queen!" I'm not the slightest bit humiliated about crawling over to her bag while she watches me. Why should I be when she's complimenting my ass the whole way? When I open the bag, I'm overwhelmed by the possibilities. My brain shuts down, and my hand reaches in and pulls out the first thing I find —an orange and teal silicon unicorn horn.

I swallow hard and crawl back to her, handing her my offering. I'm so busy staring at the thing, I don't watch what she's doing. Not until she fists a handful of hair and pulls hard, forcing me to look at the thing. She's attached the horn to a harness and I salivate.

"Good choice, Puppy. I wouldn't want to start you with one of the bigger ones."

She has dildos shaped like the giant cocks of mythical beasts, not just unicorn horns. I found them when I went through her bag a few days ago. When she stands in front of me, hands on her hips, sweat beads on my forehead. I might only be me, but it's boiling in here, and I'm as hard as the goddamn fireplace mountain rocks.

"Safe word?"

"O-octopus."

"Good, now open your mouth and relax your throat. Just like I showed you."

The old me would have argued about this, saying I wasn't into it. The new me? He opens his mouth like the greedy slut he is. All for her.

"Eyes up, Puppy. Tap my leg if you can't speak." She grips my hair and pushes my head down onto her unicorn horn dick. This one has a longer shaft and thicker base than the one she usually shoves in my mouth. I reach up and grab her hips, directing her thrusts and pushing her deeper with every word of praise and moan she rewards me with. Any noise she makes lights another fire inside me. I want more.

She pulls her hips away, and I let go of the toy with a soft pop. "My, what a greedy little whore you are. Are you ready for your reward?" I'm panting and give her a drunken half grin. She wipes the tears from my eyes and holds out her hand, motioning for me to stand.

"Hands behind your back."

I follow her command and watch her fingers guide my boxers down my legs, letting my cock spring out. There's a rush of euphoria when my cock thinks it's going to get attention, but she stares at it like it's in a museum.

"You're already making a mess, puppy." She licks the pre-cum from my tip and I groan. "Get on the bed on your hands and knees."

Once I'm in position, she tucks a pillow up by my head and two under my stomach.

"Ass up, head down. DO NOT forget the safe word, Puppy."

The snap of a cap opening sounds like gunfire and I can't control my breathing. It's not a panic attack, not anxiety. Hell, I don't know what to call it—anticipation? She's talking to me, but the roar of blood rushing through me deafens me. She knows how to get my attention.

SMACK! It's only her hand on my bare ass, but holy fuck, it's incredible. It's a sting followed by warmth that spreads through my whole body.

"What color are you?"

"Green, my queen…what…uhm…are you…?"

"I'm going to fuck you," she hums, her hands rubbing the heat of my ass cheek. "Like I said when you weren't paying attention, I need you to relax and take calming breaths. I've got lube, and you'll be okay. If it gets to be too much, what do you do?"

"Octopus."

"Good. If you can't say it for whatever reason, hit the mattress, and I'll stop right away." She's rubbing her glistening fingers together and I swallow hard. "Are you ready to have the best orgasm of your life, pretty boy?"

"Yes, my queen."

The smell of coconut fills the air as she rubs the slick out over my ass. She even helps me relax by playing the bongos on my cheeks and rubbing the horn between them as she eases me into this.

"Cynthia was right, Puppy. You have a super cute little butt." She cackles and positions herself. "Okay, one finger."

There's pressure, it's not too bad, it's just…weird. She's taking it slow like she said she would and she's talking me through everything. No secrets, no surprises. I try holding my breath when she announces she's going for a second finger, but her free hand rubs my back gently as she coaxes a breath out of me. There's a noise, it sounds so foreign, but it's coming from me.

"Do you like that, puppy?" I'm glad she has small hands, especially when the third finger goes in, stretching me and searching for that perfect angle. She knows when she hits it, too. Her fingers curl and I'm off the mattress, back arched till I'm almost bent in half.

"Oh, fuck! Yes. YES! Please, please don't stop, Ren."

"Do you want me to fuck you with my pretty cock now?"

"Y-yes."

She pulls her fingers out, leaving me with this strange, empty feeling that doesn't last long. She adds more coconut oil, and the cold sends a shiver up my spine, making me gasp.

"Breathe, handsome. Let me take care of you. Here we go. You've got this, Chase."

"I love you, Ren," I mumble with my face buried in the pillow.

"I love you too, Puppy."

The tip of the horn pushes against me as she offers me praise and rubs my back. I hug around the pillow, moaning and biting the fabric. When the tip finally pushes through, I throw my head back and release a wail followed by a string of swears.

"You're okay, baby. You're doing so good," she coaches, holding my hips the way I hold hers.

"More!" I yell out. The euphoric bands of electricity shooting through my fingertips as my toes curl. "Fuck your filthy whore, my queen!"

She rocks her hips, thrusting with short, shallow rolls of her hips. "Atta boy, taking my cock so well, aren't you?"

It's not enough, I need more. I rock my hips, pushing my ass against her. "OH JESUS! OH FUCKING FUCK!"

"Color, Chase?"

"Fuck me harder! I'm green. I'm green!"

"Do you want to take it all? Every inch of me in your pretty, tight ass?"

"Yes, my queen."

I've died, and ended up in the weirdest, kinkiest, most fucking phenomenal sex heaven. She sets a slow pace, not wanting to hurt me, and every word she says to me is laced with the rush she's getting from this. I'm lost somewhere in between pain and pleasure, as I hug the pillow harder and push back onto her.

"We need a mirror so you can see how pretty you look right now, letting me fill that pretty hole of yours while you fall apart.." Her hand travels up my spine and into my hair, teasing and playing. I let out another primal groan into the pillow and she smacks my ass again. "You've got a greedy little cunt, don't you, Puppy? Now, let go of that pillow. I need your beautiful voice to pray to me."

"Y-YES MY QUEEN! Oh, shit!"

I push onto my elbows, taking over the power dynamic and fucking my own ass while I jerk myself off. I can't hear myself screaming because of the roar in my ears, but there's soreness in my throat. My fingers dig into the sheets so hard my knuckles are white.

"I'm… I'm gonna—"

SMACK!

"AHH, FUCK!" I scream out. My head whips back and my scalp stings from how hard she pulls, but fuck, I love it. The dynamic shifts again as she forces my head down and takes over again, slowing down her thrusts and rolling her hips at her own pace.

"Do you need to use the safe word, Puppy?"

I shake my head into the mattress. "Don't stop! Harder! Please, my queen?"

"Good boys beg for their asses to be fucked, Mr. Cooper."

"Holy shit. Please keep fucking my ass? Please? You feel so good, baby. I need it. I need your big cock in my ass!" I no longer have control of my words, letting them pour out and hoping like hell they're the ones she wants me to say.

"That's better." Her calm voice sounds jarring against my wild, unhinged screams. "You like that thick cock in your tight little ass, don't you?"

"Y-YES! OH FUUUUUUCK!" I shout as she slams into me

again and everything inside me tightens. Shockwaves shoot through me and detonate fireworks in my vision every time her hips slam against my ass.

I'm worried I'll pass out until she yanks my head back again. I'm fisting the sheets as I rock with her, finding the rhythm so we're no longer fighting one another for control. She has it, she always has. I can't stop, though. Every inch of me burns for her. The tightness in my stomach will give way soon, and my fist can't pump any faster.

"Please! I'm gonna… I wanna come. Please, my queen?" Her hand comes down on my ass again and I damn near come, but she has fucking rules and I'm trying like hell to follow them. I let out another strangled cry of ecstasy just as her hips rock and thrust into me again.

"Such a good boy. Can you hear how pretty you sound while I fuck you? While I own your tight little ass."

I'm shedding every last shred of control, losing parts of myself in the most primitive, animalistic way I can imagine. My mind becomes static, my vision becomes a snowstorm. Her voice cuts through the noise in my mind as she whispers, "Let go for me, Chase."

Her fingers find my hand. I scream her name one more time, throat hoarse and tight as ropes of cum shoot onto the bed, the pillow, my chest, fucking everywhere. The world goes black.

Her voice sounds far away as she tells me how good I did, soothing me, rubbing my back. I'm too far gone to open my eyes, drifting away into my mind. Not a care in the world because she's here, and she'll take care of me.

When I open my eyes again, I'm on my side with a clean blanket over me. She's holding my head in her lap, combing her fingers through my hair and singing softly.

She didn't lie—that was the best orgasm I've had in my whole fucking life. My hands reach around her waist as I nuzzle into her soft belly. I'm exhausted and could sleep for an entire week after that.

"How do you feel?"

"Infuckingcredible," I mumble against the fabric of her corset. My fingers drunkenly fumbling with the ties in the back.

"Good. You did amazing, baby. Come on, lift your head so you can get some water."

I shift around so I can sit up, careful not to take it too fast. I'm surprised I'm not more sore, but she's done this before. She holds my drink, offering me a straw. I glance down and find my hands shaking. I also find that she's cleaned off my chest while I blacked out. I drink the whole damn bottle and half of a second one while she giggles and sips on champagne. When I curl back in next to her, she feeds me fruit and the best chocolate I've ever tasted. "No one's ever taken care of me after sex, not like this."

"I'll take care of you, Chase. From now on, I'll make sure you're praised and worshiped, just like you take care of me."

"Can we do that again? Like another time?"

"I'd love to, Puppy. You looked so perfect when you lost control for me. Like artwork." She brushes my hair back, and a whimper finds its way out of me. "Does anything hurt?"

I shake my head, finding the string from earlier and pulling it. Her breasts spill out of her corset, and I wrap around her again, resting my head on her bare chest.

I'm losing the battle with sleep and I glance up at her through lazy eyes, remembering something she said at the pier. "You know, you don't need a prince to save you, Ren."

"I don't?"

"Fuck no. You're not a princess, Renate Silva. You're a fucking queen. You're my queen."

Her soft laughter becomes even softer kisses as she pulls the blanket over me again. Just before I drift off, she whispers, "I love you so much, Chase Cooper. I'm so glad you found me. So glad you're my king."

HOLLYWOOD
Chase

CHAPTER 34
DESIRE

MEG MYERS

I FLOP down on the couch, working one shoe off with the toe of the other, while covering my face with a pillow before the dogs can slobber all over me. Between the three television interviews for the movie going to Cannes and my therapy appointment, I'm fucking beat. It takes a minute before I notice I'm missing two dogs climbing all over me and begging for attention. I don't even hear their toes tapping around anywhere in the house. But it would be hard to hear that over the loud Latin music coming from the backyard.

Pulling the pillow away and tossing it to the other side of the couch, I lean over to get a better view of the patio. This isn't the pool cleaner's jam, and not Devin's either, but he's at the rink anyhow. I spot Pongo laying on his bed, and Lulu as she bounces around with one of her toys. There's movement and I find the reason for the music and why the dogs are ignoring me. Ren bends over into a pose on her mat—showing off her perfect ass and thick thighs. God, I love yoga pants.

She's been trying meditation and yoga to see if it helps with the stiffness in her joints. In reality, she's doing it because she's sick and tired of everyone recommending it, so now she'll be able to tell them to fuck all the way off. Although, the view I have right now has me hopeful it will work for her. I check the clock and see there's still plenty of time before the guys should be here for the game.

Ren stands up again into a tree pose, holds it, and switches into a cat pose. She's on her hands and knees with her back bowed, pushing her ass up higher. I'm relieved that she doesn't do yoga naked because I'm sure I would have just died. Instead, I unbutton my pants and shove my hand into my boxers. She gives her ass a little shake as my thumb slides over the tip of my cock and I can't hold back the moan. I want her so fucking bad, but this could be fun.

Admiring her like this feels a little pervy and a lot voyeuristic, but that's also making it even hotter. I'm biting my lip so hard I should taste blood any minute now, but I'm focused elsewhere while I continue my long, slow strokes. I picture her red lips, perfect and parted as I slide into her mouth. How fucking incredible she feels when I hit the back of her throat. The thought of that thing she does before she rolls her tongue makes my hips jerk upward. I'm imagining what it would be like to have my face buried in her while she's trying to balance.

She looks like a fucking angel out there, the sun in her hair and that skin tight outfit on. My hand pumps faster, slick pre-cum beading on the tip. I don't want my hand; I want her. All of her. But there's something about seeing her like this that's making me lose my mind.

She goes into the child pose with her hand in her leggings as she plays with herself for me. My hips roll at the sight, wanting to slam up against those fucking thighs. She sits up again, still not turning to look at me as she hooks her thumbs into her leggings and pulls them over her ass. She goes right back into child pose, sliding her thong to the side so I have a front-row seat to her soaking wet cunt.

There's a loud, pornographic moan that isn't coming from

me. "Chaaase," she whines so loud the neighbors could hear her. Not that I give a fuck. "I need your big fucking cock right now."

Like she has a leash on me, I'm up and leaving my pants behind as I hurry out to the pool. "Lulu, Pongo, inside." I don't even wait to make sure they listen, kneeling behind her, spreading her cheeks wide, and diving my tongue into that glistening pussy I love so damn much.

"Oh yeah, just like that baby," she coos, still rubbing her clit in tight little circles while I devour her. I grab her legs, pulling them wider apart before I hook my arms under them and lift her to my mouth. She has to stop playing with herself so she doesn't fall over, but my tongue takes the place of her fingers and she's crooning my fucking name. Mine. Because I'm the one about to make her come so hard she sees stars. My fucking stars.

Her body shakes and I can feel the orgasm ripping through her. I drop her back onto the mat, keeping her elbows on the ground and her ass up. A second later, I bury my cock deep inside her quivering pussy as she screams my name again.

"Atta girl, Christ, you feel amazing." I lean over her, grabbing her tit and squeezing while I lick the shell of her ear. "You enjoy teasing me, don't you? Putting that pussy on display and making me wait for it. What if Steve came over early and saw you out here like this? What if the pool guy found your fingers in *my* pussy? Saw you out here, dripping wet and begging for someone's cock to fill you up."

"You like that, don't you Puppy? The thought of some other man watching me, seeing how much I beg for your cock?"

"Maybe, so long as they never touch you."

"It's your cock I want, Puppy. Only yours."

There's no thought left in my mind beyond her, how much I need her. I'm a mess of grunts and thrusts, whimpers, and slapping skin. It's fucking beautiful.

"Harder, Chase. Oh, fuck!"

I wrap my arms around her, pulling her body up so her back

presses against my chest. I haven't stopped fucking her in deep, hard thrusts, and I can't wait to see the bruises on my legs tomorrow. I've got one hand around her throat and the other pinching and teasing her swollen clit.

"Fuck, I love when you scream for my cock, pretty girl. You like that, huh? Like me fucking you hard till you black out? Tell me you want that, my goddess? For me to fuck you stupid?"

"God, yes! Yes!"

I squeeze her neck, and she's coming all over my cock. There's grunting and swearing, and it takes a moment to realize it's coming from me. I'm some kind of fucking animal right now as the rush of warmth spreads over my thighs. "You like that, my queen? Does my cock make you feel fucking good?"

She reaches up and back, finding my hair and pulling hard as her body rocks, fucking herself on me, using me. The pressure builds, telling me it won't be long now..

"Fucking use me, Renate. Come again, please, come again before I can't hold it anymore. Use me like the whore I am for you. That's all I wanna be, you're fucking play thing."

We're tangled together in the most perfect euphoric cloud as we both let go together. I catch her before we collapse, and roll to my side, still holding her to me as I bury my head in her soft, damp hair.

"I love you. I love you so much, Renate," I huff out, trying to breathe. We weren't supposed to love each other. We agreed to casual fuck buddies and nothing more. I'm so glad that failed so miserably, because now I get to hold her, and tell her how much I love her. I get to worship her for all she is, body and brains. I belong to her as much as she belongs to me. It's a bliss I never thought I'd feel.

"My sweet, perfect Puppy." She pulls my head back down to her shoulder and strokes my hair as she whispers to me and coos in my ear. I'm crying again. I don't even know who I am anymore, crying after sex, telling her I love her every minute of the day, needing her like a drug. This isn't me, but I don't want to go back to my old life. I just want her and everything she does to me.

I pull my head up and my lips find hers while my hand slides to her face, holding her in a fierce but tender way as our mouths tangled like the world doesn't exist. The shit with Lawson, the stalker, her ex, all of that could have torn us apart, but every obstacle brings us closer together. She's left marks on my skin and my soul that I hope never fade.

"Don't leave me," I whisper as we break for air. The years of games and bullshit are catching up to me and pushing all my abandonment issues to the surface, but for once in my life, I don't want to let go. I don't want to let her go. I need to be hers or I'm nothing.

"I'm right here, Chase. Right where I belong." She strokes my hair before wiping the tears away. "We should get dressed. Cynthia will be here soon, and you boys are watching Dev's game."

"Shit, I forgot about her coming over."

"Chase?" I hum my response into her shoulder as I kiss and nip at her soft skin. "I love you, too, my Puppy."

"So, do we think he's in cahoots with your stalker?" Cynthia asks as she pours herself a drink. "I mean, I wouldn't put it past him, but it seems a little—"

"Not just the stalker. He's working with my ex, too. Luis spent too much time hanging around where he shouldn't be, telling my mother lies. Lawson knew about that and other things I hadn't told anyone about."

"He's got connections, so I'm not surprised by any of this. He and Chase have butted heads more times than those damn rams on nature documentaries. I don't know about them, but it sure as fuck gives *me* a headache."

She sits at the table across from Ren and they talk while I continue zoning out across the room. I'm replaying memories, all the times Lawson has pissed me off in the past. It's not a long list since I try to avoid him, but none of our interactions went well. I'm known as a nice guy, and, except for that prick, I usually am. But he should have gone down long before I had to bother with him.

"Chase, are you even listening to us?" Cyn asks, pulling me back to the conversation.

"What? Sorry, no. I, uhm, guess I got a little in my head."

"Well, get your head out of your ass for ten minutes and get over here. Ren asked what happened between you and Mr. Personality."

Oh, uhm, I met him almost five years ago. He wanted to cast me for a movie and I came pretty close to signing on, but I found out about the wage gap between my co-star, Rosie Johnston, and me."

"Rosie?! No, that's so fucked up." Ren replies and I remember how enamored she got when Rosie sat next to her. "Why do you people go to his fake ass charity functions after he fucks you all over like this?"

"Publicity," Cyn answers.

"Ugh, always. How bad of a difference?"

"A few extra zeros at the end of the paycheck. I called him on it, and he refused to budge, so I backed out of the project. People knew me by then from a few of the higher grossing movies I'd done, so people noticed."

"Yeah, people tend to take notice of a twenty million dollar hit to avoid a court date. Rosie got her friends together and had every intention of fighting him harder if he'd gone to court.

"So this all comes down to contracts and equal pay?" Ren asks Cynthia.

"Oh, you bet your Cooper's cute little butt it is. Twenty million doesn't sound like a lot in terms of Hollywood money, but baby, you and Rosie set off a firestorm. He's seen every single contract you've turned down from his studio or studios linked to it. It made agents shy away from anything with his name anywhere near it. Last year, he had to shelve ten movies because no one with a name wanted to sign on."

"Wait, he still sends me contacts?"

"Yep, and I've rejected every one of them, like we agreed." With a heavy sigh, Cyn tosses two stacks of paper over to me. One stack has Cynthia's name, and the other, mine. "He has one of these fucked up contracts for each of us."

"Still blackmail!" Ren yells and Cyn nods.

"He'll try to use each of us to take out the other. He's an old man with idiotic grudges and more money than God. Except, he's not."

"Huh?"

"He's financially fucked six ways to Sunday, Chase. Has been for years. Lives well above his means and makes promises he can't keep. He has a string of lawyers he owes money to, and backers that have never seen a finished product or a dime in return. He also owes money for harassment cases he settled out of court. Hell, I'd be surprised if he could even get the money together to pay Ren off if she did sign this. It's a sinking ship, and he's decided you two are going down with him."

"Do you always use so many idioms?" Ren says, chuckling. Cyn laughs and responds with a shrug. "There's a lot of that— what do you call it—when it's all stories from other people and not the source?"

"Hearsay?"

"Yeah! He's coming after us with a lying, drugged up son of a bitch and a stalker obsessed with Chase as his ammunition? That's the best he's got?" Cynthia nods in agreement and shrugs.

"He's scraping the bottom of the barrel and he's using shit that won't stick to Chase. At least not for long."

"You ever thought about going into politics?" Cyn asks with a laugh.

"No. I can't even get myself a raise and a promotion to department head," Ren cackles.

"We still need to stay on our toes with what he does next. It doesn't take much of a controversy to bury an A-lister, because people don't care about the truth." She takes a deep breath. "Before we do this, I need to know you're both on board. If one of you needs to back out, do it now, before this shit hits the public eye."

"Oh, I'm all in. Let's fuck this guy up!" Ren shouts.

"You could lose your job in this, Sunshine. Are you sure?"

Ren thinks for a minute before nodding. "Someone needs to stand up to that dickhead. Plus it means I'm fighting alongside Rosie. Lawson and the principal of the school know each other, which puts my job in jeopardy, anyhow. If I help take down Lawson, there's a better chance I still have my job at the end of all this."

"God, I love you."

"Alright, I'll put together team Screw This Guy," Cyn says, staring at me. "Also, we're at the 'I love you' stage? Congrats. I've got to go meet with Mills and Dr. Clay. It's easier to clean up after a sex scandal than all this shit. Good thing I like you, Cooper."

HOLLYWOOD
Renate

CHAPTER 35
THE CHAIN

FLEETWOOD MAC

ONE MORE DAY.

I haven't taken a vacation in years, and when I did, I spent them recovering from something Luis did. This isn't any vacation, either. Chase booked our flights the second I got the approval. I'm going to France! He's taking me as his guest to Cannes! I'm certain I died and whichever god rules over Heaven, she gave me her sweetest angel, Chase.

So, as soon as class lets out tomorrow, a driver is picking me up and taking me to the airport. I'll meet Chase in New York before we fly to Paris together. I loaded my tablet with books and packed all my bags last night so Dani can drop me off at work in the morning.

Sleep won't be a thing tonight.

For now, I'm getting a bit of a break, watching over the class as they take a test. My phone buzzes on the desk, and I grab for it so it doesn't distract anyone.

> SNUGGLE PUPPY
>
> I can't wait to see you tomorrow.
>
> I wish I could fly you here tonight…I mean, I could.

I smile. I do that so much more now than I did in the past. Lexi and Dani have a bet going that he's going to propose to me on the trip. I told them both they were nuts, but it wouldn't surprise me. Mama made me promise not to rush into it. But I reminded her it has only been four months, and we're not ready for that kind of commitment.

> I have to go to work tomorrow, you know that.

SNUGGLE PUPPY

Quit. We'll move to Paris and I'll fuck you on the Eiffel Tower.

> They'd throw us out of the country so fast.

> Besides, tomorrow I'm showing the class those new toys you got.

> The drones, not the other ones 😉 😉

SNUGGLE PUPPY

Fiiiiiine. I miss you. So dies Pongo.

> I'm sure you do. I'll see you tomorrow night, silly man.

I set the phone down just as the classroom door bursts open and Marta comes in like a tornado. Someone I don't know follows her into the room.

"Class," Marta announces as she heads for me. "This is Ms. Monroe. She'll be taking over for Ms. Silva for the afternoon. Renate, grab your phone and everything else you need and come with me."

I stand there, confused. "What's going on? Did something happen to Mama?"

She takes me by the arm and in a low voice, "I saw Luis in the office with Miley. They were talking about some pictures and he said something about leaking them. I'm going to hide you in the empty classroom while you call that cute detective guy."

"Private investigator."

"Whatever he is."

"Hang on." I run to the back of the classroom and into the storage room, opening the second drawer and feeling around above it. Shit. I kept the backup drive of Miley spying on the teachers here, and it's gone. Only three people have a key to this room because it's where we keep all the expensive computer equipment.

"Marta, who watched my class last week when I had the doctor's appointment?"

"Samantha did. I would have, but I had a—"

"Who's Samantha?"

She nods to the woman standing at the back of the class as she pushes me out the door. "Samantha Monroe. She's taken over for Allison in Miley's office. Allison had a skiing accident and had to take a medical leave of absence, poor thing."

"Skiing? In April? On our salary?" Marta shrugs and we duck down the hall and into the empty room. My fingers fly across the keys as I text Mills. Chase told me to contact Mills first if I saw Luis again. "There are new warrants out on Luis, and we have a restraining order. Miley knows about that and he let him walk in?"

"I'm not sure. Samantha had a picture of Luis and knew about the—"

Before she can finish, Principal Miley steps inside, closing the door behind him. He's doing a terrible job of hiding the smug smile. "Samantha told me I could find you two in here. She's such a doll. Honestly, she's much better than Allison in so many ways."

"Mr. Miley, whatever Luis said—" I start, but I'm cut off.

"Marta, go back to your classroom. I'll take care of this," Miley demands.

"Mr. Miley, I—"

"Now, Marta. Or you'll be in the same trouble as Ms. Silva."

What? Why am I in trouble?

He shuts the door behind Marta, and I watch his hand linger over the lock. He doesn't turn it. Instead, he saunters over to the empty teacher's desk, leaning on it like he's about to start a lecture for his class of one. Me.

"The school board will request that I put you on a leave of absence as soon as they see these." Miley grins, pulling an envelope like the last one from his coat pocket. He's trying to act like he has some kind of pity for me, but he sounds more like a devil here to make a rotten deal. "At least until we can sort all of this terrible mess out. I'm sure it's a lot of riffraff and bologna. Photoshop. The kids can do wonders on it these days."

"What are you talking about?" I cross my arms, not backing down. "Luis lies, and he only gave you more lies. You should have called the cops on—"

"Violation of school policies against sexual relations with what very well could be a student while on school property."

"What?!"

He opens the envelope, smirking as he looks between its contents and me. His grin twists into something dark and lecherous, and when he licks his lips, I expect his tongue to be forked. My stomach lurches as he leans forward and slides a photo across the desk. I fall in the chair as he pulls out another photo and another. The bathroom. My clothes ripped and littering the floor. Me on the counter. Each one worse than the last as they turn a moment of passion and magic into chum for the sharks. It's only me, though. None of the pictures have any part of Chase that's recognizable.

"Ms. Silva, or should I call you Mrs. Santiago? Either way, Mr. Santiago simply came by to make sure I understood you had put the students in danger, Renate." He picks up one of the pictures, eyeing it with a smirk. "I talked to the parties concerned, and they've agreed this can all end right now—"

"Parties concerned? A felon with warrants? A blackmailing pig?"

"HOWEVER," he shouts, cutting me off. "Since you're in my school—on my turf, if you will—I'm going to add a little something to their stipulations. I'm sure they won't mind."

"I'm not signing anything! I told that slime ball I wouldn't."

"Lawson told me. Renate, let's handle this like adults. If you're willing to do something for me, work with me. I won't submit these pictures to the board. I'll even talk to Mr. Lawson about his agreement. Oh, and don't bother threatening to release your little proof of my misconduct. We've already taken care of that. In fact, we used your own cameras against you after we moved them to the bathroom."

He tilts my chin up to look at him, and I smack his hand away. He snarls as his face turns red. I'm rejecting his offer, rejecting him, and that pisses him off. That look in his eyes scares me, and I lived in fear of it for too long. He reaches over the desk and grabs me by the shoulders, shouting into my face. "I'm offering you your job on a silver fucking platter. And you just need to do what you do best. Luis said you'd be easy to convince since you're a fat fucking whore. They said I could have you. They promised me!"

"Fuck you!"

"Yes, Ms. Silva. That's exactly what you're going to do. Right on top of my desk. Maybe I'll turn that camera feed back on for a little momento. If you want your job back, you'll do as you're fucking told. Your dignity? Well, maybe we should look in your little bag of sex toys to see if we can find it in there."

"You fucking—"

"Before you fight back, you should know these aren't the only pictures. The others could easily paint your pretty little boyfriend into the same corner. God, I love technology, sometimes."

They're going to use this to hurt Chase, and I won't stand by and let that happen. I jump up, pushing Miley's hands away, seething. "You dare do anything to hurt Chase, and I will personally rip your fucking dick off and shove it down your sick, stupid throat."

"He's none of my concern. You're all I wanted, all I ever asked for. I turned down money, whores, and drugs all so I could have you. And it will go so much easier once you understand your new position: on your knees."

"You're all sick fucking pervert," I whisper, shaking with rage. Miley looks taken aback, expecting me to beg and cry for him, to let him take what he wants so I can have my job back. The world turns red.

"That may be, but once we take everyone and everything away from you, you'll learn to accept your new life. If you're a good girl, I might even marry you."

I spit in his face and he comes at me again as the door slams open and Mills runs to me. He holds me back from clawing Miley's eyes out of his moronic fucking head, and keeps me from crumbling to the floor in a mess of tears and anger.

"What happened, Ren?"

"It's his fault," I sob into his chest. "He's working with Lawson and Luis, like I told you."

"Oh, I'm innocent as a babe." Miley holds his hands up and looks down at the photos.

"Luis Santiago, a known criminal with warrants and a restraining order, gave you those. You're withholding evidence in an ongoing criminal investigation. If you want to continue playing this like a dumbass, you should know I'm friends with a few detectives in the gang and cyber crimes units. They'd love a word with you." Mills steps forward, ripping the envelope out of Miley's hands and scooping up the pictures from the desk. Miley cowers. He's not a small man by any means, but Mills has him by a few inches. I'm enjoying watching how Mills looms over Miley like an ominous cloud.

"But—"

"Don't fuck with me, or I'll make sure Luis ends up as your cellmate."

"I-I-I'll have Marta pack your things. Leave your keys," Miley says to me, his eyes never leaving Mills. "T-t-the resource officer will meet you outside to escort you to your car."

"I don't need a fucking escort to my fucking car. I need my damn job!"

"You have my offer. Now get out of my school. Both of you. Or I'll have you arrested for trespassing." Miley doesn't wait for an answer as he slips out the door.

Mills turns me to face him. "They found Luis's car a few blocks from here. Guns, rope, drugs, and a computer full of images. Evidence suggests he planned to go after Chase and your family before coming for you. When none of them were home, he decided to get you out of the way. We have him on camera driving near Chase's home, and yours earlier today."

"Fuck, what do I do?"

"We've got Chase covered, and Devin left yesterday for a week-long road trip, but we'll let him and the team know just to be safe." He goes to the desk and starts picking up my things. "I'm sending your mom and sister to a safe house. You are getting on an earlier flight and Chase will meet you in New York as planned. They won't be able to follow you through all that security and do *not* leave the airports without Chase or an escort. I'll get Cynthia to rebook all your hotels while you're in the air. Don't go home, go straight to the airport. Okay?"

"The school's new secretary knows something, Mr. Mills. She looks familiar. She stole the drive with my evidence against Miley. No one knew about that but me."

"I'll check her out. For now, we need to get you out of here. Luis poses a serious threat, and if he's set this in motion, it may draw out the stalker as well and force her hand."

"My bags… my passport… We weren't supposed to leave until tomorrow."

"Breathe, Ren. I'll have someone pick up your things and it will be at the airport before your flight takes off." He stares at me, and I swear there's pity in his eyes. "The press already has the pictures Miley tried to blackmail you with. Cynthia caught some of them, but sent me here to get you the hell out of here before it all blows up."

Mills walks me out to my car, the vultures already circling across the street. As I climb into the car, a numbness takes over. I put the key in the ignition and whisper, "If you don't start, I swear to the baby Jesus, I will light you on fire right here in this godforsaken parking lot, you piece of shit." It turns over on the first try. It hasn't done that in weeks.

"Renate, be careful. I'll text you once I have your mother and sister. I'll keep them safe and we'll figure this out." He slips me a card and I tuck it into my purse without looking at it.

He doesn't promise me everything will work out, which I appreciate. They make promises like that on Dani's crime shows —they promise they'll find the guy who did it, and the case goes cold. They promise to keep someone safe, but the bad guys get to them, anyway.

"Be careful, Mills," I say as I back out of my spot and head for the gate. Some reporters have to jump out of the way as I pull out of the lot and onto the street a little too fast. A few of them run for their cars to follow me, but I don't need a map for these streets, and in a few blocks, I duck into a public parking garage. I watch, but no one follows me, so I find a spot and pull my phone back out, dialing Dani.

"Rene, where the fuck are you? What the fuck happened?!"

I can hear my mother yelling in Spanish in the background about her language and the men on our lawn. I hope Dani has kept this from her. Everything I said couldn't happen has happened. Luis, Lawson, Miley, there's just too many of them.

"I'll tell you later, Dani. Get some things packed for you and mom."

"Fuck, are we going to Chase's? I'm supposed to move into my new place this weekend."

"No. Mills has somewhere else he's taking you for a few days."

"What about you? What about Chase?"

Her words sound like they're a million miles away. Luis. Miley. These are all my problems, not Chase's. I even blame myself for Lawson. The card from Mills falls out of my purse. I pick it up and see writing on the back.

"I'll call you back, Dani. Just do what I said." I say flatly before hanging up.

I send a text, and I drive away. Away from the city. Away from my family. Away from the man I love.

I've stopped twice, each time to buy a phone from a gas station and switch out my SIM card. Being a tech girl has its advantages when you're running away from someone. When I get to the house, I dig the key out from under a rock, where it's always been. I toss my things on the couch, not that I have much, then take my latest burner phone and go into the bathroom. I sit in the dry tub with the lights off. It's cold and silent, but it's not dark because the light from the screen blinds me as I read everything Luis leaked to the press. Every lie, every truth, all muddled together to paint me into some kind of sick monster, feeding the students lies to recruit for the local gangs. Selling drugs on campus. Parents are at the school being interviewed by the press, saying they're shocked that the school board would hire a *groomer* and an *addict* like me. Every word twists the knife in my stomach.

I'm not sure who I'm more mad at for ruining my life. My

abuser. My boss. The movie producer. Or myself. I wanted to move on, to be loved. Instead, I've ruined not only my life, but the life of the man who loved me.

I turn off the phone, pull out the sim card, and crush it. I cry myself to sleep in the tub, apologizing to Chase over and over again as I do.

HOLLYWOOD
Chase

CHAPTER 36
SOMETHING

JIM STURGESS

I'M BEAMING when I unhook the harness after the take. We fucking nailed that stunt. Johnny, my stunt guy, grabs me and lifts me into the air in a hug. Without his help, I wouldn't have been able to pull that shit off and I'm sure Cyn will appreciate that I survived.

"Coop, come over here and see how that came out," one of the PA's calls out and Johnny and I walk over to him, Johnny's arm still over my shoulder. We're watching the monitor, pointing out things they'll add in post and laughing about how everything looks. It's going to look incredible, and I can't wait for people to watch this in theaters.

More specifically, I can't wait for Ren to see this. I wish I could thank her for giving me back the confidence I needed. As I watch the clip, my thumb slides over the small sunflower tattoo on my wrist.

The stab in my gut from thinking about her just about has me doubled over and I have to play it off around my colleagues since none of them knows what's going on. To the public eye, we broke up months ago, right after Luis's photos went viral. The press were brutal as hell to her, and so were some of my fans. I left the internet behind, and Cyn staged photos of me with another woman. A few days later, they found someone more interesting to follow.

It got Ren's photos off the front pages quicker than asking them to remove them would have. If I get her back, they'll post them again, but we'll be ready. I hope.

In reality, I haven't seen her in six months. None of us have, but my gut says Mills knows where she is. The plan to meet at the airport never happened. By the time Mills got Dani and Mrs. Silva to the safe house, Ren had disappeared. They tracked her phone, but found it smashed in a trashcan, and no SIM card.

At first, we thought Luis had found her, and I lost myself in a haze of weed and booze. Theo came over to the house a few times after Dev called him, and Pongo was on non-stop alert. Jamie and Steve spent a week by my side every hour when Dev couldn't. I didn't eat or sleep for days and would have been the perfect pick for a zombie film.

After two weeks, Mills came back with evidence showing Luis sending his gang and prison connections to find her. Things he wouldn't leverage if he already had her. He's not smart enough to cover his tracks like that.

After Mills found out what I put myself through, his shell cracked, but only a little. He gave me a box, saying someone mailed it to his office. Inside I found a sunflower pin. I've given Mills envelopes of cash every few weeks since he gave me that. We don't talk about it, he just nods and sticks it in his pocket. After that, I buckled down and took on more work.

Dani and her mother moved out of the safe house about a week after the photos, since Luis never threatened them. Xander got Dani to take him back, since he'd been worried sick about her. They're dating my PA, Megan, and the three of them moved in together not long after Ren took off. I'm not sure that will last, though.

Instead of being home alone, Ren's mother has been staying with Dev and me for the time being. She tried to refuse, but she saw my breakdown and because of that, she's worried about me. Now we argue over who gets the kitchen on which nights and where the pots and pans go. She's happy to not be alone, and it's nice to have a part of Ren here. We're all just trying to pretend life is back to normal when it's anything but.

"E-excuse me. Uhm, Mr. Cooper?" I turn around and find a young woman biting her lip like I'm going to yell at her for interrupting. God, I hate the actors that feel the need to freak out people like her to flex their power.

"Yeah? What's up?" I ask, making sure I smile as she hands me a note.

"Uhm, your agent, Cynthia, called. She said I needed to have you call her as soon as you were finished with the scene. She said you should probably take the call in your trailer."

A month after she disappeared, I got the first email. No one knows about it, or if they do, they haven't told me.

I don't want to wait. I don't want to give Luis any more of my time. You shouldn't either. I can't stop you from looking for me, and I hope when all of this is over, we can find each other again. For now, just know that I'm safe and I'm okay. I love you, Puppy. Go be my movie star so I can watch you on the big screen until I can hold you again.

I'm doing what she told me, not giving Luis Santiago any of my time. I'm also not giving any to Ren, and that part hurts, but sometimes I'll get a package or a message. There's never a way to contact her back, but she already knows what I'd say. I've thrown myself into my work with more energy and passion than ever. If movies are my only connection to Ren for now, I'm going to give her everything I've got. She's going to see it's all for her.

It's also driving the press nuts trying to figure out why I got the tattoo and wear a sunflower pin to every carpet, interview, presser, everything. So far, they've guessed it's for a movie, a cult, and a stance against some government somewhere. No one knows it's just my way of telling her I love her. No one but her.

"Here we go again." I nod to Pongo as he follows me back to the trailer. Cyn and I have been playing this game for the last few weeks, and I'm pretty sure I'm close to getting Cyn to crack. I want her to take Lawson down, and she has the connections to do it, but she keeps giving me excuses. So, once again, I've taken Ren's advice and stopped giving Cyn my time.

"Don't hang up!"

"Have you found her?"

"No, but—"

"Are you going after Lawson?"

"Chase—"

"Okay, fun talk." I hang up, tossing the phone on the bed and heading to the sink to wash the dirty and grime off my face. I listen as the phone vibrates behind me, closing my eyes and letting the water drip from my face and hands. I'm too close to teetering over the edge. It's like a high-wire act, and I can't see the other side, but I'm still moving ahead. Pongo strolls into the bathroom and nudges me.

"Hey, Buddy. You wanna head back to the apartment and get something to eat? I'm starving." He hops onto the bed, pushing the phone over the edge with his nose. "No way. She knows what she needs to do."

The phone vibrates again, and I pick it up and glance at the screen—there's no caller ID. Cyn can get pretty sneaky, but she's not *unlisted phone number* kind of sneaky. I jam my finger down on the green button.

"Ren?"

"HA! Still thinking she's coming out of hiding so you two lovebirds can have your cute movie ending?" Lawson sneers. "I knew that stunt a few months ago with the smoking hot, big titty blonde wasn't real."

"I'm not signing it. I've told you that already."

"Check the news. I'll call you back in five to see if you've changed your mind."

Lawson hangs up, and I open the web browser, not finding anything. I refresh it a few times until a new headline loads, and I'm grinning ear to ear.

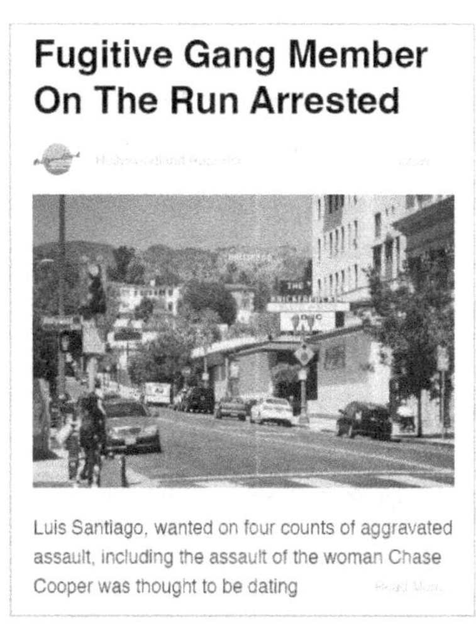

Luis Santiago, wanted on four counts of aggravated assault, including the assault of the woman Chase Cooper was thought to be dating

My phone rings again, but I'm not sure what to do. Why does Lawson want me to know about the arrest? Fuck it.

"What the fuck do you still want, Lawson?"

"You, on my payroll."

"No. I already told you I'm not signing on. It's not happening."

"Let me tell you the offer first, big guy."

"Fine, but you're wasting your time."

"One movie. One movie so people will stop blacklisting my ass. You do that, I give you the name of the stalker. I gave you one as a freebie, so you know I'm good for it."

"You're saying you ratted out Santiago, hoping I'd do a movie with your studio just to get the name of my stalker?"

When it came out that Luis Santiago had planned to come

after me, the stalker lost whatever footing she had in reality. Death threats came for all of us, including the dogs. We've stopped feeding them anything we haven't prepared ourselves, doubled the security cameras, and Mills has people driving by at random times. She even broke into Jamie's garage and defaced the mural he did for Alexis, covering the wall with photos of Ren and I. It took him weeks to clean the mess up.

Everyone thought that would be as far as she went, destroying property and threats. But she took the threats to a new level, breaking into Marta Rodriguez's home and stabbing her four times. Marta survived, but it confirmed that this girl, whoever she is, still blames Ren for getting in the way and poisoning my mind.

I glance over at the stack of unopened envelopes I've gotten from her just this week. I send them to Mills on Fridays, and he spends his weekend going through them and not finding a damn thing. Lawson could give us the break we need, and he's fucking blackmailing me for it.

"You worthless, dickless piece of shit. You fucking go after my girl, you humiliate her, you force her into fucking hiding and you expect me to come back and do a fucking movie to save your sorry ass? Buddy, I hope your damn studio catches fire and there isn't a drop of water in the lines when they go to save it."

"Hey, you and me both on that one. Insurance payout," he chuckles darkly. There's a knock at the trailer door and Pongo jumps around like a lunatic.

"Okay, this has been great, but go to hell, asshole."

"She has pictures of you." I freeze, not responding. *"Boning your bitch, on your knees and begging. She has some extra spicy ones from San Luis Obispo, too. I offered her cash money for them and she turned me down, but the longer you avoid her, the more interested in my money she gets."*

"I don't give a fuck!"

"She showed me one when I told her I didn't believe her.

Hollywood's Golden Goose getting fucked up the ass by his whips and chains whore. It's gonna look phenomenal on the covers of every magazine in the damn world. Put you both back in the public eye."

Lawson's telling the truth about knowing the stalker.

"You're a smart kid. Sign the fuckin' deal and I'll tell you who and where she is."

"Pongo, get down," I whisper as he jumps at the door. "Lawson, tell me—"

He's gone. I mumble under my breath as I head for the door and the second it's open, Pongo bolts past Megan, almost knocking her over. I catch her and apologize for him acting weird as he disappears around another trailer. It's gotta be food. Idiot acts like I don't feed him.

"Sorry to bother you, Chase, but uhm, we've had another break-in. I just wanted to make sure you were alright,"

"Break-in? Did you catch her?" My heart races.

"Yeah, we found her snooping around the trailers looking for you. She looks familiar, but she's probably someone we've tossed out before."

I check in the direction Pongo went, waiting for him to come back. There's a strange feeling in my stomach. "What, uh, what did you say she looked like?"

"I didn't, but she's short, around my height. She has a red bob, and a tattoo—"

I take off in a full run. I remember the chick that broke in last time, the stalker. Sharron. Suzan. Shauna. Something like that. Whatever she calls herself, she's much taller than Megan.

My heart hammers, while my brain tries hard to pump the brakes. If it's the stalker, she could hurt Pongo, but that's not what my gut tells me. My gut says it's the woman I've waited fucking months for. When I round the corner, there's a woman squatting down with one of the security guards next to her. Pongo's on his back as she rubs his belly. She doesn't have to turn around and doesn't need to face me when I hear that laugh.

"Sunshine!" I practically tackle her, rolling to keep her from hitting the concrete. It's a move my stunt guy taught me a few weeks back, and I never dreamed it would have real-life applications like this. I hug her to me, swearing to myself that I'll never let her go. Never. "Fuck, Sunshine! I can't believe it's you! Are you okay? Are you hurt at all?"

I don't even wait for a response, grabbing her face and pulling her mouth down to mine. It's like a game of tug-of-war, each of us fighting to pull the other's soul right out of their body. It's a miracle I keep enough of my brain intact to not strip her naked right there and claim every damn inch of her.

"Chase! Come on, let me go!" she says between gasps of air. "Seriously!"

"No, not until you use the right name. The name I've begged every fucking star in the sky to hear again. Let me hear it, please, baby?"

Her shy smile looks out of place on her, but I'll take it. "Puppy."

"Fuck, I love you!" I assail her with more kisses, grabbing her face and holding it to mine so she can't get away again. "And this new hair? Fuck, you're fucking gorgeous."

"Chase?" she squeaks out between kisses.

"Mm?"

"Can we, uhm, go somewhere less open?"

"Huh? Oh, yeah! Come on, my trailer's over here." I wave over at Megan as she stares at us. "All good, this one's legit! Sorry!"

"Not your trailer, Chase. I can't stay long, and too many people watch this place."

"What do you mean, you can't stay?"

"Let's go somewhere safe first, somewhere we can talk, okay?" I nod and pat my pocket, but it's empty. I left my phone and keys in the trailer. She holds out her own keys. "I'll drive."

HOLLYWOOD
Renate

CHAPTER 37
APT.

ROSÉ , BRUNO MARS

SEEING him again sets fires in me that had been nothing but ash and embers for months, and as badly as I want to stay with him, I can't. I'm too close now, too close to having her right where I want her. Lawson, too. I've always said people shouldn't piss off a woman in STEAM, but nobody listens. Now, they're going to pay for it. All of them, one by one.

"I have so many questions, so many things I want to know! Uhm, safe place. How about my apartment?" Chase says excitedly as he climbs into the car. My guy just became a ten-year-old with a golden ticket to a candy factory. And I'm the candy factory. Kinky.

"Buckle up and keep Pongo in the back. I can't have him licking on me while I'm driving, Puppy." He stares at me with that goofy grin I've missed so damn much.

"Sure, yeah. Uhm, do you need the address?"

"Chase, I've left you packages and you don't think I have the address?"

"Shit, I forgot. I'm just so damn happy to see you. My brain is malfunctioning. Wait! Lawson! He called me. He knows who the stalker is."

"Technically you do, too. If Mills and I are right—"

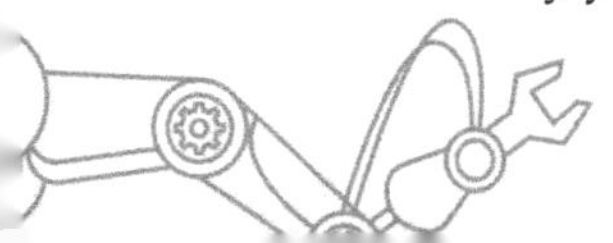

"Mills? I fucking knew it! I should fire that guy. It's the convention girl, right? The one who broke onto the set right before I met you. The fucking *day* I met you."

"That's our guess. And baby, I'm good, but I'm not *keeping myself undercover for six months* good. Mills had a plan. He passed me a note just before I left for the airport. I have an aunt that goes to Mexico every single year like clockwork, so I crashed at her house for the night until Mills could find me somewhere safer. He's helped keep me safe. Don't fire him."

"Oh, I'm fucking firing his ass as soon as I have my phone again."

"Puppy, he and I have been working together to connect all the dots. I'm finally getting to put my computer programming skills to use like I should have done years ago. He's been... amazing."

He doesn't say anything and when I finally get a red light; I find him looking out the window with his jaw clenched. I reach for his hand, but he pulls it away, shaking his head. Instead of arguing this out in the car, I get to his apartment, keeping my head down as Chase has the guard let us in. He's out of the car before I've even put it in park, storming over to the elevator.

"At least he's not making a public scene, eh, Pongo?"

When I played this moment out in my head, he ripped my clothes off in the elevator and carried me to his apartment. I pictured a scene in a dramatic period romance with wind whipping my hair and dress around. I'm not even wearing a dress. His shirt also needs to be unbuttoned and not covered in dirt and ash from the set, but I could have worked with that, too. Instead, he's punching buttons and turning away from me with his arms crossed. Chase Cooper, always the drama queen.

I haven't been to his apartment, at least not this one. I've snuck into a few places he has stayed and left little gifts for him, put on his t-shirts, or smelled his pillow—it's creepy, but I couldn't help it. I missed him. It's a spacious apartment with giant windows and a sleeping loft upstairs. The minimalist decor scattered around doesn't fit Chase at all, but I could live here.

I bet this place looks magical when the snow falls. "Does it snow in Vancouver?"

"Why did you come back?" he yells as he spins around to face me.

"I…thought you'd want me to?"

"Bullshit! Why are you doing this?"

I sit on one of the barstools, running my finger over the cold marble countertop. This isn't the welcome I had expected, but maybe I should have prepared for anger along with his excitement. He storms up to the loft and has a shoe box when he returns. I watch as he dumps the contents onto the counter in front of me. Trinkets that were meant to remind him of me and to let him know I'm okay. Sunflowers, lockets with the sun on them, a plush otter toy. There's more than a hundred little things that he's kept in this box while I hid. In retrospect, maybe sending him so many could have given away my location.

"I fucking kept them. I kept every fucking one of them, and I brought them with me everywhere! Every fucking job! Why, Ren? Are you rubbing my nose in it? Teasing me with what I'd never have again? Fucking with me? Is this how you say you're sorry? Make you feel less guilty? Because if you don't want me anymore, an email would have been fine after I waiting six fucking months!"

"Chase I don't—"

"I fucking waited! Do you know how many women throw themselves at me daily? I didn't touch any of them. Not one! I waited for you because you're all I wanted, Ren. It's only been you since I met you! But I guess you didn't feel that way, huh?" Pongo even hides under the table, confused.

"Oh, we are *not* doing this." I slide off the chair and head toward the door, but I have an idea. "Fuck it," I mumble, grabbing a chair from the dining room table. I drag it over in front of him and climb up on it so he can't yell down at me like some kind of child.

"What the fuck are you doing?!"

"I'm yelling back!" He has to look up now, which makes it difficult for me to keep a straight face and it throws him off his game a little, too. "I sent you these so you wouldn't forget about me!"

"Then…then…why are you? Wait, are you? Yeah, no! Why are you fucking him?"

"Do you speak to my mother like this?"

"What? Stop it! Stop fucking with my head and answer the question!"

"What are you talking about, Chase? I'm not fucking anyone!"

"Mills! You ran off with fu—with Mills! He's so fucking *amazing,* huh? How long have you two been… did you plan all this?"

I purse my lips and try my best not to laugh, but I can't help it. I'm doubled over and snorting from laughing so hard. When I catch my breath, he's staring at me, that confused, lost little dog look in his pretty blue eyes. I missed those eyes so much.

"Puppy—"

"No!"

"Chase Cooper!" I use a stern voice, and he straightens up, giving me his full attention. At least he hasn't forgotten about that. "I am not now, and I have never before, slept with, kissed, or even held hands with your private investigator. He helped me move around without being detected and provided me with the equipment and means to trap a few flies in our web. He also gave me the money you sent. Thank you for that."

"You didn't?" He blinks, still confused.

"No. I didn't."

"I'm such a fucking idiot." His shoulders slump and the poor man looks like he's about to cry as everything hits him at once.

"You're my idiot. And it better be you that I'm fucking in the next five minutes, or I'm leaving."

The words are still on my lips when he grabs me off the chair, throws me over his shoulder, and carries me up to the loft. There's a loud snap when he smacks my ass, and the tingle goes all the way to my toes and the top of my head. He throws me down on the bed, standing over me with that look he gets in his eyes, the look that says I won't be able to walk when he's done with me. I move back on my elbows and he climbs onto the bed and over me, our noses brushing together as the electricity sparks between us.

"Stay."

"Oh, Puppy. I—"

"No. No excuses, no bullshit. Stay!"

That simple word has teeth. He wants me to fix him, to make him whole again. He's broken, he's been that way for years, and he wants me to pick up the pieces and glue him back together one piece at a time. How could I say no to that level of trust and love?

"Please?" The strength in his voice fades, replaced by a whimper.

My chest heaves as I nod and he dives into my neck, wrapping his arms around me and tugging at my clothes while I struggle to get to his. There's a ripping sound before his hand slaps against my now bare thigh as he rips the leggings open and pushes his fingers between my legs. He remembers every spot and how to touch me. I'm putty in his hands and just as I get to the edge, he spreads my legs apart and thrusts into me. My body isn't ready for his size, and I scream his name out as he pushes into me again, both of us desperate and needy. I shove my hands under his shirt and claw down his back, not caring who will see it later, watching him throw his head back and moan for me.

His mouth hovers over mine as he thrusts one more time, bottoming out while my back arches. I'm being split in two, but it's what I want. What we need. We breathe each other in, neither of us moving as our eyes lock together. I may not have gotten my movie magic elevator ride, but I'm okay with this fantasy coming to life.

"One more request," he breathes against my mouth.

"Anything for you, Puppy."

"Marry me."

I move my head back and stare at him. "Are you serious right now?"

"Very. Renate Silva. I want you to be my queen now and forever."

"One condition?"

"Anything," he echoes.

"Ask me again when you're not rage fucking my brains out?"

"Okay."

"Okay." I cup his face and wipe the tear from his cheek as he smiles.

"Yes? Really?"

My phone vibrates, almost sending us both flailing off the bed. He digs it out from under my torn clothes and holds the screen to me.

"Mills. I need to answer—"

He hits the button for the speakerphone and answers. "Mills, bro, shitty timing. Can you call back later? I'm in the middle of fucking my wife because you're not." He ends the call, tosses the phone over the edge of the bed, and dives back into my neck as he thrust into me again.

"Chase!"

"What? Not what you were asking for?" His brow furrows. "In my defense, it's been a few months, and today has been pretty weird."

"No. I mean yes. I just, I don't think I wanted to tell Mills quite like that."

"Oh, I'm going to shout it from the fucking roof. You're my

light, my everything, my family. I'll tell the world as soon as you scream my name while I put a baby—" He stops, freezing mid sentence as his brain blue screens.

Neither of us moves. We're barely even blinking as we stare at each other.

"Mr. Cooper? Were you about to reveal a bit of a breeding kink?" He cringes as he looks down at me, swearing under his breath. "Hey, Puppy? Remember our rule?"

"Never be embarrassed by a kink?"

"Good fucking boy." I grab him by the throat and whisper, "Now knock your fucking wife up, you whore."

The clock says it's after three in the morning when I wake up. Chase has me cradled in his arms, his hand splayed over my belly. His confidence that he got the job done on the first go made me giggle, but I can't help but hope right along with him. I need to pee, though, and the dim glow from the horror movie we had on when we fell asleep helps me maneuver the apartment in the dark.

When I'm done, Pongo and I head down to the kitchen, hoping I'll fix him some food, too. Now that I'm a part time spy, my internal clock picks strange times to be wide awake or hungry. I'm starving, but, of course, his cupboards are bare. That would explain why he's lost so much weight. Skinny fucker. I'll have Mama help me fix that when we're back.

I find a granola bar and nibble on that while I search for a cup. I laugh when I open the cabinet and the mug Chase got me for his house stares at me. There's a whip and handcuffs hidden in the apple that reads 'Teachers Do It Better,' because of course Chase would find someone to make that. I doubt that will ever be true again—the teacher part.

I find my phone next to the couch and I'm surprised it didn't

shatter into a thousand pieces. I have one text from M.O.T.H.E.R.
—an appropriate name for Mills. I almost ignore it, but my brain
refuses to let me leave it until morning, no matter how badly I
want to curl back into Chase's warm arms. I click the thread.

M.O.T.H.E.R.

Leave now! She saw you! On my way.

I check the timestamp, it's from fifteen minutes ago. I've been
pretending everything can go back to normal, when it can't. Not
yet, anyhow.

I grab one of Chase's shirts from his laundry basket
downstairs and find a notepad and pen, leaving him a note so he
doesn't worry when he wakes up alone in a few hours. He'll still
worry, but not as much, I hope.

As I scoop up my keys, there's a noise by the door and Pongo
stands up, growling. I hold my hand out to him, the signal to
stay, praying that he'll listen to me as I hold my breath and stare
at the door. Minutes pass and Pongo relaxes as there's a soft,
familiar tap on the door. Mills.

As I rush for the door, I find the envelope and my heart sinks.
She's watching us still. I grab it and run out the door as quietly
as I can.

When Mills and I are safely in the car and miles away from
Chase, I rip the envelope open. Pictures of me at the film set, of
us screaming at each other in the kitchen, and of us in bed. None
of it would do much to hurt either of us. It's meant as a threat.
The closer I get to her, the further ahead of us she gets.

Fuck.

HOLLYWOOD
Chase

CHAPTER 38
AIN'T NO SUNSHINE
BILL WITHERS

I'M CURLED up with Pongo and a pillow that smells like Ren when I wake up. Convincing myself yesterday happened will take a few more minutes and some coffee. My hand feels around for her, but I only find Pongo. When I sit up to survey the damage and see if she's up here, I spot the remains of our clothes scattered around the loft. The costume guy is going to kill me for wearing that off set. I can't even return it like this, in pieces. I pick up her shirt from the end of the bed, hold it to my face, and inhale that summertime sunshine that's all Ren.

My girl. My—

My eyes shoot open dart around the loft, then back down to Pongo. "Bro, did I... Did I propose to her last night?" I try to replay it in my mind, and flop backward onto the bed, trying to stop my brain from spinning.

There's a foggy memory of tossing her phone downstairs after telling Mills—

"Holy shit! Did I unlock a breeding kink last night, and, maybe...you know...?!"

Pongo rolls over to face the other way.

"Holy fucking shit. Wait, where is she?"

I hop off the bed, pulling on boxers as I run around the

apartment. I don't know what the neighbors saw last night, but they don't need to see me running around naked this morning. Not yet, anyhow.

"Renate?" There's no answer. I head into the bathroom, smirking at the scratch marks that cover my body. Then I trek downstairs. As soon as I turn the corner, my heart sinks.

I haven't left. I'm always with you.
I love you, future husband.

-R

HOLLYWOOD
Renate

CHAPTER 39
SOME NIGHTS

FUN.

MILLS HAD cameras installed in my house not long after I did the disappearing act. At first, the cameras were to keep Mama and Dani safe. When neither of them came back to the house, it became a way to know when I could go home and pick up some essentials. I've been back twice, and it's like a time capsule. But now that Mama's moved back in, I keep the feed up all day and watch her move around the house. Sometimes she's dancing around the house making dinner, other times she's crying on the couch.

The other day, I cried as I watched Chase and Devin come over and have dinner with her, and I wanted to hug the shit out of both of them for it. I love those boys.

Today, I flip on the feed expecting to see my mother, but there's a box sitting on the kitchen table. Right off the bat, I determine it can't be a head, since the box isn't big enough for one. So, that's a bonus. I switch over to the front porch and scrub the feed backward to get a timestamp for the delivery. I scrub it back to yesterday, and forward again, slower this time..

That's when I find it. One second, there's nothing on the porch but the welcome mat. The next, there's a box.

She's hacked my fucking feed.

I search the house looking for my mother, but I can't find her. I can't find when she left, either. It's the opposite of the box. One second she's in the kitchen, the next, she's gone. I call Mills, but he doesn't answer, so I leave him a voicemail and grab the keys.

When I get to the house, I park down the block in an alleyway and go in through Dani's entrance. I poke my head into Dani's empty room first. I'm a little jealous of her, but I'm also hopeful about her big move. She's the only one of us kids who didn't move out right after high school. Her decision made sense, though, because now she has money in savings, even after dropping out of fashion school and starting a band. Good for her. I just hope this new girlfriend of hers works out, or at least that Xander sticks around for good this time. I don't think she could stand living alone.

The delicious scent of food leads me to the kitchen. My mouth waters, but my heart has lodged in my throat as I sneak through the house. I can't let Mama see me. Not yet.

I find an empty kitchen, with food in the oven that's minutes away from burning. Mama has always been terrified of kitchen fires. As a child, she lost an aunt to one, and she's been vigilant to the point of obsession over not leaving food unattended since that happened.

She didn't plan to leave.

I pull the food out and set it on the stovetop before I turn the oven off. If she comes back, she'll be confused, but the house will still be in one piece.

I peek down the hall, but nothing appears out of place. I'm at a loss, so I sit at the table and stare at the package. It's addressed to me, but that's all it says, my name. There's no actual address on it. I'm about to open it when my phone buzzes.

New Message from M.O.T.H.E.R.

I unlock the phone and a flood of ice water runs through my veins. I put the phone down on the table and feel the hand on my shoulder.

M.O.T.H.E.R.

Leave the box and get out, now!

"You should have taken the money, Renate."

HOLLYWOOD
Chase

CHAPTER 40
IRIS

THE GOO GOO DOLLS

I'M TRYING NOT to mope as I stare at the TV that isn't even on. I wanted more time with her, but her leaving again didn't surprise me. Three more weeks have passed, but this time I couldn't throw myself at roles or events. I'm tired. So I've been staying home and making Jamie worry so much that he comes by every fucking day to check on me and force me to play video games. I'm sure he'll be here any minute. With any luck, he'll get caught up talking with Devin downstairs and leave me to wallow in self pity.

Pongo comes up beside me and nudges me in the leg, so I give him a few head scratches. He misses her, too, and I don't blame him. This has been the hardest time of my life since Cassie. At least Steve finally got me out of bed and back in the gym, working me so damn hard my body hurts as much as my heart does. It's a distraction for an hour or two. I haven't cooked in weeks, but they're all making sure I'm eating. Even Dr. Clay says this qualifies as manageable depression, and I'm managing it pretty well. Whatever that means.

My stomach growls as the smell from Devin's pizza wafts its way upstairs to the loft where I'm curled around the pillow from the apartment. The smell of her shampoo has faded, but it's still there. I groan and complain to myself as I stand up, stretching my stiff muscles. I glance over at the bedroom and frown. I haven't slept in my bed in at least two months. I tried for a while, but I just gave up. It wasn't the same without her. I don't sleep much, anyway.

Something sparkles as I walk into the kitchen to grab a slice. I shift the box of cereal Devin hasn't put away since yesterday morning and find Mrs. Silva's bracelet. She only ever took this off while doing the dishes—I told her I have a dishwasher, but she doesn't trust those *damn machines*. She must have forgotten to put it back on before she moved out.

I miss the old lady going around the house and bossing us around like she owned the place, cleaning up while she bitched us out about a clean house, and chasing the dogs around while calling them filthy animals. She meant none of it, and while Devin gets a little forgetful sometimes, we're both pretty neat. She did it out of boredom. Not having Dani to clean up after or Ren to shoo out of the kitchen. She gave the house a warmth it lacked.

I stuff the bracelet into my pocket, grab a slice, and hop onto the counter where Ren used to sit and watch me cook. Instead, I've got Pongo's big eyes looking up at me—or maybe it's the pizza. I pick off a pepperoni and toss it to him as I stare out the window. I glance down at the slice, and realize I've taken two bites, but given Pongo every piece of pepperoni on it. I love pepperoni, but Ren eats like this.

"Fuck it," I mumble, hopping off the counter and tossing the rest of the slice to Pongo. "Come on, buddy, let's get some clothes on, yeah? You wanna go see your *Abuela*?"

Ren's mother and I bonded over our guilt and what Ren has gone through. Me for Lawson and the paparazzi, and her for Luis. She admitted Luis kept her away from Ren, even when they lived under the same roof. With Dani and Ren gone, she misses her family and the warmth they brought to the house. I want to change that, and I'm going to do it tonight.

I'm going to ask her if I can marry her daughter. Maybe it can give her hope like it gives me. I may even tell her how we want to make her a real *Abuela* someday. As much as I miss Ren, her mother misses her more, and I want her to know that she's part of this family that Ren and I are going to make.

"Hey, idiot. I'm going out for a bit!" I shout into the living room a few minutes later after I've gotten dressed and no longer look like a goblin hermit.

"Okay," Dev yells back. He's busy blowing off steam with his teammates and doesn't register what I've said. After being eliminated by Vegas last year in the playoffs, he and some of the other guys get their rage out by pummeling the shit out of Vegas in a weekly video game session. They call it therapy. I guess everyone handles shit in different ways.

Pongo's jumping around my feet, waiting for me to open the door. "You coming with me, buddy? Yeah, okay. Come on." I turn back toward the living room and yell out, "Lulu? You wanna go for a ride?"

"Dude, she didn't even move. I got her. Pick up some food on the way back, yeah?" I'm not surprised. Lulu and Dev are inseparable now. He even takes her to the rink for practices and has her out on the ice chasing pucks.

"You have pizza in the kitchen, fucknut."

"Shit, right!"

I open the door to the garage and Pongo bounds toward the SUV. I traded the Jag in when I got back from Vancouver. I'm hoping to surprise Ren when she gets back, a promise that I'm serious about our future together. I'm not sure she's going to approve of it since she liked the Jag, but Pongo loves it. Besides, I can buy her a Jag that's all hers. Pongo sniffs by the sensor and the back hatch automatically lifts for him. I bet this wasn't what the manufacturers had in mind when they put those in. I close the tailgate and we head out.

When we pull up to her house, I take a long, hard look at the front gate, regretting my decision to come here. My stomach did somersaults the entire drive over, and I almost pulled over to puke twice. I keep reminding myself that Ren's not here, I'm just going to drop off her mother's jewelry, profess my undying love and devotion to her daughter, and head home. Easy peasy. Unless Mrs. Silva has decided she doesn't like me and tosses me out.

If she hated you, she wouldn't have had us over for dinner the other day. Calm the fuck down.

I'm pulled out of my panic by Pongo scratching at the door, ready to be let out. He bolts the second the door lifts enough for him to squeeze through.

"Guess you really had to go, huh Bud—"

Someone screams from inside Ren's house.

I'm out of the car and jumping the fence, sprinting to the open front door. I find Pongo standing over someone, growling and ready to rip his face off. Someone else takes a run at Pongo, but I drop my shoulder and throw my entire body into him, crashing into a bookshelf.

"Ow, fuck," I groan.

"Chase!" My head snaps toward my name because that's my girl's voice. My pain disappears, replaced with a blazing rage. She has a large cut on her lip, her eye has swollen shut, and she's clutching her arm. There's someone holding a knife to her, but I can't tell who because they're wearing a ski mask.

"Chase, don't—"

Too late.

I pull the guy out from under Pongo, shove him against a wall, and punch him square in the face before I can let out my next breath. I'm inches from his face and the growl isn't coming from Pongo anymore.

"Tell that motherfucker to let *my* fucking girl go, or I'm going to beat the fuck out of you and no one will going to recognize your corpse when I'm done." The prick snarls back at me, but I don't give him an inch. "DO IT! NOW YOU PIECE OF SHIT!"

"Fuck you!"

"Chase! Let him go! Let Luis go and get the hell out of here!"

"He's not going anywhere," the guy holding her says, but it's not a guy's voice. It's...familiar. "Not unless it's with me. I told you he'd come for me. He loves me, and you're just a stupid whore that got in our way."

"Who the fuck *are* you?" I bark, still pinning Ren's ex against the wall as he sputters and swears through gasps of air.

"Oh, duh, of course you can't recognize me," she giggles, as if she's not holding a knife to someone. She pulls the mask off and steps into the light. It's the girl from the set, just like we thought.

"Sh—Shawna?" I pray I'm right. She smiles, her eyes sparkling like I've just asked her to prom. This girl gets creepier by the minute.

"Yes! I knew you'd remember me if I didn't use my stupid real name. Shawna sounds so much cooler than Julie. Nobody remembers Julie, but they will now. Julie Catherine Cooper. Isn't it so cute? I may just go with Catherine Cooper, though, since it would sound so fun with your name. Chase and Catherine Cooper...forever."

This chick has a permanent address in delulu land, but I have to play it cool.

"Shaw—uh—Julie, will you please let Ren go?"

"Oh, no. I can't. Sorry. I mean, she tried to ruin our lives, baby. Tricking you into leaving me like you did. It's okay, I forgive you, Chase." She smiles again and I shiver at the sight. "But look, it's fine. She can go be with her scummy dipshit husband again. He made it difficult since he's a fucking dumbass who can't follow simple instructions. I bailed him out so he could take her off your hands. I'm not totally cruel. She's just, you know, not your type, Chase. I'm your type. I'm your girl."

"Stupid bitch!" Luis spits, and splatters of blood appear on my sleeve.

"Please, she won't bother us anymore?" I ask again, ignoring Luis. Ren's body shakes and she keeps glancing to her left at something. Her mother's feet sticking out from beyond the couch. "No! Fuck! Ren?"

"S-she's knocked out. Bleeding. I don't, I don't—"

Julie slaps Ren across the face before pulling her head back by the hair and holding the knife to her throat. Luis struggles to get out of my grip, but I push him harder against the wall. When I turn back to Julie again, she's giggling, enjoying all of this.

"You can kill him—I don't need him anymore. It's probably easier this way, so they don't try to follow us or anything. I mean, I guess I should kill them both anyhow, but if we each kill one of them, it would be so cute!"

"No!" Luis yells, and turns to me, looking for sympathy. He *is* an idiot. "She's fucking crazy, man! Loco! She did all this! She used me, right?"

"I'm not fucking crazy, you asshole! I'm the smartest one in this house!" Julie screams, pulling Ren's hair harder. "I used you to lure this dumb bitch out of hiding, and it worked, didn't it? *You* couldn't fucking do it! You pathetic, limp dick loser."

She stops yelling and takes a deep breath, centering herself until she's smiling again.

"It would be a kind of poetic if him kicking this fucking whore in the gut earlier fixes that problem. Although, I still don't think I'll leave her alive. I mean, who the fuck does she think she is?" She yanks Ren's hair back again, and I can see a trickle of blood on her neck.

I make out the faint boot prints on Ren's stomach in the dark.

Ren wouldn't know yet. I've done nothing but google babies and pregnancy shit for the last three weeks since I wasn't doing anything else. But the possibility of her losing another baby because of him? Our baby? I swallow hard and try to focus.

"She's damaged goods, Chase. How could she make you happy when she couldn't even keep her small-dick husband happy?" She giggles, holding her finger and thumb up a few inches apart. "Seriously. So small."

"Fuck you," Luis yells back, still trying to get away again. "You liked my dick when I put it in your bitch ass! You fucking screamed for —"

Julie pulls a gun out, pointing it at him, which means also at me. "Back up, Chase. I'll take care of this, of you. This will look like domestic violence turned murder/suicide. Everyone will believe her half-pint, loser hubby ended her life, and killed himself so he wouldn't go back to jail. It's the perfect cover up. After that, you'll be with me, and no one will remember her."

"Fuckin' let me go, motherfucker! I'm gonna fuck her up so bad! My boys are gonna—!" Luis tries to punch me in the side so I head but his already broken nose. He screams like a child, but at least he stops talking. My attention goes back to Ren and Julie, but before I can do anything, Luis gets an arm free and that asshole punches me in the side of the head. "I said I'd fuck you up, stupid white boy!" he slurs and spits blood.

Luis pushes me backward before pulling a gun out of the back of his pants and leveling it at Julie. If Ren wasn't right there in the line of fire, I'd let the two of them have their little cowboy stand-off. But Luis has a broken nose, and a swollen eye. There's also a chance he's on something. No way he's that good of a shot.

Fuck.

Pongo steps next to me and I command him to heel, not wanting him to get hurt trying to be the hero. It's hard to explain that to a dog, but hopefully he gets it. I take a deep breath and do what I do best. Act.

"Baby, you're so right. It's our time. Yours and mine. Together."

She almost looks away from Luis, but stops herself. Her face twists again as reality slips back in for a split second. "Do you think they'd give me a medal for killing him? A shitty drug dealing wanna-be gangbanger who can't even get it up?"

"What?" Luis and I ask together.

BANG! Blood splatters over Pongo and me as I scramble backward.

"Jesus fucking Christ!" Luis and I stare at each other. He's coughing up blood as he moves his bloody hand away from his chest and falls to the floor. "Holy shit! Julie! Julie, we…we have to get out of here. We have to go before anyone else gets hurt!"

She holds the gun to Ren's head. "She called the cops on us, baby! She'll tell them everything and they'll take me away from you again."

"No, no, she won't. She never called the cops. Why would she? The cops don't listen to her, they never have. We'll get her to sign Lawson's contract, he'll give her the money, and she'll disappear. We'll be free." I lay it on thick, even though my voice shakes. She shot Luis; she'll shoot Ren.

"We already tried that—it didn't work. She's too much of a hard ass cunt while all I tried to save your career." She lowers the gun to Ren's stomach, pushing the muzzle hard against her. Ren flinches, but Julie just throws her head back, cackling. "Besides, Rich won't be able to give her that money anymore, if he ever had it. Unless they'll accept a DNA sample for a signature at the bank."

"What?"

"I killed him! Anyhow, she had her chance. A hundred grand would have bought her dumb Mexican ass a nice little hacienda in her home country and have her set for life."

"I was born *here*, you stupid white bitch!" Ren snarls.

"Illegally, I'm sure! Now shut up! You stole him from me, and now I'm going to kill you for it."

"He's never been yours."

"Renate!" I doubt she hears me over her own rage.

"He's mine!" Julie shouts back. "We had something together! If those fucking security guards hadn't taken me away like I was some kind of threat."

"You have a fucking gun! You are a threat!"

"REN! Seriously!"

"I can't help it!" Ren shouts back at me. "She's a fucking idiot!"

CRACK! Julie smacks the side of Ren's head with the gun and Ren drops to her knees. "Don't talk to him like that. Don't talk to him at all!"

I watch her face contort as she stares at Ren. This is my chance. I lunge forward.

HOLLYWOOD
Chase

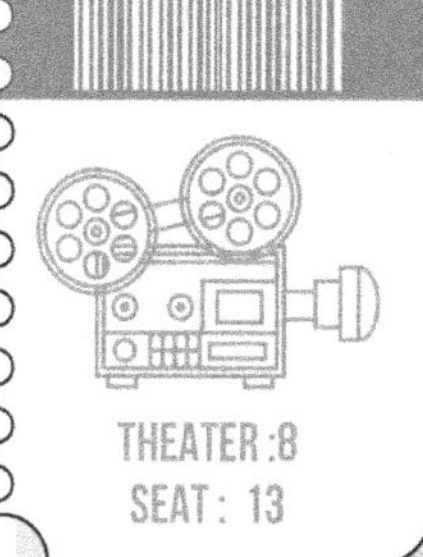

CHAPTER 41
OBSESSED

OLIVIA RODRIGO

I UNDERSTAND NOW why movies do these kinds of scenes in slow motion, because that's how it happens. The world slows down and I can swear a clock ticks at half speed. The gun fires, and I watch the knife plunge into Ren as I burst forward. I'm sure I could run faster in quicksand. There's no pain when I slam into Julie, sending us both flying through the window and out onto the front lawn. I don't register the glass in my arm and face or the dislocated shoulder. My mind has only one thought.

Renate.

"LAPD," someone announces behind me. I chuckle because it sounded so strange—the LA still in slow motion and the PD speeding through my brain while it catches up to real time. "Stay on the ground, hands out, now!"

"Chase!" Mills yells, running toward me as he waves off the cops and holds up his ID before he pulls me off Julie. "Where's Ren?"

I watch the cops pile onto Julie, shouting about a gun as she regains consciousness. I'm trying to focus, but there's something in my eye. Everything turns red, then blue, then red. Two ambulances pull in front of the house. "Ren," I whisper, trying to remember. "REN!" I scream and he helps me to my feet. I fumble past the cops and back into the house, stepping over Luis's body as I try to get to her.

"Medics!" Mills yells from behind me. "We need paramedics in here now!"

"Sunshine, talk to me." I pat her bruised and bloody face and cradle her in my arms. Pongo's on the ground next to her, licking her hand. "Come on Ren."

"Mama?" she moans, turning her head from side to side, but her eyes are still shut. I check and find her mother sitting up, touching her forehead. "She's gonna be okay. Don't worry about her. Come on, show me those beautiful eyes of yours."

Police yell about the house being clear and a pair of EMTs tell me I have to move, but I don't want to. I need her to look at me. I need to know she's going to be okay.

"Please, please open your eyes for me, Renate. I love you. I love you so much, you know that, right? Sunshine?"

Her eyes flutter open and focus on me. "Puppy?"

"Yeah. Yeah, I'm here, my queen."

"Who did that to you?" She tries to reach up to touch my face, but can't move her arm high enough. "I'm gonna kick their ass."

I reach up and wince at the glass shards in my forehead. Cyn's going to kill me for that. "Hey, scars are sexy, right?"

Mills pulls me away so the paramedics can do their thing. He takes me over to the couch and I glance around at the glass and blood that litter the floor.

Another set of paramedics comes over to me, one working on my face, the other checks my arm, but I'm more concerned about Ren and her mother.

"We've got a gunshot here," the paramedic says, and I glance down, not realizing he's talking about me.

"Hey, aren't you—" the other paramedic asks me, but I cut her off.

"Yeah. Yeah, I am." She wipes blood out of my eye, clearing

my vision. I stare at my arm as they wrap it, but it doesn't feel like it belongs to me.

"Cool. You're pretty fucked up, dude. Hope you're doing a lot of action movies over the next few weeks."

"I can't even feel this shit."

"It's the shock. We'll get you something for the pain at the hospital and make sure there's no other damage."

Someone's screaming outside, yelling at the cops about her mom and sister. Mills disappears, coming back a few minutes later with a very pissed off Dani in tow. She runs over to her mother, who's wide awake now and sitting on the stretcher as they take her blood pressure while she complains about the mess. She gives Dani an earful about her language until the EMT stops her and tells her she needs to stay calm.

Even with a knife wound, Ren tries to fight me about going to the hospital. When we step outside, we find Julie in custody and handcuffed to a stretcher. She screams about the glass in my face, and I'm tempted to walk over and point out the three-inch piece sticking out of one of her eyes. I'm pretty sure I'd puke if I stare at it for too long.

Mills stays behind to talk to the police, promising to bring Pongo to the hospital for me as soon as he's done. The paps arrive just in time to watch me climb into one ambulance with Ren, and Dani into another with their mother. I'm sure they're getting plenty of shots of my blood face and shirt. It should make them some decent money. I make a mental note to pick up the tabloids tomorrow to see just how crazy their theories get.

"Jesus, you look like hell. Tell me you've already called the plastic surgeon."

"Nice to see you, too, Cyn," I reply with as much of a smile as I can manage. "And yes, I called a place your assistant recommended when she dropped off coffee and a script for me this morning."

A few people mill around the waiting room, but so far, no one has bothered me. My head throbs, and the lights are too bright for me to take the sunglasses off, so I've been sitting here, head against the wall and eyes closed. When the door to the operating wing opens, I turn my head to see if it's her, or one of her doctors. So far, it's been everyone but them.

"How's she doing?"

"Better than expected, honestly. They're setting her arm. Said it would take a few hours."

"You know that wasn't a script I sent over this morning, don't you?"

I turn my head toward her, lowering the sunglasses and squinting my eyes against the light. The window to the face made me even more light sensitive. Or it's the concussion. I hand her my cup of coffee and shift so I can pick up the envelope she sent over. I fight with it, swearing under my breath about the damn sling, so she takes the envelope and opens it for me.

"Convenient of you to get shot in the arm you dislocated. Or you'd need me to send a straw with your coffee." She takes a sip of it and winces. "Fuck, how do you drink this?"

She hands me the stack of legal documents. Some have my name, some have Ren's.

"I don't understand."

"Mills and I have been building the case against Julie for a few months now. Although she used aliases so we had a hell of a time tracking the real her down. At first, it didn't make sense, but Ren cracked it. The brains, the muscle, and the bank. You should write this shit down, sell the screenplay."

"I don't follow."

"Initially, we thought the role of brains belonged to Lawson, while Julie and Luis played the dutiful henchmen. But Lawson didn't have brains enough for how complicated this web became. Too much to weave together for a guy paying off a stalker and a gang member using payroll checks."

"You need to take a vacation, Cyn."

"On your dime, baby. Anyhow, Julie only wanted you at first, but once she found out about Ren, she realized she needed help. Enter Lawson's money and Luis's gang affiliations."

I nod and let that sink in. "How did she get those pictures of Cassie and I?"

"Well, maybe we can figure that part out later when we talk to Mills. He wanted you to see what they found in Julie's apartment, but wouldn't give me details."

"Fun."

She takes the papers back from me and sets them on the table beside her before brushing my hair out of my face. "How are you holding up?"

"I'm, uhm…I don't think it's hit me yet, Cyn. I mean, I'm already on the verge of losing my shit and I just want to get Ren and go home. Last night when we got here, I had to answer questions for her." I stop, closing my eyes. "They asked if she could be pregnant and I—I—"

"Chase?"

"Huh?"

"You're going to be okay. So will Ren. Did they run the test?"

"Yeah."

"And?"

"No. I mean, she's—we're not. But she could have been and we—what if…"

For the first time since getting to the hospital, I finally let go. It's like a train came around a blind corner and crashed into me at full speed. I never had time to brace for it either, the full impact of everything from the last twenty-four hours. The last few months. The last four years. Everything I'd held together with rusty nails and rotted wood finally crashed down on top of me.

"Chase, when you're both out of the hospital, why don't you take some time?" Cyn says as the tears stop.

"Time?"

"Yeah, time. You've gone non-stop lately. Take some time. Take care of Ren, put a ring on her, show her you can do this. We can cut down your movies back, spread things out. I've watched too many of you go full tilt into work while trying to have a family, and it rarely works. You're busting ass on movie after movie, and next thing you know, you're at your kid's graduation and you don't know a damn thing about them."

"Time. Yeah. Yeah, I'd, uhm, I think I'd like that."

"I'm glad, because I rebooked both of you for three months in Europe as soon as Ren can travel again." She puts the sunglasses back on my face and grins. "Coop, if you two ever have a girl, don't name her Cynthia."

I laugh—really laugh—for the first time in weeks. "Deal."

My phone vibrates, and I struggle to dig it out.

MILLS

I'm with the detective at the stalker's apartment. We should talk.

Can it wait? Ren's in surgery again.

MILLS

Yeah, I'll pick you up later today when she's out.

It's raining when Mills comes to the hospital. Harder than I've ever seen it rain in Los Angeles. It reminds me of storms on the East Coast when we'd be filming out there in Atlanta or Miami. It smells comforting yet unfamiliar, and I can hear Dr. Clay in the back of my mind. I stand under the downpour for a moment and let it wash over me before I climb into the car.

"You okay?" Mills asks as we drive down to the police station, handing me a towel.

"Yeah. Sometimes, it just fucking rains."

"Ain't that the truth?"

When we get to the station, two detectives greet Mills and me before taking us to a room in the back. I'm nervous because I've only ever filmed in police station sets, not actually been in one like this. Not even when Cassie died.

"Have a seat, Mr. Cooper. Coffee?"

"No, thanks. I'm bouncy enough as it is. Mills said you needed me to identify some things?"

"Have you had any keys or locks redone at your house in the last four years?"

"No. I had more keys made…oh, and I did add a lock on the pool house since my brother moved in."

"Can I see your keys, Mr. Cooper?"

I dig them out of my pocket and hand them over, watching him take a bag with a key in it out of a cardboard box and hold them up next to each other and sighs.

"This key." He puts the bag down and taps on it with one beefy finger. "We recovered it from Julie Horowitz's apartment."

"That isn't an alias?"

"No, but she had about a dozen IDs in different names, including Cassidy Landon's. We also found clothes that are not her size. They were all kept in a lockbox under her bed, along with the jewelry and a stack of photocopies of a marriage license you applied for four years ago."

He spreads a dozen or more photos in front of me, showing the inside of someone's apartment. My brain tries to put together a puzzle, but the concussion slows me down. He lays out more photos of clothes, necklaces, and other personal items.

"Do you recognize—"

"These." I point to a necklace and a dress. I flip through the others, growing more frantic with each of them. All of them are Cassie's belongings. "I gave her these after she moved in with me. This ring she got from her mother. The dress, fuck, I got her that in…Paris."

Next, he hands me photos of Cassie and I. "Ms. Horowitz admitted to selling a copy of the key to a known paparazzi. The one who took the nude images in your home. We found evidence that she snuck in, planted surveillance equipment, and took things that belonged to Cassie."

"Why?"

"Her diary entries hint that she's been obsessed with you since before Cassie's death," another detective explains. "Based on what we found, her obsession may have begun with Cassie in high school before shifting to you."

"Coop, she's been in your house. Numerous times." Mills explains.

"The dogs?"

"Lulu isn't exactly a guard dog, and Pongo goes with you most of the time."

"What are you not telling me right now?"

Mills runs a hand through his hair before he sits in the chair next to me and faces me. "On the day Cassie died, Devin's skates weren't in his bag. Where were they?"

"I…don't remember."

"Would either of you leave skates without guards on concrete?" He pulls out one last picture. It's my garage, Devin's skates leaning against the back wall.

"Hell no. It can damage and dull the blades. I don't… Mills?"

"She put them there, Coop. She made sure Devin would come back to the house so someone would find the body."

"I want to talk to her."

"What?!" the detective shouts. "No way, no way, man."

"Please? I have to know."

Mills pulls the detectives aside and they eventually agree to it. They put her in the room next to ours so they can watch through the two-way mirror. They explain this might be inadmissible in court, and I explain I don't give a fuck. My heart and mind race when they escort her into the room and I finally see what I couldn't see last night. She cut and colored her hair to match Cassie's. I can see the polish on her nails and I recognize it as Cassie's favorite. She's even had plastic surgery to look like her.

She wanted to replace her—become her.

"I knew you'd come for me. I told them you pushed me through the window to save me. They don't believe me. They don't understand us." She's smiling again and I try not to shiver. It's even creepier with the patch over her eye and the cuts on her face.

"Jul—"

"Cassie."

"What?"

"I'm Cassie. The real Cassie."

I take a deep breath and stretch my shaking hands across the table and take hers. "Sweetheart, I need to ask you something, and it's important that you tell me the truth. Okay? We shouldn't keep secrets from each other, right?" She nods, squeezing my hand. "What happened to the other Cassie? The one they found?"

"Oh, they're trying to trick me."

"The truth."

"Oh fine, Teddy Bear. What do you want to know?"

"T-the phone call. When you tried to call me?" My mind flashes back, seeing her name on the screen and tucking the phone away, so sure I'd just call her back later. "Why did you call me?"

"To tell you that we could finally be together." Her smile grows, and I want to pull my hand back. I want to throw up. "I waited for your brother to leave, and I went to your bathroom and cleaned myself up. I knew Devin would be back, so I had to hurry. When I finished, I tried to call you, but you didn't answer. I wanted to surprise you, but the stupid cops came to check the house and ruined it. I hid in your crawl space."

"Why did you want to hurt Cassie?"

"She stole from me, Chase. She stole my boyfriend in high school, and when we were roommates in college, she did it again. She said she didn't remember, but she did. I loved you first, and she even stole you!"

I close my eyes, trying to focus and hold on.

"I went to your house that morning and brought her a coffee. I snuck into Devin's room while he showered and put his skates in the gym so he'd find her, not you. The drugs took too long, so I helped her to the bathroom and slit her wrists."

I pull my hand away, and the room turns red as the air becomes too heavy to breathe. I stand up, but my legs turn to jelly as time stands still. The door bursts open, and Mills pulls me out of the room as the detectives rush in.

I have one thought on my mind before I black out. Julie just confessed to murdering Cassie.

HOLLYWOOD
Renate

CHAPTER 42
KARMA

TAYLOR SWIFT

MY HEAD, side, and arm all hurt, but it's nothing compared to how Luis left me so many times before. When I open my eyes, I'm greeted by Mama and Dani, who tell me that my older brothers are downstairs getting coffee. Mama cries, Dani cracks jokes, and we all try to pretend we're not in a hospital room.

"Hey, you're awake!" Chase says as he comes in. He walks over and kisses my head before he sets a cup in front of me..

"If I never see ice again, I won't be mad."

"You would, because that's how you drink your coffee," Chase whispers as he nuzzles my hair, taking a deep breath in even though I'm sure it smells like a hospital, just like everything else. "And Devin would be really bummed if you never came to one of his games."

"My brothers want tickets."

"Already gave them some. They'll be in our suite, which I'll have stocked with beer and food. They've got hotel rooms and a driver, too, so they won't have to drive home after." He flashes me that dorky smile. "Least I could do after they cleaned up the mess at your house."

"Baby, tickets in the nose-bleeds would have been enough for them."

"But not enough for you."

"You two are fucking disgusting. Like, worse than Jamie!" Dani complains as she shoves a burrito in her mouth.

"And you're not supposed to be eating in here! Not until your sister can eat proper food again." Chase flips her off and Dani sticks her tongue out at him before Mama smacks her arm.

I reach up with my working arm and stroke Chase's stubble. Remembering what that feels like between my thighs sends a warmth through my body. If I weren't on all these meds, and we were alone in here, I just might make a move on this beautiful man looking down at me. He's staring at me like I'm the only person in the universe. It's the same look my father used to give my mother. The one I'd hoped someone would give me one day, but gave up on after I met Luis. It's passion and promises in a sparkling blue bow. It tells me what I knew the day I first met him, but tried so damn hard to fight.

"Ask me again."

"No."

I wrinkle my nose and pout. I didn't expect that answer from a man who rarely ever uses that word on me.

"I want more time, Ren."

My heart cracks, but I'm confused. "Oh, I—"

"Not what I mean, Renate." He presses his forehead to mine and in that moment, we're alone in the room, even if Mama and Dani haven't left. "I'm not doing it wrong twice in a row, beautiful. I don't need more time to think about us. I want more time. I want memories, adventures, and travels. I want them all with you. I want to take my time taking you apart on the balcony of a hotel in Paris. I want you to taste fresh pasta in a hotel in Italy after we've fucked on every surface in the room. I want you to dance with me at a club in Germany before we slip off to a back room and you scream my name."

"What are you talking about?"

"We had time taken away from us, and I want it back. I want

every minute back and I'm going to fucking get it. You'll say yes to me when you least expect it. When we're ready, we'll come home, plan a wedding, and start our family. You and me," he whispers the words, splaying his hand over my belly. "And as many as you want."

"Wait, did he just—"

I turn just in time to see Mama smack Dani's arm again, almost making her drop her food. "Leave them alone, *niña tonta.* You're too nosey."

"Geez, wonder where I get that from?" Dani says under her breath as I turn back to Chase.

"So, what do you say? We heal up, and we leave. Cyn has us set for three months, but I can extend it. Six months. A year. Whatever you want."

"I can't leave Mama in that house the way it is. My brothers may have cleaned it, but it needed more than cleaning, Chase."

"She can sleep at her boyfriend's place, dumbass. OUCH!"

"Daniella, stop making Mama mad. It's making me laugh and that hurts."

"We'll hire an architect and contractors." He turns to Mama. "We'll change anything you want, and while that's in the works, you can stay with Devin if you'd like."

"Okay. I'll go." I turn his head and rub my nose against his. "It's not like I have a job."

"Oh!" Chase's eyes shoot open as he pulls away and starts looking through his pockets, still struggling with the sling. He pulls out a thumb drive and lays it on the tray next to me. "Mills got that back from the cops. He said there's no charge for impersonating a teacher, so you could have this back?"

I pick it up like it's made of the finest glass, holding it in front of me and feeling my lips pull into a wicked grin.

"Renate?" Chase asks when I smirk at him. "You've got that look in your eye, and neither of us is in any shape for anything that usually follows that look."

"Chase, my love?" I swear he melts when I call him that. It's better than Puppy. "I need a computer."

Marta tries hard to bite back her smile when she comes by the hospital to check on me. Which means my plan worked. She greets everyone, blushing a little when she gets to Chase. When she gets to me, she drops a newspaper in my lap.

Once Beloved Principal Fired for Pornography, Harassment, Indiscretions

I can't hold back the snort in my laughter, even though it hurts like hell. "Beloved? Who in their right mind would ever call him that?"

"Did you do it?"

"I sure as hell didn't call him that!" She cocks an eyebrow at me, and I feign innocence. "Did I do what, Marta?"

Leaning in closer, she whispers like she's in a spy movie, "They say in the article that someone emailed a video of him to numerous outlets. The same outlets that he and Luis sent those images of you." She points to the picture on the front page. "That's his office, Renate."

"Would it matter if I did it? I don't work there anymore, and whoever sent in these images and videos probably just wanted to protect the teachers and students from a man like him. He's wicked and cruel—he had it coming."

"What am I going to do without you, Renate?" Her shoulders slump as she smiles through a pout. "You were my best friend in that school!"

"You'll have to come visit me sometime, or maybe I'll get you a new job. I have an offer waiting for me at a private school. Why don't you take it?"

"A private school? Why don't you want it?"

"Because Chase is taking me on an adventure. We're going to

take some time. Together. When I'm back, we'll see about teaching."

"Oh, those private schools are so—"

"Not always. This one had a different approach." Chase says as he moves to sit on the edge of the bed. He pulls out a business card and hands it to her. "No snotty rich kids and trust funds there."

"Not yet, anyhow. And they won't be a problem, because I'll give every one of them an earful once they get home."

Marta stares at me, and I watch the gears spinning. "Oh my sweet baby Jesus, are you saying?"

"Not yet, but I'm pretty sure we've decided on it."

"Pretty sure?" Chase teases, squeezing my leg and giving me a mischievous wink. "Oh, it's my mission now. Unless you've changed your mind."

"I haven't, Puppy. Don't worry."

Marta giggles and tucks the card into her purse. "You know, Mr. Cooper, I tried to tell her to talk to you that night you came to the school. She told me you wouldn't know what to do with a woman like her. I'm glad someone has finally proved her wrong." Chase blushes as he laughs so hard his shoulders shake. "You are a good man, so stay that way. Treat this woman like the princess she is."

"Oh, she's not a princess, Marta. She's my queen."

Marta cackles so loud, I expect a nurse to come in and hush her. "Ren, you better treat this man here like a king. You two are cute together. I'm going to go talk to your mother."

As soon as Marta sits beside my mother, the pair gossip in Spanish. Sometimes they forget that, while I don't speak it often, I understand them. Chase asks me what they're talking about, but I just smile and pat the space next to me on the bed. He doesn't need to know that every woman in this room thinks he has a cute butt.

His arm wraps around me as I nuzzle against his chest,

feeling drowsy. He's changed since that night and the visit to the police station. He hasn't told me what happened yet, but he's not fidgeting and nervous. Like he let go of something that had a chokehold on him. When I ask, he tells me it's something for another day.

"Do I want to know what you did with that thumb drive and the computer?"

"No. You do not."

"Something we'll need to tell Cynthia about?"

"Chase, we might need to keep a few parts of our lives just to us."

"I tell her everything, Ren."

I tilt my head up to his ear while I squeeze his thigh. "Did you tell her how loud I made you scream my name while I choke you and peg your perfect, tight ass?"

"Keep talking like that, Sunshine, and I'm kicking everyone out and locking the door."

"Let me take a nap first. Then kick them all out."

He swallows hard and closes his eyes. I'm interested to know how many European sights I'll be seeing only from the window of a hotel room. He presses his lips against my hair and hums the song we danced to that night all those months ago on our first date as I drift off to sleep. Warm, safe, and, most importantly, loved.

HOLLYWOOD
Renate

EPILOGUE- REN

There's a bead of sweat just above the mask Chase wears and his hand hasn't let go of mine since we walked in the door. I spent months researching this place, and it's why Germany had to be the last stop on our trip. I have a feeling he'll ask to extend our stay after tonight.

The exclusive club has a serious no camera policy and a high enough entry fee that members aren't interested in breaking that rule. Masks are optional, but almost everyone has one and so do we. It's dark and loud in the main room, with a DJ and people mingling near the bar, searching for their next hookup.

I walk Chase out toward the bar hoping a drink will help with his nerves, since he refused to get high before we came here. He said he wanted to experience everything, take it all in, so I didn't argue. If the drinks don't help, the back rooms will.

I arranged a tour a few nights ago while Chase filmed a talk show appearance. It gave me a better idea of the rooms while I made sure this would work for us. I had to turn down more than a few offers that night, and tonight, some of those men lingering around the edges of the room, eyeing Chase. They're not curious to know who he is, but why he's mine and what it would take to

replace him. There's not a thing in any world they could offer me to trade him away. Not unless he asked for it.

"They're looking at me."

"They covet you, Puppy."

"Me? They know who I am? Shit. I thought—"

"No, baby." I run my hand down the buttons of his black dress shirt and adjust his collar. "They're drooling for a chance to be at the end of this leash I'm holding, to call me mistress. Every one of them wants to know why you're fucking me later tonight, and not them. Don't worry, no one even knows you cut your hair yet."

He runs his hands through his short, wavy hair, still getting used to it. It's for a role and I almost cried when he told me he had to cut it, but he promised he'd grow it back. Thankfully, it's still enough to get a firm grip on when he's between my legs. After drink number two, he relaxes enough for me to show him the VIP rooms. I show my pin, proof that I'm a VIP and allowed in the area with whoever I choose to bring with me. As the curtain pulls back, Chase's grip on my hand tightens with excitement and curiosity, but also fear.

"Holy shit!" he gasps as we pass the occupied voyeur rooms, staring in with curiosity.

The first has two gorgeous men, one tied up and worshiping his partner's cock. In the next room, a man has a woman hog-tied while he fucks her from behind. When we pass the last window, we find two women and a man that stop Chase in his tracks. He watches as the handcuffed man gets on his hands and knees, his head moving between the young brunette's legs while the blonde with a strap-on stands behind him with a paddle.

"They were here the other night. They're amazing, all three of them."

"Can they see us?"

"In some rooms, yes. In some, no. It depends on what they're into. We're not doing that. Not tonight anyhow."

Chase jumps a little when the paddle comes down on the man's ass, but he never stops licking the brunette's pussy.

Chase whispers under his breath, "Shit."

"We don't do anything unless we both want it, you know that, Puppy."

"Yeah, okay. But, uh, can we…can we do that?"

"The paddle?"

He nods, eyes not leaving the scene playing out in the room. "And maybe the room, too. Someday?"

Even asking me that question has me fucking dripping. I reach over, pressing my hand over the bulge in his pants, and his head snaps toward me. It's hard to tell in the low light, but his eyes look blown out already and I grin.

"Shit, I'm sorry. I'm still not, you know, used to—"

"Do you like this? Me holding your cock in front of all these people?" He looks around the room. At least twenty other people roam the area, watching the shows. He nods and my firm grip pulls a moan from him just loud enough for me to hear. "Your words, Puppy. Use them."

"Yes, my queen. I… I like this. A lot."

"Do you want them to watch us?"

"Really?"

"How does it make you feel, the thought of them watching your enormous cock and how well I take it?"

"You sound like my shrink asking about my feelings, Sunshine."

"Theo talks about your cock?"

"You know what I mean."

I back him up against a wall so he's facing the paddle room before I drop to my knees and kiss his hard-on through his pants. "Re—uh—my queen? Are, should we, are you—" His head rocks back against the wall as I unzip his pants.

"Watch them, Chase. Watch them nice and close. If you look

away from them, I'll edge you all damn night. Do you understand?"

"Yes, my queen." His eyes remain glued on them as I massage him, leaving more kisses and teasing nips. Feeling him squirm at every touch. I reach into his boxers, freeing his thick, stiff cock, and licking the bead of pre-cum from the tip. It brings the sweetest moan to his lips. "Oh, shit. We're doing this."

"Good boy, now, put your hands behind your back, and don't fucking touch me, do you understand?" He nods. The instant my tongue touches the tip again, his hips jerk forward. "Tell me what they're doing, Chase. Describe it for me."

I take his cock deep as he fights hard not to look at me, describing the ongoing paddling scene taking place in front of him as he pants. I'm not ready to make him come yet, but he doesn't need to know that. His hips thrust forward again, making me gag. The people around us move about, watching me take this pretty cock that I fucking own, whispering about us. I release him with a loud pop and he whimpers, begging me not to stop.

"You taste so amazing, Puppy. How's the plug?"

"It's, uhm, weird." He tries to tuck his dick back into his pants, but I slap his hands away.

"Keep it out. Let them see your magnificent cock on display. Let them crave what they can't have." I slide my finger up the shaft and watch him shiver.

I follow his eyes as he searches the crowd. He's unsure at first, a normal reaction. But with each person staring at him, licking their lips at the sight of him, the more confident he becomes. It confirms my suspicion that Chase Cooper has an exhibitionist kink.

I stand, taking hold of the leash that hangs around his neck and pull him down to me. "I should make you take off your pants and crawl in front of all these people. Show them how obedient you are and let them see that pretty plug in your tight ass."

"I will do anything you ask, my queen."

"And that's why you're mine." I run my fingers over the letters on the collar that spell out Good Boy in diamonds. "Another time. Let's go have some fun."

I walk him down the hall, watching his cock bob as we make our way through the crowd to the room I reserved. As soon as the door shuts and we're alone, he pushes me against the wall, kissing me hard and grinding his cock against me, desperate for release. He pulls back for a breath and I slap him hard against the face.

"I'm sorry. I'm sorry, my queen."

"It's okay, Puppy," I say, like I'm talking to a child or an actual dog while I unbutton his shirt and pull it from his shoulders. "You're just a little eager, aren't you?"

His groan turns into a growl as my nails drag down his chest, leaving angry red marks. He looks at me with eyes so dark I can only make out a sliver of blue. If I gave him the command, he'd fuck me so hard I'd scream loud enough to hear me over the DJ. But that's not why we're here. I push his pants down his thick, muscular legs so he can step out of them. Licking my lips, thinking about what it will be like when we let people watch. When other people stare at this beautiful specimen of a man as he rails me.

"On the bed, on your hands and knees. Put the pillows under your chest."

He turns around, looking around the room for the first time. There's an enormous bed in the center with restraints on the posts. Two walls have thick, red curtains hiding us from the people outside, while the other two have various toys decorating them. I go straight for the paddle, not wanting to waste any time.

"Okay, you're going to count for me. I'll keep them light for now. We can work you up to where you're comfortable later, right?"

"Yes, my queen."

"And what's the safe word?"

"Voorhees." I picked the new safe word after a Halloween party Chase threw. I also told him to retire the costume for something new since he'd been the same thing for five years.

"Relax and let me take this out first." He drops his head to the pillow, groaning like a feral beast as I pull the plug from his ass and tossing it aside. "Are you ready, or do you need a minute?"

"I'm ready."

Smack.

"That was too light. One."

Smack.

"Better, my queen. Two."

"Harder?"

"Uhm." He adjusts his legs and takes a deep breath. "Please, my queen." I still don't go full force, but I give him what he asks for. He almost shoots off the bed. "OH FUCK! THREE! JESUS FUCKING CHRI—"

"Color?"

"Green, baby. Fuck!" he howls, and bites down on the pillow before turning back to look at me. It's pitiful, and I want to remember this look on his face for the rest of my life. "Ren, I'm gonna come if you do that much more. I'm sorry. I'm—"

"New. You're new, Puppy, and all this stimulation isn't something you're used to." I rub the warm spot on his ass cheek that's turning a red, and he nods. "Okay. Do you think you can take one more?"

"Yes, my perfect wife."

"Atta boy."

CRACK!

"FOUR! Holy shit, Ren! Please! Please, my goddess, my beautiful wife, please?"

I give him a bottle of water and make him drink it through his whines and whimpers; fuck, I love the noises this pretty boy makes. When he's finished the bottle, I stand in front of him, brushing his hair back. He presses his head against my hand, begging me with his eyes. I lean in, nibbling on his ear while I tease his cock.

"What do you want?"

"You, my queen."

"You want my pussy, you little whore? Beg for it."

"My greedy cock needs to be inside of your incredible pussy, my queen. To fill you until you can't breathe and our cum drips from your beautiful cunt."

"Someone's been practicing new lines," I smirk, pushing him back onto the bed and climbing on top of him. I reach over his head, pulling the straps over his wrists, but don't tighten them. He's free to let go of them when he wants. I reach down between my legs as he watches me move my panties to the side, hunger in his eyes. He's so ready, he drips down my fingers as I rub his cock through my slit.

"Please, Renate. Use me like your toys. I promise not to come until you tell me."

His words have me so wet, I slide him into me with ease as our moans echo around us. He pulls on the straps, threatening to rip them off the bedposts as I ride his cock, bouncing the way we both like. He licks his lips, watching me, craving me as I throw my head back and say his name. I can feel his eyes watching me as I run my hands over the lace dress I'm wearing—the one he wants to rip off of me.

"I have a job for you, Puppy," I say in a breathy voice, looking down at him.

"W-what? What do you want, my queen?"

"I want you to be a good boy, and fuck a baby into me. Right. Now."

I've asked him to do that in every city, every hotel room, every chance we have, and each time he gets bolder and it gets better. The transition from curious and worried he'd hurt me into this wild man beneath me has been like poetry in motion. And the way he fucks me now—with equal parts passion and primal desire—is too perfect to be heavenly. Chase isn't my sweet angel anymore; He's my ideal devil.

His wild eyes stare into mine as he lets go of the straps and flips us over, ripping my panties off. I gasp as he pulls out and teases me with short, shallow thrusts where only the tip penetrates me. Reaching up, I wrap my hand around his throat, squeezing hard enough to tell him he's being a brat. I'm torn in two as he impales me. His arms wrap around me as he picks me up and carries me over to the glass wall, pushing my ass against it.

"Open the curtains."

"Chase, are you sure?"

"You said they wanted to know why it's me on the end of your leash? I'm gonna fucking show them exactly why it's me. I'm gonna show every one of them just how devoted I am to you, and only you. I'm going to show them you're mine." His head lowers to my neck, sucking and biting while I'm still pinned against the glass. We listen to the sound of the curtains retracting, but he doesn't look up at first, but when he does, it's like a switch in his brain. He thrusts longer and harder until I'm worried the glass might break. And as I tighten around his cock, he stares out the window defiantly, daring them to watch as he lights my body on fire.

My beautiful beast transforms into a god, howling and grunting as slams into me. I scream his name until his hand wraps around my throat and our mouths collide. Raw, unfiltered passion passes between our lips, and I almost black out when my body lets go, soaking his legs.

His yell follows not long after, even though everything sounds miles and miles away through the snowstorm in my vision. When he's done, he carries me to a table. He positions my body like a doll, draping me over the table so anyone watching can see my face. It's almost too much when he laps at my cunt, bringing the stars back into my vision as he fucks his cum back into me with his tongue.

Four orgasms.

Apparently that's the number I can take from Chase Cooper before I pass out.

When I wake up, he's in the bed next to me with a tray full of food, water, and even tea. I turn my head to the side and see he's also closed the blinds again to give us our privacy. He's even wrapped me in a warm, soft robe while he lays there, covered only in scratches and bruises we're both proud of. I'm glad he's doing a voice acting gig next.

"Can I get you anything else, my love?" He asks in a hushed tone while massaging my legs. "Your bath should be ready soon. I'll carry you there when you want."

"I didn't ask them—"

"I did. You're my queen, and you'll be treated like one for the rest of our lives, Sunshine." He kisses up and down my neck before he pours me tea. It's not long before he's inside of me again, but this time his movements are more languid, like I'm in a dream. This time I feel and hear everything as he whispers how much he loves me and vows his never ending devotion to me. He makes me feel like the queen he swears I am.

He holds my gaze as he fills me, staying inside me until he softens while I stroke his hair and promise him the moon and my unending love.

When we're done, he carries me down a hall filled with people that gathered after our display. He unlocks a door with a key around his wrist, and I'm enveloped in the warm smell of cinnamon candles. Yellow rose petals decorate the floor and the steamy bath water and two bottles of champagne are on ice nearby.

"I didn't even know they had this."

"That's because we're the only ones with a key."

"What?"

"Don't be mad at me, but I kind of found out about the club before we left California. You left your laptop open. So I contacted them and, well, I kind of arranged for our own private bathroom."

"Chase?" He nuzzles my neck, distracting me, already desperate to be inside of me again. His libido has grown to an insatiable level.

"Merry Christmas, my queen."

"Chase! You are fucking kidding me, right? You have to stop this overboard crazy—"

"Shhh, beautiful. As hot as it sounds to have you walking back to our hotel covered in…well…me—yeah, that's not how I take care of my queen."

"This was supposed to be an experiment! What if you didn't like the club?!"

"Sunshine? Beautiful queen and—hopefully, after tonight— mother of my child? Why would we not come back here and make a few, you know…more?"

"Puppy, babies take timing and a little more than amazingly wonderful sex."

"Yep. So, if you're not, well, we keep coming back here until you are. Letting everyone watch me fill you night after night. And—" he stops, pursing his lips.

"And?"

"And, uhm, maybe while you're, you know, preg— pregnant?" The way he stumbles over the word melts my heart. I couldn't have asked for anyone better than my man, my Puppy, my king. "I mean, some of these people might enjoy a knocked up hottie fucking the living hell out of her man after she tied him up, wouldn't they? Maybe with that new purple dildo you got?"

"You are ridiculous."

"And you're absolutely perfect. Marry me?"

"I already did!"

"Do it again! Hell, I want to get married to you in every city and every country forever."

"You know, we were only supposed to come to Europe for a vacation. Not to get married and spend every night trying to make babies."

"What the fuck else did you want to do on vacation?" His nose scrunches up as he giggles, carrying us into the tub. "I love you, Renate."

"I love you, too. Let's go home, Chase. We can get married again, if you want, and have this baby. We'll come back and make as many as we can."

"Yeah?"

"Yeah."

HOLLYWOOD
Chase

CHAPTER 44
BELONG TOGETHER

MARK AMBOR

EPILOGUE- CHASE

"Where's Dani?"

"Making out with Xander in the pool."

"What? Oh hell no, not in my pool," Ren announces as she tries to get up out of the chair and just glares at me when she realizes she's stuck. "You did this to me."

"Damn right." I kiss the top of her head and give her belly a gentle rub before I head over to the door and look out. "They're fine. Besides, it's not like she's going to end up like—shit, you're right." I slide the door open. "Hey, assholes! No knocking people up in my pool unless it's me knocking up Ren."

"You can't stop me! Also, why are you so fucking gross, Coop?!" Dani yells back, flipping me off and laughing.

"I feel like I swallowed the fucking sun," Ren complains as return to my seat next to her. "The thermostat says seventy and you're in a hoodie while I melt!"

"We could go join them in the pool. Can you still hold your breath while you suck—"

"They're coming!" Devin yells as he whips around the corner, sliding to a stop. "They're coming. Not like that! I mean, like, in the gate, right now!"

"Okay?"

"But it's a surprise. Aren't we supposed to hide or something?"

"Devin, are you seriously asking if we're going to jump out and yell *'surprise'* when they come in? Do you think that's wise?" Ren asks, trying to hold back the laughter as I head for the door. I'm not waiting for them. I'm too stoked. "Go get Jamie and help them."

I step outside in time to see Steve sticking out of one side of the car and Ethan on the other, arms flailing as they take potshots at each other. They already bicker like it's been fifty years—it's perfect. For both of them. Ethan's become part of the family and I've never seen Steve act so natural and happy before. I jog over and hop in the front seat, looking back at the two of them as they struggle. "You, uh, get a manual with that thing?"

"No! Did you get one? If so, I need to fucking borrow it! I have no idea what the hell I'm doing, as Ethan reminds me every fucking five minutes." Steve sighs, exasperated. He only calls him *Ethan* when he's annoyed. "How the fuck do you get it out? Putting it *in* was so simple. How come pulling it *out* isn't?"

"Oh, sure, cause he's gonna know how to pull anything out? Have you seen his wife?" Ethan snipes back. He's getting a lot better at that. We're a bad influence on the poor guy. "Also, don't call her *'it'* just because we haven't picked a name!"

"Click the button, the red one. No, the other one. Just, yeah, there you go!" I raise my fists and stare into tiny green eyes as I whisper yell, "Freeeeedom!" She gurgles and tries to laugh as she kicks her feet. She's beautiful.

"I thought this was your first kid?" Ethan stares at me, trying to figure out how I learned to work a car seat. I glance out the front window at Devin and smile before I go grab the diaper bag out of the back.

Babies haven't changed since I raised Dev, but the toys and contraptions all have. Internet videos have helped. But I have the same car seat already setup in the SUV and Jamie and I have used Lulu as a test baby to make sure we know how to get the real baby out when the time comes. We give her plenty of treats and eventually Devin always comes out to rescue her. We've got it down to thirty seconds to get the whole car seat out and attached to the stroller. Ren keeps saying something about whiplash, but Lulu's fine!

The hugs and photos start as soon as Steve and Ethan step through the door. Steve even starts a game of *make Lexi hold the baby*, which makes her freak out and run away. She's convinced she'll drop the kid or warp her mind just by holding her. Lexi's more into puppies than babies; that's never going to change. Jamie's the same, but he'll at least hold the kid. Once the oohs and aahs are all taken care of, everyone heads outside to the pool to get the grill fired up and the adoption shower going.

I hang back and sit on the couch next to Ren instead of helping her up when she holds her arms out. She looks so pitiful and so beautiful all at once. I wrap my arm as far around her as I can, kissing her neck and smelling her shampoo.

"Chase, we should go outside with everyone else."

"They can wait." I kiss along her neck, my fingers playing with the hem of her dress, pulling it up her leg. "We should go back to Germany. Or to the bedroom. Or the gym. Or right here."

"How can you possibly want to make out with me right now? I'm a fucking hot-air balloon, complete with the flamethrower thing inside."

"You're beautiful. Absolutely stunning, Sunshine." She screams as I lift her onto my lap. "You better get used to it, though, because I'm gonna put so many babies in you."

"Jesus, you really do have a breeding kink, don't you, Mr. Cooper?"

"Not until I met you, Mrs. Cooper." Her and her eyes widen as she catches my smirk.

"No! Chase, don't you fucking dare! If you throw me in that damn pool, I'm going to—"

I cut her off with a kiss deep enough to take her breath away and remind her how much I love her. "I'm not throwing my pregnant wife into a pool. That's not what I want. Not what I need. I need you, Ren. I need you so fucking bad it hurts, baby."

"There are people over! Lots of people!" She tries to pull the hem of her dress back down as I grab her hips, rocking her back and forth.

"Yeah, our friends. People that have known either you or I for most of their lives, or at least know us well enough." I reply. I love every bit of her, but my favorite thing about her pregnancy has to be how horny it makes her. She's breathing heavy, chest heaving and begging me to take her right fucking there. "No one would be surprised if we disappear for a few minutes. Come on. Just a quickie?"

"I...don't wanna climb...the stairs," she whines between kisses, grabbing my shoulders and rolling her hips. "Fuck, why do you do this to me?"

"I have an idea." I shift her so I can scoop her up, carrying her toward the garage. She bitches at me, saying I'll hurt myself doing that someday, but I don't give a fuck. I carry my queen and I will keep carrying her, seven months pregnant or not. I turn her so she can't see into the room and once we're in, the lights flick on.

"SURPRISE!" everyone screams. She throws her arms around my neck and screams back at them while I laugh.

"What the fuck?! Do you want me to go into premature labor?!" I put her down, and she gasps as she takes in the room. There's no gym anymore. We moved out the equipment and replaced it with a king-size bed. There's fresh paint and new floors. I even have a locked cabinet for all our toys. When her eyes land on the back of the garage, she covers her mouth and grabs my hand.

"We ripped out the bathroom and redid it so it's bigger while you were visiting your aunt."

"But, Chase?"

"You're having trouble with the stairs and I'm worried you'll fall, so we're moving down here for a bit. Look." I run over and show her the bassinet that Jamie painted for us, and the giant mixed-media piece on the wall that Lexi did with bits and pieces of the life we've built together so far. "Your mom and Tommy can take the bedroom upstairs, at least while the contractor finishes their house. I still think they should just move in permanently, but whatever her and Tommy want, they get. We'll move back upstairs when we're done having babies."

"You think we're having more after this?"

"Oh, I know we are. We have way too much fun making them."

"Ahh, there are babies present!" Steve jokes. "Gross!"

"Isn't this party for Steve and Ethan? Did you lie to me?"

"It's a family baby party. We just paid extra to get ours delivered a little early," Steve teases, nuzzling the bundle in his arms. She looks so damn small and watching him has all sorts of new fears building in my stomach. It's not that I'm not happy as hell for Steve and Ethan, but I'm terrified for Ren and I. Dr. Clay says that's normal, and if I didn't freak out at least once a day, he'd be worried. Ren must sense the coming panic attack, because she takes my hand, rubbing her thumb on my palm to calm me as Pongo appears at my side, dripping all over the new floor.

"So like, what happens if you have a boy, and they end up dating each other?" Steve asks.

"I will punch you in the face and we'll deal with it, Stevie."

"So, nothing new?" Jamie jokes before kissing his wife's head. "We should practice harder, Angel. And…get another dog?"

"Yes, to another dog!"

Looking around the room as the group continues to laugh and joke with one another, I can't help getting emotional. We were just three idiots who used to joke about eternal bachelorhood and planned to live together in a big house someday. Now, all three of us found our soulmates. How our little family has grown. And Fast. Warm hands reach up and wipe the tears from my cheeks. I don't think I ever understood how to love someone as much as I love Ren, but now, looking at my friends—my family—I realize we have everything we need to make this work. All of us.

"Shit, I left the burger on!" Devin runs out the door. Xander and Dani follow behind him, offering to help. Ethan and Steve hang back as everyone leaves the room to rejoin the party, and I catch Ethan whispering something as he pushes Steve forward. Steve looks like he swallowed a gallon of sour milk as he steps over to us.

"Coop, uhm, we, uhm, we wanted to ask you something," he stutters. "Her name—"

"Don't hyphenate it, you guys." I sigh. They fought about this for weeks before they got married, now they're going to fight about it again. "Come on. LaVonsen sounds perfect."

"No, we, well, we wanted to know what you're naming your baby."

Ren slides up next to me, rubbing her belly as she laughs. "We're not sure yet, but we won't be bothered by whatever you two choose for her."

"I know, I know. I just, well, we…we thought it would be cool if they kind of, uhm, matched in a way? Like, all our kids had names that go together. Not like the same letter or anything, but…"

"Something that makes them family," Ethan helps Steve find the words.

"Oh, uh, we're going with Daisy Lou Mae Rae for a girl and

—" Ren swats at me as I laugh. "What? I wanted them to match that!"

"Not helping, Puppy." She pinches my side. "Chase has mentioned the alphabet. We could try filling it in, even though we already have doubles on D."

"Double Ds," Steve snorts, and Ethan rolls his eyes. "I kinda like that. So we'd need a B first."

"No, Bex has the B," Jamie says as he rejoins us, bringing us all beers and a bottle of water for Ren. "That's Lexi's sister. Lex and Bex."

"Okay, F?" Ethan asks, clearly going through girl names in his head.

"Guess I'm gonna be busy. I have my heart set on Violet and Zoey," I tease, counting letters on my fingers to annoy Ren.

"Too many babies, Puppy!"

"We'll see. So what do you guys think you want to name her?"

"Farrah?" Steve asks.

"Fallon? Ethan offers with a shrug.

"Oh, yeah, I like that one more. Fallon LaVonsen? I love it, Sweets!" Steve says before he leans over and kisses Ethan.

"So, what, we get G? Thanks, guys." I shake my head, knowing I'm on board for this idea.

"Georgie? Oh, maybe Gracie." Ren lights up. "We could work with that. What do you say, Mr. Cooper?"

"I'm okay with either of those, but if it's a boy…Graham?" Jamie locks eyes with me as his jaw drops. "Yeah, after you, dickhead."

"Graham Cooper? They'll call him Graham Cracker. You can't do that," Jamie tries to argue, knowing it's no use.

"I love it, Chase." Ren coos and wraps around me, looking down at her growing bump. "What do you think, our little Graham Cracker?"

"I love you. Of course, I'd name my kid after you. Dumbass."

Jamie laughs nervously and rubs the back of his neck until I let go of Ren and hug him so hard I lift him off the ground.

"So now it's a race to see who gets H?" Steve jokes and slaps Jamie on the back.

"If you fuckers get to V first, I'm gonna deck you. You're taking the easy way and that's cheating!"

"Okay, that's enough! I'm hungry and my feet hurt." Ren shouts above us. Ethan, Steve, and Jamie all agree with Ren and head toward the door, but I stop and pull her back to me.

"Whoa, what's the rush, sexy? You were about to soak through my pants a few minutes ago, begging for me." I wrap my arms around her. "I thought we'd lock the door and see if I can break the bed."

She takes my hands from her hips and puts them on her belly, and as soon as I tickle the sides, I'm greeted with kicks and punches. "Feisty, like their mother. Gender doesn't matter, 'cause this kid isn't going to take shit from anyone."

"The baby wants food, and so do I."

"Alright, my queen. But tonight, I'll be on my knees for you. Worshiping every single inch of your incredible body."

"Damn right you will be, my king."

LIKE WHAT YOU READ?

Let others know how much you enjoyed this book by sharing your favorite scenes or moments! It's a quick way to support the author, and only takes a few seconds.

So be sure to leave your review and help spread the word about Love The Stars Fondly by Jordyn Barnes on Amazon and Goodreads today.

Thank you.

MENTAL HEALTH RESOURCES

IT'S OKAY TO NOT BE OKAY.

This book deals with several instances of mental health issues and struggles seen frequently in the LGBTQIA+ community. If you or someone you know is struggling, the following are free and confidential resources to help.

National Domestic Violence Hotline
www.thehotline.org
1-800-799-7233 | Text **LOVEIS** to 22522

Suicide and Crisis Hotline
www.988lifeline.org | Call or text 988

Prevention & Treatment of Child Abuse
www.childhelp.org/hotline/
1-800-4AChild (1-800-422-4453) | Text 1-800-422-4453

From hrc.org:
Transgender Community
translifeline.org | 877-565-8860

LGBTQ+ Youth

www.lgbthotline.org/youth-talkline | 1-800-246-7743

www.thetrevorproject.org/get-help-now
1-866-488-7386 | Text START to 678-678

All Ages
www.lgbthotline.org/national-hotline
1-888-843-4564

For more information on Mental Health:
National Institute of Mental Health (educational)
www.nimh.nih.gov | Chat: infocenter.nimh.nih.gov
1-866-615-6464

For International Mental Health resources:
dbtselfhelp.com/resources/international-resources

ACKNOWLEDGMENTS

Mom, you're the best. Thank you for supporting me, encouraging me, and for reading my silly stories. I'll never get tired of handing you a first draft only to get it back and hear *"Okay, where's the next one?"* I love you.

To **Spellbound Books** (Sanford, FL), **White Rose Books & More** (Kissimmee, FL), and **Foxtail Coffee/Lauren Sutton**, thank you for believing in my books and letting me bring them to your stores. You are all incredible and amazing.

My **alpha readers** (Emily & Mom), thank you for keeping me going and telling me this didn't suck. Also, special shout out to Emily for checking my Spanish and keeping my LA references on point.

My beta readers (Stacey, Marta, Anna, Laura, Arundhati, Erika, Laurie, Andrea, Ashley, and Rhianna), your feedback was amazing and helped to shape so much of the finished book. You're all wonderful and so friggin cool, and I'm so glad you loved the heck out of Chase & Ren.

My street team, thank you for opening my emails, sharing my posts, making super rad posts, and being the best support squad an author could ask for. Without you, I don't think I could have finished this book. I love you!

Very special thanks to my **Kickstarter Backers**: you all helped make this book actually happen, like, physically come to life. Virtual hugs to every one of you!! I'm amazed by the support that kickstarter received.

Zoe, Andrea, Kaysie, Peggy, Tiffani, Amy, Jeff, Colleen, Janet, Stacey, Bonnie, Jessi, Sara, Valeria, Naila, Emily, Andrea

As always, extra bonus thanks to to my **editor** (Danielle), **PR guru** (Jennifer), and my **muse** (seriously, you should all know who he is by now). Two of you keep me sane, one of you will never read these.

And, as always and with the deepest love, thank you to everything that is **Los Angles, California**.

These business don't sponsor me, or even know I exist, however, they do appear in this story:

The Magic Castle- Hollywood, CA (💗 this place)

The Madonna Inn- San Luis Obispo, CA

Mersea's Seafood Restaurant- Avila Beach, CA

ABOUT JORDYN

Giving Broken Characters
Their Happily Ever Afters.

Jordyn Barnes is an author, graphic designer, nerd, & elder goth. She loves Halloween, creepy things, morally grey characters, and writing about the flawed and beautifully broken people she creates in her mind palace. When she's not writing or reading, she's rearranging the growing collection dedicated to her favorite Disney Princess: Bucky Barnes/Winter Soldier. She also enjoys Marvel movies/shows, true crime everything, and, occasionally, sports. She's a long time Disney adult who relates most strongly with Madam Mim's dislike of sunshine while envying her forest hag lifestyle.

For updates on upcoming releases, join Jordyn's mailing list at jordynbarnes.com. Don't forget to follow her on social media:

instagram.com/jordyn.writes.and.reads

tiktok.com/@Jordyn.writes.words

facebook.com/jordynbarnesauthor

goodreads.com/jordynbarnes

amazon.com/author/jordynbarnes

bsky.app/profile/jordynwrites.bsky.social

bookbub.com/authors/jordyn-barnes

THE HOLLYWOODLAND BOOK SERIES

Let Me Love You Anyway

Faith in Fools

Love the Stars Fondly

Never to Suffer

In the Hatred of a Minute

Dream Only by Night